Peta Tayler is married with two sons and lives in Sussex, where she runs a small farm and is involved in the breeding of Limousin cattle. Her interests include reading, cooking, swimming and travelling. Her three previous novels, GINGERBREAD AND GUILT ('A charmingly intricate story . . . very atmospheric and every scenario is clearly painted' *Nottingham Evening Post*), CLOUD CUCKOO LAND ('Absorbing . . . gentle humour and a perceptive insight' *Huddersfield Daily Examiner*) and CUTTING THE SWEETNESS, are also available from Headline.

Also by Peta Tayler

Gingerbread And Guilt
Cloud Cuckoo Land
Cutting The Sweetness

Somewhere In Between

Peta Tayler

HEADLINE

First published in 1997
by HEADLINE BOOK PUBLISHING

First published in paperback in 1997
by HEADLINE BOOK PUBLISHING

10 9 8 7 6 5 4 3 2 1

ISBN 0 7472 5355 2

Typeset by
Letterpart Limited, Reigate, Surrey

Printed and bound in Great Britain by
Cox & Wyman Ltd, Reading, Berks

HEADLINE BOOK PUBLISHING
A division of Hodder Headline PLC
338 Euston Road
London NW1 3BH

This book is dedicated to Luke,
with apologies for doing the unforgivable and
invading the pitch.
Also to the memory of his friend, Thomas Kenwright.
Stay young forever, Kenny.

Chapter 1

It is not given to many women, Phoebe was to reflect later, to lose a husband and gain a fortune on the same day. Not, that is, when the two events are utterly disconnected. Even in those early days of terror and uncertainty there had been a little niggling awareness that there would come a time, well into the future, when she would tell this tale at parties, and make a good story of it, too. She dismissed the thought at once, but though ashamed she was also relieved by the knowledge that her heart, while undoubtedly broken now, would be susceptible to the curative Band-Aids of time and money.

For the purposes of a good story, the two separate events must happen simultaneously, and indeed her discovery of them did, in a sense, take place on the same day, if not at the same hour. In fact, at the moment when the little numbered balls were tumbling down the chute in the magic sequence that was to bring her just over three-quarters of a million pounds (eleven people shared the jackpot that week), Leo was there, pulling the cork from rather a good bottle of claret. It came out with a satisfying pop – the showman in him made sure of that; not for Leo the discreet easing out with only a whispering sigh as the cork came free.

Phoebe heard the pop as she lit the candles. In the six months since their marriage they had evolved a weekend routine, made all the more special because Leo worked abroad during the week, disappearing on Monday morning and returning on Friday. On Friday evening they celebrated his return with a bottle of champagne and a light meal of something like lobster that involved little or no cooking, and went to bed early to discover anew the passionate delights of their physical union. On Saturday evening they occasionally went to a restaurant or, if they stayed at home, Phoebe cooked a special meal which they ate by candlelight. Sunday was a late roast lunch with all the trimmings, supper in front of the television and another early night to make up in advance for the lonely week to come.

Phoebe's eyes lingered on the table. The crocus flames of the candles there, and in the graceful wrought-iron chandelier that hung above it, were reflected in the glass of a Victorian-style conservatory. The small square dining room, originally rather dark and poky, now had a kind of lighthearted elegance, the pretty Regency furniture blending with the rioting plants and colour-washed rattan chairs. Leo had bought the cottage during those heady weeks of courtship. He had almost from their first meeting displayed a certainty about their ultimate relationship that Phoebe had found both exciting and endearing.

Their first encounter had been one of those ridiculous, chance-in-a-million things that Phoebe, a sensible and practical teacher, would have dismissed as far-fetched if anyone else had told her about it. Loaded with carrier bags after an exhausting Saturday of pre-Christmas shopping, she had run (staggered, he had jokingly said afterwards) to catch a taxi that had pulled up to the pavement to drop someone off. Unnoticed by her, he had also been hurrying to the vehicle – it was a cold day of penetrating drizzle, and every taxi that passed had been taken.

Their hands had met on the handle of the door, and he swore afterwards that he had felt a kind of electric shock at that first touch, even through their gloves. Since both of them were going to Victoria they had shared the taxi, and when he had invited her to join him for a cup of tea before her train she had seen no harm in accepting. He could scarcely do her much harm in so public a place, and besides, he was so charming . . . the cups of tea grew cold and were renewed several times as they talked. With courtesy, although Phoebe already felt she knew him well enough to trust him with her telephone number, he had refrained from asking for it, but had given her his and left it for her to decide whether to contact him. Within a day, she had done so, and they had embarked on a whirlwind round of meals, concerts, plays, and best of all endless, fascinating talk. By March, they were married.

'What are we having? Shall I open a bottle of white as well?'

Leo's voice had been the first thing Phoebe had noticed about him. Deep and clear, it was as expressive as a well played 'cello, and still even his most mundane remark gave her a shiver of pleasure.

'Crab parcels to start, and lamb fillet in a herb crust. A glass of white with the crab, perhaps? We can finish it tomorrow evening, or I'll use it up during the week.'

His voice was warm with loving amusement.

'How many times do I have to tell you, my thrifty little darling, that we don't have to worry about things like that? If you want a glass of white then I'll open a bottle, and to hell with when it's finished. Or champagne? A little drop of champagne, now, and carry it on into the meal? If those luscious-looking objects in the steamer are the crab parcels, then I should think they deserve champagne.'

'No, just wine will be lovely.' It was true that Phoebe, though she had always had enough money to live in reasonable comfort, was not used to the kind of throw-away opulence that Leo seemed to take for granted. 'What's the point of having to tear myself away from you for more than half the week, if we don't enjoy the fruits of my labours?' he would say, rolling the r and declaiming the final words. Phoebe, seeing his pleasure in showering her with luxuries, seldom turned them down, but too much champagne gave her hiccups.

'White wine it is. There's a bottle of Cloudy Bay in the fridge . . .' She heard his feet on the Italian tiles of the kitchen floor as, his initial disappointment gone, he crossed to the utility room. Phoebe gave one last glance at the table. One creamy petal had fallen from the arrangement of late roses she had cut in the garden the previous morning. About to pick it up she hesitated, then left it. Against the deep shine of the polished rosewood it glowed like an ivory shell, relieving the perfect symmetry of the carefully placed flowers and giving the table a touch of humanity. Too much perfection is unnatural, she thought, and then shivered, for was not her own life now almost too perfect to be true?

'Cold?' Leo came in with two glasses of white wine. 'Shall I turn the heating up?'

'No, of course not, it's bad enough having it on at all, when it's only September. It was just one of those shivers.'

'A *frisson*, in fact.' They touched glasses, drank. The wine was cool but not too cold, exploding in the mouth with delicate flavours. To Phoebe, who had always rather disliked white wine, it had been a revelation. But then life since she met Leo had been so full of such discoveries that she felt as though she had been in perpetual hibernation for the previous thirty-five years.

He put an arm round her to lead her to the conservatory chairs. Not particularly tall – he was only four inches over her own five-foot-six – he nevertheless gave the impression of size. Partly because of his build: he had the body of a lifelong sportsman, broad and muscled and still without an ounce of flab, although they were already planning his fiftieth birthday party the following year. Mainly, though, it was the overwhelming vitality that expressed itself in every movement he made and word he spoke. It was as though a giant had been confined in a human body, and it seemed entirely natural that his brown hair, receding now at the temples but still thick over his head, should crackle and spark with static when brushed, while his hazel eyes sometimes appeared to emit their own flashes as they gleamed with amusement, with excitement or with interest.

His arm squeezed her shoulders gently before releasing her so that she could sit down. The thick cushions received her with an almost equally affectionate hold as she sank into them. Leo put down his glass and leaned back in the twin of her chair, stretching out his arms and legs luxuriously.

'Saturday evening!' He lingered over the words as if savouring them. 'How I love Saturday evening. A wonderful day behind us, and another wonderful day ahead. Perfection!'

He had the art, Phoebe thought, of enjoying the present without thought of the past or future, something that most people lost as they left childhood behind. Relishing as he did the luxuries of their existence, he still extracted the sweetness from every small pleasure: a sunset or a moonrise; a perfect flower in the garden; the iridescence of a picked-up feather; the scent of woodsmoke from the sitting-room fire. He garnered these joys with a kind of happy greed and shared them with her, laying them as it were in her hands, like jewels.

Phoebe sipped her wine, her eyes drawn to Leo's reflection in the dark glass. Looking up he caught her gaze, and smiled.

'You're looking particularly luscious tonight, Mrs Miller. New dress?'

Phoebe glanced at her own reflection. The new dress (he always noticed things like that) was a deep red, dramatic against the creamy skin that never seemed to take the sun, and the short dark hair, newly trimmed, that had just enough curl in it to hold its bouncy shape. It was lucky, she thought, that Leo was away during the week: if she were to eat as well all week as she did during the weekend she would soon lose her slim figure. As it was the soft jersey clung becomingly, revealing no unsightly bulges.

They lingered over the meal. Afterwards Phoebe was to look back over this and all the other conversations she had had with him, trying to remember what they had talked about, searching for things that should have alerted her, that should have told her to be wary of him. But of course she never had been, not from that very first moment when they climbed into the taxi together.

'Delicious!' said Leo, finishing his crab. 'How you spoil me! You know, if it weren't that you have to work so hard to make this beautiful food, I'd say that I prefer eating here, just the two of us, to going to any restaurant you care to name.'

'I think I do too,' said Phoebe, looking round the pretty room with a pleasure as keen as when it was first decorated. 'And I don't mind the cooking. In fact, I enjoy it.'

'But isn't it dull, with just me for company? I should take you out and about, show you a bit of life . . .'

'After thirteen years of teaching English to adolescents, I think I've seen about as much life as I want to, thank you.'

'Go on with you, you know you loved those kids. Don't tell me you don't miss them even a little bit!'

'Well, yes, of course I do. All those years of seeing them grow up through the school. When I was doing it I did nothing but complain about them – well, we all did, and it's true that a few of them were awful – but then you'd have the odd one that really wanted to learn, and that made it all worth while. But that was then, and a different life. This is the life I want to see now – your face, across the table.'

Watching the way the skin crinkled round his eyes as he smiled at her, she thought how amazing it was that she should be able to say such a thing without embarrassment. There had been a time when even the thought of it would have made her hot all over. Brought up by a mother who could not have been more loving or supportive, but who regarded problems as something you kept to yourself and did not bother other people with, she had always found it difficult to show her feelings.

'And you're not too lonely? You're making some friends?'

'Well . . .' She hesitated, then, when she saw his face, wished she had lied. The truth was that after six months of living here, she still knew scarcely anyone, and then mostly by sight. The situation of the cottage itself was partly to blame. The village, in the uplands of East Sussex, was arranged down the two sides of the road that ran through it. The church at one end, and the pub at the other, marked the two social centres of the community. Phoebe had never been a church-goer, and didn't much care for pubs even if it had not meant going by herself. Their early Victorian cottage was not, in any case, in the centre of the village, but at the end of a narrow lane that went between fields to a farm. It was surrounded by a large garden, which was itself secluded by high hedges of hawthorn and holly, so that unless you knew there was a house there it was easy to miss it altogether.

None of this, of course, would have mattered if Phoebe herself had actually wanted to make new friends. The truth was that she had spent the last six months in a kind of happy daze. Never, in the wildest excesses of her youthful imaginings, had she thought she would experience anything like the bliss she was in and, like a miser, she wanted to hug it to herself, savour it in secret. Partly she feared that the touch of the outside world might burst the rainbowed bubble of her new life. It seemed almost too good to be true that she should have found, quite suddenly, a man who was intellectually, emotionally and physically exciting. Her old friends, who had once been so important to her, had now been allowed to drift to the periphery of her life, remembered with a pang of guilty shame when she realised she had forgotten a birthday, or to return a telephone call. As for making new friends, she would make an effort, of course, but not just yet.

'The vicar called,' she said now. 'Bob.'

'Aah, Bob.'

'Bob.' They patted the name backwards and forwards between them, like a tennis ball.

'With his guitar?' he asked hopefully. Phoebe grinned.

'Of course not! With a copy of the parish magazine, and a tactful sounding-out as to whether I would help with the Sunday school. Qualified teacher, all that kind of thing. I felt rather guilty turning him down, but I said that I felt it would be wrong for me to be teaching something I wasn't sure I believed in myself.'

'A masterly argument.' Leo put down his knife and fork to applaud softly. 'And that stopped him in his tracks?'

'Not exactly. He tried to get me to join a study group, and when I turned that down he moved on to the flower rota.'

'Pushy?'

Phoebe thought about the tall, thin young vicar. He had folded his long body into a conservatory chair, his awkward movements betraying a distrust of such comfort. The freshly ground and brewed coffee she gave him, however, had made him relax, as though his subconscious had decided to give in and relish the sybaritic luxury while he had the chance. His diffident manner had, she thought, hidden a sharp intelligence that was sadly unleavened by humour.

'Not pushy, no. Just doing his job, and doing it pretty well, I'd say. Anyway, he didn't manage to get me on to any rotas or committees or classes. I did promise something for the harvest festival, though.'

'Fair enough. Pumpkins? Shiny apples? Sheaves of corn?'

'Some pots of my jam, I think. The old people in the village tend to be rather insulted if people bring them apples or marrows, so he makes up hampers and auctions them off. Rather a good idea. Anyway, that was Bob. Other than that, I saw that rather odd old woman in the droopy hat, the one who marches along the lanes talking to herself.'

'Or the rabbits. Perhaps she's talking to the rabbits?'

'Possibly. I've never asked. I always say good morning to her, and she growls something back but keeps right on marching and muttering. I suppose she's perfectly safe, but she is a bit scary.'

'Care in the community, darling. Does she smell?'

'Smell? Not that I've noticed.'

'She washes, then. That's all right. People that can keep themselves clean are probably not too far gone.'

'I suppose so. I'd never thought about that. Anyway, I see her most days, and that's about all. Oh, no, I met the woman from the rather nice house near the pub. Jennifer something. She asked me for coffee the next day, said she had a few friends coming round. It seemed churlish to say no, but when I got there it was a coffee morning in aid of arthritic cats, or something. Bit of a con, I thought. I had coffee and a digestive, and bought some raffle tickets, but they were all a bit what one of my student teachers called "clicky". All talking about prep schools and au pairs and the pony club, so I didn't stay long.'

'Pity, but I can't say I'm sorry. I don't want to have to share you with a horsey clique. Click. Actually, I don't want to share you with anyone. Is that selfish of me? I miss you so much during the week, I grudge every minute of our weekends together. As long as you're not lonely? Or nervous, here on your own?'

'Never. It's not at all a creepy house, is it? Even the first time we saw it, when it was empty and full of cobwebs and dust, it still felt friendly.'

'That would have been the spiders. Friendly creatures, I always think. Always keen to share one's bath. But seriously, we are a bit isolated here. I worry about you sometimes. What about a dog?'

'I did think about that. It would be rather nice, actually, only I'm not sure I know how to bring up a dog. I can't bear them when they bark all the time, and jump up at you with muddy paws, and stick their noses up your legs. And that's quite apart from the house-training.'

'Just be firm with them. Like teaching the kids.'

'Well, most of them were house-trained. But it's true I feel more able to cope with a class of thirty fifteen-year-olds than one puppy. I suppose it's because we never had dogs when I was a child. People who grew up with them know how to go about it.'

'You didn't grow up with thirty fifteen-year-olds.'

'No, but I *was* one.'

'And you can still remember it, unlike most people. Hell, wasn't it?'

'Pretty much. Funny how people forget, isn't it? I swore I never would. I always told myself that if I had children I would remember how it was.'

Having children was a subject they tended to veer away from. Phoebe, feeling that at thirty-six she couldn't afford to waste time, had not bothered with precautions for months, but so far there was no sign of a baby. Phoebe told herself it was early days, and there was no need for medical checks yet. She cast about for a change of subject, but Leo beat her to it. As always, his question followed so naturally from their previous talk that Phoebe couldn't tell whether he was steering the conversation or not.

'And Millie? Have you heard from her this week?'

'Not a thing. I tried to call her, but she's passed on.'

Leo, familiar by now with the family code, was able to hear this without distress, correctly inferring that his mother-in-law had not died, but had simply moved to a different address.

'Already? She'd only been there about two weeks, hadn't she? She must be slipping.'

'No, I think she was being tactful. Their daughter's left her husband and come rushing home, and Millie felt she couldn't be much help with that, so she upped and offed. They were in such a state they forgot to ask her who she was going to next, and there's no reply from the London flat. Oh well, in a week or two she'll suddenly realise she hasn't heard from me, and ring me up.'

Phoebe's voice sounded faintly forlorn. Leo reached across for her hand.

'Darling, you know you're welcome to ring everyone you can think of, if you want to. You know most of her friends' numbers, don't you?'

'Yes, of course, and it's sweet of you to suggest it. I can't do it, though. She would just loathe it. She'd feel as though I was checking up on her. And she'd simply hate her friends to think that she didn't remember to phone me. She doesn't, of course, but what's new?'

'Darling Millie, such a scatterbrain, I adore her.'

'Of course you do. So does everyone. That's how she gets away with it.'

'She's amazing, isn't she? I always thought that kind of visiting went out with the last war, when nobody had servants any more. Nowadays you're lucky to stay a night, or at most a weekend, but somehow all that has passed her by. She's like a dinosaur. No, that's too ugly. Like one of those fossil ferns – so delicate and beautiful, but set in solid rock.'

'She does make herself useful.' Phoebe was not sure whether Millie was being criticised, and as always went into instant defence of her mother.

'Of course she does! She's the perfect guest. Why else would all those people have her back, time after time? She's turned being a house-guest into an art form.'

Millie Humphreys had been a notably lovely girl, and at her present age of sixty was a woman of whom the word pretty might still justifiably be used. Smaller than her daughter, she was slim, with none of the bony stringiness of some older women. Her blonde hair had silvery streaks that only accentuated its golden fairness, and the only lines on her delicately made-up skin were from smiling. Inexpensively but attractively dressed, she had a knack of always looking right for whatever setting she might find herself in; a knack that Phoebe longed to possess, but felt she had never achieved.

The one subject Millie, who was open and forthcoming to a disarming degree, was never prepared to discuss was Phoebe's father. Even to Phoebe herself she would say no more than that their liaison had been brief and had ended abruptly. The word 'lost' was implied though never actually used and the child Phoebe, accustomed to her mother's habit of losing everything from umbrellas to house keys or even, occasionally, cars, had grown up with the impression that her father had somehow been mislaid. She had envisaged him being left behind on a departing train, or wandering aimlessly through a maze of anonymous streets, both of which things had happened to her. In later years she had assumed, more rationally but with no concrete evidence, that he was dead.

In her childhood she and her mother had lived in a succession of small flats in the cheaper areas of London. Money had always been a problem, but Millie had somehow found the means to send her only child to a good school and, afterwards, helped her through university and teacher's training. When Phoebe had left home to share a flat with a group of friends, Millie had instantly moved into a tiny bedsit and embarked on the first of what proved to be an endless succession of visits to friends. From then on she spent no more than a few days of any month in her nominal home, but moved like an old-time monarch on what was scarcely less than a triumphal progress round the country.

As Leo said, Millie had re-invented the art of being a perfect house-guest. Cheerful and accommodating, she had a chameleon-like ability to adapt to whatever way of life her hosts had chosen. With unfeigned pleasure she would throw herself into helping with their plans, and she was particularly good at parties, so that friends intending to give one frequently begged her to come a week or two before to assist with the arrangements. Millie could make an armful of leaves and flowers from the garden look like a professional arrangement; she made delicious and beautiful canapés and snacks; she could be relied on to rescue people from the local bore, and she never shirked the washing up. She always arrived, moreover, with an elegant treat, like a small pot of caviar, a basket of exotic fruit, or some luscious Belgian chocolates. And, above all these other things, she was discreet, disappearing quietly to her room or for a walk at those times when her hosts showed signs of wishing to have a private discussion (or row) and never, under any circumstances, repeating any gossip to subsequent benefactors.

An equal discretion was upheld regarding her love life. Certainly she never lacked a male escort, and there had been times in Phoebe's childhood when they had known a certain affluence which was almost certainly paid for by a current man friend. At the same time, whatever sexual adventures her mother might have indulged in were always carried on elsewhere. No man ever spent the night in any of their flats, where Phoebe, until she reached the age of fourteen, usually had to share her mother's bedroom. Of recent years Millie seemed to have abandoned such things without regret; no whisper of scandal was ever heard in connection with any of the couples she stayed with, and even the most possessive wives seemed perfectly happy to risk having her in the house. Somehow, without anything being said, Millie managed to make it clear to everyone she met that she was not sexually available, and although she flirted charmingly she did so with care.

'A mobile phone!' exclaimed Leo as they stacked the dishes in the dishwasher. 'Why didn't I think of that before? It would be just the thing for Millie. You'd be able to ring her anywhere, whenever you wanted.'

'As long as she hadn't lost it, and always providing she remembered to recharge it, and switch it on.' Phoebe saw his face. 'Sorry, darling, I didn't mean to knock your brilliant idea. And it really is brilliant, only we'd have to be patient for a while, until she got used to it. She could have mine, really. I hardly ever use it.'

'Nonsense. I like to know you have it with you, for safety. I'll order another. Shall I make coffee?'

'Keeps me awake,' said Phoebe automatically.

'Precisely,' he said, with a leer.

Phoebe slept late the following morning. She woke to find that Leo, who was always full of energy at the beginning of the day, was already up and dressed. She sipped the cup of tea he brought her and smiled to hear him singing in the kitchen as he got the breakfast ready. In deference to the roast lunch they never ate much, but there was Greek yoghourt with local honey, and Phoebe had bought some peaches and a bunch of grapes that were so big they might have almost have been plums.

Phoebe had a shower, then, tantalised by the smell of coffee, went downstairs in a towelling robe. She was sticky with peach juice when she heard the muffled beeping of a telephone.

'Bother,' she said crossly. 'On a Sunday morning, too. Unless it's Millie, perhaps?'

'I shouldn't think so. It's my mobile,' said Leo, wiping his hands and standing up. Phoebe smiled. She often teased him about his mobile phone, saying it was his comfort object and that he couldn't get to sleep unless he had it snuggled up in bed with him like a teddy bear. Her jokes held more than a grain of truth: Leo never went anywhere without his mobile – it even sat on a shelf in the bathroom when he had a shower. Phoebe had noticed, too, that he never seemed to have calls on the ordinary house telephone. She supposed vaguely that there was no point – everyone knew they could always reach him on the mobile number.

Leo took the bleeping phone from the hook on his belt, and went out to the hall. He did not shut the door behind him, of course, but he had a habit of turning away when talking or listening to it, and Phoebe had learned that it was better not to interrupt him. His work abroad was something of a mystery to her. He always said it was mostly boring routine – endless travelling and hours of discussion with clients – and that most of it was slightly sensitive because in this cut-throat world his competitors were always trying to steal a march on him.

Now he was listening intently, saying nothing.

'Right,' he said at last. 'Thanks. Don't worry, I'll see to it.' He clipped the phone back to his belt, and returned to the table.

'Sorry about that, darling. Is there any more coffee?'

'It's cold. I'll make some more.'

When Phoebe returned to the table she saw that he had not moved. The remaining segments of his half-eaten peach still lay on his plate. He nodded his thanks as he refilled his cup, then stood up. Coming round the table he stood beside her, bending to hug her.

'Darling Phoebe. Such a bore, but something's come up. I'll have to go off and see if I can get it sorted out. Sorry to mess up our day, but the sooner I go, the sooner I can be back again. Forgive me?'

Phoebe turned her head to kiss him.

'Of course I forgive you! I'm just sorry you have to lose some of your precious free time. I'll get dressed and get on with the lunch, so don't worry about me. You'll be back for lunch, won't you?'

'Would I miss our Sunday lunch? Of course I'll be back. Darling Phoebe, have I ever told you that I adore you?'

'Just once or twice.' She gave him a little push. 'Off you go. Give them hell.'

She heard him run upstairs. When he came down again he had not changed from his jeans, shirt and pullover, but he carried a waxed jacket over his arm, its large pockets bulging. Automatically he picked up the briefcase that was almost as much a part of him as his mobile phone.

'All right if I take your car?' he called. 'Mine's acting up a bit, don't want to risk it breaking down.'

Before she could do more than nod he had picked up the keys. The front door opened and banged shut, and as Phoebe began to clear the breakfast table she heard the sound of the car engine purring as he reversed out of the garage. There was a pause, and she knew he was activating the remote control to close the garage doors, then the gravelled drive crunched under the wheels as he drove out.

It was, though of course she did not know it then, the last time she would ever see him.

Chapter 2

With an unexpectedly empty morning to fill, Phoebe had to make a conscious effort to be busy. During the week she knew that she would be on her own, and though naturally she missed Leo she did not allow it to bother her. In the early part of the week she fed on memories of the previous weekend, and by Wednesday she was already planning for the following one. Housework and gardening kept her physically occupied, and allowed her mind to dwell on her present happiness without distraction, and it did not occur to her to be surprised that Leo, so generous in every other respect, made no mention of employing a cleaner or a gardener.

This Sunday morning, however, the house felt echoingly empty as it never did on Sundays. Phoebe prepared the vegetables carefully. Potatoes to be roasted with garlic, parsnips with a basting of lime, honey and sesame seeds; carrots for a puree with parsley and plain sprouts – all were peeled and set out meticulously. She even dug a root of fresh horseradish from the garden and grated it with streaming eyes and nose, knowing how Leo adored it. The joint, a rib of beef that was far too large for two but which she would finish during the week, was ready in its tin, and the Yorkshire pudding batter was resting in a jug.

At mid-day she put the beef in the oven where the potatoes were already fragrantly sizzling, and made herself a cup of coffee. Leo would surely be back soon; she might as well sit down with the Sunday papers for half an hour – once he was there she wouldn't want to waste time reading them.

The papers lay on the table in the hall where Leo had left them. The shop in the village had a delivery service, but Leo preferred to walk briskly down to fetch them himself, since he was invariably awake by half past seven. Phoebe took them to the sitting room, where she had earlier lit the fire. An unusually hot summer had broken with a bang and the morning, which had started cloudy, had degenerated into drizzling rain which, though it was not cold, was damp and dismal. The sitting room, like the dining room, opened onto the conservatory, which ran along the entire length of the back of the house. Phoebe kicked off her shoes and curled up on the sofa, abandoning the larger news sections in favour of the colour supplement, which was easier to hold.

There were several unusually interesting articles, and for a while Phoebe was engrossed. By the time she laid the magazine aside the clock in the hall was striking one, and she hurried through to the kitchen. The window was blurred with rain on the outside and steam within: she flung it open but a flurry of rain blew in and she shut it hastily. There was no sign of a returning car, and she turned the oven down, telling herself that if he was going to be late he would have telephoned her by now, and that he was sure to be back soon. There was nothing that needed doing, and she returned resolutely to the papers.

The news section, however, could not hold her attention. Twice she started to read an item that looked interesting, only to have her concentration broken by the sound of a car in the lane. Each time she put the paper down, ready to go and put the sprouts on to cook and make the gravy, only to subside again as the car failed to turn into the drive. Distracted, she flicked through the pages, her eyes skimming the headlines but failing to assimilate them. Even the lottery numbers flickered past her unrecognised, and she had actually dropped the paper on the floor before their implication hit her.

Without excitement, because she disbelieved the evidence of her flurried mind, she picked up the pages which had come apart, neatly re-aligning them and crisping up the fold before allowing herself to look again. She started at them in disbelief, frowning a little. Her lips moved as she murmured the numbers to herself, the sequence so familiar that she thought she must be imagining it, reading what was not really there.

Foolishly, she had fallen into the trap of selecting numbers from birthdays and other significant dates. She bought only one ticket a week, laughing at herself but saying defensively that one pound was a small price to pay for a weekly glimmer of excitement. Having used the same numbers every week she was now trapped. If ever the numbers came up and she had not bought a ticket, how could she ever forgive herself for throwing away a fortune?

Having checked the row of numbers several times, she could no longer deny that they were the right ones. Now, with trembling hands, she ran for her bag and scrabbled through it, unable for a moment to remember which pocket she had put the ticket in, although it was always the same place. Finding it, she smoothed it between her fingers, reading the numbers as though fearing that she might, by some mishap, have marked entirely different ones last week. Putting the ticket down on the paper she checked them off one by one, marking each with the forefinger of each hand like a child struggling to read. There was no doubt about it. They were exactly the same. A jackpot of eight million pounds, the black letters screamed. She shook her head. What would she do with eight million pounds, she who already had everything she could ever want? The figures seemed almost obscene, and she was relieved when she saw that it was likely to be shared between several people.

Thrusting her feet into her shoes, she ran to the front door and out into the lane, oblivious of the rain. Hopping like a child with excitement she strained to see Leo's returning car. She could almost hear his bellow of laughter when she told him the news. He had always teased her about buying a lottery ticket.

'If you must gamble, do it properly!' he had said. 'Buy a hundred, or a thousand! Bring the odds down a bit! You'll never win with only one!'

'One is all you need,' she had pointed out, 'and anyway, I don't expect to win it.'

'Then why do it at all?' he asked reasonably. 'If you want money, I'll give it to you, you know that.'

'I know you will. You give me far too much already. This is just for fun, because it's still a new thing and it's easy.'

'Well, I won't call Gamblers Anonymous just yet, then.'

Strain though she might, Phoebe could neither see nor, more importantly since the lane was far from straight, hear any approaching car. Even the distant murmur from the main road was silent. She resisted the urge to run down the lane to the village, realised she was getting wet, and went reluctantly back indoors.

It seemed a ridiculous situation to be in. Phoebe longed to tell someone about her good fortune, but she had no way of finding Millie, and in any case she wanted Leo to be the first to know. Then her eye fell on the telephone, and she shook her head with impatience at her own stupidity. Leo's mobile! She snatched up the receiver, only to realise belatedly that the excitement had driven all memory of the number out of her head. During the week, of course, she could not telephone him on it because he was abroad, and at weekends they were invariably together so that she had seldom had need to use it. Once again she scrabbled through her handbag, this time for her diary.

When she heard a ringing tone she was relieved, having feared that it might have been switched off, but her relief ebbed away when the ringing was unanswered. Stubbornly, hoping against hope, she waited. Perhaps he was in the middle of an important discussion. More likely, he was on the road, hurrying to be home for lunch and unable to pull up. After several minutes, however, she was forced to give up, though five minutes later she could not resist trying again. Still there was no answer.

Caught between frustration and annoyance, she went back to the kitchen. Everything in the oven was cooked: she took out the joint and the roast vegetables and put them on serving dishes in the warmer. The Yorkshire pudding batter had settled, the flour forming a thick sludge in the bottom of the jug. Absently she stirred it up. The clock in the hall struck two.

The telephone rang. Phoebe started so violently that the jug of batter that she was still stirring tipped over. She ignored it, and ran to the hall.

'Hello?' She was breathless, her voice high with excitement. 'Leo?'

'Is that Phoebe Miller?' The woman's voice, strong and confident, rang in her ear because she had the receiver pressed so tightly against it. 'Jennifer here. Hope I didn't disturb you. You weren't in the middle of lunch, were you?'

'Lunch?' said Phoebe idiotically, as if she had never heard the word before. 'Oh, lunch. No. No, not at the moment.'

'Good. We have our meal in the evening – never enough hours of daylight for the garden, are there? – and I always forget. Anyway, it's good news. You've won something.'

'How did you know?' Phoebe was astonished. Surely nobody could possibly know what numbers she put on her lottery ticket?

'Well, it was at my house.' Jennifer sounded puzzled, her voice careful as though she was dealing with someone slightly deranged. 'The raffle, you know. You bought some tickets the other day, and one of them's won a prize.'

'Oh, the *raffle*!' Phoebe giggled with relief. 'I'd quite forgotten about it. I hope you had a successful morning?'

'Not bad. Eighty-seven pounds and thirty-four pee. Why, what did you think I meant? Have you won something else? Don't tell me – not the lottery?'

'Don't I wish!' answered Phoebe, with a laugh. The question, she knew, had been a joke, and she was certainly not going to admit the truth to someone she barely knew. 'I'm glad your do went so well. What have I won? I can't remember the prizes.'

'Well, just between the two of us, nothing to get too excited about. I'm afraid the main prizes had already gone, so it was a toss-up between a home-made cake from Mrs Mallory, and a crochet tea cosy. As you weren't there I made a unilateral decision and went for the tea cosy.'

'Oh . . . fine . . .'

'Well, I thought someone as slim as you probably doesn't eat cake. And besides, just between the two of us, I bought one of Mrs Mallory's cakes at the church fête, and it was full of bits of eggshell. Disgusting, crunching in your teeth, I had to throw it away. She's into one-bowl cakes, and I suspect she just throws the whole egg in with everything else. Couldn't inflict that on you. Put you off the village for life!'

'Oh, no . . .'

Jennifer forged on. Phoebe could just visualise her, standing sturdily foursquare in her jeans and riding boots, topped with a blue striped shirt with pie-frilled collar, and the navy padded waistcoat that she wore almost all the year round. Her broad face, weathered by a lifetime of outdoor living, would be innocent of make-up and the skin of her cheeks would be coated by no more than a heavy growth of down, with here and there a coarser sprouting hair. Phoebe found her daunting, with her loud voice and her blunt, sometimes tactless manner, and saw her as representing a class of countrywoman that she herself neither could nor would want to belong to.

'You don't have to use it, of course. The tea cosy, I mean. Just give it to a jumble sale, or another raffle. In another part of England, preferably! Mustn't hurt people's feelings! My sister lives in Norfolk, so whenever we meet we swap a boxful of stuff – juffle, we call it. Cross between jumble and raffle! Works a treat! You got any family?'

'Um, no. Just my mother, and she travels a lot. In England, that is.'

'Good for her. I always say we're dreadful stick-in-the-muds. Or is it sticks-in-the-mud? The girls are always on about going abroad, but as I say to them, darlings, if you want to go to the point-to-points and the shows it just can't be done! You can't go off and leave a horse for two or three weeks and then expect it to jump a clear round for you. One or the other, I say, and that usually shuts them up.'

Phoebe thought that it probably would, in fact it was a wonder they managed to get a word in in the first place. She had seen Jennifer's twin daughters out on their horses – they were seldom seen without them, and Phoebe had sometimes idly speculated that the horses lived in the house with them, everyone curling up cosily together to watch showjumping on the television.

'Couple like you are just what we need in the village,' Jennifer was continuing heartily. 'Pity your husband has to be away so much, but I expect you keep busy. Bob been to see you, has he? Did he mention the Sunday school?'

'Yes, but I told him I couldn't help. For one thing, I like to keep my weekends free for Leo, and for another, I'm not really very sure about God.'

'Oh, nor am I! I sometimes think that if He does exist, He must have a pretty weird sense of humour. Or maybe He's just a bit of a bastard,' said Jennifer with cheerful irreverence. 'What I do believe in is supporting the village church. It's so hard to keep any sense of community these days, isn't it? What about the Brownies? Brown Owl could do with a bit of help, and they meet during the week. You were a teacher, weren't you?'

'Yes, I *was*,' said Phoebe, firmly emphasising the verb. 'And I can't tell you how lovely it is, after all those years, to be free of other people's children.' She wondered, after she had spoken, whether her edginess over Leo had made her speak too abruptly. She was relieved to hear Jennifer laugh again.

'I don't blame you! That's fair enough! Well, do you want to come and fetch your sumptuous prize, or shall I drop it round some time? No trouble, I often walk the dogs down your way.'

'Yes, come and have tea or coffee with me,' suggested Phoebe, shamed by Jennifer's good nature and needing to make amends.

'Lovely. I was hoping you'd say that. I've been dying to see what you've done with the house. I hear you've had the most wonderful conservatory built, and you've turned that little bedroom into an en suite bathroom. I'll pop in one day next week, shall I?'

'Yes, do,' said Phoebe. Next week, she thought. By next week Leo will be away at work, instead of just out, and I'll be quite glad of the company.

Phoebe, her mind slightly calmed by the normality of the call, depressed the button on the telephone and then tried the mobile number again. Surely this time Leo would answer, full of apologies and explanations. She watched the face of the hall clock, hearing the rhythmic tick and seeing, in her imagination, the cogs turning as the pendulum swung, teeth meshing and disengaging. The ring of the telephone was almost, but not quite, synchronised with the ticking. She counted the rings. When she reached two hundred, which must be more than three minutes, she put the handset down and stood, leaning against the table. The clock clunked, preparing to chime again. Half past two.

Phoebe went back to the kitchen, and drearily wiped up the puddle of Yorkshire pudding batter that had dripped its way down to the floor. There seemed little point in mixing any more. Unable to settle, she roamed round the house. She was not particularly anxious. Obviously whatever crisis had sent Leo hurrying off was more difficult to resolve than he had originally thought. The sight of the table she had once again laid so carefully made her feel cross and let down, as did the drying joint and the roast potatoes that were now dark and leathery. She was hungry, but could not bear to eat any of the lunch. She cut herself a hunk of bread and cheese, and ate it standing up in the conservatory. The dry food was hard to swallow. She drank two glasses of water and felt better.

Trying to distract herself, she thought about the lottery win. She supposed she should be telephoning the lottery number, setting the wheels in motion. Without Leo beside her, however, it seemed a bit pointless. His excitement and enthusiasm would raise what was already a special event into a positive firework display; without him there, it all seemed almost meaningless.

The telephone rang again. This time, surely, it must be Leo? She snatched it up.

'Leo?'

'Hello, darling. It's me!'

'Oh. Oh, hello, Millie.'

'Why did you think I was Leo? Isn't he there?'

'No. No, something came up, from work. Some kind of crisis. He had to go and sort it out.'

'Poor Leo, on a Sunday. And poor you, too! I am sorry, darling. I'll get off the line, he's sure to ring soon. Such a thoughtful man!'

'No, it's all right.' With an effort, Phoebe pulled her mind back from Leo to her mother. 'Where are you staying? Helen said you'd left them when I rang on Wednesday, but she couldn't remember where you were going.'

'Well, I wasn't very sure where I was going myself. So difficult for poor Helen, with that drippy daughter coming home and wailing at her, crying all day and then waking her up in the night to tell her just how awful she felt! They needed my room, and I felt very much in the way, so I just retreated. I intended to go back to London, but I met such a lovely couple on the train, some Argentinians called Abercrombie. I ask you, Abercrombie! They were spending the night in London, and then travelling up to Edinburgh. They'd rented a house for a month, because he wanted to trace his ancestors. We got on like a house on fire – really, such an *interesting* family – and they thought it would be a help to have someone with them who really knew Edinburgh, so here I am!'

'Millie!' Phoebe felt the indescribable mixture of terror and exasperation that only her mother could inspire. 'Are you telling me you've gone off to Edinburgh with a couple who picked you up on a train?'

'Yes, darling, but they didn't pick me up. So sordid! We *met* one another. We made friends. I knew at once – you know how one does – that we would like one another, and I was quite right! The most delightful people, and anyway, they know the Fortescues.'

'Everybody knows the Fortescues. Or knows of them.'

'Well, the Abercrombies know them. And, what's more, the Fortescues know the Abercrombies! I checked. They stayed with them in Argentina, and the Abercrombies took them to see some marvellous waterfalls called something like Lizard Zoo . . . no, that can't be right . . .'

'Iguazu. But Millie—'

'That's right, darling, how clever you are. I knew it had a zoo in it. Iguanas, not lizards, I must remember that. And they went in a boat, right behind the water, and there were the most wonderful rainbows. It sounds lovely, doesn't it?'

Phoebe gave up.

'Yes, lovely. So you're in Edinburgh? Are they enjoying it?'

'Very much, though we haven't got round to the ancestors yet. Wonderful shopping. Isabella just loves it!' Millie adored shopping, and though she bought little for herself she always knew the best places for everything, and was good at finding things that other people would like. 'Anyway, I didn't want you to be worried about me, so I thought I'd ring and give you the number.'

They chatted, and Phoebe made an effort to sound normal. She thought she had succeeded, but Millie was, as usual, more perceptive than her daughter realised.

'Are you all right, darling? You're not too worried about Leo, are you?'

'No, of course I'm not.' To her horror, Phoebe felt her throat swell painfully, as if from a sudden onset of mumps. Her eyes filled with tears. 'No problem,' she managed huskily. There was a short, thoughtful pause, which was unusual in itself. Millie hated to waste a second of a telephone call, and was careful of her friends' phone bills.

'Right, then.' She sounded her usual brisk self. Phoebe's tears vanished. I'm not hurt, she told herself. Millie is being very sensible. She's up in Edinburgh, and I'm down in Sussex. Ridiculous to think she could do anything – a hangover from early childhood, Phoebe supposed, when 'Mummy will make it better' still carried its potent magic. They said goodbye.

With a conscious effort, Phoebe waited until the clock had struck half past three before trying the number of the mobile again. She was not at all surprised when the ringing tone continued as before, but once again she waited, counting the rings. On forty there was a click. The ringing stopped and there was a low crackling hum that always accompanied such calls. Phoebe closed her eyes with relief, and felt her knees tremble.

'Leo!' Her voice came out scarcely louder than a whisper. 'Leo, where are you? What's been happening? I've been trying to ring you for ages. Are you all right?'

There was a pause. The voice which answered was cultured and, though deep, it was not a man's.

'I'm sorry. This isn't Leo.'

'Who is it? Who are you? Where's Leo?'

'Just a minute.' Phoebe heard strange noises: creaks and splintering sounds, a grunting breath, a splash.

'What are you doing? Hello! Hello, are you still there? Hello?'

'Still here.' The voice was breathless. 'Sorry. I was slipping into the ditch. Had to get back down the bank.'

'Look, would you please let me speak to Leo? It's his wife.' Phoebe used the voice she had once used to quell her class of obstreperous teenagers.

'I'm sorry, I can't. There's no one here. It's just—'

Phoebe interrupted. 'What are you doing with his phone, then? What's happened? Is he all right? What the *hell*'s happening? Who are you? *Where* are you?'

'Blackwater Lane.'

'Blackwater Lane? You mean, Blackwater Lane outside Oakhurst?'

'Yes.'

'But that's– that's less than a mile away. Has there been an accident? Is the car there? Oh, God . . .'

'No, it's all right. No car, no sign of an accident. No skid marks, or anything like that. I just heard it ringing, and it went on and on, so I scrambled across the ditch and found it. It rang for such a long time, I thought it must be important.'

'Important! Of course it's important!' Phoebe's voice was high and shrill. She drew in a long breath, and swallowed. 'I'm sorry. It's just . . . who are you?'

'Daphne Cunningham. Old Hall Cottage. Are you the people

who've moved into Ember Cottage? Red car?'

'Yes, that's right. I'm Phoebe Miller. Look, I'm awfully sorry, but would you mind staying there for a moment, until I can come and find you? Just so I can see where you found the phone? It seems so peculiar.'

About to run out of the door, Phoebe gathered up some remnants of sense and went to fetch a waterproof jacket, and her wellingtons. It was still raining, and a nasty gusting little wind had risen, blowing the rain into her face as she hurried down the lane towards the village. Blackwater Lane was another turning off the village street, but unlike her own lane it was not a dead end, but wound a tortuous way through to the main dual carriageway and was frequently used by locals as a cut-through. Phoebe was out of breath by the time she reached it. The figure waiting for her was, alarmingly, the odd old woman she so often saw striding through the lanes muttering to herself. Only the fact that Phoebe could see that she was holding Leo's mobile phone in her hand prevented Phoebe from turning tail and disappearing. Instead she broke into a run, feeling the dampness of sweat round her body and under her arms inside the heavy waxed jacket.

As Phoebe approached, the older woman silently held out the telephone. Phoebe took it, clutching it in her hand, her last hope evaporating at the sight of its familiar scratches. Hardly aware of what she was doing she punched in her number at home, and heard the ringing tone. Numbly she turned it off, and slipped it into her pocket. The woman – Daphne Cunningham, she remembered, the name seeming incongruous for the scarecrow figure beside her – watched incuriously, the water collecting on the drooping brim of her battered waterproof hat.

'Where did you find it?'

A long arm gestured.

'Up there. Want me to show you the place?' Her voice was gruffer than it had sounded on the telephone, her cut-glass accent unselfconscious in its exaggerated clarity. She stepped from the grass verge across a muddy ditch, overgrown with weeds. Phoebe followed her, grabbing at tufts of grass in the opposite bank to help her over, and scrambling up the bank. The old lane had sunk over the years – the roots of the hedgerow at the top of the bank were almost as high as Phoebe's head when she stood on the verge. It was a tangle of hawthorn, blackthorn and bramble, thick and untrimmed, with here and there a cascade of scarlet rosehips. Daphne pointed. Her hand, Phoebe saw, was quite badly scratched.

'It was right in there. I heard it from the lane, but it took me a while to find it.'

'Your hand . . . I'm sorry.' Daphne dismissed the injuries with a casual wave.

'Don't mind that. Half of them are from gardening, anyway. The thing is, how did it get there? I've been thinking about it. Nobody climbed up and put it there. Not a mark on the bank before I started scrambling about – I noticed. Can't have come from the other side – hedgerow's too thick. Only one explanation I can think of, I'm afraid. It was thrown up there. Probably from a car.'

Phoebe looked at her dumbly.

'Passenger side, if you're going towards the village. Driver's side going away,' continued Daphne. Phoebe's feet slid on the wet grass of the bank, and she felt herself steadied by a strong hand. 'Might as well get down.'

Phoebe, back on the rough-edged tarmac, looked up at the hedgerow and tried to imagine the throw.

'Why from a car?' She still clung stubbornly to the hope that someone might have stolen the phone and then, on impulse, got rid of it. Daphne stooped and picked up a short piece of branch, weighing it in her hand.

'Awkward throw, from a car window,' she said. 'Standing up, it would have gone further.' She flung the branch, and they watched it turning end over end against the sky as it cleared the hedgerow completely. Phoebe winced at the thump of its landing, clutching at the hard rectangle of the telephone in her pocket. She felt as though some part of her had gone with that piece of wood.

'Sorry about that,' muttered Daphne. 'You all right?'

Phoebe nodded, clenching in the muscles of her stomach and pulling her spine up straight.

'It's very odd, but I expect there's a perfectly simple explanation,' she said. 'I'd better get back to the house.'

'Right. Daphne thrust her scratched hands into the pockets of the disreputable old mackintosh that looked, Phoebe noticed, as though it had been expensive in the long-ago time when it had been bought. She frowned at Phoebe, who saw that she was wondering reluctantly whether she ought to accompany the younger woman back to her house.

'Thank you so much for your help,' said Phoebe firmly. 'Perhaps you could come and have tea or coffee with me one day soon?'

Daphne frowned.

'Kind of you, but I don't take coffee. Or tea. I expect I shall see you on one of my walks. Tell me how things turn out. If you want to, of course. Don't have to tell me anything. Can't abide gossip.' She was, Phoebe saw, reassuring her that this curious episode would not be spread around the village, and imagining what Jennifer, for instance, would make of it, she was grateful.

'Thank you,' she said again. Daphne nodded her head, a bobbing movement that made the brim of her hat jerk. She turned away and strode off.

The cottage felt cold and empty. Phoebe boiled the kettle and made tea, but found herself unable to drink it, her throat closing against swallowing. Unable to settle, she roamed round the house, looking for something to occupy herself with. They had lived in the house such a short time, even the cupboard under the stairs was still tidy. She foraged through Leo's desk, finding nothing but neatly ordered receipts. No letters, or diary, or even a jotted note, just businesslike arrangements. Guarantees, service contracts for boiler, washing machine, dishwasher – everything she might need, carefully to hand. As if . . . Phoebe closed the desk with infinite gentleness, as if it held something sleeping. Or dead.

Suddenly cold again, she returned to the fire and sat on the rug in front of it. As the warmth soothed her aching limbs she felt her eyelids closing. Reluctant to move, she reached for a cushion from the armchair, and fell into a heavy doze.

The sound of the doorbell jerked her awake from a troubled dream. Her heart pounding she pushed herself into a sitting position, groaning at stiffened joints. The ringing of the doorbell, which she half thought she had imagined, sounded again. Phoebe stood up and went to the door in a stumbling run. Her fingers fumbled at the locks in the dark hall, and when she looked through the spyhole Leo had insisted on installing she could see nothing in the unlit porch. The bell sounded a third time, right in her ear, and instead of switching on the outside light Phoebe twisted the knob and opened the door. Phoebe saw the suitcases first. Bulging, their expensive surfaces scuffed, they were as familiar as her own face in the mirror.

'Millie!'

Her mother stepped into the hall.

'Hello, darling. Goodness, it's dark in here. Shall I put some lights on?'

'How did you get here?' Phoebe felt slow and stupid.

'I flew down. I must say, it's a very good service from Edinburgh, such nice girls, gave me a drink, couldn't have been more helpful. It's very convenient, your living so near Gatwick. The taxi-driver – a delightful man – remarked on it.' Automatically, Phoebe bent to pick up the cases. 'Thank you, darling.'

'But . . . what about your friends? The Argentinians?'

'Oh, they *quite* understood. In fact, they insisted I should come down and be with you.' Phoebe mentally translated this into 'they paid the fare', knowing that her mother could not have afforded it herself.

'How kind. But there was no need.'

Millie tilted her head to look up into Phoebe's face.

'Darling, of course I had to come,' she said briskly. 'I am your mother, after all. Who else should be here with you, if not me?'

Phoebe's eyes filled with tears. Millie patted her arm.

'Now, I've got an especially good bottle of whisky in my bag, the Abercrombies practically *forced* me to take it. Let's find it and pour ourselves a stiff drink, and then you can tell me all about it.'

Chapter 3

Afterwards, when Kate had time to think about it, she was profoundly thankful to have been alone in the house when the two men in suits came to the door. At the time she had assumed that their arrival had something to do with the fact that her three children were all out searching the streets for her missing mother. Their sombre clothes (so inappropriate for Sunday in Brighton) and serious faces made her think, irrationally, that they were undertakers. She had a moment of sick horror when she opened the door, which lurched into panic as they pulled plastic-coated identity cards from inside pockets, and flashed them at her. Assuming they were from the police she failed to take in anything they said, but pulled the door wide to let them in.

'Where is she? Is she all right?'

The two men exchanged a glance.

'Mrs Miller? Is your husband Leonard John Miller?' It was the older, taller man who spoke, his voice as cold and brusque as his manner.

'Len? Yes, of course he is, but he's not here. He's never here at weekends. Never mind him, it's my mother I'm worried about. Is she in hospital? Or – she's not *dead*, is she? I mean, she's not ill, there's nothing wrong with her physically, she just forgets—'

'Mrs Miller.' He broke into the torrent of words with which she was trying to stave off what she didn't want to hear. 'Mrs Miller, I'm afraid we don't know anything about your mother. We're from the bank. Carver and Greenwood,' he explained, seeing her blank expression. 'We'd like to talk to your husband.'

'Oh.' She sagged against the doorframe, relief warring with renewed anxiety. Whatever they wanted, it was irrelevant to her at that moment; Len's work was his problem, her mother was hers. 'Well, he's not here. I told you.'

'Quite so. Perhaps we might come in, Mrs Miller? Sorry to disturb you, but it would be helpful if we could talk to you for a little while.'

Somehow they were already both inside the house. The hall was high and rather gloomy on this sunless early morning. The men seemed to loom at her out of the shadows. Kate switched on the lights, which made them only slightly less menacing. Before shutting the front door she stepped outside and looked up and down the street, as she had done every few minutes since discovering her mother's empty room. No sign of her. Sighing, she came back in and shut the door.

'I suppose I ought to ask you to show me your identity cards again, though I wouldn't know whether they were the real thing or not,' she said, attempting a mild joke. Neither man smiled. Their eyes, she saw, were busy; sharp assessing glances up the stairs, through open doorways. The taller man who had so far done all the talking stepped across the polished wood floor, the soles of his shoes snapping crisply, and opened a door, his eyes flickering swiftly round the cloakroom. Kate watched him, speechless with affronted fury, as he opened the door to her mother's room. When he walked into it she started forward to stop him, feeling as though his official presence both contaminated the room, and made her mother's disappearance official.

'That's my mother's room,' she said sharply. 'I told you, she's not there.'

He ignored her, crossing the room to glance into the little bathroom that had been neatly fitted into the far corner. On his way back he went to the wide double windows that looked out over the garden. He leaned over the deep sill to see the flowerbed beneath, put his hand on the window latch and tested it. The window, fitted with restrainers, opened no more than a few inches. Kate saw her mother's crochet work, a half-finished square that would eventually be joined with others to make a blanket for the Save the Children charity, lying abandoned on the windowsill together with one of the many pairs of glasses she owned. Her eyes filled with tears, and she pushed past the other man to snatch up the work and the spectacles, clutching them to her protectively.

'How *dare* you! I tell you this is my mother's room, her private room! Leave it alone!'

'Just checking, madam.' It was the other man who spoke. He was short and plump, and his flesh looked as soft as dough, while his voice was as soothing as honey is meant to be. Only honey, Kate thought, invariably gave her a tickling catch in her throat, much as the way he called her 'madam' made her want to knee him smartly in the groin. The only people who ever call one madam, she thought, are the ones who are out to get you.

'Perhaps you'd like to "check" the rest of the house?' she asked sarcastically. 'Do feel free. Or should I perhaps ask whether you have a warrant? And what on earth are you looking for, anyway? I've told you already my husband isn't here. He never is at weekends.'

'As you said, madam. And where does Mr Miller spend his weekends?'

'How would I know? It's to do with work. If you're really from Carver and Greenwood, you should know more about it than I do.'

For the first time since she had let them in, the two men both looked at her. Kate's heart did a lurch. Oh, blast it all, she thought. Bloody, bloody Len. And to think that after all that's happened in the past, I believed him this time! Or did I? I never thought he could be so blatant, going away every weekend like that, I thought it had to be work. Well, this time is the end. I don't have the time or the energy to be worrying about him as well. I suppose I've got to cover for him this time, though, damn it all.

'He's a busy man,' she said defensively. 'He works very hard, and his job involves a lot of travelling. At the moment that means he is away at weekends. I don't like it, but I'm getting the benefit so who am I to complain?' She gestured towards the large, comfortable room that had been built for her mother. The men exchanged glances again.

'Doing well, is he?' An odd question for a bank employee to ask about a colleague, but Kate was too distracted to notice.

'Very well. At least,' Kate amended, 'I suppose he must be. He doesn't discuss business with me – some of it's rather confidential, particularly the foreign stuff – but he's been very generous. My mother—' She broke off, her anxiety returning in a rush. 'Look, is this really important? Only my mother's been missing for nearly two hours now, since very early, and I really can't think straight . . .'

She closed her eyes for a moment, and brought up her hand to rub her forehead. The skin felt tight, with an underlying ache that seemed to be located in the actual bones of her skull. She did not see the two men look, once again, at one another. The one who had checked her mother's room gave a little nod, and the other spoke.

'We can see you're under a great deal of stress, Mrs Miller, and we're very sorry to be disturbing you at this worrying time. You'll understand, though, that we have a job to do. Now, isn't there anywhere we can sit down for a minute – the kitchen, perhaps? And could I make you a nice cup of tea? Good at that, I am. My mother trained me well – boiling water, warm the pot, all of that. Now then, what do you say?'

Kate sagged limply. It was obvious that these men were not going to leave until they had found out what they wanted. For the first time, a little worm of alarm stirred in her stomach. Such persistence, and on a Sunday too, meant something serious, something beyond a simple sexual infidelity. She wrenched her mind away from images of her mother tumbling from the pier into a grey sea, or squashed by a lorry, or simply wandering out of the town and getting lost in the countryside, prey to hypothermia, and started to wonder what was the problem with Len.

Her mind seething, she led the way into the kitchen. The plump man – Mr Nice Guy was how she thought of him – made movements towards the kettle, but she turned him down firmly and filled it herself. Swiftly she set out mugs, milk, sugar, teaspoons.

'What's the problem with Len?' she asked as casually as she could, keeping her back to them.

'Oh, just a bit of a mix-up,' said Nice Guy. 'Something we needed to check with him.'

'On a Sunday? At this time of the morning?' She glanced at the kitchen clock, scarcely able to believe that it was still only eight o'clock. Waking early, she had come downstairs to make a cup of tea. Taking a cup through to her mother's room she had found it empty, the front door unbolted. Rousing the children – no easy task in the pre-dawn gloom of Sunday morning – she had sent them out to search, staying at home herself as usual to co-ordinate things.

'No rest for the wicked.'

She poured the tea, glad to have something to do with her hands. Both men said yes to sugar, and as they sat stirring their mugs she looked at them and thought, these are not the kind of bank employees I have ever met. These are policemen. She looked back. Len had always been a generous man, with both his time and his money. It was part of his charm, that easy way of giving which was so apparently a pleasure. He rarely discussed money with her, but it was always there for meals out, for holidays and nice clothes and other treats. In the last year or two he had paid out large amounts for the extension for her mother, bought a new car for Kate and a good quality secondhand one for Nick when he had passed his driving test in the summer.

Kate had scarcely queried all this. Len, she knew, worked in a field where high achievers made considerable salaries, with generous bonuses as well. In their drifting marriage she had seen this as part of the bargain. Her side was to run the house and care for the children, his to provide the wherewithal. She had long ago learned not to rely on Len for more than this. His series of secondary love affairs had taught her that however much Len might love her and adore his children, he would never resist the impulse to pleasure. He was scarcely able to see such infidelities as harmful, and was honestly amazed by her inability to dismiss them as separate from his life with her.

It was many years, now, since Kate had looked with clear eyes at her husband and her marriage, and made the choice between dignified and lonely independence, and acceptance of the status quo. Inevitably there were times when she despised herself, but generally the aphorism about half a loaf being better than no bread held true. Len was generous, devoted to his children, devoted apparently to her though constitutionally unable to be faithful. She did not trust him or rely on him as a friend, but he was an amusing companion who was still able to make her laugh. It was hardly perfect, but what was?

She took a mouthful of tea, scalding her tongue without noticing.

'There's trouble, isn't there?' She spoke bluntly, her words more a statement than a question. Nice Guy opened his mouth, but before he could speak, the other – Mr Nosey? – spoke.

'I'm afraid there is, Mrs Miller. It could be very serious. If there's any way you can get in touch with your husband, it would be as well to help us to do it. It may be that he has nothing at all to do with it' – he looked as though this was something he would find hard to believe – 'and in that case, we can clear it up straight away.'

Kate frowned down at her tea. Could she believe that Len had been doing anything wrong? While he would never mean to hurt or injure anyone, his attitude to his own money was, surprisingly, as casual as that towards sexual mores. Kate had come to assume that because the sums he dealt with were so huge that they seemed almost unreal, it was difficult for him to see amounts of less than a million as meaningful. He would happily lend small sums even to casual acquaintances, without ever expecting to be repaid, and by the same token would borrow similar amounts from friends, having gone out without his wallet, and never think to give the money back. When challenged he would pay up cheerfully, but with an air of surprise.

Kate came to the conclusion that she could accept the idea that Len had been, so to speak, casual in his interpretation of what was the bank's money, and what was his. With a feeling of incipient doom she realised that two men in suits were not going to land on her doorstep on a Sunday morning over a missing fifty pounds. It was something big, and it was not likely to be a simple mistake. She saw that Nosey was watching her, and blanked out her expression.

'I do have a number for emergencies, of course,' she said with apparent helpfulness, 'but you probably know it already. It's the message service for the bank.'

He shook his head.

'And that's the only way you can reach him?' He sounded disbelieving.

'Well, he's travelling so much. But it's a very efficient service. I've never had any problems with it.'

A difficult hour ensued. There were endless questions, which Kate had to answer carefully but without her wariness being apparent. They gave her no time to think, firing queries from both sides almost before she had finished her previous reply. His friends, his clubs, holidays, car, registration number, hobbies . . . Kate answered honestly, glad that she was unable to remember the number of his car, which was fairly new. By the time they eased up, she felt exhausted, mentally and physically.

'Well, that's everything, for the moment,' said Nice Guy. 'Sorry about all that, Mrs Miller. Let's hope it all turns out OK, mm?'

She looked at him in silence. Her eyes felt hot and gritty, she wished she could cry and rinse them with tears.

'If you should remember anything that might be helpful,' said Nosey, 'or, of course, if Mr Miller should contact you, you would naturally call us. Wouldn't you?'

She turned her eyes to him with an effort. She felt she could hardly bear to look at him. He was holding out a rectangle of card to her. Dumbly she took it, read the words 'Private Investigators' on the card.

'I thought you said you came from the bank?'

'We are employed by them. If any anomalies show up, they do their own internal audits, and if there seems to be an irregularity they ask us to check it out.'

Irregularities, thought Kate. What a horrible word. Irregularities. Is Len an irregularity? My Len? The man who is, in spite of everything, my husband, father of my children?

She had a sudden, vivid memory of how fascinating she had once found him. They had met when she was in her early twenties, a meeting that was a chance and yet inevitable, because she had been going out with a close friend of Len's. They had met for a drink, and she had ended up spending the whole evening talking to Len. By the time they left the pub she had been drunk, not on the glasses of cider but on the exhilaration of meeting someone as extraordinary, as fascinating, as altogether wonderful as Len. When they married three months later – and it said much for Len that her former boyfriend consented to be their best man – she had been in a daze of happiness that seemed, now, to have no connection with her but to have been experienced by someone else.

'One other thing,' said Nice Guy, as if as an afterthought. 'Have you had any reason to suppose that Mr Miller might be seeing anyone else?'

His tone was discreetly hushed. Kate almost laughed.

'Another woman, you mean?'

'A man who spends so much time away . . .'

Kate thought quickly. She was so accustomed to covering up for Len. Not for him, so much, as for herself and, above all, the children. The older two, at least, were aware that their father had not always behaved as he should. Kate had done her best to shield them, but knew from the things they did not say that she had not altogether succeeded. This, however, was a very different thing. Nevertheless, the habit of covering up was uppermost. There was some small advantage, too, in the fact that she was telling the truth.

'He told me he was working away, and I believed him.' The two men were looking at her. Behind their professionally blank faces she was sure she could see contempt and, which was worse, pity. She pulled herself straight, struggling for some remnant of dignity. With her chin in the air she walked to the front door, opened it.

On the doorstep an old lady hesitated. At first sight she was neatly, even smartly dressed, but a second look revealed that one of her shoes was brown, and the other navy. An oddness about her hat was explained when one realised that it was on back to front. She stood ramrod straight, imperious.

'Mum! Oh, Mum, where have you been?'

Her mother smiled, the old brilliant smile that even now was so infectious.

'Just out for a walk, darling. Why, did you want me?'

'Oh, Mum.' Kate felt her eyes fill with tears. More than anything, quite suddenly, she wanted her mother, the mother of her childhood. Someone bigger and older than her, and comforting; someone who always knew what to do, who could always make things better. She wanted to climb into a lap and be cuddled and comforted and crooned over. She looked at the frail, confused woman in front of her.

'Is Dad back yet?' asked her mother brightly. Behind her, Kate felt the two investigators stiffen like pointers.

'No, Mum. Not yet,' she said gently. 'Come on in, I'll make you a cup of coffee. You'd like that, after your walk, wouldn't you?'

'Lovely, darling. Or should we wait for Dad?' Her mother came through the door. 'Hello!' she said. 'I don't believe we've met, have we? Joyce Carpenter.'

She offered her hand. Disconcerted for the first time, both men shook it gingerly, muttering inaudible names. If only I could laugh at that, thought Kate. Old Lady Routs Private Eyes.

'Come and sit down, Mum,' she said. 'They're just leaving. Aren't you?'

'Oh, what a shame! Such nice young men! I'm sure Harold would be interested to meet them! Why don't we all have a cup of coffee when he gets in? I'm sure he won't be long.'

'Harold?' said Nosey.

'My father,' said Kate. She put an arm round her mother's shoulders, steered her firmly towards the kitchen. 'Why don't you put the kettle on, Mum?' She waited until she heard the rush of water into the kettle, then spoke in a lowered voice. 'My father Harold died fifteen years ago. She knows that quite well, some of the time. Sometimes she prefers to forget.'

She hoped she saw a slightly shamefaced look on Nice Guy's face. Nosey's revealed nothing. She shut the door firmly behind them, thankful to have got rid of them before the children returned.

Back in the kitchen the kettle was beginning to steam. Kate was glad to see that it was plugged in properly: once or twice her mother had put the electric kettle on the fast burner of the cooker, and only the fact that she had forgotten to turn on the gas had saved them from a nasty fire. Kate felt the tea she had drunk with the two men washing around uneasily inside her. She felt sick, told herself she should eat something. The telephone rang, shocking her like a drenching of cold water.

'Hello, Mum, it's Nick. No sign of her.'

'Darling, I'm sorry. She's just this moment turned up. Where are you? Are the others there?' During the last few months they had established a pattern of searching. Nick, the oldest at seventeen, took one section of streets, while Tashie and Sam together took another. Tashie, being fifteen, thought that she was looking after twelve-year-old Sam, though in fact in Kate's mind it was rather the other way round. They had set times and meeting places, and one or other would telephone back at regular intervals.

'Yes, we've just met. We'll come back, then. She OK? You sound a bit funny.'

'She's fine.' Kate stretched her face into a smile. 'I'll start some breakfast. You must be starving.'

'Just a bit!'

Kate laughed. In the last two years Nick had shot up to six foot, with a corresponding increase in appetite that never seemed to put a millimetre of fat onto his spare frame. 'Is Tashie all right?' She lowered her voice.

'Well, you know . . .'

'Yes,' sighed Kate. 'Yes, I know.'

'And we have to call her Natasha, instead of just Tashie.'

'Oh, God. Thank you, Dominic.'

'Mum!' Nick disliked his name, thinking it silly.

'Sorry, darling.'

Adolescence, which had affected Nick little beyond raising his height and lowering his voice, had struck Tashie like some kind of cyclone. Kate, aware that she could not altogether blame her daughter for what was an act of nature, a kind of natural disaster that one could not, unfortunately, insure against, still found living with a moody teenage daughter almost unbearable. Petulant, sulky, demanding, she was possessed with an almost demonic ability to sow havoc and discord wherever she went. Kate often thought that her mother, even at her most exasperating, was not a fraction as much of a worry as Tashie was, and closed her eyes to the fact that her mother could only get worse, while Tashie would surely emerge, sooner or later, from the emotional war zone she appeared to be inhabiting. Sam, thank God, was still swimming happily in the sunlit lagoon of childhood. Kate prayed that when he finally encountered the reefs of adolescence he would float serenely over them, as Nick appeared to have done.

Back in the kitchen, her mother had set out three cups and saucers. Kate heated milk – coffee, to her mother, was a thing that flavoured milk, not a drink in its own right – and took food from the fridge. Bacon, eggs, mushrooms, tomatoes. Another loaf from the freezer. That should do it.

'Hungry, Mum?'

'I'll wait for Dad, dear.'

Kate sighed again.

'Have a slice of toast to keep me company,' she suggested. The thought of food made her throat close, but she told herself she must eat something. Better now, before the kitchen was rich with the smell of cooking breakfast. She and her mother sat opposite one another. Kate couldn't bring herself to put anything on the toast. It filled her mouth with sharp crumbs, impossible to swallow. She sipped her coffee, relishing the bitterness.

'Where did you walk to, Mum?' Sometimes it was risky to ask such questions, her mother being upset if she was unable to remember, but Kate could not sit in silence with her head exploding with clamorous thoughts.

'Oh, here and there. I had thought I might go to early communion, but they've moved the church.' Like a small child, Joyce would fabricate and believe the most unlikely explanations. 'It's completely vanished. And the sea is much nearer than it used to be.'

'It is, Mum?' Kate was listening for her children's return.

'I'm sure it is. Coastal erosion, isn't that what they call it? I'm not sure it's safe to go on living here. Neap tides, equinoctial storms . . .'

Kate switched her attention back, hearing the beginning of an anxiety that must be allayed before it had time to grow.

'Now, Mum, you know Len told you all about how safe this house is. Think how steep the hill is, coming up from the beach. The sea would never reach up here. Len said so, and so did – so did Dad.' Kate hated that kind of pretence, but she had once found her mother in the garden filling plastic carrier bags with soil (and new plants) as a defence from an imagined flood. Much of her energy was spent on keeping her mother on a steady course between anxiety and euphoria.

'Did he, dear? I'd forgotten. That's all right, then.' Harold Carpenter, the mildest of men, had assumed godlike powers in his widow's mind. She returned cheerfully to her toast and coffee. Kate gave up on hers and went to put the bacon under the grill. A few moments later she heard the front door open.

'Hi, Granny!' Sam came bouncing in. Joyce's face lit up. She was devoted to her grandchildren, particularly Sam who even at twelve resembled his grandfather closely.

Kate busied herself with cooking, glad to have something to do. Tashie rejected the hot food with loathing, taking a bowl of muesli with an air of conscious superiority.

'You're all up early, darlings,' said Joyce brightly. 'Have you been out for a walk too?' Tashie groaned and clapped a theatrical hand to her brow, scowling. Nick flicked a glance at her.

'That's right, Gran. Tell you what, why don't we all go together, next time?'

'Oh, Nick!' said Tashie crossly. 'Serve you right if she remembered,' she muttered. 'I wouldn't put it past her, silly old bat.'

Kate tightened her lips, reminding herself that, of all her three children, it was Tashie who became the most distressed when her grandmother was missing.

'This *is* nice,' said Joyce, beaming round the table. 'All of us having breakfast together – though we should really have waited for Harold.

What a shame those nice young men couldn't stay, Catherine. It would have been quite a party!'

Three pairs of eyes swivelled enquiringly (and in Tashie's case accusingly) to Kate.

'Something to do with work,' she said, flustered. 'Dad's work. They were from the bank.' Sam returned his attention to his plate, young enough to find adults' behaviour unworthy of question. The other two were less easy to satisfy.

'On a *Sunday*?'

'They just dropped in. Happened to be in the area, I suppose.'

'Such smart young men. Properly dressed in suits, not those sloppy jeans.'

Nick was frowning. Kate got to her feet, began to bustle with empty plates.

'I think that programme you like will be on in a minute, Mum. Shall I come and turn the TV on for you?'

'What about Harold's breakfast?'

'Don't worry about that,' Kate soothed, gently chivvying her mother out of the kitchen. 'I don't think he'll be back for a while, and I can make him something if he wants it. Or call you,' she added, seeing a mutinous look.

'Oh, all right. No, I can turn the television on for myself. I don't want to be a nuisance.'

Kate waited while her mother hunted for the remote control. It took a while, but it was eventually located down the side of the armchair. While Joyce pointed it and pressed every button in turn Kate quietly turned on the set and put it to the right channel. Nick had taken the batteries out of the remote some weeks back, because Joyce de-programmed the set every time she used it. Fortunately, once it was on, she was happy to sit and watch whatever happened to be showing, and rarely wanted to change the channel.

Kate returned to the kitchen. The table was cleared and wiped, the dirty crockery stacked in the dishwasher and the pans soaking in the sink. Nick, Tashie and Sam sat at the table, their faces turned to her. She hesitated in the doorway, feeling like a candidate for an interview.

'Darlings, how kind of you! Don't you want to go back to bed, catch up on your sleep?'

'Come and sit down, Mum.' Nick patted the chair beside him.

'Rather busy . . .'

Their faces told her it would not work. Reluctantly she sat with them.

'Come on, Mum, *tell* us. He is our father, after all. We have a right to know what's going on!'

'I wish I knew. All I can tell you is that two men turned up on the doorstep wanting to speak to Dad. They said there was some kind of problem.'

'Who were they? Police?' Nick's blunt question made Kate's eyes fly anxiously to Sam.

'Of course they weren't!' Tashie's furious answer came before Kate had time to say anything. 'Honestly, Nick, you really are the pits sometimes. Why on earth would the police be after Daddy?' Nick's steady gaze did not leave Kate's face. She felt her skin tighten with the effort to look normal, knowing from his expression that she was not succeeding.

'It's trouble, isn't it?'

Kate's glance flickered to Sam once again. He was frowning, more in puzzlement, she hoped, than in worry.

'Perhaps. It's probably not very serious. I'm sure Dad can sort it out.'

'Sure.' Nick, unconvinced, went along with her. Kate's own anxiety notched itself up another rung. That Nick, sensible Nick, should have no difficulty in accepting that his father might have done something wrong frightened her almost more than anything that had gone before.

Tashie stood up.

'Well, I think you're all being perfectly *shitty*,' she said tearfully. 'Of *course* Daddy isn't in any trouble. It's *ridiculous*! And I'm not staying to listen to another word!'

She slammed out of the room, and they heard her feet pounding up the stairs. Kate half stood up, then sat down again. Distantly, another door crashed shut.

'Girls,' sighed Sam. Kate tried to smile, felt her lips wobble and abandoned the attempt.

'Have you heard from him?' Nick kept his voice low.

'From Dad? No. I haven't even got a proper number for him, just the message service. Not much point in ringing that. We'll have to wait until he contacts us.'

'He'll be back tomorrow evening, won't he?' Sam, obviously, thought the whole thing was a storm in a teacup. Nick's eyes met Kate's.

'Sure he will,' said Nick. 'No point in thinking about it until then.'

Kate knew, with absolute certainty, that Nick was very afraid that he wouldn't see his father again for a while.

Chapter 4

While Kate's feelings during the course of Monday could not be compared with Phoebe's anxiety and terror, she still spent the day in a state of mental turmoil. During an evening of watching television with her mother she had drunk quite a lot of whisky. As a result she had avoided the insomnia she had been dreading, falling instead into a black hole of unconsciousness, rather than sleep, from which she woke feeling unrefreshed. Strong tea and dry toast quelled some of the churning in her stomach and contained her headache to manageable proportions, but she still felt desiccated, her brain seemed shrivelled like a dried fruit, and her legs ached.

The three children went off to the private day school they all attended. Sam, who seemed to have put the whole thing out of his mind, was concerned only with finding his gum-shield for rugby, whirling through his room like a tornado until Kate found it in the drum of the washing machine.

'I'm always telling you to check your pockets.'

'Tashtes dishgushting,' he mumbled through it. 'Still fits, though,' he added cheerfully, having taken it out again. 'Thanks, Mum. See you. Bye.'

Tashie, or rather Natasha as she was still insisting on being addressed, had refused to eat any breakfast and picked a quarrel with Nick.

'. . . Been using my special ointment again. I don't want your disgusting germs on my face!'

'I'm no germier than you.' Nick looked pale, his usually equable temper out of kilter.

'Yes, you are. Repulsive zits everywhere. Boils, practically. Pullulating pustules. It's revolting.' Nick, fortunately, was amused by her vehemence, probably because his skin was, if anything, rather better than his sister's.

'Two spots isn't pullulating. Anyway, how do you know I used it?'

'The lid was back on.' Tashie spoke sullenly.

Nick laughed and so, rather unwisely, did Kate. Tashie turned on her.

'It's all very well for you! You don't have to put up with being harassed like this! It's so unfair! Why do I have to have two brothers? Or, if I must have them, why do they have to be so vile? Is it too much to ask that I have a little privacy? Daddy always says—'

'Now, that's enough.' Kate felt she could bear quite a lot, but not having Len quoted at her. 'Nick, please respect your sister's belongings. But if you don't want anyone to use your stuff, Tashie – sorry, Natasha – don't leave it in the bathroom.'

'But it's mine! And it was really expensive . . .' Tashie's voice tailed off as she remembered that it was Kate, not she, who had paid for it.

'Precisely. Now for goodness' sake have a bowl of muesli, or something.'

'I hate muesli.'

'You liked it yesterday.' Kate knew that such sudden changes of taste were normal, but she had just bought a jumbo-sized packet of a make that only Tashie had liked.

'Yesterday was the past,' said Tashie, dismissing the past as irrelevant. 'Today is a whole new universe. Haven't we got any Weetabix?'

'As a matter of fact, we have. On the shelf. Next to Sam's Honey Nut Circles, or what ever it's called.'

'It's not fair.' Tashie, caught out, made a quick recovery from finding that there was some Weetabix. 'Sam's so spoiled. You never bought Honey Nut Loops when I was his age. I had to make do with boring old Rice Krispies.'

'Rice Krispies! Rice Krispies! You were lucky to get Rice Krispies! Let me tell you that when I was a girl—'

'Oh, I know.' Tashie broke in before Kate could get going. 'Bowls of gravel. Ha bloody ha.'

After they had gone, Kate pottered in the kitchen until her mother joined her. Joyce woke early, but preferred to avoid the early morning rush of getting the children off to school. Mother and daughter usually had a leisurely breakfast together once the house was quiet.

The morning was so normal that Kate found it easy to push the problem of Len to the back of her mind. The first few hours were taken up with a trip to the supermarket, always a lengthy procedure since Joyce, who liked to go too, invariably insisted on going slowly up and down every aisle, and examining new products that caught her eye, however unnecessary or unsuitable. By the time they were back at the house it was close to twelve o'clock. Kate was upstairs, putting rolls of lavatory paper away in the bathroom cupboard, when the telephone rang. Dropping the bulky packets she ran for the bedroom.

'Kate? It's Brian.'

'Oh, Brian.' Stretching the cord of the telephone to its limit, Kate pushed the bedroom door shut with her foot. Then, as carefully as if any sudden movement would dislocate her joints, she sat down on the side of the bed. She pictured Brian as she had seen him the previous Christmas, his smoothly plump face and quiet manner hiding the ruthless intelligence that had kept him the head of Carver and Greenwood's overseas trading for ten years. Kate had always liked what she had seen of him, and thought that she could trust him. 'Brian, what's going on?'

'It's not good news, Kate.' As she had known he would, he came straight to the point. 'In fact, it looks very bad. I wanted you to hear it from me.'

'I had two men here yesterday, looking for Len. Investigators.'

'Yes, I'm sorry about that. It was authorised from the top, I didn't hear anything about it until this morning.' His voice was wary. If anything dishonest had been going on, Kate realised, Brian would also have been under suspicion.

'Have they found anything? Do they know where Len is?'

'They can't trace him at all.' There was no question in his voice, but she answered it anyway.

'I just don't know. I really don't. All that stuff about travelling at weekends, I just believed it. I feel such a fool.'

'You're not the only one.' His voice was dry.

'Oh, Brian. Are you . . . is this going to make problems for you?'

'Bound to. One way or another. He was my responsibility, in a sense. I picked him for that job. The buck stops here, and all that.'

'I'm so sorry, Brian.'

'Yes, well, I'm sorry, too. This is going to hit you more than it does me, I'm afraid. Particularly if we can't find Len.'

Kate hugged her free arm tight across her stomach, curling her body forward in an unconscious effort to protect herself. She felt sick.

'What has happened, exactly? If you can tell me?'

He sighed.

'I don't know much myself, yet. Only that it looks increasingly likely that Len's been helping himself to the bank's money.'

Even though she had suspected it, Kate still felt a shock. She thought of recent news stories.

'Is it a lot? I mean, will the bank be all right?'

Amazingly, he laughed.

'Oh, it's not that bad! Half a million, at the most. Peanuts, really, by our standards; it could have been much worse. As it is, we're hoping not to have to call the police in. If only we can find him – or the money, of course.'

'Yes.' The bank, of course, would want to hush it up. No police, no court case, above all no publicity. Kate knew she should be grateful for that, but at the moment it was impossible to see much good in anything that was happening. She was overtaken by a tide of anger, so fierce that her head felt congested and the skin on her face and neck burned.

'Kate? Kate, are you all right?' Brian's voice in her ear recalled her. She found that she was pressing the receiver so hard against her ear that it hurt, and eased it away.

'Yes,' she muttered. 'Yes, I'm all right.' It was hard to speak. Her tongue felt rigid, her lips chilled and numb against the heat of her cheeks.

'There's no pleasant way of doing this, I'm afraid, Kate. We have to try and find out where the money's gone. Look, I know Len. Damn it all, I *liked* the man. He's not the type to steal for the hell of it, and money as such doesn't really interest him, does it? I mean, the dealing he did, it was like a game to him, a game of skill and chance that he enjoyed because he was good at it. And he was – very good. But the money itself . . . no. He liked to spend, to give people things, but squirreling it away in a Swiss bank account to gloat over in private, well, it just wasn't him, was it?'

'No.'

'He'd have spent it on something.'

'Or someone.'

'Yes.' His voice was calm. If he heard the bitterness in her voice, he gave no sign. 'I'm afraid we have to start with what we know, Kate. Do you know where he keeps his paperwork? Statements, income tax returns, that kind of thing?'

'Of course. It's all here. We had a joint account. The men who came yesterday checked all that.'

'I know, and they said there was nothing unusual. Not surprising, if it was a joint account. He wouldn't want to risk you noticing anything. With any luck that means you're in the clear.'

'In the clear?' Kate's anger returned, her ears buzzed. 'You don't think I had anything to do with all this, do you?'

'No, of course not. I thought I'd made that obvious. When I said in the clear, I meant safe. Financially speaking, that is. You do understand, don't you, Kate, that the bank must recover this money, or as much of it as is possible? No one wants to punish you or your family, but if it can be proved that he paid for the house, say, or a car, out of stolen money, then the bank would be entitled to claim their value back.'

Kate's blood, that had been humming round her head in boiling anger, now puddled and congealed somewhere deep inside her. She couldn't understand why she had been so stupid. Misery, anxiety and disgrace she had foreseen, but not the loss of her home. Panic gnawed at her mind, scurried through her body so that she felt her muscles twitching. That her children would have to learn to live without a father was something she thought she could deal with, since his parental presence had never been more than nominal. That they might lose the home that had been theirs for fifteen years was a different matter. And her mother! What was to become of Joyce? The thought of incarcerating her in a 'home' was unbearable, even if it had been possible to pay for it.

'What can I do?' she asked numbly.

'Well, the first thing is to find out. And the sooner we do that the better. Have you got all the statements there? Bank, building society, that kind of thing?'

'Yes. The men who came yesterday, the investigators, had a look at them. I think they wanted to take them away, but I wouldn't let them.'

'Right. I'd like to say I'll come myself, but . . .' The anxiety underlying his calm tones was apparent. He felt that the bank no longer trusted him.

'No, of course, I see you can't do that. But thank you.'

'I'll make sure the person who comes is all right. If I can.'

'Thank you,' said Kate again. All right? What, she wondered, constituted all right, in these circumstances?

In the event, and rather to her surprise, 'all right' turned out to be a young woman – so young that to Kate's tired eyes she scarcely looked old enough to have left school. Meek and inoffensive, she seemed almost apologetic about her presence. Kate, realising that this disarming appearance was probably intended to lull her into a state of confidence that would encourage her to open up, still found herself relaxing her guard. It was not, after all, as though she had anything to hide.

Two hours later, she felt as though she had been put through a mangle. Every bank statement had been gone through and checked against receipts. The largest outlay, which was the building work to create Joyce's rooms, was examined minutely. At the end, the girl pushed the piles of papers away from her and leaned back in her chair.

'Well, Mrs Miller, it's only what you might call a superficial examination.' Kate looked at her in horror, and she smiled faintly. 'Oh yes, just skimming the surface. But even so – and please don't quote me on this, because I shan't admit to having said anything at all – it looks as though you're in the clear. There's nothing coming in that can't be accounted for by his normal salary and bonuses.'

Kate's knees quivered as muscles she did not know had been clenched suddenly relaxed. She sat down abruptly.

'As simple as that?'

'Well, no, I'm afraid not. There's bound to be quite a lot more checking to be done, at our end, if not here. I'll need to take all these away with me. But it doesn't look to me as though you have anything to worry about. At least . . .' She looked stricken with embarrassment, blushing awkwardly. Kate's eyes filled with tears, and the girl looked even more worried. 'I'm so sorry, of course you must be dreadfully upset about all this.'

'It's all right,' Kate sniffed. She felt her mouth wobbling and put her hand up to hide it, her ears pulling back and her chin corrugating with the effort of control. 'It's relief, more than anything,' she managed.

'Can I get you something?' The girl made ineffective gestures with her hands, patting and soothing the air between them. 'A drink of water? Something like that?'

Kate shook her head, dislodging the tears that wobbled against her lower lids so that they tickled their way down her cheeks. She wiped them away with shaky fingers, seeing in the girl's appalled expression confirmation of the suspicion that in her eyes Kate was too old to cry.

The young woman left, carrying bundles of paperwork for which she had written, meticulously, a receipt. Kate, looking at her watch, was horrified to see that it was five o'clock. The dining room, where they had gone for privacy and the convenience of the large table, felt both chilly and stuffy. Kate wrestled with the window, the lock stiff with disuse and the heavy sash grating awkwardly in its frame, and heaved it open, breathing in the cold air in gulps. The street was empty, sunk in the deceptive calm between the return of children from school and of adults from work. The wind was coming from the sea, carrying a tang of salt and some wheeling gulls, their hoarse cries so familiar as to be unnoticed unless, like now, she listened for them. One was sitting on the low wall that bounded the narrow front garden. It turned its head and looked at her with mad, wild eyes. The vicious beak opened soundlessly, then snapped shut. Kate drew back from the open window, and pulled the sash down.

She left the dining room, pulling the door shut behind her as though to contain the unpleasantness it had held. As she stood in the hall the house felt unnaturally quiet. Only the faintest murmur of television voices, the jolly positive tones of a children's show, came from Joyce's suite. Having spent the afternoon hunting through receipts, Kate remembered with a pang that Len had insisted the rooms should have good sound insulation. 'That way, we don't have to worry about the kids' awful music disturbing her, and we don't have to listen to her choice of telly if she gets more deaf,' he had said with a grin. It had been typical of Len, whose thoughtfulness invariably had selfish roots.

Where was everyone? By now all the children should be back from school, and at this time of day would usually be doing homework upstairs, conflicting music seeping round each closed door. When Kate thought about it, she remembered hearing them come back, and feeling grateful for their tact in not seeking her out. Perhaps, aware of a visitor, they were working in unnatural silence? She went up the stairs, using the handrail to pull herself and regretting, not for the first time, that the exigencies of a town house meant that two of their three bedrooms were up an extra flight of stairs, above the floor that housed her room, Tashie's room, the spare bedroom, and the large bathroom.

The bedrooms were empty. Heaps of abandoned school uniform showed that the children had come home and changed. Automatically Kate picked up and shook out trousers, blazers, pullovers, a skirt; gathered shirts for washing, put shoes carefully side by side under chairs . . . The activity was obscurely comforting, a return to a simpler time when her role as mother was the most important part of her life. What am I doing? She thought. I'm always saying I'm not going to run round after them any more. And where are they? They couldn't have . . . gone? With recent memories of them searching for Joyce she imagined them combing the streets for their father, then realised it was ridiculous. She bent to glance at herself in Tashie's mirror, surprised to find that the trials and tears of the afternoon had left no mark and she looked, as far as she could tell, exactly as she always did. Then she went downstairs.

All three of them were in the kitchen. The room was warm and smelled of toast, of the yeasty tang of Marmite overlaid with the sweetness of Sam's chocolate spread. The smell of children's afternoon teas, so homely and normal, was as comforting as a warm, soft blanket. Kate saw that their plates and mugs had been cleared away and stacked in the sink, the butter dish, jars and pots put away, and that her offspring were seated round the carefully wiped table, each with books and notepads, doing homework. Kate wondered whether she had suddenly been transported to a parallel universe – one inhabited by the perfect families featured in old television advertisements, perhaps. Three faces lifted to look at her, and she saw in each of their looks, even Tashie's, the anxiety that made them huddle together in family unity, and try to placate some angry god with offerings of good behaviour.

'Hello, darlings,' she said as cheerfully as she could through a tight throat.

'Hi, Mum.' Sam was the only one to answer. 'We had our tea, and cleared it away,' he pointed out with careful pride. 'We took some to Granny, too.'

Kate wanted to hug him, to hug all of them, but was afraid of losing what fragile control she still had over her emotions.

'Thank you, my dears,' she said a shade too heartily. 'You've been a wonderful help.' She heard the rough catch in her voice, and stopped speaking, turning away to fill the kettle. The discovery that not only was it full and hot, but that a tea tray had been carefully set beside it with her favourite mug, and milk in a jug, was too much. With a little wail she burst into tears and stood bent over the kettle, her hands to her face to contain the tears and her sobbing breaths.

At once they were round her, chairs scraping on the tiles and one falling over with a crash. Clumsy arms and awkwardly patting hands, bumping against each other and her in the struggle to be with her. They ended up in a huddle. Kate, with Sam's arms round her waist and his head butting into the middle of her back, and Tashie's face pressing against her neck, leaned her own head against the rough pullover of Nick's bony chest and was comforted to her soul.

Presently, when her breathing was under control again, they unwound themselves. Nick, the practical, reached for the kitchen roll and handed it round. Eyes were wiped and noses blown, and there was a general easing of tension and even some laughter at Sam's uninhibited trumpet blast into his handful of paper towel. Nick switched on the kettle, and Kate allowed herself to be led solicitously to a chair. They watched anxiously while she sipped at her tea, and she smiled at them.

'Sorry about that,' she said. 'I can cope with the bad bits – at least, I think I can – but it's much more difficult when you're all so kind to me.'

They looked at one another, and sat down in their abandoned chairs. It was Tashie's, Kate saw, that had been knocked over. She sipped at her mug again, to give her time.

'You are going to tell us what's happening, aren't you?' There was a hint of aggression back in Tashie's voice. Nick gave her a look.

'I think you should, Mum,' he said. His voice sounded deeper than Kate had ever heard it, a man's voice now.

'I know,' she sighed. 'I am going to tell you. Not that I know a great deal, really.' She glanced at Sam, hoping he would not notice. His eyes met hers steadily.

'It's all right, Mum. You don't have to protect me.' It was said quite calmly, with none of his sister's underlying resentment. Kate smiled at him.

'I don't know how I've managed to produce such sensible children. I don't want to get all emotional again, but you really are the bee's knees, all three of you.'

They grinned awkwardly, embarrassed but clearly pleased. Kate took a deep breath, then told them the bare facts as far as she knew them. She was thankful to be able to say that it looked as though their home was safe for the time being, though how she was to continue to afford to run it was a different matter that she ignored at present.

Kate finished her short recital. There was a charged silence.

'Somebody must know where he is!' said Tashie fiercely. '*Somebody* must!'

'Somebody obviously does,' said Nick. They all looked at him. He frowned, tracing patterns on the table with his fingertip. 'He's disappeared, hasn't he? At least, that's what we have to assume. Unless he comes home this evening as usual.' Kate found herself glancing at the kitchen door, as if expecting to see Len open it in his usual flamboyant way. Turning her eyes back to Nick, she saw that the other two had done the same.

'He might,' said Sam hopefully.

'He won't, darling. I'm sorry, but I really think he won't.' Kate spoke firmly. Better, she thought, to douse that hope before it was more than a glimmer than to have Sam living in a fool's paradise.

'I don't understand what Nick means,' said Tashie crossly. She hated it when anyone, but particularly Nick, made her feel slow-witted. Kate raised her eyebrows at Nick.

'Well, he wouldn't have gone if he hadn't known something was up. The bank would have been pretty careful, I'd have thought, not to let him know they were, um, checking up on him. So how did he know? Presumably he didn't turn up in Prague last weekend.' Kate said nothing, but he saw the expression on her face. 'Oh. I see. Not Prague?'

'Not Prague.'

'What do you mean, not Prague?' Tashie's voice was sharp. Kate and Nick looked at her helplessly.

'They mean, Dad hasn't been going to Prague.' It was Sam who spoke, his unbroken voice oddly adult in tone. 'It was pretend. A front.'

'That's *stupid*! This isn't some kind of television programme! You're making Daddy sound like a *crook*!'

There was another silence while they all thought about that word. No one looked at Tashie.

'He's not! Not Daddy! Not a crook! Oh!' She burst into tears and ran from the room. Kate began to stand up to go after her, but Nick stopped her.

'I should leave her alone,' he said. 'She'll come round. She's just got to get used to the idea.'

Kate looked at him.

'Will she?'

'Of course she will. She's not stupid.'

Kate glanced from Nick to Sam, and considered the implications of that remark. Tashie, of course, had always been her father's darling, his special pet. With him she had scarcely ever displayed the prickly side of her adolescent nature, but had been the little princess he had sometimes called her, loving and beloved. The boys had appeared to accept this as normal, and had got on well with their father in their own ways. Len, with his knack of adapting himself to his company, had talked books with Nick and rugby with Sam. Kate had judged the relationships successful, compared to what she heard and read about in other families, but now she wondered how the boys had really seen their father.

'You don't seem very surprised,' she said sadly to Nick.

'Well . . . not really, no. I mean, in a lot of ways Dad was great. Good fun, generous, always ready to listen. But . . . he listened without hearing, didn't he? He'd be there, nodding, saying yes and no, laughing in all the right places, but he never really *said* anything. My friends envied me, said their fathers were always giving advice and what a drag it was, but – isn't that what fathers are about, to give advice, even if all you do is fly off in the opposite direction? He was a great guy, but you couldn't really rely on him, could you?'

Kate, speechless, looked at Sam. It occurred to her that for him, younger as he was than the others, his father had been more absent than present. In the last few years, and particularly in this past year, Len had spent less and less time at home. Certainly it was a long time since Sam had asked whether his father was likely to come and watch him play in a match, though Kate turned up on the sidelines regularly, and had gradually learned the correct things to shout, and even (by listening to other parents) to make appropriate comments on the team's performance during the match tea afterwards.

Sam nodded.

''S right,' he said laconically. Kate found herself with an irrational urge to defend Len from their seeming indifference and quelled it. In truth they said no more than she herself had felt. Len's increasing absences had accustomed them to managing without him. There had been times, recently, when his presence in the house had brought almost an awkwardness, as if he had been a guest, welcome but intrusive enough to upset the household routine.

In that case, the worst they would have to face was some financial insecurity – no uncommon thing these days, and at least their school fees were all paid in advance – and the possibility of embarrassment at school if their father's misdeeds were made public. Since it seemed almost certain that the bank would hush everything up if they possibly could, even that could be avoided. Later on, particularly for Sam, there might be long-term effects from his father's abandonment of them, if that was what had happened. For the moment, at least, he seemed to be coping. Kate decided to accept that thankfully, and worry about the future when it happened.

The kitchen door crashed open again, and Tashie burst in.

'Mummy! Oh, Mummy!'

The childhood name, rarely used in recent years, had Kate on her feet and holding out her arms almost in a reflex action. Tashie clung to her, sobbing noisily.

'It's all right, darling. It's awful now, but it won't always feel like this. Poor little love, I know, I know.' Kate murmured the words, scarcely thinking about them. Nick began to clear away Kate's tea things, and Sam fetched himself a packet of crisps from the box in the larder.

'You don't *understand*!' wailed Tashie. 'It's not what you *think*! It's . . . Oh, Mummy, I'm sorry! It's all my fault! And now – and now – oh, it's just *horrible*! I can't *bear* it!' Her breathing changed, suddenly, from hiccuping sobs to quicker, shallower breaths. She sagged in Kate's hold, whimpering through the uncontrollable gasps. 'Can't . . . breathe!' Her face was terrified.

'She's hyperventilating,' said Kate, lowering her into a chair and holding her upright. 'It's all right, darling. You'll be all right. Get me a bag. A paper bag. Something like that. It's all right, Tashie, you can control it.'

Round-eyed, Sam quickly tipped the crisps out on to the table and offered the empty packet. Nick, already at the sink, put down the teapot with a crash and jerked open the drawer where Kate kept odds and ends, grabbing for one of the pretty bags Kate kept for emergency wrapping of small gifts. He shoved the crisp packet aside. 'Here,' he said. 'I'll hold it.'

Between them they got the open bag over her mouth and nose. Kate chanted, 'In two three, out two three,' gradually slowing the count. Beneath her hands Tashie's shoulders softened and relaxed, and at last she put up her hand and pushed the bag away.

'I'm all right,' she said. 'Honestly, Sam, a crisp packet!'

Sam grinned sheepishly.

'Well, it was there in my hand. Besides, if I felt ill, I'm sure the smell of salt and vinegar flavour would revive me.' He picked up a small handful from the table, and crunched them with enjoyment.

'Gross,' said Tashie, not without affection. 'Oh, Mummy!'

'So, what was it all about?'

Tashie hung her head.

'It's my fault. That Daddy's gone, I mean.'

Kate ignored a snort of irritation from Nick, and hoped that the sound of Sam's crisp eating might have drowned it.

'Of course it's not your fault,' she soothed. 'How ever could it be?'

Tashie shivered.

'You know those men who came round yesterday?' Kate nodded. 'Well, I rang him about them.'

'What do you mean, you rang him? Rang him where?'

'On his mobile.'

Kate felt her blood run cold.

'Natasha Miller! Are you telling me that you know your father's mobile phone number?' Tashie nodded. 'And it didn't occur to you that you might tell me it?' Tashie shivered again. Kate suppressed an urge to slap her. 'So you rang him yesterday morning, and told him about the men coming here? What did he say?'

'Nothing much. He said he'd sort it out.'

Nick snorted again, this time with laughter.

'Well, I suppose he did. From his point of view, anyway.'

'Now he's gone, and I'll never see him again!'

'You wouldn't have seen much of him if he was in prison, anyway.' The brutal words made Kate frown at Nick, but they seemed to shock Tashie back into her wits.

'It's not just that,' she said, more calmly but with more unhappiness in her voice. 'I tried the number again. In fact, I've been trying it lots of times, since yesterday. Up to now the phone's been switched off, but just now it rang, and someone answered it. Not Daddy. A woman. And she kept asking if I was Leo.'

'Leo!' said Sam. 'Leo the Lion. You should have roared at her.'

'I didn't say anything. I couldn't. Oh, Mummy, what's going on?'

'I wish I knew,' said Kate grimly. Leo, she thought. Leonard. Oh, Len.

Out in the hall, the telephone rang.

Chapter 5

Phoebe stood in the hall, staring down at the telephone in her hand as if she expected it to explode within seconds.

'It rang!' she said wildly. 'It rang. Oh God, was it Leo? Why didn't he say anything?'

'It's hardly likely to be Leo. He wouldn't expect anyone to be in a ditch to answer his mobile phone.' Millie was showing herself in a new, startlingly practical light. Phoebe found this, if anything, more alarming than reassuring. She felt her mind swooping into hysteria and clutched at details to slow its descent.

'Hedge, not ditch. If it was him threw it there in the first place.'

'Who else would?'

'Oh, I don't *know*. He might have been abducted. Or someone could have stolen it. And anyway, how come it was switched on?' They had been in the kitchen at the time, and at the sound of muffled bleeping Phoebe's first reaction, in spite of everything, had been to leave it for Leo to answer. Then, on the instant, she had rushed to the hall. Unable in her panic to remember where the mobile phone was she had finally tracked it down to her jacket pocket, almost jerking the hook from the cupboard wall in her frantic haste to find the thing before it stopped ringing.

'I'm afraid that was me,' admitted Millie. 'I borrowed the jacket when I went to the shop this afternoon. I was fiddling with it, you know how I do.' Phoebe knew only too well. Her mother had a fascination with gadgets of all kinds, particularly electronic ones, that was equalled only by her total inability to use them. It was the idea of them she loved: faced with the reality, she was as likely as not to press every button she could find, just to see what happened, and then be astonished to find she had wiped its memory, or set off some kind of alarm. 'Sorry, darling.'

'No, no, it's good. I should have had it switched on all the time, in case. And the battery – I must recharge the battery . . .' Phoebe, still cradling the phone, rummaged with the other hand in the drawer for the charger.

'Never mind about that now,' said Millie soothingly. 'The first thing is, who telephoned?'

'But I don't *know*.' Phoebe continued to scrabble. 'He didn't say anything.'

'I know, darling, but—' Millie tried to take the phone from Phoebe's hand. Phoebe resisted, clutching. 'Don't be silly, darling. Let me have it.' Unpeeling Phoebe's fingers, Millie pressed numbers and listened, then scribbled on the pad by the normal phone.' There,' she said in triumph. 'Oh one two seven three – where's that? I hate these codes, they don't tell you anything.'

'Brighton,' said Phoebe automatically. 'What are you doing?' Her brain seemed to have gone numb.

'Finding out who telephoned. There you are.' Millie held out the piece of paper torn from the notepad. Phoebe took it gingerly.

'He hates people knowing his mobile number,' she said. 'He didn't even want to give it to me, and then he said I should only use it for emergencies. He was always ringing me, I never really needed to use it. In fact, I don't think I ever did, until now.'

'Well, somebody knows it. Let's ring them and find out who it is.'

'Yes.' Phoebe stretched out her hand to the telephone, then pulled it back.

'Do you want me to do it?'

'No, I will. I might recognise the voice, or something. It might make a difference.' Phoebe picked up the receiver. Looking at the number Millie had written down, she began to press out the numbers.

'Stop!' Millie's hand came down, cutting off the dialling tone. 'No need to give them this number too. Dial one four one, just to be on the safe side.'

Phoebe nodded, feeling new respect for her mother. Obediently she dialled again. The new touch phone was so quick, there was no pause at all between putting in the numbers, and a ringing tone.

It rang, and continued to ring. Phoebe counted to ten, eleven, twelve. Stubbornly she hung on, and at last there was a click and the telephone was answered.

'Hello?' A woman's voice, certainly. Wary, non-committal. 'Hello?'

'Hello.' Now that it came to it, Phoebe couldn't think what to say. 'Um, did you just call, er . . .' Unable to remember the number, Phoebe had to look it up again. 'Sorry.' She read it out.

There was a pause, and Phoebe thought she heard whispers.

'Yes.' She sounded unsure. Phoebe felt more in control.

'Who did you want to speak to?'

More whispering.

'Mr Miller. Leonard Miller.'

'And you are?'

A long pause.

'It's . . . a private matter. Nothing to do with business.'

'What sort of private?'

'Family.' The answer came back faster this time, more firmly.

'In that case,' said Phoebe with equal firmness, 'you can tell me about it. I'm his wife.'

'I beg your pardon?' The tone of voice was a strange mixture of outrage, dismay, and something that could almost have been hysterical amusement. 'What did you say?'

'I said, I'm his wife. I'm Mrs Miller.'

'Oh dear.' Surely that wasn't pity Phoebe heard? 'Mrs Leonard Miller? How long have you been married?'

'Six months,' responded Phoebe automatically. 'Hang on a minute,' she added crossly. 'Who are you? What gives you the right to ask me questions like that? And if you're in Leo's family – which I don't believe – how come I've never heard of you? Why hasn't he told me about you?'

'Why indeed?'

Whoever it is, thought Phoebe, at least I can be fairly sure it isn't the police. They certainly weren't interested when I rang them this morning, and they, surely, would never sound like this. Not uncertain. Not having hurried, whispered conferences with some other person. And not the bank, either, for the same reasons. So, who?

Leo had told her, when they first met, how much he wished he had a large, close family. An only child of elderly parents, he scarcely remembered his grandparents and his own parents had both died when he was in his twenties, leaving him alone in the world. His only relative, a cousin, was the daughter of his mother's younger sister. He seldom saw her, but was fond of her three children. He had shown Phoebe snapshots of them, two boys and a girl, and had seemed touchingly pleased when she praised them. Could this be Leo's cousin? But this was a Brighton number, and he had told her his cousin lived in Wales. Still . . .

'Are you Kate?' Phoebe remembered the cousin's name just in time.

'Yes. Yes, I am.' She sounded wary again, and also astonished, which was odd.

'Oh, why didn't you say so? Thank goodness! Leo's told me about you. I should have realised sooner, only this is a Brighton number, and I thought you never left Wales.'

'Is that what he said?'

'Yes, of course. Why, isn't it true?'

'Not exactly. What else did he tell you?'

'Nothing much. Just that you have three lovely children that he's very fond of.'

'Ah.'

'That's true, surely? I've seen photographs of them.'

'It's true, all right. And who did he say they are?'

'Their names, you mean?' Phoebe's mind span again. 'I'm afraid I don't remember. And I don't see that it matters,' she added, striving for reality.

'No, not their names. Who they are, in relation to him. And me, too, come to that.'

'Well, some kind of cousins, I suppose. If you're his first cousin, that makes them . . . I can't remember how it goes.'

'First cousins once removed,' said Kate automatically. 'The bastard. The *bastard*!'

'Who? Not Leo? How *dare* you?'

'Leo?' Kate made a spitting noise. 'Sod Leo, it's Len I'm talking about. My husband, Len Miller.'

'Your husband? But I thought—' Phoebe broke off as the implications of the name hit her. 'Len Miller? You said Len Miller? Leonard Miller? But that's—'

'Yes.'

'You mean – they've got the same name . . .' Phoebe, frightened and confused, clutched at any possibility rather than confront what awaited her at the bottom of the chasm into which she seemed to be falling.

'I mean,' said Kate grimly, 'that they're the same man.'

'He was married before,' guessed Phoebe, whispering through lips that felt as though they were ineptly moulded from plasticine. 'You're his first wife. He should have told me.'

'His only wife,' said Kate, not ungently. 'We're not divorced.'

'Oh.' Phoebe shook her head, more to clear it than in denial. 'When – when did he leave you?' I didn't know, she wanted to say. Please believe me, I had no idea. Did he leave you for me? Surely not. Surely it was long before.

'He didn't.'

'You left him, then?' Phoebe could not keep the hope out of her voice.

'I'm afraid not. As far as I knew, we were still together.'

'Still together? You mean, he was still . . .? I don't believe you.'

'I don't care whether you believe me or not. But it's true.'

'No!' Phoebe held the phone away from her ear, at arm's length, looking at it as though it were something slimy and wriggling. Then she dropped it with a clatter onto the floor, and sat suddenly down on the bottom step of the stairs, her head bowed into her lap and her arms clasped over it. Millie retrieved the telephone.

'Are you still there?' she asked cautiously.

'Yes. Who is this?'

'Phoebe's mother. She's – I think she'd better speak to you later.' Kate's voice was still questioning as Millie clicked the phone off.

'I don't believe it! I just don't believe it!'

Millie had brought Phoebe a drink, and made her swallow it.

'She says – she says . . .' Phoebe shook her head as if something in it were obstructing her speech, 'she says she's his wife. That she's still married to him.'

Millie said nothing. Phoebe looked up at her.

'You don't think it could be true, do you? Not *Leo*!' Still Millie said nothing, but looked at her. 'I know,' said Phoebe as if her mother had answered. 'I know. It does make sense, doesn't it? All that secrecy – why didn't I notice it like that before? Normal people are proud of their new wives, not secretive. And not ringing him. And using my car. We always went in my car, when we went anywhere. He said it was fun to drive something different, a change for him, and I believed him! And all the time, he was just worried about people noticing him with me. Oh, Millie, you don't think it can be true, do you?'

Phoebe knew that her mother was not going to tell her what she most wanted to hear. She knew it, because she herself thought, despite her unwillingness to believe it, that what Kate had told her was true. At some deep instinctive level what Kate had told her rang as true as the note of a firmly struck tuning fork.

She buried her head in her arms again, taking refuge in the warm blackness.

'I'll have to speak to her again,' she said wearily. 'I have to know what's going on.'

'Why not leave it until the morning?' Millie suggested.

'No. There's no point. I don't think anything's going to look much better then, do you? Maybe,' she said without much hope, 'maybe they are still married, but have separated. Maybe that's what she meant.'

Millie handed her the telephone, and Phoebe pressed the redial button.

'It's me,' she said baldly when the telephone was answered. 'Just tell me. You had split up, even if you weren't divorced, hadn't you?' She knew what the answer must be, but she still clung to the idea of Leo going abroad during the week.

'No. As far as I was concerned, we had a normal marriage.'

'But you must have wondered . . . Where did you think he was . . .?' Phoebe was still unable to accept the truth of what had been happening.

'At weekends? Abroad. Working abroad. I must have been a mug to fall for that one.'

'But he was abroad during the week! That was his work! To Gatwick on Monday, and back here on Friday!' Tears were running down Phoebe's face, she smeared them away impatiently with her hand. From the telephone at her ear came nothing but an eloquent silence. 'No,' said Phoebe. 'Oh, no. He wouldn't. He *couldn't.* Not that. Oh, please, not that.'

'I'm sorry,' said Kate. 'You have to know. He wasn't working abroad at all. During the week he lived here, in Brighton, and went to London each day on the train. Just as he'd always done.'

'No! I don't believe you! You must be mad!'

'I'm afraid it's true. You'd better start believing it, because there's worse to come. It looks as though he's been taking money from the bank. They've been round here, and it probably won't take them long to find their way to you. He doesn't seem to have covered his tracks particularly well. So if you know where he is . . .'

Phoebe was shaking her head. In her mind, the word NO excluded any other thought: not so much in denial as in an attempt to remake the world, to force it back into its previous familiar mould. It was as though the two huge letters were physically present inside her skull, hard as concrete and yet organic, growing as if feeding on the cells of her brain. If she had attempted to speak it would have been the only word her lips would have been able to form, and she knew that if she once started to say it, her voice would soon degenerate into the howl that she could feel building up in the pit of her stomach, the base of her spine, all the places that seemed to house the centre of her being. She closed her eyes, squeezing them shut until flashes of light danced inside her lids, then opened them before they could form into neon letters.

'Phoebe!' Her mother's hand grasping her own pulled her back from the edge of disintegration.

'I don't believe you.' She was amazed to hear her own voice speaking collectedly into the telephone. 'You must be mad.'

'Mad? I wish I were. Right now, there's nothing I'd like more than to be safely put away in a nice padded cell.' Kate's voice betrayed bitter fury. 'So you'd better start believing it pretty bloody quickly, because you're going to have the bank on your doorstep at any moment, looking for Len. And, more particularly, looking for their money. Do you want to ring them, or shall I?'

'He's gone.' It was the only thing Phoebe seemed to be able to focus on. The certainty of Leo's departure filled her mind, excluding everything else. 'He's really gone.'

'Look,' Kate said, 'I know you've had a shock. Come to that, we both have. But we haven't got time to howl and tear our hair just now. I've got my kids to think of. The bank seems to think we're in the clear, financially speaking, but it's early days yet. You've got to work out where you stand, and what you're going to do about it. Are you really sure you don't know where Len might have gone? If we can find him, and somehow persuade him to give back as much as he can lay his hands on, then we might all be able to get out of this without too much of a stink.'

'I don't know where he is. I don't know . . . anything.' Anything, she meant, about Leo. No, not Leo. Len. Lennie the Lion, she thought numbly, seeing a big floppy puppet, hearing a silly voice. A person who didn't exist: a construct, animated by the puppeteer with one hand inside him. A puppeteer who grinned a febrile, twitching grin through which his voice came, distorted, to speak for his creation. Or was it me? Was I the puppet, after all?

In the silence she thought she felt a wave of disbelief coming through the telephone.

'I really *don't* know where he's gone,' she repeated. 'I mean, when you rang, I thought you must be him.'

'All right, then. Neither of us knows where he is. Frankly, I've got better things to do than look for him. I'll leave that for the bank. You know he works for Carver and Greenwood?'

'Yes, of course.'

'Not much "of course" about it, I wouldn't have thought. I'll have to tell them, you know. I'm sorry. I've got to protect myself, and my family. What's your address?' Kate asked curtly. Meekly, Phoebe told her. 'East Sussex? Not all that far away. I suppose you never came to Brighton?'

'Not with Leo. I did suggest it once, but . . .'

'But he put you off. Didn't you question it at all? Didn't you find it strange?'

'Not really. We were happy here.'

'Quite.'

'Oh God. I'm sorry.'

'Yes, I'm sure you are.' Kate sounded weary. 'I'll tell them, shall I?'

'Yes, please.' Phoebe knew she should get in touch with the bank herself, but the prospect of the explanations involved were too daunting. She knew no one there, had no name to ask for other than Leo's own, and the thought of speaking to some receptionist, of being passed from one office to another, of the disbelief, the questions, the thinly veiled accusations, was more than she could bear to contemplate. 'You'd better have the telephone number too,' she added drearily. 'It's ex-directory. Of course.'

Too late, now, to see why this should be so. Too late to wonder at the absence of telephone calls, the shunning of London theatres and restaurants, the lack, now she came to think of it, of old friends. Wrapped in her shimmering veil of newly wedded bliss, Phoebe had failed – or was it refused? – to notice anything odd about Leo's seeming isolation.

'Right.' Kate's brisk voice was curiously reassuring, but the pause that followed was not. Phoebe felt strangely reluctant to end this conversation, strange and terrifying though it had been. While it continued, she was at least doing something. It kept her from screaming, or curling up into a foetal ball, or being sick. The telephone was a protective barrier: once she put it down, she would have to find some way of dealing with the present and even, hideous thought, the future.

'That's about it, then,' said Phoebe slowly.

'Yes. I'll ring the bank in the morning.'

'Don't worry. I'm not going to run away.'

The word 'too' hovered between them. Is that what I thought? wondered Kate. Was I warning her, giving her time to disappear?

'I never thought you would,' she said, and was surprised to find that it was true. She might not be sure of Len's probity where other people's money was concerned, but she found that she still trusted his judgement of people. For some reason this made her feel even angrier with him. 'Goodbye,' she snapped, and crashed the telephone down before she could hear any answer.

Phoebe and Millie looked at one another. Phoebe still held the telephone in her hand. Now she laid it down gently, as though it were as fragile as the finest blown glass.

'Did you hear it?' The thought of having to explain to her mother, to put it all into words and speak them, was unbearable. Millie nodded.

'Yes. I'm so sorry, darling.'

'I know.' Now that the telephone call was finished, and Phoebe no longer needed to keep up her barrier of control, she thought she would be able to weep. She wanted to sink into a featherbed of tears, to sob with open mouth like a child until she was limp and swollen and exhausted. She blinked experimentally, but her eyes felt dry and gritty. She wrinkled her forehead, tried to bring the tears that were boiling deep inside her gushing through arid ducts, but they stayed where they were, making her feel swollen as an over-filled hot water bottle.

'What do we do now?' she asked helplessly.

'Have another drink,' suggested Millie. She drank very little – another reason why she was seldom an unwelcome guest – and Phoebe looked at her in surprise. 'A bottle of champagne,' continued her mother briskly, astonishing Phoebe still further. 'It's a good pick-me-up, and I don't think we should get stuck into spirits, do you? We're going to need to keep our heads clear for tomorrow. You go and sit down by the fire, darling, you're shivering. I know where everything is.'

Meekly Phoebe went back to the sitting room. It was true, now she came to notice it, that her hands and feet were icy cold, the blood supply having withdrawn to go, apparently, to her head which was hot and buzzing. She crouched by the fire, and put her hands to her face, welcoming their cool touch on her forehead. The effort of thinking was too much for her: it was as much as she could do just to exist.

Millie came back with a bottle and two glasses. Skilfully she eased the cork from the bottle – helping at her friends' parties had given her several useful skills – and poured the wine. Phoebe sipped, welcoming the sharp coolness in her dry mouth. The tingling bubbles prickled at the back of her nose, reminding her that she did not greatly care for champagne. That, too, was probably just as well. Tempting though it might be to drink herself into temporary oblivion, as Millie had said she would need to have her wits about her to face whatever might be coming tomorrow.

The first glass was drunk in silence, but it was companionable rather than tense. Millie refilled the glasses, watching surreptitiously until she saw the infinitesimal relaxation of taut muscles in neck and shoulders.

'It was too good to be true, wasn't it?' said Phoebe at last. 'I should have known.'

'Why should you? There's nothing like being happy for stopping you seeing things. It has a sort of dazzling effect. You only see the good bits.'

'Rose-coloured spectacles? Yes, but I'm thirty-six. Too old to be taken in by a . . . by a con man.' She forced the words out, making herself look at them.

'No one's ever too old, or too young, for that. Besides, I don't think he was. A con man, that is. Not really.'

'A bigamous embezzler? Oh, come on, Millie.'

'Con men set out to deceive. They're cynical about it. I don't think he was like that. In his own way, he believed in what he was doing as much as you did. Bigamy didn't come into it. He could just as easily have lived with you without any formal commitment. You wouldn't have minded, would you?'

'Not a bit.' Phoebe's mouth twisted wryly. 'He was the one who wanted us to be married. Insisted on it, even.'

'There you are, then. In his own way, I think he really did love you, Phoebe. Whatever else he did, you can hang on to that.'

'That's about all I will be able to hang on to. Or can you find excuses for stealing the money, as well?'

Millie ignored the anger, knowing it was not for her.

'Of course not. There are no excuses for that. No *excuses* for any of it. And I'm not really trying to stop you from feeling angry with him, or blaming him. I just don't want you to start blaming yourself.'

Phoebe thought about it. The champagne, oddly, had cleared her head.

'Yes,' she said. 'Yes, you're right. How did you know?'

'Because that's how I was. It's so much easier to blame yourself, isn't it? I mean, who else knows all your faults and weaknesses? It took me years to stop thinking everything was all my fault. It's very self-destructive, you know, taking all that guilt on yourself. Very tiring. You're going to need all your energy, you can't afford to squander it on trying to see where you went wrong, and all that. You're going to have to fight for yourself, and you can't do that if part of you is thinking you should be punished and you deserve everything you get.'

Phoebe looked at her mother in amazement. She tried to remember whether Millie had ever spoken to her like that before. She realised that for the last twenty years, since Phoebe had left childhood and adolescence behind her, her mother had scrupulously avoided offering any unsolicited advice or suggestions. Even on the rare occasions when Phoebe had asked for it, Millie had been wary of anything but the barest generalisation. While Phoebe had never doubted that her mother had a strict personal code of beliefs and behaviour, she was so accustomed to her non-interventionist policy that her present advice struck her with all the force of a bombshell.

'Your father was a married man,' said Millie now. 'Before he died,' she added.

Phoebe choked on her last mouthful of champagne. Her coughing turned to laughter. She gasped and rocked, hugging herself as her stomach muscles ached. Her eyes ran, and even she never knew at what point her laughter turned to crying. She was scarcely aware that her mother had come to hold her, the small slender arms surprisingly strong around her.

Phoebe cried until she was exhausted. At last she sat up straight, wiped her eyes and blew her nose on the handkerchief that Millie handed her.

'Thanks,' she said hoarsely.

'Do you want another drink? There's half a glass of champagne left in the bottle.'

'No, you have it. What I really fancy is a cup of tea. A bit odd on top of champagne, but it's just what I feel like.' Millie started to get up. 'Don't move. I'll go and make it, I need to move around a bit, get my blood going again. My legs feel dead.'

The routine of filling the kettle, laying a tray, and making the tea, was curiously soothing. Phoebe carried it back, and sat down in her usual chair.

'That's better,' she said, sipping. She looked at Millie who sat, neat and composed, opposite her.

'You've never mentioned my father before.' Phoebe was careful not to allow it to be a question.

'It seemed . . . right, and it never felt like that until now. There's not much to tell you. He was married, as I said, and quite a lot older than me. I was only seventeen when I met him, and he was forty-five, and a friend of my father's. I'd been to a girls' boarding school, didn't know any boys, and when he was kind to me I developed a tremendous crush on him. At least, that's how I see it now. Then, of course, it was True Love, the Real Thing, all the romantic slush I'd ever read rolled into one and tied up with pink ribbon. He resisted quite hard, to be fair, but he never stood a chance. I practically served myself up naked on a plate, garnished with watercress.'

'Poor little Millie.' Phoebe was fascinated, but appalled. It was impossible to connect this with herself and her own life. 'What about your parents?'

'They didn't notice. I was a disappointment to them,' said her mother placidly. 'Not the kind of daughter they wanted. An old-fashioned debutante, who would be presented in a fluffy white dress and then make a suitable marriage (preferably to someone with a title) in another fluffy white dress, that's what they intended. They tried so hard, poor things, all those dancing lessons and deportment and tennis lessons and visits to the dressmaker, and I hated it all. Always watching and prodding and "don't sit like that, don't speak to those people, don't read that book" – but when it came to advising me about real life, they just washed their hands of me. And by then my mother was ill, and my father was absorbed in looking after her, so I just went. Got on with it. You know.'

'Did they know about me?'

'I wrote to them. I'm afraid they didn't answer. My mother died a few months later, and when I went to her funeral my father told me it was all my fault, that I had killed her. Ridiculous, of course. She'd been ill for years, long before there was any trouble with me, only she wouldn't go to the doctor about it. Still, he never forgave me. I went to see him later on, when he was ill himself, but he didn't want to know. I was sorry, but not heartbroken. They never really wanted *me*, just some kind of image they had in their minds.'

Phoebe sat quietly, not daring to interrupt the flow. In her childhood she had learned that questions about her mother's past would be answered only by vague generalisations. Millie lived in the present, and neither the past nor the future had any interest or even any relevance for her.

'Anyway, it's your father we were talking about. I persuaded him into an affair, but after a few months, he seemed to be cooling off. Not that he'd ever said he'd leave his wife for me – on the contrary, I came very much a secret second place in his timetable – but I was convinced I could force the issue. So, I got pregnant. Poor man!' Millie, looking back, actually laughed. 'He was appalled! And terrified, too! It was his wife who had the money, you see. They hadn't any children, and she'd always let him assume that was his fault. He offered me money – quite a lot of money – to go to a clinic and get rid of you. I suppose that was what opened my eyes, at last. I knew what it was, you see, to be a child that wasn't particularly welcomed. So I told him where he could put his money, and that was that. About five years later I heard, quite by accident, that he'd died. And do you know, I found I couldn't even remember what he'd looked like. Ridiculous, isn't it?'

'Is that the word?'

'Of course it is. Completely ridiculous.'

Phoebe, thinking about it, supposed that it was. She thought that she should have been excited, fascinated to hear at last something about her father, but she found it hard to summon up much interest.

Once, she would have been full of questions, and she supposed that in the future she would want to know more, much more, about the man who had fathered her. At present, however, he seemed an irrelevance in her life. Millie, looking at her, saw the thought in her expression.

'But it was all worth it, because I had you. So you see.'

'Silver lining? I don't feel much like Pollyanna just now.'

'Of course you don't. But one day, you'll be able to laugh at this.'

'Yes,' said Phoebe politely, not believing her. 'One day. But what am I going to do until then?'

Chapter 6

Kate put down the telephone after the first call. The skin on her face and head felt hot, almost scalded, but inside her skull her brain seemed to have congealed into a lump of cold shrivelled putty. So many emotions were churning inside her that she didn't know what she felt. Fury, anguish, resentment, disbelief and even a kind of angry pity were so closely knitted together that they seemed almost to cancel each other out, heat and cold combining to create something tepid that, like water at blood-temperature, could scarcely be felt. If anything, the thing that predominated was surprise. Not, she realised, surprise that it had happened. Looking back, it fitted all too well with the Len she had known, the Len she had been reluctant to admit was the real man she had married. No, what was surprising was that she was not surprised. It was as if Phoebe's call had been a confirmation of something that she, Kate, already knew, rather than a revelation.

Later, perhaps, there would be time to unravel her complex emotions and try to deal with them. For now that must be in abeyance, the whole tangled mess put aside like a muddle of old ends of knitting wool shoved into the back of a drawer. At the moment, she must consider her children. Len's children, who had listened to every word of her side of the conversation. She looked up into a circle of enquiring faces.

'Tell me,' said Tashie. 'Tell me I didn't hear what I think I just heard.'

'I don't understand,' said Sam. 'Who was that?'

'Oh, darlings,' said Kate. 'I'm so very sorry.' She thought that it would have been easier to have told them that Len had been in a car crash, been suddenly killed. 'I'm sorry,' she repeated helplessly.

'It's all right, Mum.' Nick's voice was husky, but controlled. 'It's not your fault.' Tashie opened her mouth as if to speak, but Sam broke in first.

'But who *was* it? Mum, please tell me what's happening!'

Kate drew a long breath. She put her hands on Sam's shoulders.

'Sam, there's no easy way to tell you this, darling. You know that Daddy had – well – other friends? Women friends?'

'I suppose so.' Sam's eyes shifted sideways, away from hers. He looked ashamed. 'Was she one of them?'

'In a way, yes. The trouble is, she thinks she's married to him. It's a mistake, of course, but that's what she believes.'

'Married to Dad? But she can't be. He's married to you!'

'You're such a *baby*, Sam.' Tashie spoke scornfully.

'I'm not! I'm not a baby! I know you're not allowed to be married to two people at the same time, and Dad was still married to Mum, wasn't he, Mum?'

'Of course he was.' Kate, seeing his sudden deep insecurity, put all the certainty she had into those words. 'Dad and I were still married. We *are* still married, come to that.'

'Then why does she think . . .?'

Kate hugged him, and he buried his face against her.

'You know Dad, Sam. You know how he used to get carried away when he made up stories? How he'd get so involved in them that he almost began to believe in them himself?' She felt his nod. 'Well, I think it was like that. He didn't do it to hurt you, or me, or any of us. He just wanted to make her happy, so he gave her something that wasn't really his to give. Like that time when you played at finding buried treasure, and you took my brooch and gave it to your friend Simon, because you really believed you'd found it.'

'But I gave it back, later.'

'I know you did. But some things are easier to give back than others.'

He rubbed his face against her. She pulled out a handkerchief and gave it to him, and he blew his nose.

'But he's not really married to her? She just thinks he is?'

'That's right.'

'And she can't . . . do anything to us?'

'Not a thing.'

He thought for a moment.

'I suppose Daddy took that money for her, didn't he?' He sounded like a little old man, and this time it was Kate whose tears flowed. She nodded.

'Don't cry, Mum. You've still got us.' He was young enough to believe that while she had them, she needed nothing more, and at that moment Kate believed it too. Then the telephone rang again, and Kate grabbed to answer it. At the end of the second conversation with Phoebe she felt exhausted, and saw the same feeling mirrored in

Nick, Tashie and Sam. They looked back at her helplessly.

'Who was that, darling? It wasn't Daddy, was it?'

Joyce, unheard, had come from her room and was standing behind the little group that was still huddled round the telephone. All their eyes had been fixed on its innocent ivory plastic, and none of them had seen her join them. If only it had been, thought Kate. She would have welcomed some soothing kind of communication from beyond the grave. 'All will be well . . .'

'No,' she sighed. 'No, dear, it wasn't Daddy.'

'Oh, well. He's sure to call soon. I expect it was Len, then. How is he? He's usually back by now – he's not had an accident, has he?'

It was uncanny, thought Kate, how in her muddled way Joyce somehow picked up a thread of what was going on. Her memory might be shaky, but she was extraordinarily sensitive to emotional vibrations. She saw that all three children were looking at her. She gazed back helplessly.

'An accident!' said Tashie bitterly. 'Some accident!' Joyce's face puckered with anxiety, the soft skin crinkling like crushed silk taffeta.

'Oh dear! Is he badly hurt? Shouldn't you go to the hospital? I'll take care of the children.'

'We don't need taking care of,' spat Tashie. 'If anything, it's—'

'Oh hush, Tashie,' Kate broke in. 'Don't make things worse.'

'Worse? How could they possibly be *worse*?' Kate, unfortunately, could think of several ways, but kept them to herself.

'But what about poor Len?'

Tashie rounded on her grandmother.

'*Poor Len* doesn't need any help from you! *Poor Len* has done a runner with the bank's money, and some haggish *tart*, so *poor Len* is doing very nicely, thank you! And what I want to know is, what are you going to do about it?' Her voice was rising, and she turned to glare at Kate, her pupils contracted to near invisibility.

'Do about it?' Kate repeated stupidly.

'Yes, *do* about it! You're the one he's married to, aren't you, not that slag, so why don't you bloody well *do* something instead of just standing there looking all feeble and dreary? This is all your fault! You shouldn't have let him do it! You should have looked after him better, been nicer to him, then he wouldn't have gone to her. Your fault! It's your fault!'

'That's no way to talk to your mother,' said Joyce firmly. Most of what Tashie had said had passed her by, incomprehensibly, but she was quick to react to the tone of voice. 'Shame on you, Tashie, to treat your mother like this when she's worried about your father.

What would Grandpa say, if he heard you?'

Tashie rounded on her.

'Well, he's not *going* to hear me, is he?'

'I shall have to tell him—'

'You *can't* tell him!' Tashie pushed her face up close to her grandmother's. 'He's dead, you silly old bat! He's been dead for years! Ooh!' She gave a sobbing wail. Kate reached out to comfort her, but was pushed away so hard that she staggered and would have fallen if Nick had not caught her. It was Joyce who reacted first, administering a sharp slap to Tashie's cheek. Tashie's mouth, pulled to a square crying shape like a small child's, closed and then opened in astonishment. She lifted her hand to her face then looked at it, as though expecting to see it covered with blood.

'You hit me!' She sounded more surprised than affronted.

'Hysteria won't solve anything.' Joyce, for a moment, looked almost like the mother of Kate's childhood years. 'Now, go and wash your face, and then I think you should have a little lie down on your bed.'

'I can't sleep! Not now!'

'I'm not saying anything about sleeping. Just a little quiet time, that's all. Up you go.'

To Kate's astonishment, Tashie turned obediently away. She brushed past Kate as if she were invisible. Nick and Sam moved to let her pass between them, and she trailed up the stairs. Her shoeless feet made no sound, but they heard the creak of the landing where there was a loose floorboard. Usually, Kate knew, Tashie avoided the place as a matter of habit. The bedroom door clicked decisively shut. Kate turned back to her mother.

'Oh, Mum.' She wanted to thank and to apologise, but in the few moments of Tashie's going, the old Joyce had disappeared again. In her place was a tremulous, confused old woman, shrunken and diminished, who looked up at Kate helplessly. 'Oh, Mum,' repeated Kate in a different tone of voice. 'Come back to your room and sit down. I'll make you something to drink.'

'What's happening? I don't understand. Where's Harold?'

Kate had not thought it could be possible for her heart to sink still further, but it did. Joyce had often been confused before, but this was the first time Kate had heard that tone of fear in her voice. Until now she had, if anything, been amused rather than scared by her lapses.

'Come on, Mum,' she said gently. 'It's all right.' With her arm round the trembling shoulders she led her mother back to the familiar safety of her own room. Nick and Sam came silently with them, and

Kate was grateful for their presence although she suspected that they derived as much comfort as she did from being together. Between them they settled Joyce in her room.

'I ought to go and see Tashie,' said Kate, when at last Joyce was in bed.

She was soon downstairs again. 'Fast asleep, I think,' she said to the boys. 'I suppose we'd all better go to bed. It's quite late.'

'I don't want to go to bed.' Sam's lip trembled.

'Why don't we have supper, than make some hot chocolate, and go up to Mum's room?' suggested Nick. 'That way we'll hear Tashie if she wakes up, and we can talk if we want to.'

'Good idea,' said Kate with relief. She could see that Sam would probably go to sleep the minute he sat down, and the thought of the three of them being together was very comforting. She wished that Tashie would join them, but recognised that it wasn't likely to happen. Still, she told herself, two out of three isn't bad.

Upstairs, Tashie was huddled on her bed. Her head was buried against the familiar roughness of her old teddy bear. Although she pretended to her friends that she only kept him on her bed to please her parents, Tashie still found his patchy fur, balding where she had chewed him as a small child, and the faintly dusty smell from his stuffing, as comforting as they had been in her early years. She could not remember a time when he had not been there, for he had been her father's first gift to her, brought to the hospital after her birth. That event, which he had described to her so often that she sometimes believed she could remember it happening, had always endeared the toy to her. Until now.

With a sob of fury she dragged him from beneath her face and flung him into the corner of the room. He hit the wall with a thud and lay, face down, his legs twisted and his arms above his head as if in surrender. The pillow, without him, was cold and smooth, smelling only of fabric softener. Sniffling, Tashie wriggled off the bed and went to pick him up again, straightening his limbs gently. The feel of his firm body within her hands was more like the sensation of holding a real baby than any of her dolls had ever been, and she could not rid herself of the feeling that there was, within him, some glowing spark of consciousness.

'I'm sorry,' she whispered, hugging him to her. 'It's not your fault.'

Cradling him in her arms, she lay down again, pulling the corner of the duvet over them both. She felt suddenly very grown up and responsible and although she was still crying her tears were gentler, and quiet. She felt the warm onset of sleep, her thoughts fragmenting and her body floating away, and surrendered thankfully to the escape it offered. When Kate came in to check on her half an hour later, she did not stir.

She awoke, suddenly and completely, to darkness broken only by a dim orange glow from her window. Her room was at the back of the house, overlooking the garden, but the night sky was never completely dark in this urban area, and she had not closed her curtains the evening before. Still dressed in jeans and a sweatshirt she was hot and sticky under the smothering warmth of the duvet. Her throat was dry and her mouth tasted stale and disgusting. She sat up.

The house was silent. The once luminous hands of her bedside clock had long since lost their glow, but the watch she had been given on her birthday had a face that lit up if you pressed a little button on the side. The small disc seemed blindingly bright and she screwed up her eyes, suddenly aware that they were puffy and sore. Half past three. She longed for a drink. There was cold water from the tap at the wash basin in the corner of her room. It wasn't what she felt like, though: what she wanted was something cold and sharp like the fresh orange juice that she knew was in the kitchen refrigerator, but it was an effort to move. She dreaded the effort of going down the stairs; dreaded still more the thought that her mother might hear her. So she waited, knowing that she would go in the end but postponing the moment, until the taste of the orange was so vivid in her mouth that she could no longer resist.

She stood up, pulling the waistband of her jeans away from her creased flesh and shivering as the cool air touched its dampness. She eased open the bedroom door and began to creep downstairs, remembering this time to avoid the creaking board. Kate's bedroom door was ajar and Tashie crept past it as though it contained something menacing and deadly.

The kitchen welcomed her with its warmth and the faint scent of food. Sniffing, Tashie detected stir fry with prawns, one of her favourites, and at once her stomach growled protestingly. Shutting the door carefully she dimmed the lights before turning them on.

The litre bottle of orange juice was still half full, and she drank straight from it. She held the first mouthful before swallowing it, savouring the way the fresh flavour cut through the sticky coating that lined her mouth and tongue. Even the way it stung her throat when she gulped it down was pleasurable, she could almost feel the dehydrated tissues softening gratefully.

Her first thirst assuaged, she became aware that the acid was churning in her empty stomach. Putting down the bottle she foraged in the fridge. A dish of peeled prawns left from supper – it did not occur to her that Kate had put them aside especially for her – and a plate of cold potatoes made a good start. Tashie spooned on mayonnaise and mixed it all together, adding some cooked peas and, as an afterthought, a squeeze of tomato puree. It turned a rather nasty streaky pink, but she spooned it up eagerly, and followed it with a large slice of treacle tart. Its sweetness made her screw up her face when she washed it down with orange juice, but she felt much better. Taking an apple and a banana from the fruit bowl, she crept back up to her room.

Once there she sat cross-legged on her bed. For the first time she felt able to confront the events of the evening. Chewing thoughtfully on her apple she considered the revelations of the past twenty-four hours.

In spite of her earlier protestations, she had no difficulty in believing that her father might have stolen from the bank. Nor, unfortunately, was she particularly surprised to find that he had fallen for another woman. Her mother, in her eyes, was middle-aged and dull, which was how a mother ought to be. She had often been thankful, seeing friends' mothers borrowing their daughters' clothes and clinging with determination to their youth, that her own mother was content to be cosy and safe and, well, mummyish. But her father, although he made no attempt to dress like a teenager, still very often thought and even behaved like one, which was what made him such good company and was why, perversely, she had adored him. Her own strongly developed instincts of right and wrong went into abeyance where he was concerned, and moral considerations appeared irrelevant to him.

What she could not accept was that, as a result of her telephone warning, he could have disappeared off into the blue without so much as a word to her. That he might be dead never even crossed her mind. However bad things might be, it would never occur to him to doubt that he would be able to sort things out, to talk himself out of a tight spot. She could imagine him faking his own death – and getting considerable amusement out of it – but not him actually doing it.

Impossible to believe that her father could have abandoned her. His relationship with this other woman who said she was married to him might threaten her mother, but Tashie could not see that it made any difference to her. Accustomed as she was to being told that she was the most important person in her father's life, the apple of his eye, his little princess, she could not imagine that his love for her could change. In the end, he would call her, send for her perhaps. Meanwhile he was – what? A fugitive. Yes, that was it. A fugitive. A mental picture of Harrison Ford on the run from the law – never mind that his character was innocent. Her father was on the run, outwitting the forces ranged against him. Her heart seized on the romantic image.

It was a tremendous relief. Against all reason, she could not bear to be angry with her father, or to blame him. The anger was still there, of course, burning so hot inside her that by contrast the surface of her skin felt cold. The need to blame was very strong. Unconsciously she lifted her hand, again, to the cheek her grandmother had slapped. Not her mother, not really. She felt angry with her as well, but beneath the anger was the need for the comfort of her mother's presence, the Mummy figure of her childhood. No, the responsibility for all this anguish was easy to place. That woman, who had answered her father's phone, and who claimed he had married her. As if he would! She turned aside from the niggle of doubt over him, and concentrated on her hate.

A silly, breathless voice. Much too young-sounding, and obviously belonging to someone mindless, thoughtless, cruel and horrible. A siren who had tempted her father away from his responsibilities and his wife, away, above all, from Tashie herself. She was to blame, there could be no question about it. She had probably encouraged him to steal, egged him on, demanded diamonds and a yacht and a flashy car, blackmailed him . . . Tashie piled up the words and the ideas, feeding her anger and her hatred. She felt a surge of heat through her body as the anger erupted like lava, flowing out from the centre of her being until her skin flushed and tingled. Her hands clenched and stretched like a cat's claws and her face, though she was not aware of it, was screwed into an ugly mask. Her father, had he been there, would have been shocked to the core and would have had trouble in recognising her.

Now, of course, this woman would get what Gran would call her come-uppance. In the morning, the bank would hear about her, and then she would be the one getting the telephone calls, the visits, the kind of investigating that had made Kate look, Tashie had thought, suddenly ten years older. They would take back the diamonds and everything else, leave her homeless and destitute. Tashie liked that idea. She went to the window. The curtains were still open – she had not thought to draw them earlier – and a cold autumn wind was gusting round the house and splattering rain against the glass.

Tashie opened the window and leaned out. The rain was fresh on her face, washing away the gritty feeling of past tears from her eyes.

She lifted her head, breathing in the cold salty air, aware that it chilled her but rejoicing in her own shivers, transferring them in her imagination to that woman. She pictured her wandering the dark streets, wrapped in smelly rags and festooned with carrier bags, looking for a bench or a sheltering doorway to sleep in. There were many such homeless relics in Brighton, washed up in the town in much the same helpless way that oiled seabirds or the abandoned rubbish from passing ships drifted in from the sea to litter the high-tide line on the pebbly beaches. Until now, the sight of them had aroused in her a complex mixture of pity, anger, embarrassment and shame. Now, for the first time, she thought of how they lived, and rejoiced.

The rain was beginning to drip from her face and hair down her neck. She closed the window and drew the curtains, then went to her wash basin. Half in a dream she rubbed her head with the towel, then stripped off her damp clothes. Dropping them on the floor where she stood she rummaged for the old T-shirt she liked to sleep in, thin and soft with many washings. She found it at last under her pillow, neatly folded, and frowned at the evidence of her mother's intrusion. As she pulled it over her head she was suddenly aware of being exhausted. Her eyes were already closed as she climbed into bed and pulled the duvet over her. One hand automatically grasped the teddy bear and pulled him to her, but she was asleep before she had finished the movement.

Phoebe, for her part, would have given anything to have been able to fall asleep so simply. She lay rigid in her bed. Every part of her body ached. The muscles in her legs twitched with tension, as sore as if she had run five miles. A dull grinding pain at the base of her back spread round to her stomach and up her spine, sending tendrils like acid trails over her shoulders and neck and up to feed her headache. Her eyelids felt hot and swollen, but though they were heavy they would not stay closed.

She had felt so exhausted, when she had finally come upstairs, that she had been sure she would sleep. Millie, she knew, had hovered on the landing listening to the sounds of her going to bed. Phoebe, lying huddled in her bed, had heard her going slowly and quietly to the spare bedroom. Millie's footsteps, which all her life had sounded so brisk and rapid, were dragging. For the first time, Phoebe took account of her mother's age, and an irrational guilt joined all the other emotions that were churning through her.

Tashie, in her present state of angry misery, would have been delighted to know that Phoebe's own image of her future was in many respects similar to her own. Not, of course, financially or physically. Cushioned by the memory of the lottery win, it did not occur to Phoebe that she might be homeless or destitute. In her innocence, she could not believe that the bank would try to take her money, as well as Leo's. In emotional terms, however, she felt herself to be as deprived as any street dweller. Of what use was a beautiful cottage if she must live in it alone, without Leo? Without, moreover, the future she had planned for them. The children she had planned and longed for, until now no more than insubstantial dreams, now took on a kind of life in her mind. Two, three, four of them – lying in cradles, tottering on bandy unsteady legs across a sunlit garden, climbing trees, opening their Christmas stockings, going off to school – they processed through her mind, their childish voices turning to shrieks and gibbering.

Sleep, when it came, was more of a sudden unconsciousness than a gentle drifting off. In her dreams she returned to her childhood, and a nightmare she had sometimes experienced then. She was in a maze – the dreams had started after an early visit to Hampton Court had frightened her – and running through the narrow paths after a figure that was always vanishing round a corner. She knew that he was her father, and that if she wanted to keep him she must somehow see his face, but run as she might she never caught up with him. This night, for the first time, she did, but when she peered up into his face she saw that he was Leo. He turned away from her, melting backwards through the hedge until he was gone. She tried to follow him, but the hedge was spiked with thorns and twining brambles that trapped and held her.

She woke suddenly in the morning, snapping out of sleep and straight back into the nightmare of reality with none of the gradual coming of awareness that usually cushions such awakenings. Her mind resumed its anxious circlings at the exact point where they had ceased in the night, and only the glimmering of light round the edges of the curtain convinced her that time had passed. She thought for a moment that it might be moonlight, but remembered how heavily the rain had been falling and knew no moon could penetrate that heavy cloud, and that this was dawn.

The relief was tremendous. However awful the day might be, whatever it might bring in new discoveries and miseries, it would be real. She would have something to do, even if it were only answering accusations and questions. Her joints creaked as she climbed out of bed, but she was thankful to be moving. Her bed, hitherto a place of comfort, safety and pleasure, was now somewhere filled with nightmare images. She would not attempt to sleep in this room tonight, she thought. It was difficult to imagine going to bed in a different room: still more difficult to imagine a time when she would be able to go quietly to bed and sleep. Still, the day had come and must be faced. She put on dressing gown and slippers, and went down to the kitchen to make a cup of tea.

When the doorbell rang at half past ten, Phoebe was as ready as she thought she would ever be for the ordeal to come. She had dressed early, choosing a sensible wool skirt and matching pullover over a cream shirt, all from Marks & Spencer, that were left over from her teaching days. Careful make-up failed to hide the shadows beneath her puffy eyes, but the effort gave her confidence. Not for anything would she seek anyone's sympathy by looking as washed out as she felt, and for the first time she appreciated the truth behind calling make-up 'warpaint'.

At half past eight she had been telephoned by a man with a voice so carefully neutral that she read volumes into it. Kate had, in fact, telephoned Brian at home the night before and told him of her discovery, so the wheels were already in motion. Phoebe gave her caller her address, and assured him that she had no intention of leaving the house. Something in the quality of his reply made her think that if she were to do so, her departure would be noted and she would not get far. Raging impotently, she kept her voice as bland as his, and agreed to his suggestion that she should get out as much in the way of bank statements and bills as she could find.

It was not difficult. Possibly in unconscious reaction to Millie's chaotic lifestyle, Phoebe had always been meticulous in such matters. Leo, too, with his bank training, had left all the paperwork connected with the house neatly filed. Looking through it, Phoebe was appalled to see how much money had gone into it. No expense had been spared on renovations or decorations, and a rough addition of the total sum involved made her blink.

When the bell rang Phoebe was in the dining room – like Kate she had considered it the most appropriate place for what she could not help thinking of as her interrogation. At the sound of the bell she jumped, not having heard a car, and felt the kind of internal sinking she had not felt since her days as a student teacher. She heard Millie's brisk footsteps as she walked across the hall floor, then Phoebe heard her mother's voice sounding oddly disconcerted. Then the answering voice rang out.

'Morning! Is Phoebe in? I'm Jennifer Dobson, I promised her I'd drop in with a prize she won. At my coffee morning. I meant to do it yesterday, but you know how it is.'

'How kind of you!' Millie was moving smoothly into her social best, years of practice at dealing with awkward situations in other people's houses going into that sweetly non-committal voice. 'I know how busy all you girls are, with your jobs and your charities and your families – not to mention animals!' In spite of everything Phoebe smiled, seeing in her mind's eye Millie's swift assessment of Jennifer's appearance. 'As a matter of fact, Phoebe's rather busy herself just now, I'm afraid, which is why I can't very well ask you in just at the moment. I'm her mother, Millie Humphreys.'

'How do you do. I must say, I'm glad that you're here, Mrs Humphreys. I did wonder . . . That's really why I came. Phoebe's not been here long, and she doesn't know many people yet, so . . . The thing is, I was in the shop just now, paying my paper bill, and there was a rather unpleasant little man asking questions about Phoebe and her husband.'

Phoebe felt her skin contract, with much the same sensation as if she had inadvertently touched something wriggling and slimy. She laid down the pile of receipts she had been leafing through before Jennifer's arrival, and went through to the hall.

'Phoebe!' Next to Millie's neat diminutive figure, Jennifer looked enormous. 'My dear, I was just telling your mother—'

'I know. I heard. You'd better come in, Jennifer.' Phoebe led the way into the kitchen. 'I'd offer you a coffee, but I'm expecting some people.'

'Of course, of course! I won't stop, but I thought you ought to know . . .' Phoebe reflected that whenever people said that, they always proceeded to tell you something that you would infinitely rather *not* have known. 'Such a nasty little man, and so persistent! Of course, Mrs Jennings is very discreet – well, running a village shop you have to be, or you wouldn't last a month! – but it was very awkward for her, so I asked him straight out who he was, and why he wanted to know. He gave me a look, and said it was a private enquiry, so I told him I was the co-ordinator of the Neighbourhood Watch scheme, and that I should be obliged to report this to the police. Yes, and then I remembered that when Soppy – my daughter Sophie, that is, we call her Soppy – came back from walking the dogs first thing this morning, she said there was a man in a car sitting in the lane just outside your gate. Not looking at a map or anything, or even pulled up to have a pee or a cup of coffee. Just sitting there. So you see . . .'

'Yes.' Phoebe sighed. 'Yes, I see. It's very good of you, Jennifer, to be so concerned. You don't need to worry about those men, I don't think they're burglars or anything. It's something to do with Leo – rather hush-hush at the moment.' Good grief, she thought, I'm beginning to sound like an old film. Jennifer was looking at her expectantly, looking so much like one of her own dogs hoping for a biscuit that Phoebe could have laughed. 'I know I can rely on your discretion,' she lied. Jennifer nodded violently.

'Oh, absolutely,' she breathed.

'I'm afraid Leo has left me. Everyone will have to know in the end, of course, but it's all rather a shock, and I'm sure you'll understand that I'd rather not discuss it just yet. I'm expecting my – my advisers – any minute.'

Jennifer nodded again. She reached out a large hand, on which two fine rings sat incongruously against the work-stained and roughened skin, and patted Phoebe awkwardly. If I had been a horse, Phoebe thought, she would have patted me like that, and I might have been comforted. Rather to her surprise, she found that she was touched by the gesture, and lowered her eyes to hide a sudden rush of tears.

'I won't hang around, but I want you to know that if there's *anything* I can do to help, you've only got to call. Any time. No, I really mean it. I think you're doing *exactly* the right thing, and I do so admire the way you've taken the bull by the horns, as it were. No point in sitting there meekly, waiting to be crapped on. So remember – you can rely on me!'

She strode out, leaving Phoebe obscurely heartened. That she could rely on Jennifer's moral and physical support seemed beyond question – how far she could really count on her discretion was another matter.

Chapter 7

A bare quarter of an hour after Jennifer's departure, the doorbell rang again. This time Phoebe answered it herself, and she could be in no doubt that these were the people from the bank. Two men in dark suits – the same who had arrived on Kate's doorstep the previous Sunday, had she but known it – flanked a businesslike young woman with a briefcase, and behind them came an older man who introduced himself as Brian Harper.

'Len's boss, as you might say,' he added with a wry smile.

'Yes,' said Phoebe. There didn't seem to be anything else she could add. She stepped back and led the way to the dining room, keenly aware of their eyes on her as they followed, and walking as stiffly as an automaton.

The two hours that ensued were a bizarre mixture of anxiety, embarrassment and, strangely, boredom. It was obvious to Phoebe that however he might try to hide it, Brian Harper's feelings for her were a mixture of suspicion and distaste. It did not surprise her – in his shoes she would have felt much the same. It soon became apparent that he had known Leo for a long time and also, presumably, the person Phoebe's mind stubbornly referred to as 'the other woman'. After an hour of questions she thought that his attitude had thawed from the icily polite to a tepid kind of sympathy. If anything she found this more trying, as it penetrated the protective shell of unreality which was her only defence against the unbearable present.

The questions were exhaustive, and exhausting. At two o'clock, Brian Harper pushed a pile of bank statements away from him, and leaned back in his chair.

'Time for a break, I think,' he said, glancing at his companions and receiving a small nod. 'I'm afraid we have been holding up your lunch.'

'Lunch?' said Phoebe, once again as though she had never encountered the concept before. 'Oh, yes, lunch,' she said vaguely. For an insane moment she wondered whether she should have been offering them something to eat (beyond the coffee and biscuits which Millie, silent for once, had brought in some while earlier). She looked at them helplessly, half expecting them to produce neat packets of sandwiches from their briefcases. They stood up. Brian Harper waited until the other people from the bank had left the room before speaking.

'We'll be back in an hour,' he said. 'I imagine you want to get this over with as quickly as we do. Um . . .' For the first time he displayed some hesitation. 'We won't – that is, we'll find a pub outside the village.' Phoebe looked at him blankly. 'We don't want to make things . . . awkward for you. I know what villages are like for gossip.'

'Oh yes. Thank you.' Phoebe struggled to feel grateful. At the moment she scarcely cared whether the whole world knew what had happened. Perhaps something of that showed in her face.

'We do, of course, require an equal discretion on your part.' Phoebe nodded. Her neck felt as though it were made of wood; she almost thought she could hear her vertebrae creak at the movement. Brian Harper probably thought the gesture lacked conviction; his face hardened slightly into severe lines that sat uncomfortably on a face that was built to be benign. 'Your position is a difficult one,' he continued. 'If we can prove to the bank's satisfaction that you are not . . . involved, then we are prepared to be, shall I say, understanding. In return, I must emphasise, for your signing a confidentiality agreement.'

'You'll buy my silence.' Phoebe spoke with dull bitterness.

'Bluntly, yes. Not, I would have thought, that you have any great wish to publicise what has happened. Though you might sell it to the *News of the World*. Bigamy and fraud, that ought to be good for a few thousand.'

For the first time Phoebe looked him directly in the eyes.

'That's a bloody offensive thing to say.'

'I apologise.' He did not say that his intention had been to jolt her out of her zombie-like state, but with awakened sensitivities she saw the satisfaction in his eyes at the renewed life in hers.

'I've got some money.' Phoebe spoke softly, her eyes turning to the half-closed door and back to his face. 'I could pay you back.' The words were childish, but her eyes clung to his with desperate appeal. Make it not have happened, they begged him. Put everything back how it was.

'He wouldn't come back,' said Brian gently, answering the emotion rather than the words. 'It isn't as simple as that.' In his turn he glanced at the door, lowering his voice. 'I probably shouldn't tell you this, but you would be wise not to say that again. If you had no knowledge of what he was doing – and I believe you didn't – then you have no need, or rather no moral duty, to repay what Len has taken. I've known Len for years. He'll move on without a backward glance, write all of this out of his life, out of his mind. He was my friend – or I thought he was – but I owe him nothing now, and nor do you. Buy his share of the house from us, if you like, but keep your money. You'll need it. So don't put any ideas into my colleagues' heads. I'm not saying they're unscrupulous, but . . .'

'But they want the money back.'

'Naturally. They're bankers.' For the first time a tinge of humour lightened his face. Phoebe thought, sadly, what a nice man he was.

'You're very kind.' She felt the beginning of a tremor in her lips and tightened them, feeling the surface of her chin indent with the effort. He shook his head, hesitated for a moment, then followed his colleagues out of the room.

Later, Phoebe was to realise that she had got off lightly. At the time she felt she was on the rack, her joints popping as the inquisitors stretched her. On the day after Brian Harper's visit she was questioned by an anonymous, hard-faced man, who made it clear that he regarded Brian as at least partly responsible for, if not actually an accessory to, Leo's actions. Phoebe refused an offer to have her solicitor present mainly because she didn't have one, at least not one she knew well enough to rely on for support and advice in something like this. She found herself regretting it once she discovered how aggressive the man was, but was pleased to find that her combative spirit revived under the attack. No one, she thought afterwards, who had survived Form 4J – whose creative nastiness had been equalled only by their complete unwillingness to sully their minds with any kind of meaningful information – could be browbeaten by this kind of heavy-handed approach.

By the time he left, reluctantly but tacitly conceding, if not defeat, at least an absence of victory, she felt mentally bruised but also stimulated. Brian Harper, though she was grateful for what she recognised was both genuine kindness and equally genuine good advice, had been too sympathetic. His gentleness had only weakened her.

The process moved inexorably forward, gathering pace under its own weight like an avalanche. Phoebe had an unpleasant moment when it looked as though her lottery ticket had vanished, but after half an hour of frantic searching Millie discovered it in the bottom of the log basket. Phoebe was grateful to be busy, to have her days filled. At night she lay wakeful, aching with tiredness and with a heartache that was physical as well as spiritual. The easier solace of tears escaped her most of the time: her eyes were as dry as though her tear ducts had atrophied. She longed to be able to sob herself to sleep. Instead, she lay hot-eyed and shivering, mind and stomach churning in mutual sympathy.

'You must eat, darling.' Millie's behaviour could scarcely be faulted. With the tact that made her presence as a guest so popular, she seemed to have an instinctive awareness of when to be silent, when to speak and in what manner. Only occasionally, as now, did her own anxiety obtrude. Phoebe, for reasons that she understood but was unable to contemplate, could not bear to see herself in a mirror, going so far as to turn the pretty Regency cheval glass to the corner, and even unscrewing the bathroom mirror off the wall. She dressed and brushed her hair out of habit, her face receiving no more than a wash with cold water that was more for refreshment than cleanliness. As a result she had no idea how her face had thinned and fallen in, the hollow cheeks echoing the purplish bruising shadows under her eyes. The sight of food nauseated her, though from time to time she would force down some dry toast, or a few biscuits.

'I can't,' Phoebe answered shortly. 'I'm sorry, Millie. I really can't. It would come straight back up again.'

'I know, darling.' Millie sighed. She wondered, but dared not ask, whether Phoebe were pregnant. For a moment she contemplated that, her face softening at the thought of holding a baby, her grandchild, in her arms. 'Is there anything you could fancy? I don't mind what it is. I could pop up to London on the train, go to Harrods . . .' Her voice tailed away as she saw the negative in Phoebe's body language.

By the time the business with the bank was finally settled, Phoebe had lost more than two stone. Her clothes hung off her, but because she was so thin she felt cold most of the time, the bulk of the extra layers of clothes helped to pad out her body shape.

The money from the lottery – and never was any large prize received with so little interest or pleasure – funded Phoebe's repurchase of her cottage from the bank. As Brian Harper had indicated, the bank was prepared to accept a reasonable settlement, in exchange for her promise of confidentiality. The amount they had lost, though large by personal standards, was small enough to write off without causing the auditors to blink, and public confidence was more important than pursuing Leo.

From time to time, Phoebe wondered vaguely about Kate. The feelings of guilt and resentment that flooded over her made her reluctant to do anything other than push the memory away as quickly as possible. She told herself that Kate would be all right, that she had her children and her friends to give her comfort and support. Also, Phoebe suspected, the help of Brian Harper who had betrayed his powerfully protective instincts towards Kate. Phoebe had no energy to spare. She knew that Kate was deserving of pity, but could not get beyond the wall of guilt and despair that separated her from the rest of the world.

There came a morning when Phoebe woke from a shallow doze, which was the nearest she currently came to proper sleep, with the knowledge that the day ahead of her, and all the days after that, would be free of intrusion by the bank. It should have been a relief. She told herself that it was a relief, but the emptiness in her mind betrayed her. Dealing with all that had to be sorted out had at least been a link with Leo, with the happy past. Now she must relinquish that, put it behind her, get on with the rest of her life. The words were hollow, as hollow as the future that stretched so drearily ahead of her.

It was not that there was nothing to do. Her solicitor was already hard at work untangling the legal problems that her unwittingly bigamous marriage involved her in. There were papers to sign, decisions to be made. She was at once anxious and reluctant to relinquish Leo's name – somehow going back to her maiden name was too much of a backward step, when she needed to be going forward. In her lighter moments she even wondered, with some seriousness, whether to go through the formal process of changing her name to something completely new. Her lethargy, born of depression, prevented her from doing anything so radical.

Outside, cold grey drizzle lived up to the worst elements of late November. Phoebe pulled the duvet up round her ears, pushed her face deeper into her pillow, and closed her eyes with determination.

Two hours later she woke again, drenched with sweat, and with a grinding ache in her stomach and back. She turned over, aware of warm stickiness between her legs. She reached for the box of tissues on the bedside table, snatched out a handful and wadded them against her, pushing back the duvet with the other hand and rolling from the bed. The air, though the central heating was on, struck chill against her clammy skin as she stumbled to the bathroom, half bent over and with one hand between her thighs in a posture that was a grotesque parody of the graceful modesty of a naked Venus, or Eve.

The flow of blood was thick and dark, but the eviscerating pain inside her told her that this would be the kind of flooding period she had not experienced for several years. Since Leo's departure, her one period had been irregular and sparse, but any hope that she might, by some wonderful last chance, be pregnant died in the face of repeated negative tests. It was as though her body, shocked out of its comfortably regular existence, had put that side of her life on hold. Now, with the release of other tensions, it was striking back with a vengeance. Grimly, Phoebe hunted out tampons and pads, and turned on the shower.

As she went down the stairs she was surprised, and rather irritated, to hear voices coming from the kitchen. Millie's of course, and a gruff female voice she recognised as Daphne Cunningham's. An unlikely friendship (given that they had almost no interests in common, and Daphne was known to shun human companionship) had sprung up between the two women during the weeks following Leo's disappearance.

It had started on the first day of the bank's investigations. Brian Harper had done his tactful best, but it was too much to expect that the village, accustomed as it was to Phoebe and Leo living an isolated existence, should fail to notice the presence of two or three strange, and in some cases expensive, cars parking all day in the drive. Leo's non-appearance at weekends, when he had always fetched the newspapers and bought things at the shop, had not been missed either. Jennifer's visit, delivering the tea cosy (which did not fit any of Phoebe's teapots) had added spice to the simmering pot of speculation. Millie, visiting the shop for eggs, faced a barrage of enquiries that were too genuinely sympathetic to be resented, but which she had great difficulty in answering.

During the afternoon, while Phoebe was incarcerated in the dining room with Brian Harper, Millie had taken advantage of a burst of sunshine to go out for a brisk walk. Turning firmly away from the village she had discovered a footpath that, in the manner of such by-ways, led her across several fields and through a small wood and then vanished, leaving her not precisely lost but certainly not very sure of where she was. She could, of course, have retraced her steps, but like many who occasionally walk for pleasure rather than those who are committed to a twice daily dash to exercise themselves or their dogs, she wanted a circular route. Casting about for the absent footpath markers she failed to notice the threatening clouds until the first heavy drops signalled a coming downpour. Resignedly she sought shelter in the wood, and with her vision blinkered by the floppy hood she had pulled over her head, almost jumped out of her skin when she rounded the trunk of a large oak and found a still figure already leaning against it.

'Oh! I'm so sorry!'

The figure did not move. Rivulets of water ran down the disreputable old coat, and her head in its floppy waterproof hat was lifted so that drips from the leaves overhead fell on to the leathery skin and into her half-opened mouth. As Millie surveyed her in some alarm, an even larger drop fell into one of the woman's open eyes. Millie's own eyes screwed up in sympathy, but the scarecrow figure simply blinked once. Her stillness made Millie uncomfortable: she had the sensation of being intrusive, of blundering into some kind of private meditation or even sacrament. Millie edged away. To leave the shelter of the wood – the rain was by now heavy – was more than she was willing to do, and although the woman looked odd her face was so peaceful that Millie felt no unease. Quietly, as one not wishing to disturb someone at their devotions, she moved round to the other side of the tree.

Almost at once, as if her being out of sight made her easier to deal with, the woman spoke.

'Are you lost?' The gruff voice was, as Phoebe had noticed, clearly articulated and educated. Millie stayed where she was, her back to the rough bark, and spoke to the empty air in front of her. How odd we must look! She thought. Like something out of *Alice*.

'Not exactly.' She pitched her voice above the sound of the rain on the canopy of leaves that were, in late September, still green though dusty-looking. 'I don't know where I am, but I do know the way back home. I wanted to carry on, but I seem to have mislaid the path.'

'Haven't we all?'

'It looks rather like it at the moment.' Millie thought of Phoebe, her own stomach twisting in sympathy for what her daughter must be enduring, and which she herself could do so little to alleviate.

There was a thoughtful silence.

'Where do you want to get to?'

Millie thought about it.

'Spiritually? Metaphorically?'

A grunt of laughter.

'Geographically. Further than that, I wouldn't presume.'

Millie smiled, knowing that it would be heard in her voice as she had heard it in the other's.

'Ember Cottage. It's in Forge Lane, in Oakfield.'

'Yes, I know.' Millie waited out the silence, willing to volunteer more but interested to know whether she would be asked. The voice, when the other spoke again, was carefully indifferent.

'My name is Daphne Cunningham. I live at Old Hall Cottage.'

'Millie Humphreys. How do you do.'

'How do you do.'

The formal greeting, spoken by two women with their backs to one another, nevertheless did not sound totally ridiculous. It was as old-fashioned and solid as the oak tree between them. The silence that ensued was friendly. Millie felt relaxed, as if the easing of Daphne's own tension was transmitted through the living timber. Like Daphne she lifted her head (though keeping her eyes and mouth closed) and let the rain fall on her face, breathing in the damp air that was as rich as old-fashioned fruitcake with the smell of the woodland.

'There is a way . . .'

'Mmm?' Millie dragged herself back to the present.

'A way back. It's quite a long way. No roads. I could show you.'

'I should like that. If you're sure? I mean, it's not private?' She knew that Daphne would understand her.

'I don't mind showing you. The rain's easing off now. Or do you want to wait?'

'I don't mind the rain,' said Millie cheerfully. She stepped away from the tree, as Daphne did also. They made an odd couple – Daphne tall and bony, her ancient raincoat flapping and dripping round legs that appeared to be clad in an old pair of men's tweed trousers; Millie short, slim rather than thin, her elegant country clothes undimmed by Phoebe's waxed jacket. Millie, whose tolerance for the foibles and even downright eccentricities of her friends sometimes alarmed even Phoebe, looked at the clear grey eyes that seemed oddly youthful in Daphne's leathery face, and thought she had found a friend. Daphne, who shunned human contact from ancient habit reinforced by more recent unpleasantness, saw her candid friendliness, and was amazed.

'Let's go, then.' Accustomed to her solitary walks, Daphne set off at her usual rapid, loping pace. Millie trotted uncomplainingly beside her, and after a few yards Daphne shortened her stride. 'Sorry. Didn't think.'

'It's all right.'

As they walked, Millie thought about her companion. She knew very well from Phoebe that Daphne had been instrumental in finding Leo's mobile phone. She was interested that Daphne had neither mentioned this event, nor even said that she had met Phoebe. Millie had deliberately refrained from stating their relationship – and their lack of physical similarity made it easy – in order to see whether Daphne would make any comment. It was obvious, by now, that

Daphne would say and ask nothing, even though she was willing to share her own secret. Millie understood just how important her private knowledge of the hidden country paths must be to Daphne, and she was fully alive to the honour which was being paid her. She realised that Daphne would mention nothing of Phoebe unless she herself did so first.

'I'm staying with Phoebe Miller.' The statement elicited no more than a sideways glance, and a brusque nod. 'I'm her mother.'

'Ah.'

Daphne, obviously, was not going to rely on the ideal of complete confidence between parent and child – unless she found mobiles ringing in hedgerows so frequently that she didn't think it worthy of remark.

'Phoebe told me you were very helpful the other Sunday. About the telephone.'

'Ah.'

Millie, rightly, saw the monosyllabic answer as a lack of conversational skill rather than a lack of interest.

'It was lucky you were there at the time. Anyone could have found it; it could so easily just have been stolen. Finders keepers, and all that.'

'I wouldn't know what to do with it anyway. Don't much care for telephones.'

'It was brave of you to answer it. Rather a surreal experience, hearing it ringing in the hedgerow.'

Daphne smiled for the first time, revealing large, strong teeth that looked startlingly white against her weathered skin and increased her resemblance to a horse.

'Scared me witless,' she admitted. 'I was tempted to ignore it, but it sounded . . . desperate. Silly, really.'

'Not a bit. I know just what you mean. And you were right, anyway. Phoebe was pretty desperate, even then.'

'Umm.' The agreement was given, clearly, as no more than that. There was no curiosity, no enquiring lift to the voice, not even the kind of sympathy that invites further revelations. That Phoebe had been desperate was accepted without judgement and without question. Millie found it extraordinarily soothing. It was, she thought, almost like talking to an animal – an intelligent dog, say, or (more probably) a horse: an animal with whom one had a close relationship and which gave, without words, the impression of understanding what you said. She drew in a long breath.

Millie had always thought of herself as self-sufficient. She had had to be. The many friendships she enjoyed had been built on the fact that if she had problems, she kept them to herself. With an endless and unfeigned interest in other people's lives, she never gave more than a superficial and joking account of her own. Partly out of pride, and partly from a strongly held belief that her own problems were rather dull, she never revealed her innermost self even to Phoebe. Particularly to Phoebe, in fact. Her own upbringing had given her a horror of possessive parents, and she had always tried to give her daughter the freedom she herself had suffered to gain.

In Daphne, unalike though they might appear, she perceived a kinship. They were of a similar age (though Daphne was some years older than Millie), and the marks of an old-fashioned strict upbringing such as Millie had endured were clearly to be seen in Daphne. They were there in the crisply articulated voice; in the almost obsessive politeness and in the deep lack of self-confidence that had made Daphne withdraw from society, and had led Millie to keep her contact with the world, though outwardly gregarious, superficial.

'I'll be staying with Phoebe for a while,' she said without the explanation that she knew Daphne would have found intrusive. 'I don't know that I can help her much, but someone should be there. Some of the time, at least. She doesn't want me fussing over her every minute of the day.'

Daphne unlatched a gate, and held it for Millie to go through before shutting it carefully.

'Stupid things, sheep,' she remarked. 'Never know when they're well off.'

'Do any of us? Except with hindsight?'

Another smile delighted Millie.

'Leo certainly didn't. Phoebe's husband, that is. Can I tell you about it?'

'If you're sure you really want to.' The answer came after a pause. Millie smiled at the reluctance.

'I think I do. Phoebe doesn't know anyone in the village, and nor of course do I. It would be nice to have someone to talk to, get it off my chest a bit.' She glanced at Daphne, who looked surprised, but gratified.

'I don't know that I can help much, but I don't mind listening.'

'That's what I need. And Phoebe too, in time. I'll stay as long as she needs me, of course, but . . . she's very independent, we haven't shared a house for so long that I'm not sure whether having me there won't do more harm than good, after a while. I'd like to think there was someone around she could talk to. The only other person she knows at all is Jennifer – can't remember her other name. She organises things like coffee mornings.'

'Dobson. Organises the whole village. She'd organise Phoebe too, given half the chance.'

'Exactly.'

Millie proceeded to tell Daphne, as far as she could, just what had happened. Daphne showed neither surprise nor shock, merely nodding in token of understanding, and Millie found this very soothing. At the edge of the village they separated, Daphne saying sensibly that if they were seen together she herself might well end up being interrogated by one of the village busybodies, but after that they met frequently for walks. Daphne seemed to enjoy Millie's company, and as she got to know her better, Millie discovered an ironic vein of humour that gave an added bite to their conversations. From time to time she visited Daphne's home, which had once been the gamekeeper's cottage of her family's house. Very rarely, as on Phoebe's first morning of freedom from the bank, Daphne visited Ember Cottage.

Phoebe, hearing the sound of Daphne's voice as she came down the stairs, hesitated. Not that she did not like Daphne – rather the reverse, if anything, for she had all her mother's appreciation for eccentricity, and she was grateful for the discretion Daphne showed. Grateful, too, for her companionship of Millie. As Millie herself had foreseen (though Phoebe had not), Phoebe was too used to her independent and semi-solitary existence to want even her mother around the house all the time. Now, she heard Millie's clear voice rising above Daphne's gruff tones.

'. . . Don't know whether I should accept it. Lovely people, and of course I've always wanted to go to India . . .'

Daphne's voice growled an indistinguishable reply.

'Yes, they even offered to pay for my ticket, though I'm not very happy about that. I know Phoebe would do it for me out of her money, but should I go? I don't want her to feel I'm abandoning her.'

How do I feel about it? Phoebe wondered. Do I want to be on my own? After a few moments she decided that she didn't really care much either way. That being the case, it seemed a pity for Millie not to achieve her ambition. She went into the kitchen. Millie, sitting at the kitchen table, looked at her with an absurdly guilty expression.

'Oh, darling, there you are! I thought you were still asleep! Daphne's here!'

'Yes, so she is. Good morning, Daphne.' Daphne nodded. She was leaning against the sink – Millie had noticed that she felt uncomfortable sitting down in other people's houses. Her boots and the old army greatcoat that was her winter protection were in the lobby by the back door, so the full glory of an ancient mud-brown pullover and her baggy tweed trousers was revealed. The pullover had been washed into a felted mass which had prevented the knitting from unravelling round the holes, and the trouser pockets bulged with the pieces of baler twine that Daphne made it her business to retrieve from fields and hedgerows. She looked, as always, like a country version of a bag lady, in wonderful contrast to the cut-crystal clarity of her speech.

Phoebe joined her mother at the table.

'Did I hear something about an invitation, Millie?'

Millie, who rose effortlessly above any awkward situation when staying with other people, was thrown into a fluster by Phoebe's calm question. She stood up quickly, and began fussing with the kettle.

'Oh, that's nothing. I was going to tell you about it later. Now, you must have some tea – or would you prefer coffee? The kettle's just boiled. And what about a piece of toast? You should eat something, you only picked at your supper last night.'

'I'm not hungry. A cup of tea would be nice, though. Now, Millie—'

'Your mother's been invited to go to India,' said Daphne, who believed in the direct approach. 'She doesn't know whether to go or not. I think she ought to go.'

'Of course you must go. What's the use of my ill-gotten gains if I can't spring you a trip to India? Who's it with?'

'The Abercrombies. That couple from Argentina. But I really don't think—'

'Of course you don't. But I do,' said Phoebe with a firmness that surprised even herself. 'Come on, Ma, you know you'd love it.'

'Well, I would. But I hate to leave you.'

'I'll be fine.' Phoebe summoned up all the acting ability she had perfected when facing classes of recalcitrant children. 'Really, I will. All the business with the bank is sorted out, thanks to The Win. Leo, all of that, it's all over. I'm going to put it all behind me, get on with my life.' The phrases sounded trite in her ears, culled as they were from dimly remembered magazine advice pages, but Millie was looking reassured. 'Let's face it,' Phoebe continued with well simulated enthusiasm, 'I've got it made! I'm young – well, pretty young – and I've got both the indispensable attributes.' Millie smiled reluctantly, but Daphne looked puzzled.

'Sound teeth, and a good digestion?' she hazarded. 'Read it somewhere,' she added with embarrassment, as though it were an admission of dubious taste.

'No, that's a different one. I meant the one about no woman ever having too much money, or being too thin.'

'But you *are*,' Millie was distracted from her Indian daydream. 'Much too thin.'

'Well, never mind that now. I promise I'll feed myself up while you're in India. Now, when is it to be? You'll need all the inoculations, of course. We'd better check that out. And what about clothes? What time of year is it over there?'

'I don't know. Phoebe, are you *sure*?'

'Sure I'm sure. Never been surer. Come on, let's ring the Abercrombies, get all the gen. Half the fun of a holiday is planning it beforehand.' And so Phoebe, with smiles and cheerful words, beguiled her mother into believing that all was well.

Chapter 8

The little Christmas tree was crooked again. Crossly Kate grasped it by its trunk rather as though she was intending to strangle it (which was not far from the truth), and winced as its spiny prickles drove themselves viciously against her flesh. She jerked it straight, making the sea-smoothed stones in the pot grate against one another. Where, she wondered fruitlessly for about the hundredth time, had Len put the Christmas-tree stands? The tree stayed straight for the moment as she sucked her finger, tasting the bitter stickiness of gummy sap on her skin. Then it slid inexorably sideways in the opposite direction until it was canted almost at forty-five degrees. Kate suppressed a scream of fury and pulled it straight, cramming the stones more firmly round the chopped-off trunk.

'You can't buy that. It hasn't any roots.' Tashie's voice echoed disgustedly in her head. 'It's been executed. It'll die in no time. Besides, I thought you didn't like this prickly sort? The needles stick in the carpet. Look, there's a much nicer one, all planted in a pot. The colour's better, too, sort of blueish.'

'It's twice as expensive.' In spite of her good intentions, Kate heard herself snapping. 'That one is much prettier, I know,' she agreed in tones that were meant to be companionable, but which came out patronising. 'It's just . . .'

'I *know*. I *know*. Cheap and nasty, everything's got to be cheap and nasty. I don't know why you bother.'

'Nor do I. And it's cheap and cheerful, not nasty.' Kate wished she hadn't brought Tashie with her. In the past, buying the Christmas trees had been a happy outing, the three children competing to find the best and bushiest, a big tree for the hall and a little one for the sitting room. Even last year, the two teenagers had swiftly come down to Sam's level and insisted on checking every tree at the nursery before making the final choice. Kate, asking if Tashie would like to accompany her while the boys were out doing Christmas shopping, had hoped to recapture some of the past magic. Tashie, however, had made a favour of it, trailing reluctantly down the rows of trees and shivering, hunched in the old duffel coat of Len's that she had taken to wearing. Kate could have slapped her, but she made the choices as quickly as possible and headed back to the house.

She was trying, as far as she could, to keep everything the same as it had always been. Not, of course, that anything was the same without Len. He was at his best at Christmas: funny, inventive, producing presents that ranged from the hilarious to the opulent, filling the house with an atmosphere of fun and excitement. They had always had two trees – the big one for the children, with decorations of all colours, bought and home-made, crammed on to it. By well established tradition the three children decked it themselves, bickering happily over what should go where, and greeting old favourites with cries of joy.

This year, though Nick had done his best, it had been a subdued occasion. Only Sam had seemed to derive any pleasure from it: Tashie joined in reluctantly and rushed away in tears on discovering a tattered silver-foil star that she had made with Len about eight years earlier. Nick and Sam worked on in silence, until Kate implored them to play some music.

'Carols?' asked Nick dubiously. When they were younger, Kate had always played recordings of King's College Choir to put them in the mood.

'Heavy metal, if you like. Anything.' Brightening, they had fetched a tape, and soon the hall was filled with something that sounded, to Kate, like road works set to music.

The little tree in the sitting room was, also by tradition, the adults' tree. Over the years Kate had collected an assortment of clear glass baubles: iridescent balls as fine as bubbles; chains of little stars and faceted beads; glass bells that chimed softly when the tree was touched; stars and angels and birds that caught the light of the strings of tiny white bulbs. Kate decorated it herself.

'Which is why', she said now to the little tree, 'I am standing here at two o'clock in the morning, instead of in bed where I should be. So if *you*', she gave the stones another grating shove to embed them, 'would just stay still, I can get on with this jolly Xmas task and get it over with.'

The tree, miraculously, held steady. The string of lights failed, as always, to light up when she plugged it in, but after tightening all the bulbs one by one she was rewarded with their sudden acquiescence. As quickly as possible, and cursing the almost invisible loops of fine fishing line that she used to hang them, she arranged the decorations on the branches. A few needles were falling already in the warmth of the room, and she tried not to remember the previous year's tree with its softer leaves that never dropped. This one looked somehow dusty by comparison, and it seemed already to have lost any scent it might once have had.

Still, when it was done it looked pretty. Kate stepped back to admire it, deciding that she had made a good choice. The branches were well spaced and even, and the little lights shone as bravely as they had ever done. Kate wondered why it was that the little economies, sometimes, were harder to bear than the big ones. She could cope easily with no holidays, with buying cheap clothes or no clothes at all and managing with what she had, but she bitterly regretted having to buy supermarket sliced bread instead of the local baker's loaves. Still, this little saving was a success, she told herself, blinking hard to dispel the blurring of tears that she refused to acknowledge. The sofa next to her looked soft and welcoming but she resisted its temptations, knowing that if she sat down she would fall asleep and wake, later, stiff and cold.

'Time for bed,' she told herself firmly. The trouble was, however easy it was to fall asleep on the sofa, or a chair, or even at the kitchen table, the minute she got into bed she felt all inclination to sleep desert her. Partly because she was so physically exhausted that she ached in every limb, but mostly because she had reorganised the whole house and now slept on a divan behind a screen in her mother's room.

Faced with the knowledge that Len's income had disappeared with him, Kate had spent several days in anguished calculations. She had several thousand pounds in a deposit account, saved over the years from Len's gifts. She had what was left of the housekeeping and her own allowance. Of her mother's money, some had been used to help in the cost of the extension where she lived and the rest put by: Kate was only too uncomfortably aware that it might soon be needed for nursing-home fees. Other than that, her sole asset was the house.

Len had finished paying off the mortgage only the previous year, and Brian had assured her that the bank would make no attempt to claim any of its value from her.

'It doesn't look as though he used any of the – the other money – on this place. Only his salary, and his bonuses. Even so . . . shall you be able to manage? What about school fees?'

'Paid in advance. Len got several extra-good bonuses a few years ago, and put them into the school scheme as a lump sum. You save a little bit that way, and if they leave early you simply get the remainder back. I did wonder whether to do that – I'd be perfectly happy for them to go to the local state schools. But I just don't want them unsettled, if they're happy where they are. That's why I want to hang on to the house, too, if I can. We've lived there so long . . . and there's my mother. She has her bad days, but by and large she's hanging on quite well. I can't bear to think how it might affect her if we had to move.'

'You know, Kate, if I can help in any way . . .'

His plain, kind face was troubled. Kate stiffened the muscles in her face and throat, and patted his hand.

'I know. And I promise I'll ask you, if things get desperate. I just hope they won't. I have', she said portentously, to lighten the mood, 'a cunning plan.'

'A cunning plan, Baldrick?'

Kate blinked at him in astonishment. She had never taken Brian Harper for the kind of person who would watch *Blackadder*.

'A cunning plan, Mr B. I just hope the family won't rise up in revolt when they hear it.'

'Move out of my *room*?' Tashie was appalled by the suggestion. 'But I can't! All my things, and my posters . . . You said you'd try to keep everything the same!'

'At least you still get to have a room of your own,' Sam pointed out gloomily. 'Not that I mind sharing with Nick, exactly, but we don't really like the same things, do we?'

'I know, darlings. I know it's not what you like, but if we want to stay here at all, we've got to have some kind of income.'

'Can't you get a job?' Tashie's anger was, Kate knew, largely a front for her distress, but the knowledge didn't make it any easier to bear. 'There must be something you can do. Be a secretary, or something. Work in a shop.'

'For heaven's sake, Tashie!' Nick, goaded beyond endurance, rounded on his sister. 'Can't you *ever* think of anyone but yourself?'

'I *am*! I'm thinking of Mum too! Do you really think she wants to move out of her nice room, and share with Gran? If she got a job, she wouldn't have to.'

'If I got a job – which in the current market, at my age, and with negligible experience or secretarial skills, is pretty unlikely – then someone would have to be here to be with Gran,' Kate pointed out wearily.

'Don't you worry about me, dear!' It had been impossible to exclude Joyce from the family conclave, and now she looked brightly at Kate. 'I'm fine! No need for anyone to be with me. Harold will be back soon, he'll keep me company.' Kate's eyes challenged her children to dare say anything.

'But *lodgers*!' Kate could almost have smiled at Tashie's disgusted tone: she might just as well have said 'cockroaches'. 'It's so – so sordid! Nobody has lodgers!'

'Nonsense, all the best people are doing it. Paying guests, not lodgers. Bed and breakfast – half the stately homes are opening for people to stay in.'

'But we're not a stately home.'

'No more we are, thank heaven. I don't want to be having Tudor banquets. No, my idea is to do bed and breakfast in my room, and use the space from the big cupboard next door for an en suite bathroom. It won't be large enough, of course, we'll have to pinch a bit of the spare bedroom as well, but not too much, I hope. Then we can turn the boys' old attic rooms into bedsits for a couple of students.'

'Students? What sort of students?' Tashie was still suspicious, but patently she was beginning to imagine a house full of interesting hunks. Kate, who was hoping for a couple of quiet girls, did not disabuse her.

'I don't exactly know yet, but there are so many colleges, not to mention the university, that it shouldn't be difficult. So, the boys get your room, because it's the biggest, and you can have the old spare room.'

'What's left of it,' muttered Tashie. Kate ignored her.

'New curtains, if you like – so long as they're something not too expensive. And I can go in with Gran, if she doesn't mind. There's that old screen in the attic – I thought we might paint it up, and I can screen off the bed so she has a bit more privacy.'

'Whatever you say, dear.' Kate blessed her mother's equable nature. 'I'm not sure about Harold, though.'

'Well, if he complains we'll think again,' soothed Kate. 'I know it's not great, but with luck it will mean we can stay here.' This remark silenced even Tashie.

So far, things had worked out reasonably well. The bedsits, to Tashie's disgust, had quickly been let to a pair of earnest German girls, friends who were supposed to be studying English but who seemed to Kate to spend most of their time with a group of fellow German students. To Kate's delighted relief they were both quiet and tidy. There were no drunken parties, and the smells that drifted down from the top floor were of sauerkraut rather than cannabis. Tashie found them boring, and said so, but Renata and Greta treated her with quiet superiority as befitted their years. They went home for

Christmas, having meticulously paid their rent until January and leaving gifts of chocolate, neatly wrapped and nicely graded in size, for all the family. Joyce had the biggest.

The bed and breakfast had proved to be harder work than Kate had bargained for. It was not the guests themselves – they were generally undemanding and even the awkward ones had only to be endured for a night or two. Worse than them were the inspectors – it had seemed sensible to Kate to register with every agency and body that was concerned with the business. To her dismay she found that she was expected to provide a huge number of accessories that she herself had never thought might be necessary, while it seemed that every inch of paintwork, every scrap of grouting between bathroom tiles and every stitch in the soft furnishings had been examined with a magnifying glass.

'The way they carry on, you'd think I was offering to adopt the visitors for life,' she complained to Brian Harper. He called in from time to time, and Kate welcomed his visits. He was a link with the outside world, and a link with her past and with Len. Surprisingly, Kate found this comforting. She seldom missed Len in terms of his company or his support – she had had little of either for some years. What she missed was the sound of a man's voice, the input of a male point of view, and the kind of conversation that she could not have with anyone else in the house.

Brian, she thought, felt a kind of responsibility towards her and her family. An old-fashioned man, he still retained an almost Victorian attitude to the paternalistic nature of employment. He would, she thought, feel more at home in some Japanese company which expected to oversee its workers' homes, marriages and social lives than where he found himself, in the cut and thrust of city banking in the nineties. He took an interest in all the children (being, in fact, Nick's godfather) which, to Kate's surprise, they accepted without resentment.

'I know just what you mean,' he answered her comfortably. 'We thought of adopting, at one stage. Filled in the forms, jumped through the hoops, had the inspections. The questions they ask! Bloody impertinent, some of them. I mean, I know they have to be careful, but really . . . And the house must be clean, but not *too* clean – and where does that leave you?'

'Oh, Brian, I didn't know. I hope it wasn't tactless of me?'

'Not at all.' Brian leaned back in the kitchen chair, causing it to creak in an alarming fashion. He was putting on weight, Kate thought, noticing the gently rounding stomach beneath his hand-knitted pullover. 'It's many years ago now. Of course even then we were considered rather borderline, age-wise. Naturally, we wanted a baby; but so many people do, and there are so few babies to go round.'

'And nothing came of it?'

'Well . . .' He reached out absently for the biscuit tin, and Kate pushed it nearer. 'As a matter of fact, we were offered a baby. A little boy, with hearing problems.' He paused, and Kate willed him silently to continue. She had never known Brian's wife very well. She had died two years earlier, and for several years before that had been an invalid. Kate remembered Len saying something about a child that had died, and Brian's wife never getting over the loss.

'It was extraordinary, really.' Brian took another biscuit. 'I got home from work one evening, and Lesley said she'd had a call that morning from the adoption agency about this baby, and that she could have had him more or less there and then. "He could be here now!" she kept saying; "I could be a mother right now!" '

'And you took him?' Kate knew that the child they had lost had had some kind of problem, but she hadn't thought it was as simple as deafness. Brian looked surprised.

'No, we couldn't. You see, Lesley had learned only the day before that she was pregnant, finally, just when we'd given up hope. A month earlier, and – who knows? Anyway, she had to tell the adoptions people, and of course the baby went to someone else. I've often wondered . . .'

'How it would have been? Terribly difficult, surely. Two children so close in age, and the – the problems.'

'Yes. Impossible really. I believe the baby was profoundly deaf, so he would have needed a tremendous amount of extra help and attention, and of course with Tom – you know he had CP? Cerebral palsy?'

'I knew there was something wrong, but I never knew that. How tragic for you both.'

'Yes, and no. Tragic for him in a way, except that he was such a happy little chap! It sounds extraordinary to say it, but he really enjoyed life, and I've always been thankful that he died before he had time to lose that enjoyment. And Lesley was already ill, by that time. Diagnosed, I mean. It had started some time before, only of course nobody realised. There was never much hope, though they did everything they could. I think it was a relief to her, really, when Tom died. She was so worried about what would happen to him in the future.'

Why did I never hear all this? Kate wondered. Len must have

known about it. But then Len, though he would always appear interested and always say the right thing, never really cared about other people's problems. Or even his own, come to that.

'Len never told me any of this. I wish I'd known.'

'Well, you know now. And you didn't really know us then, did you? But I remember the letter you wrote when Lesley died. I've still got it, as a matter of fact. It was so simple and straightforward.'

Simple and straightforward, Kate thought as she bent to switch off the Christmas tree lights. I don't recognise that in myself, but perhaps in those days I was. My life was, anyway. But now? Should Brian come and see me as often as he does? He's lonely, of course, and so am I. But is that enough? I certainly don't want things to progress any further than this, at the moment. Perhaps I should put him off. But maybe that would make things worse – putting ideas into his head, as it were. Oh, dear.

The hall clock struck three. Exhausted and confused, Kate began to climb the stairs. Fortunately she remembered that her bedroom was no longer up there before she burst in on the current guests – a couple from Norfolk who had come to make the acquaintance of their future daughter-in-law's family. Grimly, she turned and came down again. Creeping into the annexe room she shared with Joyce, she was relieved to hear the regular sound of light snores coming from her mother's bed. She was too tired for the noise to keep her awake, and at least Joyce was safely asleep.

Christmas passed, and was less of an ordeal than Kate had feared. Tashie, predictably, was emotional, but fortunately for once in her life this rendered her quiet and introspective, rather than aggressive. All three children were pleased with their presents and with the stockings that Kate still did for them. With little money at her disposal she and Joyce had spent several afternoons going round the numerous charity shops. In the past, Kate had always looked for gifts in the beautiful but expensive shops in and near the Lanes; now she abandoned them for the colourful, if sleazy delights of the maze of little streets below and beyond the station. Their purchases, judiciously cleaned and imaginatively wrapped, proved to be a tremendous success. Nick and Tashie, who had both found holiday jobs, had joined forces with Sam to buy Kate a bottle of her favourite Penhaligon scent, a luxury she had tried to persuade herself she could now manage without.

On New Year's Eve, Kate was only too thankful to make her mother the excuse to refuse all invitations. New Year had never seemed madly significant to Kate, who loved Christmas and, having made the most of all of its traditions, was usually too tired of eating, drinking and generally celebrating to enjoy anything else. Len, of course, had always been in his element. He liked Christmas, naturally – particularly the present-giving and the meals – but he found the religious aspect of it embarrassing and unnecessary. Kate, brought up in a church-going tradition, loved all the services from Stir-Up Sunday onwards. One of the benefits of Len's departure, for Kate, was that she was free to attend midnight mass without his complaining that she was breaking up the evening.

Kate fully intended to celebrate this New Year by going to bed early, preferably with the new book that Joyce had given her and which she had not, as yet, had time to start. Nick was at a party and staying the night; Tashie was also at a party, but was being brought home by the strict parents of her current best friend at half past one. The bed and breakfast guests were at a dinner dance, and only Sam was there with her and Joyce. Uninterested in parties, Sam was happy to watch the videos Kate had taken out, and eat his favourite supper of deep pan pizza washed down with copious quantities of cola.

Kate was in bed by eleven, and even the new book could not keep her eyes open for longer than ten minutes. She had left the door just slightly ajar, and even in her sleep registered the return of Tashie and, not much later, of the guests. She thought vaguely that she could shut the door now, but the bed was warm and it didn't seem worth the effort.

Some time later she woke, abruptly, with the impression that some sudden sound had roused her. Lifting her head from the pillow, she listened intently, but heard nothing. Telling herself firmly that she had imagined it she lay back again, but her eyes were wide open and her ears, in spite of herself, still listening intently. In the end, knowing that she would not sleep until she had checked, she crawled reluctantly out of bed and put on dressing gown and slippers. The house was warm – thanks to the guests who, rather like tiny babies, needed to be kept warm at all times, but also because of the guests she was unable to wander around in her nightie.

A swift check of the downstairs rooms showed nothing amiss. No forced locks, no broken windows, nothing moved or fallen down. Upstairs, she listened for a moment outside her old bedroom, then moved on to the room that Sam and Nick now shared.

As she reached the door, she heard a low groan. It sounded as though Sam was about to be, or had just been, sick. Kate burst in, switching on the light. Sam was on his hands and knees on the floor.

'Sam!' Kate went to him. 'Sam, what is it? Come on, love, let's get you to the loo.'

Sam did not move. Kate put her arms round him and tried to lift him to his feet, but his sturdy body was too heavy. She bent to look at his face. His eyes were half closed, the pupils visible but turned away from her, and he breathed in a heavy, almost snoring way. There was a trickle of bloodstained spittle at the corner of his mouth.

'Sam! Oh God. Tashie! Tashie, wake up! Tashie!' When Tashie did not appear, Kate called with increased urgency, but to no avail. She was reluctant to leave Sam, although his breathing had now quietened. Never had Kate felt so alone. If only, she thought, if only Nick were here! It would have to happen the one night he's away! She peered into Sam's face again. There was no smell of alcohol about him – had he . . . taken something? Her mind shied away from a more specific thought. Not Sam, surely? He hadn't even been out that evening, and he was still a child, wasn't he? Once again Kate shouted for Tashie. She, at least, might have some idea of what Sam might have been up to. Or should she call for an ambulance?

'Mum?' Sam had turned his head, and was looking at her blearily. 'What's going on, Mum?' At the same moment the door behind her opened more widely and revealed the male half of the bed and breakfast guests, incongruously clad in a dinner jacket over striped pyjamas, his feet bare.

'Is something the matter?'

'I'm so sorry to have disturbed you.' Kate and the guest, whose name completely escaped her, spoke at the same time. 'I'm so sorry,' Kate continued. 'Sam isn't very well, and I was trying to call my daughter. How can she sleep through all this, I can't imagine!' She suppressed the horrid thought that Tashie was unconscious rather than asleep. Sam was struggling to his feet, and both Kate and the man moved to help him.

'I'm all right,' he muttered. He sounded embarrassed, but his speech was clearer.

'It's very good of you to come and help, Mr Pritchard' – Kate's head was clearing, and his name suddenly came back to her – 'but I think he's all right now. I'll sit with him for a bit. Thank you, and I'm so sorry to have woken you. I hope your wife wasn't alarmed?'

'She sleeps with earplugs – says I snore,' he said with a smile. 'I'll be off, then, if you're sure there's nothing I can do.'

Tactfully he closed the door behind him. Sam was already back in bed, his eyes closed. Kate put her hand on his forehead, which was cool, and his eyes opened heavily.

'Tired,' he said.

'I know, darling, but I must ask you. Have you – have you been drinking? Or taking anything? Pills, or . . . you know.'

'Substances?' He grinned. 'Really, Mum! Course not!'

Kate studied his face. Like all parents, she knew the risks. Knew that drugs of all kinds were available everywhere, in and out of school, and particularly in Brighton which had an exceptionally bad record in this respect. She thought she was aware of the danger signs, and she knew her children. Of all of them, Tashie was probably the most at risk, and Sam as yet the least. She was fairly sure he was telling her the truth. His eyes had closed again, and he slept as tranquilly as a baby. Kate went to the basin and dampened a facecloth to wipe away the bloody dribble by his mouth. He never stirred as she did it. Kate switched on Nick's bedside light and turned off the main switch.

After ten minutes, during which time Sam continued to sleep normally, Kate crept from the room and into Tashie's. She turned the desk lamp away from the bed before turning it on, but even so Tashie woke up at once.

'Who's' that? What time is it? Ugh, it's half past three! For God's sake, put the light out!' Her voice sounded unnaturally loud, and when Kate looked at her she saw that she was wearing the little earphones attached to her Walkman.

'No wonder you didn't hear me,' said Kate crossly.

'What?'

'For heaven's sake, take the bloody headset off!' hissed Kate, miming the action. 'You'll wake the whole house!'

'No, you're the one who's doing that,' Tashie pointed out with heavy patience. 'What's the matter? Oh no, don't tell me – Gran's disappeared! Honestly, Mum, if you can't even take care of her when you're living in the same room—'

'It's nothing to do with Gran. It's Sam.'

'Sam's disappeared? Good.'

'No! If you'd just listen. He was making funny noises.'

'He does it all the time. He calls it talking.'

'Please, Tashie, I'm really worried!' Tashie gave an exaggerated sigh, but she opened her eyes again. 'He was making a sort of groaning noise, and he was on the floor. He was . . . strange. As if he was still asleep, only his eyes weren't closed.'

'Perhaps he was sleepwalking.'

'I suppose so.' Kate, pleased that Tashie seemed to be taking it more seriously, was reluctant to dismiss her suggestion. 'Only, I just wondered . . . He says he hasn't, and I do believe him really, but I must just ask you because you'd know more about it – being older, I mean—' She floundered to a halt.

'Whatever are you on about?' Tashie, who had already experimented with smoking pot and had several times been offered Ecstasy tablets, searched her conscience as she played for time. Had she left anything around that Sam might have got hold of? There were several people at school who, if not precisely pushers, were known to be able to supply drugs. Had she ever seen Sam talking to any of them? She was sure she hadn't. 'Oh, you mean drugs. No. Not Sam.'

'Thank goodness. Oh dear.' Kate sat down abruptly on the edge of the bed. Tashie patted her awkwardly.

'Don't worry, Mum. He'll be all right. It was probably just a bad dream or something – not surprising, after all the food he's been stuffing down. Did you see how many mince pies he ate yesterday?'

Kate sniffed, and gave a watery smile.

'I suppose I'm over-reacting. It's because it's the middle of the night. Thanks, Tashie.'

'Do you want me to go and check him? I could set my alarm.'

Kate was touched.

'No, darling, it's sweet of you, but I think I'll just stay with him. I can sleep in Nick's bed.'

'Well, if you're sure. Aaaagh!' Tashie yawned, and huddled down into her bed. Kate kissed the top of her head, which was all that showed, and went back to the other room. Sam hadn't stirred. Wearily, Kate climbed into Nick's bed. She had thought she would spend the rest of the night lying sleepless, listening to Sam's even breathing, but as the bed warmed she relaxed and fell headlong into sleep.

Chapter 9

When Kate woke she wondered for a moment where she was, then she struggled upright in Nick's badly made bed and looked across at Sam. He lay, as he had so often done as a baby, flat on his back and with his arms flung wide. For a horrible moment Kate thought he wasn't breathing, then she saw the slow rise and fall of his duvet. Outside it was still dark, but the cries of the seagulls – so much a part of their daily existence that she seldom heard them but missed them when she went away – told her that for them at least it was morning. She glanced at Nick's alarm clock. Half past six. She felt exhausted but wide awake. A cup of tea, she thought longingly. Wouldn't it be lovely if someone were to bring me a cup of tea. Banishing the wistful thought she climbed quietly out of bed and went down to the kitchen.

Sitting at the table, her hands wrapped round a steaming mug, she thought she had never missed Len so much. Even at Christmas, when his absence had been as tender as the hole in a gum when a tooth has just been pulled, she had been able to push the pain to the back of her mind. Now, at this moment of crisis, she felt utterly alone. No matter that Len, faced with illness in one of his children, had always shied away like a startled horse. Like many healthy men, he regarded illness as something faintly shameful. He was alarmed and affronted if he himself went down with 'flu; if Kate got it, he was alarmed (in case he caught it) and irritated. Where the children were concerned, he alternated between a brusque 'pull yourself together' attitude, and a morbid fear of serious consequences.

With her rational mind, Kate knew that if Len had been faced with the events of the previous night he would either have shrugged them off as the effect of a bad dream, or have been thrown into an alarm that would have worried Sam more than anything else. Even so, Kate wished she had someone close to her she could discuss it with. Impossible to expect her mother, her own mental equilibrium so uncertain, to provide emotional support. Even Nick, so adult and helpful, should not be expected to shoulder this sort of worry, with his A levels coming up.

For a brief half hour, Kate allowed herself the luxury of letting her misery take over. Safe in the knowledge that no one was likely to be awake for hours – even Joyce had stayed up later than usual the previous night – she loosened the straitjacket she had been exerting on her feelings. Lacking even the privacy of her own room, Kate had been forced to suppress her unhappiness and anxiety. Now she cried, letting the emotions take control of her body and sobbing aloud.

She pushed her fingers into her hair, grasping it tightly so that her scalp was pulled up from the skull beneath. The pain felt, if not good, at least appropriate. She pulled harder, aware with a part of her mind that she had never before realised that the phrase 'tearing my hair out' was so literally true. Only the thought of how alarmed everyone would be if she actually appeared with a bald head made her slacken her grip. When, at last, she had no more tears to shed, her mouth was dry and her face hot and puffy, but she felt, surprisingly, much better. Her scalp was tender, but there were no clumps of hair, no bald patches. Rather ashamed of herself, she made a fresh pot of tea, then went to wash and dress.

When the Pritchards came down for their breakfast, Sam and Tashie were still asleep. Kate had checked Sam several times, and he looked perfectly normal. Joyce had breakfasted, and was engaged in doing some ironing in front of the television. She did it exquisitely, in painstaking detail, and Kate was always grateful for her help as long as she didn't have to watch the agonising slowness.

'My dear.' Mrs Pritchard bustled into the dining room, where the table was already laid for the guests. She was a large, firm-fleshed woman whose clothes looked as though they had been upholstered onto her by a well trained soft furnisher. 'My dear, how is your boy? Eric told me about it, you must have been worried.'

'I was, rather,' Kate admitted, 'though he seems perfectly all right. He's not awake yet, but I wouldn't have expected him to be, considering how late he stayed up. You know what these kids are like – they hardly ever wake up until lunchtime. I'm just sorry Mr Pritchard was disturbed – it was so kind of him to come and help.'

'Oh, that's nothing.' Mrs Pritchard dismissed her husband's lack of sleep with an airy wave. 'I told him he should have woken me, but he said you wouldn't have wanted too many people fussing around. So, what do you think was the problem? Has he ever walked in his sleep, perhaps?'

Her interest was real, and it was impossible to resent her curiosity.

'No, never. I've never seen anything like it before, not with any of them. When they were little and had high temperatures they sometimes hallucinated a bit, but he didn't have any temperature. It seems unlikely, but I wondered whether it was some kind of – of fit. Only he's never had one before, so perhaps I'm just over-reacting. It was probably just a very vivid dream, or something. It's just . . . he'd bitten his lip, or his tongue, there was a bit of blood . . . I'm really not sure what to do.'

'Take him to the doctor,' said Mrs Pritchard firmly. 'How old is he? Twelve? A friend of mine's son developed epilepsy at just that age. It's quite common, when they're coming up to adolescence, and particularly in boys, for some reason.'

'Epilepsy.' Kate was alarmed. Like many people, she had a picture of epileptics that involved a vague but frightening image of a shambling figure falling to the ground, twitching and frothing.

'It's only a possibility,' said Mrs Pritchard sensibly. 'Ten to one it's nothing of the kind, but if it is, it's very treatable nowadays. My friend's son takes pills that keep it under control, and he's just passed his driving test. Oh, there you are, Eric. I was just telling Mrs Miller about Richard. Jenny and Matthew's boy, you remember. Now they took him to a very good neurologist in London. I could get his name for you, if you'd like.'

'Jumping the gun, aren't you?' Eric Pritchard smiled ruefully at Kate. 'My wife should be with the UN – she'd soon have the whole world's problems sorted out.'

'Well, I couldn't do worse than the rest of them,' responded his wife cheerfully.

'Oh no, you've been very kind. I'll take him to the doctor tomorrow, and if I need to take it further, perhaps I could ring you?'

'Any time, my dear. Now, Eric, I suppose you want to have a full cooked breakfast? I don't let him eat like that at home, but this is a holiday! And I'll just have the continental, and coffee for both of us. Hot milk, if it's not too much trouble.' Kate found herself meekly returning to the kitchen, where the food for breakfast was already laid out since she had asked the Pritchards on the previous evening what they would like. She felt slightly buffeted, as though she had been out in a high wind, but there was something very comforting about the benevolent energy that had been unleashed upon her.

When Sam came downstairs, he complained of a headache but remembered nothing of the night before. He seemed to take it calmly, and refuted with disgust any suggestion that he had taken anything illicit. When Kate asked him if anything else had happened that he could recall, he looked unhappy and evasive.

'Not really,' he said. 'Nothing much, anyway. Can I have a cooked breakfast too, or is it only for guests?'

'Of course you can. What do you mean, nothing much?'

'Oh, it was ages ago. I had a funny sort of thing when I was with Daddy, my head kept turning one way and my eyes – he thought I was putting it on, but I wasn't. I felt a bit funny once or twice, at school. I told Daddy about it, but he said it was probably nothing, and I shouldn't worry about it. He sounded a bit cross, really, so I just left it.'

Kate felt such a spasm of rage pass through her that if Len had been there, she really thought she could have killed him. It was true that he had never been much help when the children were ill, but to dismiss something like that . . . It seemed a betrayal of his fatherhood, even more so than his infidelities and his bigamous marriage. That Sam, of all her children the least inclined to make a fuss about his health, should mention any kind of problem to either of his parents should have been enough to alert Len that there was something wrong, something more than an attempt to get out of a test or to play the fool.

'How long ago was that?' she asked, when she had got her voice under control again.

'I don't know. The beginning of the summer holidays, something like that?'

July, then. Half a year ago, and whatever was causing this was still going on, had perhaps got worse.

'Anything else?' She dreaded hearing the answer.

'Not really. Nick was moaning on about me snoring, only I didn't take any notice of that. I don't snore. I know I don't.'

'That's what everybody says. Your father was convinced he didn't snore, either.'

'There you are, then. Perhaps it's hereditary. Perhaps what I had last night was just an extra bad snore.'

There seemed no point in alarming him.

'Yes, I expect it was. How many rashers, and one egg or two?'

'Six, and two, please. And can I have fried bread? And are there any mushrooms?'

Whatever might be wrong with him certainly hadn't impaired his appetite, Kate thought as she set about the cooking.

When the telephone rang later that morning, Kate was surprised by the pleasure she felt on hearing Brian's voice. It had crossed her mind that he might invite her to go for a meal on New Year's Eve, and she had made up her mind to turn him down. It was, she felt, too significant a date for her to feel comfortable going out with him. When he failed to ask her she told herself that she was relieved, and refused to acknowledge that she was actually rather disappointed.

'Brian! Happy New Year!'

'And to you too. All of you. I didn't want to ring too early, in case you were all nursing hangovers.'

'Amazingly, none of us are – is? Unless it's Nick, and he stayed the night so I don't have to put up with it. What about you?'

'I'm not a great one for New Year. I'm afraid I celebrated it by staying in with a good meal, and a book. Does that shock you?'

'Not at all. In fact, that's how I celebrated too. We should have done it together.' Too late, she remembered her earlier reservations.

'But then we wouldn't have stayed in, would we? We'd have felt honour bound to go out somewhere, and then we'd have been trapped into waiting until midnight, because that's what it's all about.'

'Yes,' agreed Kate, reservations forgotten, 'and even then, you can't just leave at five past twelve, can you? It still looks as if you're a spoilsport if you don't stay until at least half past.'

Brian laughed.

'Fogeys of the world, unite! Anyway, I would have invited you to spend the evening with me, only I thought that New Year seemed a bit . . . particular. If you know what I mean.'

'I know exactly what you mean. And I would have said no, for the same reason.'

'That's all right, then,' he said comfortably. 'I know that when Lesley first died, the people I felt uncomfortable with were the ones who were always inviting me round for meals, because they were "sorry for me", and the people I was relaxed with hardly ever did. I suppose that's why I was relaxed with them. That sounds very ungrateful, but . . .'

Kate nodded.

'Yes,' she said in heartfelt tones. 'I feel just the same. It's the friends who treat me the same as always, instead of as a Poor Thing, or some kind of emotional cripple, or a husband stealer. Whoops, sorry. I must be more tired than I thought. I'm not usually that bitchy.' She told him about Sam.

'Don't wait,' said Brian firmly. 'I know I shouldn't interfere, but health is the only thing worth worrying about.'

'I know,' said Kate, recognising that he knew what he was talking about. 'But the National Health . . .'

'The National Health is great. Most of Lesley's treatment and all of Tom's were done on it. But with something like this, very specialised but not particularly life-threatening, you could be waiting months. I know the tests can be expensive, but if you won't bite my head off, I'd like to offer to help with that.'

'Oh, Brian.' Kate sighed. 'How could I bite your head off? It's so very kind of you, but how can I accept?'

'You can accept because it's for Sam, not you. It's amazing what you can bring yourself to do, for your children's sake. I would have paid anything, taken anything, if there had been anything that could have helped Lesley or Tom, but there wasn't. Look, I'm fond of your kids. If it were Nick you'd let me, because he's my godson, wouldn't you? Nick will be affected by this too, remember, with his A levels coming up and everything. You could say it's for him, really.'

His tone was calm, friendly, undemanding. Kate saw, however, that this was something he needed for himself, and that by helping Sam he was, in fact, making a gift to his dead wife and son. She relaxed.

'If you're sure?'

'Of course I am. That's settled then.'

'And will you come to supper? This evening?'

'As long as you're not just asking me out of misplaced gratitude.'

'Of course I'm not. I'm going to see what else I can wheedle out of you, while you're in an expansive mood.'

Nick came home in the afternoon. The rest of the family was watching an adventure film on television in varying stages of somnolence.

'Hey, Nick!' Sam bounced out of his chair. 'Guess what? I woke everyone up in the night with my snoring. It was really loud, Mum heard it from downstairs, and the guests, and everyone!' He sounded, if anything, rather proud of himself. 'And I was out of bed, and I bit my mouth – look!' He pulled down his bottom lip, cheerfully displaying the pink inside marked with a small red cut. 'And there was blood!' he finished proudly. Nick raised an eyebrow at Kate.

'I'll tell you about it later,' she said hastily. 'It's probably nothing.'

The day passed quietly. The Pritchards left in the morning, and no more visitors were expected for several days. Kate, though she needed the money, particularly after Christmas, was relieved not to have to change the beds and furbish the room and the bathroom. There was still a lot of cheese and other leftovers in the fridge, so Kate made some soup, opened a bottle of wine, and felt more cheerful.

Brian seemed happy with such homely fare, and since there was a good film on television they opted to have the soup in the kitchen, then fill their plates and move back to the sitting room. Going back to the kitchen for more bread, Kate almost ran into Sam. He was standing just inside the doorway, a plate piled with food tilting dangerously in one hand. His eyes were flickering sideways, and his head turning slightly in the same direction. Fuddled by the wine and the lack of sleep, Kate's first thought was for the food that was about to slide to the floor.

'Sam!' She grabbed at the plate, pushing the food back from the rim. 'Sam, what on earth are you doing?'

For a moment he didn't answer, his eyes still flickering and his head twitching to his right. Then, painfully, he turned it back to her, and his eyes stilled.

'Sam! What is it?'

He looked at her, puzzled. 'I don't feel well,' he said. 'I've got an awful headache.'

Something cold clutched at the pit of Kate's stomach.

'Poor old love,' she commiserated. 'Don't worry, we'll get you off to the doctor tomorrow, have you checked over.'

'It was my eyes, wasn't it? And my head. I couldn't stop it.'

At least, thought Kate, he was aware that something was happening. Does that mean it wasn't a fit? Oh, please.

'Yes, but don't worry about it. Is this what happened that time with Daddy? And when you said you felt funny at school?'

'Yes. Only I was in a lesson, so I just put my hands up and held my head still. Nobody noticed.'

Kate's heart wrenched. She wanted to put her arms round him, contain and protect him with her body. But he was no longer a baby, so she just smiled and said, 'If you can do that, I should think that must be a good sign. Was it just the once?'

'I think so.' He looked anxious, and Kate thought it better not to press him.

'Well, don't worry about it. It doesn't sound like anything too desperate. Now, how do you feel? Do you still want this?' She glanced at the plate she was holding, which had a mound of strong pickle, a chunk of cheese, a large number of cold roast potatoes, and a mountain of salad. Almost half a loaf of French bread was balanced precariously on one side.

'Of course I do! I'm starving!'

Kate relaxed and smiled.

'There can't be too much wrong with you, then. Do you want anything for your head?'

'No, I don't think so. I'll take something later, if it doesn't go off.'

Back in the sitting room, Kate found she had completely lost track of the plot of the film. She gave up trying to watch it, and spent the evening keeping an unobtrusive eye on Sam, who seemed completely normal. She thought no one had noticed, but as he was leaving Brian took the chance of speaking to her at the front door.

'Did Sam have another turn? I thought you looked a bit distraught.'

'Did I? Oh dear, I thought I was covering it rather well.'

'Yes, very well. I know the signs, that's all. Don't forget I spent a lot of my life covering up, as well. So he did?'

'Yes. Nothing much, but . . . I'll ring the doctor in the morning.'

'Yes, do that. And try not to worry. It may well turn out not to be as bad as you're imagining. And even if it is, you can deal with it.'

'Can I?'

He leaned to plant his usual chaste kiss on her cheek. Kate found herself having to fight the urge to clutch at him.

'Of course you can. And don't forget, I'm always there. You can ring me any time.'

Kate returned his kiss. He smiled of soap and clean washing. A homely, comforting smell.

'You smell nice.'

'So do you. Like a very good florist's.'

'The kids gave me a bottle of my favourite scent for Christmas. Extravagant, but I do love it.'

'There you are then.' It was a meaningless phrase, when she came to consider it afterwards, but at the time it made sense.

The doctor leaned back in his chair.

'Well, I should say it's quite likely that it was an epileptic episode.'

An episode, thought Kate numbly. Part one of our great new serial. She glanced at Sam, who was looking bored.

'What about the other time? It was only his eyes and his head.' She knew she was clutching at straws.

'The same. A minor episode. You'll need to see a specialist. There's a good man in Brighton. He'll organise some tests.'

'Will it take long?'

'It shouldn't be too bad. A month or two, maybe a bit more. Of course, if you've got medical insurance you can see him at once, but I should warn you that the scans and things are very expensive, so unless you've got cover . . .'

'Not for outpatients. But I'd rather get on with it.'

'Waste of money.' Sam spoke with decision. 'Honestly, Mum, it's not worth getting in a stew about. I'm fine.'

'Well . . .' Kate felt torn, not wanting to make Sam any more worried by seeming in a hurry, but anxious herself for some answers.

'It's something that needs to be investigated,' said the doctor, 'but as things stand, it's not desperately urgent. Having the tests sooner is for your mother's peace of mind, and yours, rather than a medical necessity.'

'We'll do it privately,' said Kate decisively. 'I have some money put by for crises. Not that this is a crisis, exactly,' she added hastily, 'but for anything unexpected that might crop up. A sort of "just in case" fund.' She hated to lie to Sam, but felt unable to endure the kind of speculation that would be engendered by his knowing that Brian was paying. She wished, now, that she hadn't used her bit of capital on the house alterations, but it was too late to regret that.

'Right. Well, meanwhile, there are a few rules for you.'

'What sort of rules?' Sam looked wary.

'Well, you shouldn't swim on your own. Don't go mountain climbing or scuba diving. Don't drive. Keep off the drink and, more particularly, steer clear of recreational drugs. OK?'

Kate could see that Sam was rather flattered by the assumption that he might be going mountaineering or scuba diving any day now, not to mention driving. As a result he entirely failed to resent the reference to drink and drugs. Kate's opinion of the doctor, a young man she had only seen once before (their own doctor was on holiday), rose.

'What about sport? Rugby,' she amplified.

'Again, it shouldn't be a problem. Generally speaking, exercise is beneficial rather than otherwise. The great thing is that Sam should continue to lead his normal life.'

'Except for the mountaineering,' put in Sam with mock disappointment.

'Yeah, pity about that. You'll have to stick to that bungee jumping.' Kate's opinion of the doctor went up another notch.

Kate stood, shivering, on the touchline. She told herself that she had been far colder, in the past, watching Nick's prep school cricket matches. At least with rugby she could keep moving, follow the play up and down the pitch, and there was some excitement to get the blood moving. Cricket was a quiet, static game for the onlookers, and though it was played in the summer term that was no guarantee of hot weather. The January sun was doing its best, and one could rely on a rugby game to finish in under an hour and a half, which was by no means the case with cricket.

Behind her, Joyce was chatting to one of the other grandparents.

They both rather enjoyed coming to these matches – there was a little group of devoted parents and grandparents who met up nearly every week. After several years, Kate prided herself that she knew the whereabouts of the ladies' cloakrooms at every local school. She was also a connoisseur of match teas, which she and Joyce graded on a scale of one to ten. Today's, she reminded herself hopefully, was usually an eight. She thought longingly of hot tea and egg and cress sandwiches.

The game was over the far side of the pitch, groups of boys clustering and breaking apart at the sound of the referee's whistle. Sam, who played on the wing, was quite near her. Kate resisted the temptation to go to the other side of the pitch at half time, knowing that Sam didn't like her to look too partial.

'You're supposed to support the team, Mum,' he had told her seriously, aged about nine. 'You don't just come to see me play.'

'Of course, darling,' she had replied, equally seriously. Nevertheless her eyes were invariably fixed on him. There was always the sneaking fear that he might be hurt. She knew, also, that if she looked away for more than a few seconds he was bound to be passed the ball and score a try, and be mortified if she had to admit she hadn't been looking at the time. Now the game was moving towards them, and her eyes automatically sought him out.

To her dismay, he seemed not to be attending to the game at all. As the struggling group moved nearer to him his head was turned away and he seemed to be looking up at a small plane that was buzzing overhead. As Kate, puzzled more than alarmed, watched him she saw him turn slowly to the right, his whole body shifting until he was sideways on to the game. Around her, other parents were calling out.

'Wake up, Sam!'

'Come on, Sam! Look for the ball!'

His body turned a bit further. Surely, thought Kate with some embarrassment, surely he's not watching that plane. Not at his age, and not in the middle of the match.

'Sam!' she shouted out. 'Come on, Sam!' His body twisted a bit further, still to the right, so that he had turned almost completely round. In a moment of horrid clarity Kate knew what was happening. Knowing that she was doing the unforgivable, but unable to do anything else, she ducked under the loose rope that marked the edge of the spectator area, and ran on to the pitch. As she put her arm round Sam he staggered, and she had to exert all her strength to hold him up.

The referee, blowing his whistle, was upon them. His face, hot and red, was angry. Kate brought her other arm up to support Sam who had stopped turning and had both hands up to his head.

'Mum . . .' he said, confused. 'Mum . . .'

'It's all right, Sam. I'm sorry,' she said to the referee. 'I'm sorry. He was having a fit.'

His look of disbelief faded as Sam lowered his hands and revealed a face the colour of skimmed milk. Sam's sports master, who had been watching from the other side of the pitch, came running over.

'What's up, Sam? Mrs Miller?'

'Sorry, sir,' Sam mumbled. 'Mum . . .' His tone of voice changed to horror as he realised where they were. 'Mum!' He pulled away from her.

'I'm afraid he was having a fit,' Kate said to the coach. 'I'm sorry, darling, I know I shouldn't come on the pitch, but I didn't think anyone else would realise what was happening, and the play was coming straight for you.'

'Yes, you were quite right. Come on, old chap.' The coach signalled to one of the substitutes, who started pulling off his tracksuit.

'I'm all right now,' said Sam. 'I can carry on, I'm all right!'

'Better not, I think.' The master caught Kate's eye, and she nodded. Sam burst into tears.

'I'm all *right*,' he insisted vehemently. 'I've just got a headache. I'm *all right*!'

'I know, darling. Come on, let's get off the pitch. You know they can't let you play again straight away. They're not allowed to take chances like that, and it's not fair on the rest of the team.'

'But we were winning—'

'Yes, and your try put us in the lead,' said the coach briskly. 'Your mum's quite right. The headmaster would have my guts for garters if I let you play on.'

Sam, still protesting, agreed reluctantly to go and sit in the minibus, with one of his non-playing friends to keep him company.

'The ultimate sin,' said Kate ruefully, watching him go. 'He'll probably never forgive me. But I knew nobody else would recognise what was going on – no one but me has seen him have one of these fits, as far as I know. It was because he was turning to the right, I suddenly realised.'

'It's a good thing you did. They'd have knocked him for six. I knew he'd been having some trouble, but I wasn't sure how it took him. I'll be on the lookout, in future.'

'They won't tease him, will they?'

'They'd better bloody well not try!' Looking at his large, muscled shape and no-nonsense face, Kate thought that it would indeed be a foolhardy boy who did anything to displease him. She couldn't help smiling, but some doubts remained.

'You can't be there all the time.'

'Of course not. But they're a nice little lot, this year. I wouldn't say that about every year, but on the whole I can't think of one of them that would say anything untoward. Sam's very popular, you know. And pretty tough, too – he wouldn't put up with any nonsense.'

Three days later, Kate had confirmation of this.

'I had another fit in maths yesterday,' said Sam airily, over supper. 'It was great.'

'It was great?' Kate looked up from her tagliatelle. 'Sam, I don't want to fuss, but you must tell me when you have one, you know the doctor said we should keep a record for the specialist. Yesterday, did you say?'

'Yes, in the morning. I meant to tell you, but I forgot. Sorry. Anyway, it was really funny because I felt it coming on, so I made it look really bad – you know, groaned, and twitched my head and much more and things. You should have seen Potty's face, he was really frightened! I kept it going a nice long time, and he was in such a state he let us go to break ten minutes early!'

'You little monster!' Kate might be inwardly relieved, but she knew her duty. 'Poor Mr Potter. And what about the rest of your class? You didn't frighten them, did you?'

''Course not.' Sam was scornful. 'We'd fixed it up beforehand. I had been going to fake one, but when the real one came along it was even better. They all wanted me to do it again in French, but I thought it was a bit too soon. Besides, Mr Stone's much tougher than Potty. You know, Fiona tried that trick with the fake blood in netball last term. It worked really well on Miss Harrison, but Mrs Stone just said "wrap it in your handkerchief, and make sure you don't get it on your shirt".'

All in all, Kate thought, Sam's response to his new problem seemed, if not precisely to be applauded, at least healthily unworried.

Chapter 10

Phoebe closed the front door with relief. She wondered fleetingly who was more pleased that the day was over – herself, or Daphne. Not, of course, that she did not like Daphne. In many ways, she was inclined to think of her at the moment as one of her greatest friends. Millie, whose trip to India had been so successful that the Abercrombies had easily persuaded her to carry on with them to a tour of the Far East, had telephoned in early December from Hong Kong.

'Darling, I hate to think of you being alone at Christmas. Why don't you come out and join us? You know we're going on to Thailand next, it should be wonderful. There's a trip up the Mekong River on a bamboo raft, you could join us for that, it sounds simply fascinating and so romantic! Oh, *do*, darling! I'm sure you'd enjoy it, and after all you know you can afford it!'

Phoebe frowned. She knew that she ought to be jumping at the opportunity, but all she felt was irritation. It was rare for Millie to have that effect on her: even during her years of rebellious adolescence – which had not in fact been particularly rebellious – she had never felt oppressed by her mother's care.

'I don't think so,' she said vaguely. 'I don't really feel up to it at the moment. Socialising, I mean,' she added quickly. She didn't want Millie worrying about her health.

She believed – and hoped it was true – that her present state of apathy was only a passing phase; that tunnel we all see as having a light at the end of it. She had always been so energetic, so full of plans and ideas. From time to time she tried to think of something she could do, some enthusiasm that might bring her back to life. Not teaching – she had loved it, but somehow to return to it now would be a retrograde step – but perhaps something else to do with children and young people.

She spent mad moments wondering whether she should sell everything and go off to India or Africa, offering her services and her remaining wealth to one of the charities there. The thought of being useful, of making some difference in the world, was seductive, but she retained enough common sense to know that to go flying off, in the kind of state she was currently in, was to risk doing more harm than good. Such a life called for true dedication, not a self-indulgent need to wrap oneself in good feelings.

At other times, and curiously it was often when she felt the most depressed, she found herself thinking that if she survived this, she would be able to help other people to survive also. Perhaps some kind of counselling, she thought? She did not need to be earning: with the security of her lottery win behind her she could perhaps go back to university, take a course in psychology. Physician, heal thyself, she thought wryly.

Millie was persistent.

'What will you do, then? What about those friends we invited last year?'

Phoebe thought back. Leo's departure constituted a kind of insurmountable barrier in her memory. It was as though her real life had come to an end then, leaving her a shadow in this empty place. She knew that there had been a time when she had been ecstatically happy with Leo. She knew that there had been an earlier time when she had been normally happy with her job and her friends. It was just that none of it had any substance, and it certainly didn't seem to have anything to do with her present self.

Last Christmas, she realised, she had only just met Leo. She and Millie had spent the holiday together in her flat, and another couple, also teachers, had joined them for the meal. It had been a cheerful time, tinselled over with the sparkle of excitement that had overcome her every time she remembered Leo.

'I don't really hear from them any more,' she said now, allowing an edge of hardness to creep into her voice. She knew that she had been foolish to let her old friendships lapse. When she had been with Leo they had seemed, if not absolutely irrelevant, at least something she could afford to put on hold. After he had gone, it had seemed too much like making use of people to revive relationships she had turned her back on. There was, besides, a reluctance to admit to anyone that she had been taken for a ride.

'I'm sure they'd love to hear from you . . .' Millie's voice, after the disconcerting time lapse that made speaking long distance on the phone so difficult, was pleading. Phoebe gritted her teeth.

'If you really insist that I must be convivial, I'll invite Daphne,' she said tersely.

'Oh, Phoebe. You don't have to invite anyone just to please me. You know I don't want to interfere. It's just me fussing because I feel guilty, having such a lovely time here instead of being with you. Not that it isn't lovely being with you, but . . . oh, bother.'

Phoebe couldn't help smiling. Millie never got flustered like this with anyone else.

'It's all right,' she said, knowing that Millie would hear the smile in her voice. 'I know what you mean. Now really, don't worry. I'll ask Daphne, I promise, and if she says no I'll ask Jennifer and her family. I've seen her a few times recently – I must say she's been very kind. I had supper with all of them a couple of weeks ago. I learned more about horses in that evening than in all my life up till now, so I'll ask them. And the horses. I'm sure they never go anywhere without the horses. Will that do?'

'Well, as long as you'll be all right . . .'

'I'm fine, Millie. You get off to Thailand and enjoy yourself. Are you sure about the bamboo raft? Is it safe? It sounds rather flimsy.'

'Oh, I'm sure it's fine,' said Millie airily. 'Bamboo grows very *big* out there, you know.'

The next problem Phoebe encountered was issuing the invitation. Since Millie's departure, Phoebe had left the house as little as possible. The weather was dismal, endless days of grey drizzle that dripped off the limp autumn leaves, and turned the fallen ones into a squelchy morass. At first painfully thin, Phoebe had felt cold all the time. Even indoors, with the central heating on full and the fire lit, her feet and hands were white and bloodless, and she shivered deep in her body so that her muscles ached. The raw outside air was physically painful, almost as difficult to breathe as seawater in her lungs.

All this was her excuse, of course. In reality what she shunned was other people. She imagined that wherever she went, people were staring at her. Their eyes flayed her like knives: the flesh over her bones felt raw, tender nerve-endings exposed. She was, she was sure, the object of derision, and it seemed right that this should be so. Her own self-doubt and self-dislike were so strong that all she wanted was to be invisible, to drag out a half-life in the parallel universe that events had flung her into. Her evening with Jennifer's family, though she had been grateful for the kind thought, had been uncomfortable for all of them.

Curiously, her appetite for food revived almost at once. With Millie cooking delicious little dishes for her she had found it impossible to swallow. Now, on her own, she ate voraciously. She craved sweet, rich food in particular. Doughnuts, chocolate biscuits, slices of new bread spread thickly with butter and jam – these, washed down by endless cups of tea, formed the main part of her diet. In the evenings, dreading the prospect of sleepless nights, she would have one drink after another. The wines she had once enjoyed with Leo tasted thin and metallic in her mouth: instead she drank liqueurs, preferably cream-based, the sweeter the better. Even as she ate and drank she was disgusted by what she was doing, but the disgust fuelled self-hatred and she punished herself by eating and drinking still more.

As a result she slept heavily and late, seldom rising before mid-day. Although she was still fastidious about washing and showering, it never seemed worth the bother of dressing attractively. Instead, she dressed for comfort in an old tracksuit, or leggings and pullovers. When they began to feel tight, she bought larger leggings. Her shopping was all done in Tunbridge Wells. Unwilling to go to the village shop or even the local town, where she was sure to meet people she knew, she preferred to drive the longer journey once or twice a month, filling the larder and the freezer with cream cakes and other sticky goodies. She told herself that she needed the comfort of this kind of food, that it was only for a short time and then she would eat sensibly again, that she deserved a treat after all she had been through.

Her body, which had been bony to the point of emaciation, acquired layer upon layer of soft fat. Her skin without make-up was sallow and pasty, her untrimmed hair long and out of shape, straggling round her neck. Phoebe took a perverse kind of pleasure in watching her own disintegration. When the greasy food gave her spots she examined them with a sort of morbid fascination. She welcomed them as the outward and visible sign of her misery: like a medieval flagellant she mortified her flesh with the destructive pleasures of self-indulgence.

Daphne, of course, was not on the telephone. For most of the day she was out roaming the countryside. After Millie left, Daphne had called in three or four times, but her visits were so obviously carried out under the compulsion of duty that Phoebe stopped answering her knock on the back door (she never came to the front). Daphne, who was nobody's fool and who hated visiting people's houses anyway, soon got the message.

Phoebe waited for two weeks after her call from Millie, hoping that Daphne might come round. In the end, with Christmas only ten days away, she realised she would have to take matters into her own hands. Reluctant to meet anyone, she waited until seven o'clock, when even the most tardy of commuters would be home and tucked up in front of the television, then wrapped herself up in an old winter coat of

Leo's (her own was too tight to be warm), and set out.

She knew, in principle, where Daphne lived. Old Hall, which had been her family home, was at the far end of the village. The big old house, with gardens large enough to be referred to as 'grounds', lay within a high crumbling wall and beyond an imposing entrance. The stone pillars of the gates still bore the remains of carved eagles on top of them, though one had no head and the other was badly pitted where generations of small boys had used it for target practice. The buildings, left empty for several years after the death of Daphne's parents, had been owned for a while by a religious commune of dubious provenance. The village had drawn aside its collective skirts, wondering just what kind of community this was likely to be. Saffron robes and joss sticks vied, in imaginations, with fringed and beaded hippies or dour evangelicals who would try to convert everyone, and who would regard the drinking of tea or coffee as drug-taking.

In the event the commune seemed harmless enough. If people were foolish, or desperate, enough to believe that the founder of the group was divinely appointed by God to take possession of everything they owned, the village reasoned, that was their lookout. As long as they lived quietly, paid their bills, and left their neighbours alone, most people were happy. The vicar tried to involve them in the church, but was told politely that they held their own services. The news that they were intending to house down-and-outs was greeted with some alarm, but once again rumour outstripped reality. A few young people came and went, but by and large everything went on much as before until one of the inmates, who was later found to have a history of arson attacks, set fire to a store of tinder and logs in the cellar.

It smouldered unnoticed until the timbers and joists of the ground floor were well alight, at which point the smell of smoke alerted the community, who were holding a meeting. They left without delay, and in the excitement everyone thought that somebody else had telephoned for the fire brigade. By the time the firemen arrived the ground floor had already collapsed into the cellar, and the building was burning well. Practically every inhabitant of the village over the age of five gathered in the grounds, and a party atmosphere quickly developed. Sandwiches, biscuits and hot drinks appeared from nearby houses, and for the first and last time the commune was a part of village life.

The building was left a ruin. The commune, which had been well insured, decided against rebuilding and withdrew to its parent house. The grounds, already neglected, soon grew into a jungle-like state much appreciated by local children, and it was not long before people almost forgot that the house had once been the centre of village life.

Daphne's cottage was in the middle of an area of woodland on the far side of the grounds. Phoebe knew that it was isolated down an unmade track, but it was not until she had to try and find her way there in the impenetrable darkness of a winter evening that she realised just how isolated it was.

The first part was easy, since the lane ran beside the wall that surrounded the old gardens. There were no street lights, but there were enough houses with outside lighting on the other side of the lane to illuminate the narrow road. While the houses lasted there was also a narrow pavement, and when this finished a white line marked the side of the roadway. Phoebe followed its glimmering path, childishly setting her feet one in front of the other on it as if it had been a tightrope. When she reached the dark gap that was the turning into the track to Daphne's cottage she felt reluctant to leave the line. Stepping off it she found herself holding her breath, as if she were plunging into deep water.

The surface of the track was not metalled, but it was fairly level. Winding through the woods it was mainly used by walkers, and the occasional tractor used by the woodsmen had not rutted the surface. The darkness, however, was well nigh impenetrable. Phoebe shuffled through soggy leaves, feeling her way with outstretched hands. A stray twig snatched at her hair, and she ducked. She was, she knew, quite mad to carry on. She should go back home and fetch the powerful torch that was set, carefully to hand, near the back door. She imagined the beam slicing through the darkness, throwing the trees into two-dimensional reality, like stage scenery. In her mind's eye the torch was trained, not on the path, but like a spotlight on her. She set her lips and carried on.

After a while she noticed that the heavy canopy of trees over her head was withdrawing, and a glow from the sky was dimly gleaming on the track. Under her feet the squelching leaves had turned to a soft carpet of needles, from which rose the ghostly memory of pine scent. To left and right the trees marched in their ranks, unnaturally straight and tidy, like rows of plastic bottle brushes. There was no undergrowth, and nothing moved on the bed of fallen needles; it was a dead world.

Still, it was lighter, and Phoebe stepped out with more confidence. It was as well she could see more, for the track twisted and turned. It seemed long, too – Phoebe began to wonder whether she had missed a turning. She thought of retracing her steps, but as with the torch she was reluctant to go back, so she carried on. The track made a sharp turn to the right, precise as a geometric diagram, and at last she saw a gleam of light from a window. It was no more than a narrow crack where the curtains did not quite overlap, but it seemed brilliant against the darkness, a golden promise of warmth and shelter.

On the doorstep she hesitated. There was a smell of woodsmoke, incense-sweet on the damp air. No spitting, turpentine-smelling pinewood was being burned here. Fruit wood, or lime, Phoebe guessed. There was no garden at the front of the cottage – the line of trees simply stopped some yards away, leaving an area of roughly mown grass without even a path to the door other than a track where the grass was trodden thin. A low thick hedge on either side of the building protected a garden that was given over entirely, from what Phoebe could see, to vegetables. It was astonishingly neat, rather to her surprise, with rows of leeks, winter cabbage and brussels sprouts in serried rows reminiscent of the fir trees.

There was no sound. No gabbling of television or radio voices, no music, no one speaking. Only the line of light on the bleached winter grass hinted at habitation. Even so, Phoebe was reluctant to knock, and if it had not been for the thought of leaving that glow of light and finding her way back down the dark track, she would have turned tail and scurried back to her cottage. As it was she looked in vain round the door for some kind of bell or knocker, and ended up tapping on the heavy painted wood. Her woollen glove muffled the sound, and after two tentative attempts she was driven to giving a hearty blow that thudded on the timber.

There was a pause, and then the corner of the curtain next to the door was pulled aside. There was no outside light, so Phoebe stepped sideways so that the gleam from the window fell on her. A moment later the door was unbolted and pulled open. Two cats shot past Phoebe's feet, startling her.

'Come in,' said Daphne gruffly. 'Don't mind them. They don't like strangers. I don't get many visitors.'

Phoebe stepped over the wooden sill.

'I'm sorry. Am I disturbing you?'

'Not at all,' said Daphne politely, shutting the door again. They stood looking at one another, each unsure what they should do next. Phoebe looked wildly round her for inspiration, and for a moment all thoughts of her own affairs deserted her.

It was an extraordinary room. It took in the entire cottage, being kitchen, living room and bedroom all in one. At one end was a large, old-fashioned range, the stack of logs beside it showing how it was fuelled. A vast painted dresser flanked it on one side, and a deep sink with a wooden drainer and plate rack on the other. There were no taps over the sink, only a long-handled pump. On the side of the range next to the sink stood a square container with a tap at its base that must have been for hot water. Two deep armchairs stood in front of the range, heaped with what Phoebe took at first to be a collection of mottled cushions until she saw the pricked ears and wary eyes, and realised they were cats.

A large round table of varnished pine stood in the middle of the room, with an assortment of chairs round it that ranged from a wheelback Windsor to something that Phoebe suspected might be genuine, though battered, Hepplewhite. The walls were lined with shelves holding ranks of books, leather-bound tooled with gold mixed haphazardly with modern paperbacks. At the other end of the room from the range stood a small four-poster bed, complete with tattered hangings. The floor was of brick, covered here and there with rag rugs. The corners of the room were gloomy, because the only source of light was a large oil lamp that stood in the middle of the table.

'What a wonderful room!'

Daphne looked around her, as if assessing something she had not previously noticed.

'Is it?'

'Of course it is! I've never seen anything like it!'

'That makes it wonderful?'

'Well, it does to me. You'd better watch out – if any of the interior design magazines got wind of this, you'd have them all camping out on your doorstep wanting to do features on it.'

Daphne looked hunted. Phoebe even thought that she made a suppressed movement towards the door, as if to bolt it against the encroaching hordes.

'Don't worry. Your secret is safe with me.' As she spoke Phoebe remembered that she had no one, except perhaps Millie, to tell about it, and Millie had presumably seen it already. 'Why didn't Millie tell me?'

'Probably thought you wouldn't be interested.' Daphne spoke without any hint of criticism. 'May I take your coat?' she asked in exactly the same tone. 'Won't you sit down?'

Phoebe struggled out of her coat, and since the armchairs were full of cats took a chair by the table. A faint smell of paraffin came from the lamp.

'I don't have any tea or coffee, but would you care for a sloe gin? I make it myself. Otherwise it's elderflower cordial, or water.'

'Sloe gin would be lovely, thank you.' The bottle – one of many,

Phoebe saw – came from a cupboard in the bottom of the dresser. Two glasses came from the top. One was instantly recognisable as a free gift from a petrol station, and the other was, as far as Phoebe could tell, eighteenth century, with a hollow twisted stem in which the richly coloured drink glowed. It seemed by accident rather than design that Phoebe got the antique glass. Daphne appeared not to differentiate between them, but simply gave her the first one that came to hand.

'Have you heard from Millie? Is she well?' No amount of eccentricity could disguise Daphne's upbringing, and the social code it imposed sat surprisingly comfortably with her weatherbeaten appearance.

'She's very well. She telephoned from Hong Kong, and they're off to Thailand for Christmas.'

'Thailand?' Daphne looked vague. 'Which one is that?'

'What they used to call Siam.'

'Ah.' For Daphne, obviously, Millie might just as well have journeyed to the far side of the moon. They drank again, and Daphne topped up their glasses. The hospitable movement seemed to galvanise her. 'Will you be on your own, then? Want to come here? On Christmas Day, I mean?'

The invitation brought Phoebe up short. She was well aware that this was an unprecedented honour, due partly to Daphne's friendship with Millie, and partly to Daphne's sympathy for someone in her unusual and difficult position.

'I don't want to put you to any trouble. I came to ask if you'd come to me.'

Daphne thought. Phoebe could almost see her trying to decide which was the lesser of two evils. Village legend had it that Daphne, being the daughter of the Old Hall, must be a rich miser, but from what Millie had said Phoebe was fairly sure that Daphne had a very small income, and what little she had was spent mainly on feeding her cats. A Christmas meal of any kind, she thought, would not be cheap.

'Oh, do come to me,' she said warmly. 'I love cooking, and it's no fun for one.'

A look of relief mixed with resignation flitted across Daphne's face.

'Thank you, then,' she growled. They sipped their drinks in silence. The sweetness exactly suited Phoebe's present preferences. She finished her glass, and Daphne did the same, refilling them both. They sipped again.

'Last Christmas,' said Phoebe, 'I had just got to know Leo.' It was a painful pleasure to speak his name. 'It was all – just starting. And now it's all finished.' She heard the whine of self-pity in her voice, and sat up straighter. 'A new beginning,' she heard herself say, and wished she could mean it. 'Today is the first day of the rest of my life,' she quoted hollowly. Daphne grinned.

'Ghastly thought. I'd rather say, today is the last day of that bit of my life. I don't bother with the future, much.'

'Nor did I, really. I mean, I suppose I always had, well, certain expectations. Rather old-fashioned ones really . . . a husband, children, that sort of thing. I mean, I wasn't exactly in any rush, but I was beginning to think it ought to happen soon. But I wouldn't have done anything about it – joined an introduction agency, or anything. If Leo hadn't turned up, I suppose I'd have drifted on for a while. I mean, you hear of people who make the decision to have a child even if they don't have a man around. I don't think I could have embarked on that, though you never know what you might do when the hormones really start biting, or whatever it is makes women suddenly desperate to have a baby.' She stopped suddenly, wondering if she'd been tactless.

'I'd have done it, I think,' said Daphne. 'Not so easy thirty years ago, of course. None of this artificial insemination, and test tube babies, and all that. I've never met a man I could fancy going to bed with, even to get pregnant. Never really liked men. If you'd known my father . . . I daresay, if I'd been born thirty or forty years later, I'd have been a lesbian.' She spoke quite matter-of-factly, lifting the bottle of sloe gin. Speechless, Phoebe held out her glass. She took a large gulp, and choked on it.

'Don't worry,' said Daphne. 'You're quite safe. And so's Millie, come to that. I've never been interested enough to do anything about it. Tell the truth, I've often thought that sex was a bit overrated. I expect babies are, too. I prefer cats, really.'

Phoebe found that her mouth was hanging open. She closed it.

'Tell me about your father,' she begged. 'Was he really so awful? What did he do?'

Daphne topped up their glasses, then looked dubiously at her own.

'This stuff is pretty strong, and I don't usually drink much. Am I talking too much? Don't want to be a bore.'

'A bore?' Phoebe heard her voice rise incredulously. 'I'm absolutely riveted! Please do tell me! Only not if you don't want to,' she added reluctantly.

'I don't mind. It's not a secret. He was a complete bastard.' Daphne spoke robustly, but without heat. 'That's not just my opinion. I doubt whether you could have found anyone within a twenty-mile radius who had a good word to say for him. Violent, aggressive, obsessive . . . He liked hurting people, you know. Oh, not physically,' she added quickly, seeing Phoebe's horrified face. 'Mentally. He knew just where to stick the knife in, how to twist it. He was a psychopath really, I suppose. A very sophisticated one. He knew just how far he could go, within the law. Studied it up. He had disputes with every person who owned land next to his, and because he was richer than them, and more aggressive, he always won. He'd get bored, when the court cases were all settled, and buy up more land so he could start all over again. It got so that nobody would sell him anything, round here. He was hated. It was . . . shaming.' She paused, then said calmly, 'I think I decided, quite early on, that God didn't exist. I just couldn't encompass a universe that contained my father, and a loving God.'

Phoebe imagined it. She looked at what she had thought of as her own suffering, and was humbled.

'What about your mother?'

'She gave up. You know how some Victorian women became professional invalids? Rather like that. Headaches, palpitations, fainting. We scarcely saw her.'

'We?'

'My brother and I.'

'I didn't know you had a brother.'

'I haven't. He died when he was fifteen. Killed himself, actually, only of course they hushed it up. My mother died the following year.'

'So you were left alone with your father? Oh, Daphne!'

'No, I ran away,' said Daphne calmly. 'I was three years older than my brother. As soon as my mother was buried, I left. Went to work on a farm. It was wonderful, you can't imagine! By the time my father died he'd got through all his money, mortgaged the house. There was nothing left, really. I managed to hang on to this cottage, and a few things like my brother's bed,' she nodded to the far end of the room. 'It was plenty. I didn't want any of that – the big house, all that stuff. Too many memories. This does me fine. And do you know?' she peered owlishly at Phoebe, 'I'm happier than I've ever been! When the house burned down—' She looked a question at Phoebe, who nodded. 'Well, I went along there. There were still people in the village who remembered my father. We watched it burn, and they didn't say anything, but we all knew. I was glad, and they were glad. If we'd had some fireworks, we'd have set them off.'

Much later, Phoebe reeled home. Daphne had offered to accompany her, but Phoebe didn't want her to be walking back on her own afterwards, and she reckoned that she was marginally the more sober of the two of them – or the less drunk. She gratefully borrowed Daphne's torch, however.

She woke in the morning with a crashing hangover. Christmas, she thought, might be less awful than she had anticipated. With something nearer enthusiasm than anything she had felt since September, she began to plan a menu.

In the event, however, the day was a disaster. Daphne, whom Phoebe had not seen since their evening together, arrived looking sallow under her weathered tan, and seemed withdrawn. Phoebe thought that the revelations under the influence of sloe gin had been regretted subsequently. When Daphne refused to drink anything but water, and went practically catatonic every time Phoebe mentioned anything to do with the past, she was certain of it.

The food, too, was a disaster. Phoebe had splashed out, indulging her present need for rich food and enjoying the chance to show off her cooking skills. With no need to consider cost she had bought caviar, foie gras with truffles, lobster and smoked salmon, Belgian chocolates, every luxury that Harrods and Fortnums could supply. Daphne, who lived mainly on the vegetables she grew and who was more likely to give the cream from the top of the milk to her cats, could scarcely manage more than a few mouthfuls, though she persisted politely.

Phoebe, who had been looking forward to her meal, felt greedy when she looked at her piled plate, continued to eat defiantly for a while, then gave up when she found her enjoyment gone. They made stilted conversation, and were both grateful to the BBC for providing a film during which they could sit in silence, filling up the afternoon. An early supper culled from the mountain of leftovers was soon finished, and when Daphne said she should be getting back, Phoebe made no attempt to keep her. A bag of titbits for the cats was received with the first genuine pleasure Phoebe had seen from Daphne.

'I'm afraid I wasn't a very good guest,' said Daphne as she was leaving. 'I've not been feeling too well recently.' She made the admission as if ashamed. 'Nothing catching,' she added.

'Oh, Daphne, you should have said. I'm so sorry. Is there anything I can do?'

'No.' The response was brusque, and she softened it. 'No, thank you. It's just something I have to sort out.' She dived out into the darkness, like an animal making for its burrow. She had not, Phoebe noticed, said goodbye. The telephone began to ring, so she shut the door quickly and went to answer it.

'Hello?' she said into a listening silence. 'Hello? Millie, is that you?'

A faint sound, like the murmur from inside a seashell, was the only response.

'Hello? Hello?' Phoebe spoke with increasing urgency. 'Leo, is that you? Oh, Leo, if it is you . . . please say something. Please . . .'

The line went abruptly dead. Phoebe continued to hold the telephone to her ear, unaware of the tears running down her cheeks. Then, very gently, she put the receiver back in its holder.

Chapter 11

In later years, when she looked back on this period of her life, Kate wondered endlessly how she had been so blind to Tashie's increasing unhappiness, and found it difficult to forgive herself. She had tried so hard, always, to make sure that her three children were treated fairly. Aware of the problems that can face the middle child out of three, she had always been thankful that Tashie was the only girl, which in itself made her something special. The main trouble was, of course, that Tashie had always been considered, and considered herself to be, her father's favourite. Although he talked books with Nick, and enjoyed hearing about Sam's sporting exploits, he had never made any secret of the fact that Tashie was very special to him. The boys had accepted this without any sign of jealousy, and in fact made use of this partiality by getting Tashie to put forward their own requests.

Tashie, of all of them, had been the most blind to Len's faults. To her he was the king to her little princess. Because he never criticised her, and indeed seemed not to see the flaws in her character that sometimes provoked mother, brothers and teachers to plain speaking, she found him perfect also. To discover that the man she adored, rather than simply having feet of clay, was second-grade earthenware practically from the neck down, shook her to the core of her being. If her father was not perfect then she, whose self-image had been built on his partiality, must be flawed also, an idea which she found it almost impossible to accept.

Tashie had been certain first of all that it was no more than some kind of ghastly mistake. When, inexorably, it was borne in on her that Len was guilty of all and more than they had originally suspected, she was filled with fury and the hatred that is the converse of love. To hate her father, however, was to come too close to hating herself, so without any difficulty she transferred the hatred to his girlfriend, Phoebe.

For the first few weeks, Tashie was convinced that her father was bound to get in touch. If not with her mother, at least with her. She understood that he could not telephone her at home – that would be too risky, and she had no wish to see him caught. At the same time, surely he could manage some means of contact? He had always excelled in making up games with all three of them: in the past he had often created magical treasure hunts with cryptic clues. Once, for a summer holiday, he had arranged one that lasted for two weeks. It had taken in visits to the Pavilion, to the pier, and to Anne of Cleves' house at Lewes. Somehow he had arranged for clues to be there for them, and the first clue of all had been in code in the local paper.

Tashie took to studying the newspapers every day. She pored over the announcements and the small ads, trying to see some cryptic message in them for her. She checked her pigeonhole at school twice or three times a day, and all her friends were nagged into examining their family's mail early in the morning, in case he wrote to her there.

When the first weeks had passed in silence, she decided that he was allowing time for the furore to die down. He would wait for the bank to settle things, and then he would – what? Send for her? Wild visions of South America floated in her head – a place which for her meant little more than beaches of white sand, fringed with palm trees. She saw herself, lean and tanned, sitting on a lounger and sipping something delicious out of a flower-decked coconut, while a circle of admiring dark youths stood around her. This daydream kept her happily embroidering it for some while, and she never noticed that her father figured in it not at all.

By early December, Tashie was beginning to feel desperate. Then, like a flash, the thought of Christmas came to her. Of course! That was when it would happen. For as long as she could remember, her father had been at the centre of the Christmas celebrations. It might be her mother who shopped, and cooked, and bought the trees, and put up the decorations, but it was her father who brought it all to life, gave it its magic. It was unthinkable that he would not, somehow or other, be in touch with her.

As the days went by, and Christmas approached, her tension mounted. She resumed her frantic scrutiny of the newspapers, and spent her lunchtimes, quite against school rules, roaming along the sea front and loitering on the pier. Her school work was abysmal – she did as little as she could possibly get away with, knowing that some allowances would be made because of problems at home and taking full advantage of it.

On Christmas Day she jumped and ran every time the telephone rang. The first time, in the morning, the sound of a man's voice sent shivers right through her until she had time to recognise Brian

Harper's familiar tones. After that it remained stubbornly silent throughout the afternoon, although she stayed within reach of it and kept putting off going to pee in case she should miss it. Late in the evening, after a day of tension had exhausted her, it rang once more. This time the caller hung up after a second, though Tashie continued to say 'Hello? Hello?' into it for half a minute.

'Who was it?' Kate, too, had half expected Len to call.

'Wrong number,' said Tashie shortly, not wanting to believe it.

As Boxing Day drew to a close she tried, forlornly, to persuade herself that New Year rather than Christmas might be the time. Christmas, she told herself, was too obvious. The wicked people who were accusing her father, driving him away, would be expecting him at Christmas time. For all she knew, they had probably been watching the house. Bugging the phone, even.

By the time she got to the New Year's Eve party, Tashie was beginning to have to face an unbearable reality. Her father was gone. At the party, surrounded by friends whose life still continued, she was filled with fury and anguish that she scarcely knew how to contain, yet could not express. She longed to be back home, and yet when she was there she hated that too, because nothing was the same and she had a different, smaller room.

Sam's epilepsy was the last straw. The thought of anyone having a fit filled her with disgust and terror – suppose she, Tashie, should have the same problem? How could she bear it? Her mother's attention was focused only on Sam, and to make things worse Sam himself was taking it all so well, being so brave and mature about it. Everyone was impressed, everyone was sorry for him and yet admiring him too. Tashie, wanting to hate them all, transferred that feeling, also, to Phoebe.

She became obsessed with the other woman. At night she dreamed of her in many forms, foul and fair but always faceless like something in a horror story. In her dreams it was Phoebe who pursued her, but in her waking moments it was the other way round. Tashie spent every moment dreaming of revenge.

When the telephone rang, Phoebe nearly didn't answer it.

For the past two weeks, ever since just after the New Year (which she had celebrated by eating, on her own, a large meal of choice bits and pieces culled from the freezer and the larder, drinking a great deal of Bailey's and being extravagantly sick) she had been plagued by silent phone calls. Not every day, but two or three times a week, at different times of day. It was impossible to guess which they were;

equally impossible not to answer in case it should be Millie, who phoned at erratic hours several times a week, and would be anxious if she didn't get through.

The first call had come on a Sunday afternoon. Phoebe had been lying half asleep on the sofa, not really watching an old black-and-white film on television but leaving it on for the cosy sound of the voices – "Eio, *thenk* you, Jimmy dahling!" "Think nothing of it, eold thing" – and eating her way through a box of Belgian chocolates. Thinking it might be Millie she had rolled from the sofa and started searching through the jumble of books and magazines from which the agonised bleeping of the cordless phone was emanating.

'Hello?' It had taken her a while to find the phone, and at least it was still ringing when she eventually located it. Whoever was calling was determined to reach her. 'Hello? Is that you, Millie?'

For a second or two the silence at the other end did not disconcert her. Calls from the Far East were subject to some hiccups. Then she noticed, rather blearily, that instead of the usual crackling and interference she usually got on such occasions, there was an echoing silence. Echoing in the sense that she was aware that the line was live. There was none of the deadness of a call cut off, and, besides, the dialling tone would have reasserted itself. Phoebe grabbed at the remote control and turned the television sound off. She remembered the call on Christmas night.

'Hello?' she whispered, her vocal chords tight. 'Is there someone there?'

There was no answer, but as she pressed the telephone tight to her ear Phoebe heard a faint rustling sound of movement, and the distant rhythmic hiss of someone's breathing. Not a heavy breather. Some years earlier, when she was teaching, she had for a while been plagued by one. The gasping and grunting had been pathetic, in a nasty kind of way, and she had hesitated to complain to the police. She had finally seen him off by borrowing a loud whistle from one of the sports teachers. She tried to still her own breathing, quickened as it was by activity and stress, and listened again. Distant but clear, the harsh wailing cry of a seagull, repeated several times.

'Who's there?' Her voice was stronger now. 'If you don't say anything, I'm hanging up.'

There was a pause, then.

'Phoebe . . .' The whisper was so low she only caught it because it was her own name. 'Phoebe . . .' The vowels stretched out long, Phoeeeebeee. She shivered. The whispering voice was asexual, ageless.

'Leo?' Oh, Leo.' Her voice cracked on a sob. She put her hand over her mouth to hold back the sound, but found that her nose was blocked with the overflow of the tears that were aching in her throat. She took her hand away, and drew in a hiccupping breath. At the other end, only listening silence. Even the breathing sound was stilled, as if the other person were holding his breath. Surely, his breath? Between hope and horror, Phoebe had to believe it was Leo there, though could this be the tender-hearted Leo she remembered, who seemed to hate to see her upset? The seagulls called again, mocking her. 'Leo,' she begged. Abruptly, the line went dead.

Disbelieving, Phoebe continued to press the phone to her ear. Only the sound of a dialling tone released her with its dull impersonal hum. She took the phone away from her head and looked at it. Beep beep beep, it went on a rising tone. Please hang up, and try again, said the sensible voice that just stopped short of admonition. Automatically she shifted the button, then remembered Millie and reactivated it, pressing one four seven one with shaking fingers.

'You were called. Today. At. Four. Forty-three Hours.' The electronic voice was almost as precise as the actors in the black-and-white film. Phoebe found herself glancing at the television. The monochrome couple, faintly out of focus so that their skins were impossibly smooth and perfect, mouthed at one another with sharply defined dark grey lips. 'The caller. Withheld the number.'

Withheld the number. The caller withheld the number. The words rang in Phoebe's head. She threw the telephone across the room, where it crashed off a wall and, more by luck than judgement, landed harmlessly in an armchair.

'You bastard!' she screamed at it. 'You bastard!'

Tashie looked at the telephone in her hand as if she scarcely knew how it came to be there. She felt sick, ashamed and triumphant all at once. The shame was hidden deep, unacknowledged, but it was there. She concentrated on the triumph. She had been clever, she thought. Clever, and resourceful. She had planned it carefully. Now she put the phone down, and went to curl up on her bed. She picked up her teddy bear, meaning to hold him cuddled under her chin as she usually did, but when she looked at him his face had a withdrawn look, almost disapproving. It seemed to her that his shiny boot-button eyes were refusing to meet hers. She sat him in the corner of the bed, his face turned to the wall, but that look seemed to bounce off the wall and come back in her direction, so she pushed him under the bed with the old magazines and other litter. That would teach him, she thought childishly.

She hugged her pillow instead, clutching it so that her arms went right round it and came back to embrace her own body. She screwed her eyes up tight.

'I did it, Daddy,' she said in her head. 'I did it for you. She cried. I hate her. I made her cry for you.'

'That's my little princess,' said her father's voice. 'That's my clever girl.'

'I got the number. I went through Mummy's desk, when she was out. I can do it again, lots of times. In the daytime, when she's busy. Or at night. I could wake her up. That'll give her a fright.'

She heard her father's approving words repeating themselves in her mind. She felt warm, safe, close to him. It was the best she had felt for months, since he had left them. She concentrated on the good feelings, pushing out of her mind recent memories of Sam's illness; her mother's worry; Nick's scathing attack, two days earlier, on her selfishness.

'Mum's worried sick, and all you can do is whinge, whinge, whinge about yourself.'

'It's not my fault. I can't help it if Sam's worse. Anyway, he doesn't seem very worried about it, except that it stops him playing his stupid rugger. Well, that's a bonus, for a start.'

'Not for Sam, it isn't.'

'Well, for Mum it is,' Tashie retorted virtuously. 'She used to worry about him getting hurt, and now she doesn't need to.'

Nick shook his head.

'That's not the point. The point is, couldn't you at least stop bickering with him in the evenings? And complaining about supper not being ready? I mean, you could actually have got something ready yourself, couldn't you?'

'I had homework to do. And I did help, when she got in. And it was really late, you know it was. And I didn't see you setting to and producing a meal, either.'

'I had homework, too.' Nick refrained from reminding Tashie, yet again, that this was his last complete term before taking his A levels. 'I had a sandwich earlier. Mum had told us she might be late. You know how long hospital appointments always take, and then they had to get back from London afterwards.'

Tashie shifted uneasily, unwilling to admit that she had forgotten the appointment. Sam's fits, from being a rare occurrence, had suddenly increased until he was having, first two or three a day, then two or three an hour. Alarmed, Kate had contacted the Pritchards, her New Year guests, and got the name of the consultant at the Hospital for Neurology in London. It was, Kate thought, no time for pride, and she had made a private appointment to see him almost at once.

Sam had been put on medication, which began to control the fits but which brought him out in a rash. The change to new medication took time – it had to be done gradually over two weeks – and meanwhile there were endless tests.

'An EEG,' said Kate wearily over the hastily cooked spaghetti with mushrooms, tomato sauce and cheese that Tashie had grudgingly helped to make. 'And a CT scan. And an MRI scan.' She paled at the thought.

'What', asked Nick, 'is an MRI scan?'

Kate shook her head. Sam spoke through a hearty mouthful of food.

'Magnetic Resonance Imager,' he said loftily. 'It was cool. I had to take off anything with metal – you know, like the rivets in my jeans – and they said it was a good thing I don't have train tracks fixed to my teeth, because of the metal, and then I went into this white tunnel thing, it was really cool, like something out of *Star Trek*, and I had to lie still, and it did slices of my brain.'

'Slices of your brain. No wonder you talk like a salami.'

Nick frowned at Tashie, and glanced at Kate who was pushing her spaghetti round her plate without eating it.

'No wonder it took so long,' said Nick calmly.

'Yes. And we had to wait for it, because there was an emergency. Some woman who'd been in a car smash. They were all rushing around, it was just like *Casualty*.' He twirled a knot of pasta expertly round his fork, balanced half a mushroom on top, and stuffed it into his mouth. Tashie looked at him in disgust.

'That poor woman, can't you show a bit of sympathy?'

'Well, I don't know her, do I? Anyway, what about a bit of sympathy for poor me?'

'Poor you? You've had a day off school, and a trip to London, and I bet Mum took you out for lunch too, didn't she?'

'Yeah, we found a place called Cagneys – like Cagney and Lacey, you know? – and they were really nice to us. They said people from the hospital often eat there. I had—'

'Spare us the sordid details,' said Tashie coldly. 'So what earth-shattering conclusions did they come to, after all that? Apart from the fact that they needed to cut your brain in slices, of course.'

'They didn't *cut* it,' said Sam crossly. 'It's like photographs. Or X-rays. And they don't tell you the results there and then, stupid. They have to – to process the data, and that sort of thing. I'm seeing Dr Salmon again next week, or the week after. To discuss it with him.'

'He won't want to discuss it with *you*, squit-features. It's *Mum* he has to discuss it with. You're not old enough.'

'I am too!' Sam spluttered, his face red and his eyes shiny with tears. 'I *am* old enough, and he wants to talk to *me*. It's my head. And he was really impressed, because I told him I had an aura.'

'Oh really! Did it show up on the scans? What colour is it, baby blue?'

'Oh *Tashie*, for heaven's sake!' Kate was driven to protest, but Sam was crowing.

'Not that kind of aura. You don't know anything, do you? An aura is when you know you're going to have a fit, just before it happens. Not everyone gets them, but it's jolly useful if you do, because you can warn people, or sit down, or get someone to hold your head still.'

Tashie remembered seeing him watching television on the sofa, mumbling 'Another one, Mum', and her mother with her arm round him clasping his head to her shoulder, as he felt happier if it was kept still.

'Well, I can't be expected to remember every detail of your nasty diseases,' she said crossly, knowing herself beaten. Even as Sam crowed over his victory she wanted to hug him. She remembered the cuddly fat baby he had been, that she had played with like a living doll for as long as he would allow her to. Sam, her little brother, going through a long and frightening day of questions and tests. She hated herself for teasing him, and she hated him because he made her hate herself.

She refused to admit to herself that she was jealous of all the fussing he was getting, jealous of the time her mother gave up to him and of the lines of strain and worry that made her face look frighteningly unfamiliar. Her mother, although she had lost weight and was pale and tired in the first weeks after Tashie's father had left, still looked much as she had always done. Since Sam's fit at the New Year, her face seemed to have lost not only flesh but firmness. Her skin, at times, seemed to sag into deep folds beneath and round her eyes and mouth. All the colours of hair, eyes and skin seemed to have faded. It was not that her hair had gone grey – it was rather as though its natural colour had simply paled all over.

Tashie knew that it was wrong, but she could not help blaming Sam for the effect his illness was having on their mother. She resented the fear that welled up in her when she thought of Sam in the night, and wondered whether he had a brain tumour and was going to die or, perhaps worse, become some kind of vegetable. Her feelings were as tangled as the spaghetti on her plate, and she retreated from the whole thing back into her hothouse world of vengeance against Phoebe. Two days later, she made the first call.

Cleverly, as she thought, she resisted the temptation to ring too often. For one thing, it wasn't always easy to find a telephone where no one would notice what she was doing. During the next two weeks she called three more times, once from a call box in the town, and once in the middle of the night for which she stayed awake, the blood pounding in her head and her fingertips tingling. The third time was from a call box in a club where, in defiance of her mother, she had gone on Saturday evening with some friends from school. It had been expensive, and she felt nervous and unsure of herself in the smoky, noisy surroundings. The idea of phoning Phoebe flashed into her mind. Phoebe, of course, would hear the music and voices in the background, but that might be all to the good, it would keep her guessing.

This time, however, she had no time to say anything. After Phoebe's initial 'Hello? Hello?' had gone unanswered, Tashie's ear was suddenly assaulted by a loud whistle blast. It seemed to echo inside her skull, ricocheting backwards and forwards like a bullet on rocks. Tashie thought of Sam's brain being sliced as, her face screwed up with pain, she slammed the telephone back into its cradle. She imagined Phoebe, though faceless, grinning in triumph. Furious, her ear ringing and her head aching, she fetched her coat from the cloakroom and went home. Too angry to think of the danger, she walked back through the dark streets. Her friends, missing her, panicked and called the house at midnight, waking Kate and incurring her wrath, since she found it impossible to get back to sleep. Tashie, seething, went back to her bed after snarling at her friends and being snarled at in turn by her mother, and began to make new plans.

Phoebe was surprised to get the parcel. Not that it was precisely a parcel, just one of the strong envelopes lined with bubble plastic that come from the post office, addressed with a printed label. It lay on the mat with two colourful envelopes of junk mail, a similar one from a charity, and a postcard from Millie. Phoebe thought it was probably some kind of advertising gimmick, and sat down to read the postcard, which was from Japan. Then she put the junk mail aside for the bin, glanced quickly through the charity letter, and opened the envelope.

She was slightly surprised to see that the flap had been sealed with strong tape.

There was something square inside, as she had felt with her fingers. She tipped the envelope and it slid out to lie on the kitchen table. A small box, carefully wrapped in dark gold tissue that caught the light in dull gleams. It was finished with narrow gold ribbon, criss-crossed and tied in a small curly bow. Phoebe looked at it as it lay, pretty and unthreatening, on the wooden tabletop, and she felt for a moment as though her heart had stopped beating. Then it gave one huge thud that reverberated through her body, and realising that she was holding her breath she released it in a rush. She gasped in another breath, feeling her head spin. Only then, as she looked at the box, did she remember that it was Valentine's Day.

Gold tissue. Leo's gifts – and he had given her many, with inventive excuses ('It's exactly one hundred and fifty days since we first met'; 'It's your three months' birthday'; 'It's the third Saturday after Easter') – had always been wrapped in gold. Even a packet of Smarties or a paperback book would get the full treatment. Neat-fingered, he would have done it himself in some variety of foil or paper, and tied deft bands and bows of matching ribbon.

The box was quite small. Bigger than the one that had held her engagement ring, smaller but deeper than a cassette. Phoebe picked it up as though it were red hot and held it in the palms of her hands, cradling it as if it had been a wild bird.

Her feelings for Leo were still ambivalent. In her mind she hated and despised him – told herself so every day, every hour – but in her heart there still lingered the warmth of the memory of how happy he had made her. If he had been there, had put the parcel into her hand, she would still not have known whether to throw it at him, or fling herself bodily into his arms. It seemed to her that she must somehow resolve her feelings before she could undo the ribbon and open the box. She felt that once she pulled the loose ends of the ribbon to undo the bow she was committing herself to forgiving Leo.

Was it possible? With all her mind and spirit she denied that it could be. How could any woman accept what Leo had done to her, and keep a fragment of self-respect? And yet . . . Her treacherous body betrayed her, aching for the strength of his arms, the skill and tenderness of his love-making, the warm glow of his love for her. Somehow the one thing she never doubted, in spite of everything that had happened, was that love. And that, it seemed, still outweighed everything else. Slowly, with stiff fingers, she pulled the ribbon undone.

Under the gleaming paper was a pretty box of strong cardboard, which had a lifting lid like a little treasure chest. It was not until she lifted the lid to reveal a lining of tightly folded plastic that the smell, pungent and unmistakable, assailed her. Her hands snatched back almost before the message had passed from nose to brain, then gingerly, to be sure, she pulled back a fold of the plastic to reveal the brownish lumps within. The smell became overpowering, and she hastily shut the box. As she did so there was a perfunctory knock at the door of the lobby, which immediately opened.

'Cooee! Only me!'

Jennifer Dobson, thought Phoebe. It would be. As before, she thought how extraordinary it was that Jennifer, whose cheerful presence she would often have welcomed, always seemed to arrive just when she would be most in the way.

'Come in,' she called unwillingly. She was too late. Jennifer was already coming through the kitchen door.

'Phew, what a pong! I haven't trodden in anything, have I?' She lifted her feet and inspected them. 'No. Not even any horse, for a miracle! Sorry, rude of me to mention it, only I was once lent a car by someone when I was stuck in Hertfordshire, and I didn't realise until it was too late that one of the twins had trodden in some dogshit. It was the devil's own job getting the carpets and seats clean again, and I never did get rid of the smell! So embarrassing, I still go hot all over when I remember it.'

She was relentlessly jolly, but there was an innocence and naivety about her that robbed her pushiness of offence. Phoebe found herself smiling.

'How awful! Did they say anything?'

'No, nothing at all, which made it worse! She was at my school, a prefect in the year above me, and you know how that feeling of inferiority hangs on, however old you get. She still made me feel about six inches tall.'

'But surely you were a prefect too?' Jennifer, Phoebe thought, would have been classic prefect material. Jennifer flushed an unbecoming brick colour.

'Yes, I was. Games captain, actually. But she was in the *year above*.'

'Yes, that makes all the difference. Would you like a coffee?' Phoebe glanced at her watch, and saw that it was already half past twelve. 'Or lunch, perhaps?' She tried to remember what, besides cream cakes and chocolate, she had in the fridge.

'No, no, I mustn't stop. I've got one of the girls home with a cold – really, these days they send them home at the drop of a hat. In my day we had to go to the san where we were looked after by a terrifying old woman we called the Hag. There weren't many malingerers then, I can tell you! Although,' she added thoughtfully, 'we did get cornflakes for breakfast, instead of that everlasting porridge. Quite exotic, that was. Still . . . I say, I don't mean to be rude but that pong's still there. Are you sure?'

'Quite sure.' Phoebe reluctantly gestured to the little box, still lying in a nest of crumpled gold tissue. 'It's that.'

'That dear little box? But surely . . .?'

Phoebe just looked at her helplessly, and Jennifer picked up the box, opening the lid.

'Heavens, how disgusting! Have you got an old newspaper, and a plastic bag?' Meekly Phoebe fetched both, and Jennifer bundled the box, wrapping paper, envelope and all, up in paper and then in a plastic carrier bag. Knotting the top firmly she carried it out to the dustbin. 'There,' she said briskly as she came back in. She washed her hands at the sink, and glanced round for a towel. Phoebe silently handed her one. Jennifer looked at her face.

'It was all right for me to get rid of it, wasn't it? I mean, you weren't – well – saving it, or anything?'

'No. No, of course not. It was horrible. It came in the post, and I'd just opened it.' Phoebe felt her eyes fill with tears. 'Sorry,' she sniffed. 'Just reaction.'

An arm strong enough to be called hefty clasped her warmly round the shoulders for a moment, and gave her a little shake.

'You poor thing! What a nasty thing to do! No wonder you're upset. But who on earth – I mean, it wasn't your, um, your ex, was it? I mean, you told me he'd gone off. Funny, really, I always thought he was so nice, and madly fond of you. Oh, sorry, sorry, Phoebe. Me and my big mouth. My husband always says I only open it to change feet.'

Phoebe wiped her eyes on her sleeve. Jennifer gave her a hastily torn-off piece of kitchen roll, and she blew her nose.

'It's all right. It's nice of you. I'm glad you got rid of it for me, I couldn't bear to touch it. It made me feel sick.'

'I'm not surprised. Spiteful thing to do. Childish, too.'

'Yes.' Phoebe thought about it. 'It's not Leo. I'm sure it's not. I mean, he's a bastard in all sorts of ways, but not that sort. It's just . . . that was the kind of wrapping paper he always used, and I thought . . . I thought . . . you know.'

'You thought he'd sent you something. What about the writing?'

'There wasn't any.'

'There must have been. On the envelope, I mean. And the postmark?'

'I didn't notice the postmark. The address was typed. I didn't really look at it, I thought it was some kind of advertising thing.'

'You, Mrs Miller, have been chosen to receive our free gift? That sort of thing?'

'Yes. Oh dear.'

'We'd better have a look.' Jennifer headed for the door. Phoebe stood up.

'Oh, really, don't worry. I mean, I'm not going to do anything about it. I don't want to tell the police, or anything. It was just a prank, really. No harm done.'

'Bloody spiteful sort of prank, if you ask me. Stay there, I'll go and fetch the envelope. I'm the one that threw it away, after all.'

She was gone before Phoebe could protest again. She was soon back with the envelope. Phoebe looked at it dubiously, but Jennifer sniffed it robustly and put it down on the table.

'It's quite all right,' she said. 'I'd shut the box again, and wrapped it separately in a couple of pages of newspaper. It doesn't even smell. I suppose I should have put gloves on, but it's too late now.'

'Do you want to wash your hands again?' Phoebe was confused.

'No, I didn't touch the box. No, I mean *fingerprints*,' she said impressively. 'Come to that, I suppose we should keep the box.'

'Oh, no.' Phoebe was firm. 'No. And I don't want to involve the police. I'll just look at the envelope, now you've brought it. Yes, the label's just typed, or printed on a word processor or something. And it's a bit smudged, but the postmark is London, which doesn't get us much further. I don't have to keep it, do I?'

'Not if you don't want to do anything about it. But I think you should watch out. If anything similar arrives, I mean. It might not be so harmless, next time.'

'Tarantulas? Scorpions? Severed ears?'

'I was thinking of fire bombs. Sounds a bit dramatic, I know, but . . . well, you do read about these things, and you always think they only happen to other people, but I had a cousin who was hurt by an IRA bomb in London, so . . .'

Phoebe shivered.

'Why should anyone do that? Nobody hates me that much. Unless . . .' She thought of Kate, Leo's real wife. She hadn't sounded like the type of person who would do something like this, but how could you tell? Phoebe shivered.

'Look, why not come back and have a bite of lunch with me?' Jennifer spoke with rough sympathy. 'I know you've not been going out much, but you can't shut yourself up here for ever. I won't let

Lottie give you her cold. You won't even have to see her, she's stayed in bed, lazy little brat.'

'I don't really think—'

'Now, I won't take no for an answer. After all, isn't that what village life is supposed to be all about? Neighbourliness, and all that? Come on, where's your coat? And some shoes, you can't come out in slippers.'

It was like being organised by a large, hearty version of Mary Poppins. Phoebe found herself carried along on a flood of the other woman's certainty, and decided it was easier to give in than to argue.

'And we'll throw that nasty envelope on the fire. I lit one in the sitting room, in case Lottie felt like coming down. All ready? Got your key? Awful how we have to lock our houses these days; when we first moved here nobody bothered. I've got some nice home-made soup, and a bit of real Cheddar, with rind on it. I can't bear that shrink-wrapped stuff, looks like soap and tastes like it too.' Afterwards, Phoebe's overriding impression was that she had been carried down the lane to Jennifer's house. Certainly she felt her feet had scarcely touched the ground.

Tashie thought that the parcel, though tremendously satisfying to organise, was disappointing as an event because she could not be present at the crucial moment of its arrival and opening. She was particularly proud of the way she had managed to get Phoebe's address. Having answered several telephone sales calls, she was able to reproduce the bored, flat tones of someone endlessly repeating a formula, mimicking the drawn out vowels and the false friendliness.

'Mrs Miller?' She extended the last syllable on an upward note. 'BT Directories customer services here. Can you spare me a few minutes?' Without waiting for an answer she had reeled off a few standard questions, ending with; 'Are you satisfied with the service you are receiving? And may I check we have your correct address? Let me see . . .' Phoebe, unasked, had repeated her address without thinking, and Tashie, hugging herself, wrote it down while saying, 'That's all correct, then. Thank you for your co-operation, Mrs Miller.'

After that, the only problem had been to collect the dog mess without anyone asking her what on earth she was doing. She solved that by buying a handy little pooper scooper set in a pet shop, then hanging around the public gardens until someone's dog squatted down by a path. When she saw an owner who stood with her back turned, gazing into the distance as though the dog at the other end of the lead she held were nothing to do with her, Tashie was ready. As dog and owner walked off she put on a smug, tut-tut sort of face and collected the mound of warm turds. She walked off looking superior. 'Well done, dear,' said an elderly man on a bench. 'Shouldn't allow dogs in here at all. I've always said so. Proper health hazard, they are.'

It was easy enough to find some of her father's old wrapping paper and ribbon, still in the cupboard where Kate kept such things, and she went to London to post it, arranging to meet some friends at Covent Garden but leaving an hour earlier, so she could find a post office. She worked out that it was pretty certain to arrive on Valentine's day, which she thought a particularly good touch, and she looked forward to that morning, and picturing its arrival.

In the event, however, Phoebe's parcel was completely driven from her mind. Going downstairs early to check the post, she saw that there were three envelopes addressed to her. One card, of course, was from her mother. Tashie saw the other two to her brothers, with no attempt to disguise the handwriting. It was nice of her, of course, and it meant she could say at school that she'd had three, but her father had always made a great effort to disguise his handwriting, and to post the card somewhere unlikely. He'd once sent it in another envelope to a friend in San Francisco, who'd obligingly posted it back to Tashie.

The second card, she thought, was from someone at school, a boy in her class. She had noticed his eyes sliding sideways towards her, but since he was shorter and younger than she was she wasn't particularly thrilled. The third one . . . she looked at it dubiously. The writing was unfamiliar, the postmark, quite clearly, was London. She opened it.

A fairytale princess, in flowing gown and crown, was perching on the back of a motorcycle, clasping trailing-sleeved arms round the waist of a leather-clad biker. She opened the card.

'You're my princess' was printed inside. No signature, but a heart with a cross in it. She stared at it, then gathered up the cards and ran up to her room, shutting the door and sitting on the floor with her back to it so nobody could get in. Then she looked again.

It was a heart, right enough, drawn in black ink with a thick italic nib. It was misshapen, though. The right hand curve was rounded, the left flattened almost away, so that it could almost have been . . . a capital D.

A capital D, with a kiss in it, had been how her father had always signed his cards and letters to her. And he had always, for as long as she remembered, used an italic pen and black ink. Feverishly she turned back to the picture on the front, and studied it.

Chapter 12

Tashie stared at the picture on the front of the card. It was a cheap card – in the past her father had always found something expensive and special, a pop-up or a cut-out, and once a reproduction Victorian card with satin and lace. This one, on thin, poor quality card, was drawn in a jokey cartoon style with the muted colours of scented cachous. It was the kind of thing that Tashie would normally have considered embarrassingly naff, but now she studied it with as much care as if it had been a priceless work of art.

She could accept that her father might be short of money, but there were plenty of cheap cards around that would have been more to his, and her, taste. This one, therefore, had been chosen for a reason. She remembered the treasure hunts, with their coded clues, and nodded to herself. There was no message inside, beyond the heart sign and the word princess, which was what he had so often called her. The picture, then, must carry the meaning.

If the princess was her, then who was the biker? She knew that her father had ridden a motorbike in his youth, though he had always been very much against Nick or Sam ever having one. Of course, that had been long ago, but still . . . was her father proposing to carry her off, like the princess? Her heart both leaped and quailed at the thought. Even if not, some kind of meeting was implied, and when she looked at the background it was not difficult to work out where.

Behind the princess was a castle. Not a fairytale, Sleeping Beauty type castle with slender pointy turrets, but an English castle with crenellations, standing foursquare on a mound, with portcullis and drawbridge. One of the square towers was taller than the rest, and from the flagpole at the top of it was hanging a rope of garments knotted together. When you looked closely, you could pick out dresses, and bras, shirts, and even an outsized pair of bloomers. The princess, obviously, had escaped from her tower down this.

Now that she was looking more carefully, Tashie could see that something had been added. Perched on top of the tower, by where the rope met the flagpole, was a small bird drawn in black, with an outsize beak. Another bird, larger because nearer, stood on the grassy mound. A crow? A jackdaw? Tashie wasn't very good at birds. Not a blackbird, certainly, with that beak. Somewhere in her bookcase was a little pocketbook of birds, left from a transitory childish enthusiasm. Feverishly she hunted for it, pushing other books onto the floor in her haste. She riffled through the pages, saw nothing, started again more slowly, page by page.

A quarter of the way through; halfway; three-quarters – nothing. About to give up she turned another page, and there it was. A raven. The book, intended for children rather than ornithologists, gave 'Interesting Facts' about ravens. Several pairs were kept, it said, at the Tower of London, because of a superstition that – she stopped reading and dropped the book. The Tower of London. Of course. The postmark on the envelope had been London, and now she came to look at it again, the idealised castle in the picture was similar in its overall style to the Tower.

Thinking about it, she remembered going to the Tower. Not with her father – he rarely joined in any outings that involved crowds, or queueing, or ice creams. She remembered mostly waiting for what had felt then like a lifetime to see the Crown Jewels, and then being hurried through so rapidly that she retained no more than a dim memory of sparkle. The arms and armour had been both boring and scary, the Beefeaters corny (Corned Beefeaters, Nick had joked), and only the ravens, to her childhood mind, were especially memorable. She had sat on her father's knee, later, and told him about them.

So, she was to meet him at the Tower of London. On Saturday, of course – he would know that that was the only day she would be able to go without causing surprise. There was no hint at time – no clock faces drawn on, neither the biker nor the princess were wearing watches. She would just have to go, and hope for the best.

'I'm going to London on Saturday.' Her insides quaked with the effort of sounding normal.

'Again? But you only went last weekend, didn't you?'

'So?' Tension made her voice come out more aggressively than she had intended. 'Is it rationed, or something? Have I used up my quota? Or haven't I got parole from this prison?'

Kate was stung into a reply.

'I only meant, what about your Saturday job? And can you really afford to go again, now the train fares have gone up. I know you didn't spend much last time, but even so . . .'

'I know, I know, money doesn't grow on trees, waste not want not, look after the pennies . . . God, I hate being poor like this. Anyway, it's my money. I earned it myself.'

'Well, you won't go on earning it for long if you keep skipping Saturdays.'

'I can get another job. Anyway, I'm going. Or are you forbidding me to?'

Kate sighed.

'Of course I'm not. When did I ever, without good reason? And of course you can spend what you earn however you want. I just wondered, that's all. We're not exactly in the back of beyond here. I would have said the shopping in Brighton's pretty much as good as London. That's what you always used to tell me.'

'Depends what you want to get. Actually, I'm going up to get some drugs, and have a wild afternoon of sex with half a dozen pushers. OK?'

'Oh, *well*, if it's only *that*. I was afraid you might be going to visit a museum, or something really dodgy like that.'

Tashie melted.

'Oh, *Mum*!' her eyes stung with tears, and she flung herself at her mother. Kate patted her.

'I know. I know,' she said. 'It's just . . . I worry, a bit.'

Tashie sniffed.

'I know you do. You don't need to, honestly.' Well, she told her queasy conscience, surely her mother shouldn't be worried about Tashie seeing her own father? It was only normal, after all. Half her friends had weekends visits to the absent half of divorced parents, and thought nothing of it except how to play one off against the other to get more money out of them.

Tashie dressed with care on Saturday. Everything must be new, ultra-modern. Her father must see that she wasn't a little girl any longer, but a grown-up young woman with a mind of her own. However much Tashie intended to forgive him, she wanted to make him suffer a bit first. A long black skirt, figure-hugging, teamed with her new jacket that might not be very warm, but was certainly smart. A hat, of course, one of the squashy, crushed velvet ones that everyone was wearing just now, and the chenille scarf and gloves that had been part of her mother's Christmas present. At least they might mitigate the cold of the inadequate jacket.

Almost sick with excitement when she woke up, Tashie felt more and more nervous the nearer she got to London. The train journey seemed agonisingly slow, but when it was almost over she wished it were longer. Crossing the Thames she looked, as always, for the little Buddhist temple upriver. The gold on its spiky roof glimmered dimly between the bare grey branches of surrounding trees, and she told herself that seeing it would bring her luck. The train stopped, as it almost always did, just outside the station, and Tashie stared blindly at the advertisement hoardings on the grimy walls. The jerk when they moved again caught her unawares, and she staggered on the platform heels and soles of her new shoes. An elderly man put a hand on her arm to catch her.

'Steady, love! Want to take a bit of water with it, you do!' His breath was offensive, but his voice was friendly and Tashie forced a smile.

'Thanks. I was miles away.'

'Ah.' Tashie could have reeled away from the smell of the prolonged syllable. 'Thinking about your young man, no doubt!'

No, my old man, Tashie thought she could have answered, but the train was slowing by the platform and she needed do no more than smile again before climbing down. The marble-like white flooring of the station rang beneath her heavy shoes so that she sounded, at least, brisk and excited.

After the fusty warmth of the underground she came up into dank cold that struck straight through her thin jacket and seemed to penetrate to her very bones. In her haste she had failed to look at the signs, and now, as she came into the wintry air she found that, though she could see the Tower, she was separated from it by a wide road, the traffic roaring by in a continuous stream. It was as impossible to cross as a river, and she stood shivering for a minute, looking at it.

Common sense reasserted itself, and she looked down. There was a subway, of course, a wide tunnel under the road. Welcome to the Tower, it said above its gaping maw. A stall sold postcards, flags and other tourist mementos. The air in the tunnel was dead, with a tang of stale urine mixed with the concrete smell and the fumes from the traffic. In spite of the weather and the time of year there were people in the tunnel: a neat group of Japanese tourists hung about with cameras that looked too heavy for their slight frames; a party of French schoolchildren, wild with the heady freedoms of being abroad, screeching into the echoing space; British families dragging reluctant children, the parents already irritable at having given up their Saturday for this. The clamour was comforting, but at the other end of the tunnel all the other visitors headed purposefully forward, washing round Tashie's indecisively halted figure. A pushchair, passing too close, snatched at her skirt, and the mother

of its sleeping passenger glared at Tashie as though it was her fault.
Awkwardly, Tashie moved to the railing. Facing the Tower she looked down into the grassy space that had been a moat. The path led to her right, a halfway house between the moat and the higher road. A bank of small trees and shrubs, edged with roses that might have looked pretty in summer but were now a depressing tangle of thorny twigs, sheltered the tourists from the sight of the traffic, if not the noise.

Turning her back to the building, Tashie faced the tunnel again. Anyone coming by underground would have to come this way, but by road? On, say, a motorbike? By standing on tiptoe she could just see the tops of coaches standing by the pavement, and the roofs of passing buses and lorries. Anything smaller was hidden. Uncertainly, she walked back through the short subway.

On the far side, unnoticed when she had come out of the station, some steps led to a small square of grass fronting on to the road. A statue, life-size, stood looking past her. The Emperor Trajan, she read. His face was almost familiar in spite of the fancy-dress clothes. One arm was lifted, the hand showing or admonishing, a finger ready to wag reprovingly. Tashie gave him a conspiratorial look, and felt she would have liked to talk to him. Instead she passed by and stood by the railing, watching the traffic as it flowed past in surges, like waves that never retreated. She looked at her watch. A quarter part eleven. She looked all round, expecting and slightly dreading the sight of a familiar figure bounding towards her. But there was no one, only groups and families. She shivered again.

After half an hour she was so cold that her stomach was aching, and the tears she kept blinking away were running down the back of her throat. She stamped her feet, as much out of fury as to try to get the blood flowing again. Her hands, in their chenille gloves, were clenched into fists. Still the tourists arrived and left, debouching from the tunnel like latter day Orpheuses, passing her by until she began to think herself invisible. Still the traffic roared by, slower or quicker, hooting and revving and braking.

A deep throated roar was from a black motorbike that cut its way through the traffic like a shark through a school of porpoises. Tashie's eyes were drawn to it, but it had two black-clad riders, so she dismissed it. Then the motorbike swerved in to the kerb and stopped with a flourish. The passenger dismounted and removed his helmet, bending to thrust it into a large pannier. He slapped the driver on his hunched shoulders. Without, apparently, checking for a gap the bike roared off again, and the man turned to reveal the face of Leonard Miller.

Tashie stood still, frozen by cold and the feeling of unreality that had come over her. Her father glanced round, spotted her, and raised an arm in extravagant greeting. The roadside was railed all along, but he put his hands on the top and with a little spring vaulted over like a boy. Tashie was embarrassed, but impressed despite herself. She stood where she was, not wanting to look too eager.

No hint of shame or embarrassment clouded Leonard's face. He strode up to her, catching her up in his arms and swinging her round in a circle. The feeling of the strength of his hug was so familiar that her senses reeled, but at the same time the touch of the stiff leather – or was it plastic? – of his clothes was as alien as armour plating, more alien than the bronze armour of the Roman emperor. Tashie put her hands on his shoulders, feeling the chenille of her gloves slip and catch on the cracked edges of what was certainly plastic. He kissed her, his face warm against her frozen skin. The feeling of unreality persisted, and even grew stronger. Close to, he smelt unfamiliar, wrong.

As Tashie turned her cheeks to receive his kisses without kissing him back – she was not prepared to commit herself that far – she breathed in again. The suit itself smelled of diesel and of old plastic, and beyond that he smelled of cafés – the oily warm effluvium of chips and sausages, stale tobacco, and an underlying something that she recognised as the dank smell of clothes that have been bundled away while still slightly damp.

Tashie pulled back from her father's embrace, and frowned.

'Tashie! Darling princess!' His voice, at least, was the same: warm, rich and rounded, what Tashie to herself called a golden-brown voice. People passing by turned and smiled, hearing the simple pleasure in his words. He glanced round, drawing them in to share the occasion. Tashie shrank back. She was glad the statue was facing the other way.

'Daddy!' It was a reproach, an accusation.

'But darling, you can't expect me not to be happy to see you, after all this time! Aren't you pleased to see me?' His voice rang out. Once again he was performing to the gallery. Tashie, her face flaming, could feel the looks from the passers-by condemning her. Waves of 'typical teenager – always difficult at that age' came almost tangibly from them. How could I have forgotten, thought Tashie, how embarrassing he can be? Something of this must have shown in her face. He came closer, speaking intimately.

'Darling, you're frozen. Poor little love, sorry I've kept you waiting. It's just so wonderful to see you, I can't tell you . . .' His voice was husky, his eyes damp. It was, Tashie knew, perfectly genuine. His easy emotional response, so far from the stiff upper lip of so many of his class and generation, was part of his charm. Of this, too, he was aware.

'Where are we going?' Tashie felt she must get him moving and away from their audience, even if it meant going into the Tower with all the crowds. He flung an arm round her shoulders.

'Somewhere! Anywhere!' He glanced around, as though he expected a magic doorway to open for them to some exciting place. 'Somewhere lovely. I know!' He paused, looking at her expectantly. In spite of everything, Tashie felt her spirits rising. This was so much her father's familiar style. She waited. 'Greenwich!' he exclaimed. 'Just the place! Beautiful architecture, beautiful river, beautiful trees and grass! You've not been to Greenwich, have you? It's wonderful, you'll love it!'

'Is it far?' Tashie glanced around, half expecting the motorbike to materialise again.

'Far? No, no distance at all. We could go there by boat. That would be fun, wouldn't it? Come on.'

He grabbed her hand and whirled her off before Tashie could protest that a boat trip in February was pretty low on her agenda of treats. She was relieved, when they reached the pier, to find that the boats only ran in the summer months. Her father, predictably, was outraged.

'Not running the boats in winter! Ridiculous! What is the matter with these people? I've never heard of anything so pathetic. No enterprise. No *savoir vivre*. No—'

'No customers,' put in Tashie tartly. 'No one wants to go pleasure boating on the river in February, Dad.'

'I do.'

'Oh, you—' But he was off again. Nothing ever cast him down for more than a few moments: every setback was an opportunity for taking a new direction. 'There's the train!' His voice was joyful, as if he'd just invented it personally for her. 'The Docklands Light Railway – wonderful – up on a monorail – great fun.'

At the station, faced with a ticket machine, he patted his pockets helplessly.

'No change, princess, no change. You haven't got any, have you? Pay you back, of course.'

The machine, Tashie saw, stated clearly that it gave change. She said nothing, however. There were subtle changes in her father's appearance which she could not help noticing, in spite of his frenetic state of almost constant motion. His hair, that he had always been so proud of, was too long and looked straggly and unkempt. The collar of his shirt that had worked its way above the cracked plastic jacket was clean but frayed, and even his cheek had been rough when he had kissed her. In the past he had always been immaculately shaved, his skin smooth and faintly scented with expensive aftershave. She guessed that he must be short of money, but surely it was not impossible to keep shaved and clean? Not easy, of course, but wasn't it worth the effort, today of all days? Of course, in the past it had been easy, and looking back she saw with unpleasant clarity how rarely he had done anything that involved positive effort. She was sobered by the thought. For a moment, as she pushed coins into the machine and bought the tickets, she felt suddenly very mature, almost motherly towards him. She smiled as she gave him the tickets.

'You'd better look after them, Dad.'

As they boarded the little train, he made a great thing out of sitting at the very front where the glass windows came right down and they had a good view. Tashie was rather glad there was almost nobody else on the train when her father kept pointing things out to her, as if she had been about six.

'I'm not a baby, Dad,' she snapped in the end. 'We've got a lot to talk about. I need to know—'

'Darling, you know you'll always be my little girl, my little princess.' He squeezed her fondly, and she shrank inside from the smell of poverty that hung about him.

'All the more reason to tell me what's going on,' she said briskly, sitting very straight in her seat. 'You've got a lot of explaining to do, Dad.'

'I know, I know. And darling, if you knew how sorry I am it's all worked out like this . . . I never meant it to, you know that. I never meant to hurt you, or Mummy, or the boys.' His eyes were full of tears again. 'The boys . . . you didn't tell anyone you were coming, did you?'

'I certainly didn't. After all, I couldn't be all that sure I'd see you at all, could I?'

He looked astonished.

'But darling, surely you understood my message? I thought it was so clear.'

'Yes, I understood it, obviously I did. But Daddy, it's been five months. *Five months*. Five months of not knowing where you were, what was happening. Five months of thinking . . . well, thinking a lot of things, really. And as for telling Mummy, or the boys – they've all got enough to worry about, without worrying about this as well.' She felt virtuous as she said it, as though she had indeed acted with her family's best interests at heart. There was more of her father in her than she knew.

'Worrying? What are they worrying about?'

Tashie turned to look at her father.

'What do you mean, what are they worrying about? Don't you think having their husband and father disappear without a word might be just a tad unsettling? Or having horrible grey men from the bank coming for days on end and poking about and asking questions about everything and not believing the answers, and having poor Granny getting more gaga by the minute and wandering off all the time, and not having any money to live on, and having to do ghastly B and B and moving out of our proper rooms and Mummy having to sleep in with Granny and finding out about your – your *woman*, don't you think that might be something to worry about!'

He seemed to deflate beneath her avalanche of words. Even his flesh seemed to shrink, the skin suddenly crêpey and grey. He buried his head in his hands.

'Oh God!' It was a mumble, muffled by his hands. 'Oh God, I know. I never meant it to be like this. I don't know how I . . . it just happened . . . like a madness. But I never meant to hurt you . . . any of you. Your mother, she's so strong, so capable, I knew she'd cope. I made sure the bank couldn't take anything, thought she'd be fairly secure with the house . . . Brian would help, he's a good chap. It's not that bad, is it? Say it's not that bad!'

'It's not that bad.' Tashie spoke dully. 'Mum coped, of course she did. Only Nick's got his A levels coming up, and Sam's been having fits, and—'

'Fits!' His face was lifted from his hands. 'What sort of fits?'

'Not very bad ones. Not lying on the ground and twitching and frothing, just his head turning. Like this.' Tashie did a quick imitation of Sam's eyes and head. 'It's not so bad now, he's taking pills. They've done all these tests, but we haven't got the results yet. At the moment they think it's just his age, that he'll grow out of it.'

Deliberately, she played it down. He was as easy to reassure as a child, and the anxiety left his face like a cloud blowing away from the sun. He's not really worried, Tashie thought. Not worried like Mum is. For a moment she hated him for that. Then she looked into his face, that had always until now been the most beloved in the world to her, and saw that it was all he was capable of. A wave of sadness engulfed her. Once again, and more profoundly than by the ticket machine, she found that she pitied him because he was not the man she had thought him nor, apparently, the man he had thought himself.

The pain of it was as sharp, as physical as a stab wound. She saw, for the first time, that she had lost him. Lost him without hope of redemption, because what she had lost was not, had never been, there to be found. She felt very grown up, and very alone. She could have hated him for making her feel like this, if she had not been so empty. Beyond misery or anxiety, she felt drained of all emotion, just tired and cold. Her body was heavy and solid, as though all her blood had jelled in her veins, or been drained out by some monstrous invisible vampire.

The train stopped.

'Come on, Daddy,' she said, very gently. 'It's time to get off.' This time it was she who took his hand, who led him through the old Victorian tunnel with its tiled walls. They came out of the lift doors into thin winter sunshine – the clouds had lifted. The *Cutty Sark* looked as unreal and pretty as a Disneyland exhibit, and beyond it the great park and the buildings rose up. It was almost deserted. Leonard looked about him, his eyes narrowed against the sun, almost helplessly.

'Come on, Daddy,' said Tashie again. 'Let's go and get a coffee, and something to eat. I've got some money.'

He stood still.

'Tashie,' he said. 'Tashie.'

'What is it? It's all right, Daddy. Everything's all right.'

He shook his head, more like a swimmer shaking the water from his hair and face than in denial.

'I need you to help me,' he said hoarsely. 'I . . . I need you, Tashie. I'm . . . well, a bit desperate really.'

'I'll help you, if I can. Don't look like that, Daddy. Let's go and find somewhere out of the wind, and have that coffee. Somewhere must be open round here. You can tell me what you want while we're eating.'

'No.' He wouldn't budge. 'No. It's too private. It's . . . it's a secret, Tashie. A secret, our secret. Just the two of us.'

With a pang she remembered how she had always thrilled to those words. They had had so many secrets, the two of them, in her childhood. Secret presents and surprises for Kate, or the boys. A new car, a goldfish, a special cake. A day in France. Fish and chips on the end of the pier. So many happy, innocent secrets to whisper about, to exchange knowing glances and smiles over, to announce at the right time. This secret, she knew, would not be like that.

'Look, Dad,' she said. 'I'm cold, and I expect you are too. I didn't have any breakfast. Did you?' He shook his head. 'Well, then. We'll go and have a meal, in the warm. And I want to go to the loo. If I'm going to be doing something for you, I need to be able to concentrate, which I can't do when I'm hungry and cold and want to pee. So we'll go and do that first, and then you can explain what you want. We can walk outside, in the park, where no one can hear us.' She fished in her bag, pulled out two ten-pound notes, and gave them to him. 'That'll get us a good breakfast, at any rate.'

He folded the notes, and tucked them into a zipped breast pocket. He pulled himself straight, taller.

'I'll pay you back, Tashie,' he said.

'I know you will, Dad. Come on, let's eat.'

Meekly, he followed her.

Chapter 13

'Did you have a nice day, darling?'

Kate's voice was preoccupied. She was rather relieved that Tashie had come home unexpectedly early from London – she had been a bit strange about the trip – and she had too much on her mind to realise that Tashie's being back by three o'clock could be a bad sign.

'It was OK.' Tashie was already turning to the stairs. Kate noticed, with a little feeling of guilt, that she looked cold and tired. Her black clothes made her seem skinny rather than slim, and the heavy-soled shoes weighed her down, looking almost too heavy for her to lift on to the first stair. Kate rallied her distracted mind and made an effort.

'Shall I make you a cup of tea? You look a bit pale, darling. Are you all right?'

'I'm *fine*. Don't *fuss*.'

Tashie would have loved a cup of tea, and to be able to sit with her mother and tell her what had happened. She longed to unload everything into her mother's capable hands. Despising herself for feeling like that, she felt angry with her mother, resentful that she didn't somehow know by instinct what was wrong. When Kate turned away and let her go on upstairs, Tashie felt unfairly that she was being neglected.

'It's all bloody *Sam*,' she muttered to herself. 'Sam, Sam, Sam, Sam.' She stamped his name into the stairs. 'That's all she cares about. It's not *fair*.'

She didn't really believe it, not deep down, but in fact at that moment it was true. Kate, with all three of the children out that morning and her mother in bed with a cold, had answered the telephone unsuspectingly when it rang.

'Mrs Miller? Dr Salmon here.'

'Dr Salmon? Oh goodness, is something wrong?'

'Wrong? Why should you think that?'

'Well, I mean, it's Saturday. Not a working day, surely.'

'Oh, you know us doctors. Dedicated professionals, day and night, week in week out – particularly when you're paying. No, joking apart, I quite often do telephoning on Saturday mornings, I'm less likely to be interrupted.'

'Oh, good.' Kate, who had been braced for something awful, found that her leg muscles were tightly clenched and let them go, feeling her kneecaps wobble as she did so. She sat down. 'Is there any news, then?'

'Yes. I got the test results back late yesterday afternoon, and I've had time to study them. The EEG is normal.'

'Oh. That's good, isn't it?'

'Yes, it is, in the sense that it rules out some of the classic forms of epilepsy. And you have to bear in mind that he was already on the medication when it was taken, which might have had some dampening effect. No, the most significant result is from the CT and the MRI – particularly the MRI. You understand what it is?'

'Sort of. Sam explained it to me. He thought it was great fun.'

'Good. Now, there's nothing huge. I mean, he hasn't got a brain tumour, or anything like that, OK?'

'Good.' It came out as a whisper. Kate cleared her throat and tried again. 'That's good.'

'Yes. And what's even better is that we can clearly see what it is that's causing the problem. On the CT, and even more clearly on the MRI. Do you know what a naevus is?'

'Um – a kind of birthmark?'

'That's right.' It was the voice of a teacher encouraging a not very bright pupil. 'It's sometimes called a strawberry mark, a little raised pink area on the skin. Now, it looks as though Sam has one on the surface of his brain. It's not at all uncommon – if I were to bring in a hundred people off the pavement and scan them I might find as many as ten with something similar. It's not dangerous, I do want to stress that.'

Kate licked her lips.

'Right.'

'What seems to have happened is that the naevus, since it stands a little higher than the surface of the brain, has rubbed against the inside of the skull, and there has been a little bleed. Nothing major, I don't want you imaging brain haemorrhages, more like a slight oozing.'

Kate nodded speechlessly, then, realising he couldn't see her, managed a strangulated noise of assent.

'Now this isn't particularly dangerous in itself. If the fits are controlled by medication, we could perfectly well leave it at that. But because it's so clear, and because it's on the surface of the brain, it presents us with an opportunity of treatment that I thought I should discuss with you, before I see you and Sam together. That way you can talk it over with him, tell him about it in your own way and time, and then we can perhaps make a decision next week. Is that all right? Are you able to talk now, or is it awkward?'

Kate swallowed. Her mouth was dry, and she gulped air which caught in a lump in her chest.

'No, it's fine. There's no one here. Well, my mother, but . . . please carry on.'

'Right. So, as I said, we could do nothing except control the fits with drugs – and of course it would be advisable to give up sports like rugby where his head gets jarred. That's the first choice. A second is to go for surgery. It would be a relatively simple operation to remove the naevus, and the surrounding tissue where the blood is. The area is very small, and it isn't dangerously near any significant part of the brain. I can't promise that this will stop the fits – there's still so much we don't know about epilepsy – but I think there's a good chance it would. The idea is to prevent further bleeding, and if the fits are cured then that's an added bonus. Do you understand?'

'Yes.' Now it had come, Kate felt surprisingly calm. It was all so matter-of-fact, and at the same time so impossible to believe. She felt that she had somehow fallen headlong into a soap opera. The thought was reassuring. Didn't things like this always work out happily, in soap operas? Unless, of course, they needed to write a character out . . . She shook herself. 'What's the third option?'

'Well, it's halfway in between. To do nothing now, and operate later when he's older. You might feel he'd cope better with it later on, or you might want to wait and see whether things get any worse, or better, in a year or two.'

'No.' Kate spoke at once. 'It would be awful, having that hanging over him. Besides, I think he'd cope with it better now than later, when he's adolescent and has his GCSEs to worry about, or his A levels. No, I think it has to be operate now, or never.'

'It's a big decision. You understand that I can only advise you, but that the choice must be yours? Yours and Sam's?'

'I know. Um, I know this sounds trivial, but at the moment the thing he'd mind most about would be giving up rugby. Later, I suppose, it'll be driving, but we'll cross that bridge when we come to it. So, you said he'd have to give up rugby if we don't go for the operation. What if we do?'

'If we operate, and there are no complications, he would be able to play after three months.'

'Goodness! Three months!'

'You have to remember that where bones are broken, the mend is stronger than the original bone. Sam's skull – or at least the bit of it we'll be operating on – will be stronger than before.'

'Yes. I hadn't thought of that.' That was a short silence. Kate could picture him – thin and intense, with the kind of intelligence that seemed to have burned away his flesh with its energy. His patience was imposed by the strength of his will; his instinct was to move on at top speed. She knew she should not keep him. 'Well. I'll talk to Sam. And the others. His father . . . his father isn't around to consult, so . . .'

'So it's for you to decide, then, with Sam's agreement. Is there anything else you want to ask me?'

As always, that question promptly emptied Kate's mind of every idea in it.

'No, I don't think so. I can't think of anything. Except when it could be done, if we decide to go ahead.'

'As soon as you like, within reason. It depends on the surgeon, really. So, you'll think it over, and talk to Sam, and I'll see you both next week.' He rang off briskly, Kate put the telephone down, and went to see Joyce.

Her mother was asleep. Kate stood looking down at her. The little figure looked so small, so frail, it scarcely seemed to mound the duvet that covered it. Her hands, clasped beneath her chin like a small child's saying its prayers, were mercifully still. When she was awake they fidgeted, almost all the time.

Joyce's face, though wrinkled round her eyes and her mouth, where the little lines radiated and carried faint traces of lipstick, was still soft-skinned. The pale ivory colour of it still took well the make-up Joyce carefully put on every morning. If the eye-shadow was sometimes smudged, and the smoothed-on colour in the cheeks too strong, nevertheless she could still look bright and even attractive. Only those giveaway hands, liver-spotted, the veins standing up like worm casts under the tissue-thin skin, betrayed her disintegration with their incessant movement.

She breathed steadily, her lips puffing out with each breath and making a little popping sound. Recently she had been quieter, and it was some while since she had wandered off. She seemed content, most of the time, to stay in her room, though she would still sometimes go to church or the shops with Kate or one of the children, and had enjoyed Sam's matches until he had had to stop playing because of the increased fits. Although she was still confused she asked fewer questions, seldom wanting to know now when Harold would be home.

Kate had the feeling that Joyce was drifting away from her, a paper boat blowing from the shore, blowing away and disintegrating at the same time. It was, she knew, merciful for them all. She had visited too many nursing homes in her quest for somewhere suitable, should Joyce ultimately need it, not to know how aggressive, even violent, patients far gone in Alzheimer's could be. Kate was thankful that Joyce showed no sign of being like this, but she still had moments of minding, quite dreadfully. There were times when she wanted to shake her mother, to shout at her, to drag her back from the mists in her mind and restore her old wit and good sense. Now more than ever, when she so much needed someone to consult, to talk things through with, even to advise.

Joyce gave a little cough and Kate waited, but she subsided back into sleep. Sadly, Kate left her and went back to the kitchen, where she drearily set about cooking a casserole for supper.

Tashie locked the bathroom door behind her. For once, her usual refuge of her bed seemed to offer no comfort. Her body ached with exhaustion as though she had been beaten, and her head was pounding, but she knew that if she were to curl up under her duvet she would do no more than go through and through the morning, over and over. It was running through her head right now, like a tape on a continuous loop. Her father's voice boomed and whispered, begging, demanding, explaining.

'It's the money, Tashie. I must have some money. I've got nothing. You can't imagine what it's like, Tashie. I always gave you everything, didn't I? Everything you wanted? So do this thing for me, this little thing. It's not stealing. Not really. How can you steal something you bought yourself, bought and paid for? And she doesn't need it. Probably doesn't even want it, it's not her kind of thing. I bought it for an investment, something I could sink the money in, something easy to carry and to dispose of, if the need arose. Well, it's arisen now, and with a vengeance. I *need* it, Tashie. You've got to get it for me.'

Tashie couldn't hear her own voice, though she had protested, refused, protested again. Only her father's voice, that beloved voice, wearing her down like a file rasping through metal, like an electric saw slicing inexorably into wood.

'It's so easy, Tashie. You don't have to break in. There's a key, I kept the key. No,' in answer to her desperate query, 'no, she won't have changed the locks. How do I know? Because I know her. I know how she is. She loved me. She won't want to lock me out.'

Tashie, remembering that moment, wanted to be sick. Her stomach heaved, but she had already vomited on the train, locked sweating into the cold, smelly little lavatory compartment, the ammoniac smell of stale urine from the stained bowl cutting through the sour smell of her sick. She had retched up the half digested meal they had shared, that she had forced herself to eat because she could see his hunger. The fried food, sausages and chips, egg and bacon, had sat heavily alien in her stomach, it had been a relief to be rid of it. With no water to rinse her mouth she had spat and spat, wiping her face with tissues from her pocket that turned grey from the tear-run mascara that stung her eyes.

Now she went to the basin and turned on the cold tap. The water was icy, her teeth ached with it as she rinsed and spat, rinsed and spat. She put her mouth directly under the tap, feeling sure that her hands were filthy but unable to wait until she had washed them. Once her mouth was cleaner she drank. The cold water sat like a stone, but she managed not to be sick again. When she could drink no more she turned on the hot tap to wash her hands, then on an impulse turned it off again and went to the shower. Kate had squashed a proper shower cubicle into the corner of the family bathroom when she rearranged the house, since they all preferred showers to baths, and with the three children sharing the bathroom it was quicker, in the long run, to have a proper independent shower with its own pump. Tashie turned it on and left it to run hot while she dragged off her clothes.

The hot water was wonderful. Tashie stood still under it, feeling it drumming on her skull and running down her body. Her cold flesh softened, came up into goose bumps and then flushed pink with returning circulation. Suddenly her stomach churned again, lower this time, and she shot out of the cubicle to run, half crouching, to the lavatory where she sat hunched, dripping and shivering, as her stomach cramped with diarrhoea. Afterwards, limp but feeling oddly better, she returned to the shower where she shampooed her hair and washed herself, then just stood with her eyes closed and her head thrown back, letting the hot water run soothingly down her aching body and hoping it would take with it some of the misery she felt.

The hot water soothed her physically, but it could not remove the unclean feeling deep within her, that she had agreed to do what her father wanted. It was against her instinct, against her own nature, but because of the pity she had felt for him she had been unable to refuse.

Even so, she felt besmirched, dirty in a way that soap and water could not touch.

By the time she came out, stepping over the puddles that had run off her when she went to the lavatory and using Nick's towel as well as her own to dry and wrap herself (Sam's towel she used to mop the floor), her skin was spongy damp and shrivelled. She brushed her teeth three times, the third time leaving some of the toothpaste in her mouth, then bundled her clothes into the laundry basket. Having touched them, she fastidiously washed her hands once again before going back to her room.

It was five o'clock, and dark. Tashie dressed in some old leggings and a long T-shirt, then pulled her warm old dressing gown on top, wrapping it round her and tying it tightly. Then she sat on the end of her bed, looking out of the window. The street lights were on, casting a lurid glare over the yellow and blue colour scheme she had picked for her bedroom, but she was too used to them to notice. In the other houses in the street lights were on, sometimes shining through or around curtains and blinds, sometimes offering a view of a room. Tashie had always loved to do this. Her mother called it spying on people, and had tried to discourage her, but Tashie argued that if people had left their windows uncovered, they must know that people could see in and they obviously didn't mind.

Other people's lives, seen in glimpses, tantalisingly brief for the most part. Silent conversations, guessed at from gestures and facial expressions. Unknown meals being prepared or eaten; children playing or fighting; television programmes no more than blur of colour; everyday people who were suddenly fascinating because they appeared like actors in some incomprehensible drama. With all her heart, Tashie longed to be one of them. Their lives looked so uncomplicated. Even when there were rows they seemed no more than play-acting. She tried to project herself outwards, to transport herself into one of them. For a little while she was distracted, living that half-glimpsed other life, then a blind was pulled abruptly down and her spirit returned, twanging like overstretched elastic, to her own body and room.

The trouble was, she already knew that she would do it. For all her protests, all the vehemence of her refusals, the turning away, the silence, she knew that she would give in. The key her father had given her, that she had wrapped in paper napkins from lunch and hidden deep in her bag, burned in her mind. Incandescent, it shone through the layers of paper and cloth and leather. Like a deadly snake, it both fascinated and repelled her. The feel of it – so ordinary a key, and yet so unique – was branded into the flesh of her fingers.

It had been on a keyring. The fob was a golden winged lion, exquisitely made, the wings springing so naturally from its shoulders that you wondered why all lions didn't have them.

'It's from Venice,' her father had remarked, in passing. 'St Mark's lion, you know? Pretty, isn't it? You can keep it, if you like. It was a present, but . . .'

A present, obviously, from Her. Tashie had clawed open the catch, breaking a nail and chewing it off angrily, then run to the riverside and flung it into the water. It made scarcely any splash, and the tiny lion had glimmered for a second before sinking into the murky water.

'Steady on, princess!' Leonard had come after her, puffing a little. 'That was real gold, you know! I could have sold it, if you didn't want it.'

'Why didn't you?' she had spat back. A sheepish expression crossed his face.

'Well . . . it was rather recognisable. Not many of them, you know. I wasn't sure . . . perhaps it's better where it is, after all.'

He had told her, so carefully, what to do. It had been brisk, efficient. An army briefing, or the preparation for a difficult practical exam. Nothing must be written down, it must all be remembered. Addresses, day and time, how to get there.

'Couldn't be easier,' he assured her. 'You get yourself to Three Bridges – no problem with that, plenty of trains from Brighton – then just walk through to Crawley bus station. There are buses from there, I've checked it all out. You get off here.' His finger followed the road on a battered map that he had produced from an inside pocket. The fingernail, she noticed, was ragged and not very clean. 'Got that? You must look out for the sign at the entrance to the village before, this one, and be ready to get off. You don't want to have to ask anyone, draw attention to yourself, eh? Pretty girl like you, they'd be bound to remember you.'

Tashie shrugged impatiently. The compliment was too pat, too much a routine, almost a chat-up.

'Come to that, you ought to wear something anonymous. Jeans, that kind of thing. An anorak, if you can, something to cover your hair . . .'

'A wig and dark glasses?' suggested Tashie sarcastically. 'A black balaclava? Or I could go Muslim, wear a chador.'

'Now you're being silly.' His impatience was carefully controlled, his voice indulgent, but she knew him too well.

'I don't see why you couldn't take me. It's all for your benefit, after all.' She knew she sounded sulky, but was beyond caring.

'Darling, I can't possibly. You know what villages are like – someone would be bound to recognise me.' Very slightly, he preened himself. Tashie knew he prided himself on being known, remembered and liked. The sour taste of hatred filled her mouth. The thought of his other life in this village, with this woman . . . She pushed it away from her.

'You could take me on the motorbike. The helmet would hide your face.'

'Angel princess, you know how your mother feels about motorbikes! You can't expect me to go against the one thing she's always forbidden you! Besides,' he added awkwardly, 'it's not mine. He just – gave me a ride.'

Tashie knew how much it must hurt him to make the admission. Against her will, she softened towards him again.

'No, it's all right, Daddy. I can do it. So, I get off the bus, then what?'

Carefully, he described to her how to skirt round the village by the footpaths that would bring her to the cottage without passing many other houses.

'Walk as if you know where you're going. As if you're just out for a stroll, not going anywhere in particular. As if you were walking a dog. It's a pity we couldn't have a dog for you . . . Still, it would be a nuisance on the bus. Anyway . . .'

Tashie had a moment of panic wondering whether her father would expect her to beg, borrow or steal a dog as well, and was relieved when he continued with his minute instructions of how to find the house, how to get into it and how, once inside, to find what he wanted.

'A matching set, in a leather case,' he said, sketching the size with his hands. 'Necklace, earrings, bracelet, brooch.' His hands moved again, miming the layout of the pieces. 'Not too big, they'll easily go in your pocket. Wrap them up in a handkerchief or something, and leave the case where you found it. Ten to one she won't notice they've gone for weeks. Months, even. She hardly ever wore them, said they were too formal, too sparkling. Just occasionally, if we dressed up to have a special meal, or something . . .'

'How do you know they're still there?' Tashie spoke sharply, hating the thought of her father and That Woman having a special meal, trying not to picture him doing up the clasp of the necklace as she had seen him do up her mother's strand of pearls. The pearls, she remembered, that her mother had sold to help pay for the alterations to the house when she decided on bed and breakfast. She had apologised, very sadly, to Tashie at the time.

'I'd always expected to give them to you,' she'd said, blinking. 'As the only daughter, and all that.' Her laugh had been a wobbly thing that scarcely made it past her lips. Tashie, who found it impossible to envisage a day when she might even consider wearing anything so dreary, had reassured her briskly, but now she remembered the subtle gleam of them, their cold smoothness against her fingers.

'She's probably sold them off,' Tashie said now, viciously. 'She'd need the money, after all. Like we did.'

'Oh, no, she wouldn't do that.' He was bland, ignoring the last part of her remark as he so often ignored what was uncomfortable. 'She doesn't know they're worth anything. I told her they were fakes, that I'd bought them for a laugh, just for the fun of it. The Blackpool Illuminations, we used to call them. They were a kind of investment, you see. Something to put the money into, something portable and saleable. Like the Russian nobles in 1917, fleeing to England with their jewels stitched into their corsets.' He smiled happily at his own cleverness.

Tashie gritted her teeth.

'And are you quite sure she wouldn't have changed the locks? And supposing she's had a burglar alarm put in? Did you think of that?'

'No burglar alarm. She hates them. Says they're an expensive waste of time, that the police don't bother to answer or that if they do they're always too late. Did you know that they only reckon to catch about eight per cent of burglars who set off alarms? Or it might be less. I don't remember.' He shook his head, appalled at this unexpected lapse. 'But no burglar alarms, that's for sure,' he added more cheerfully.

'And the locks? The changed locks?'

He turned a look of blank astonishment on her.

'Lock me out? Phoebe would never do that to me! She loves me – she'd always be hoping I might manage to come back.' Taken unawares, he had reacted without thinking, but now he noticed the look on Tashie's face. 'Darling,' he crooned, 'darling princess, it's gone. It's in the past. I was mad, it was all mad, but it's over now. You're my daughter, my only darling precious daughter. Nothing can change that, nothing can take that away from us. You know that, don't you?' His voice was honey-sweet, but as honey can catch at the back of the throat it caught at the edges of her heart.

And like her heart, her mind was torn also. She loved him, and hated him, pitied and despised, needed to hurt him and help him at the same time. The conflicting emotions seemed so huge that she could not contain them. Somehow they cancelled one another out, leaving her apathetic.

'Well, I'll do it. Next weekend. I don't know whether it'll be Saturday or Sunday. How can I be sure she'll be out? Away for the weekend?'

'Nothing simpler. Send her a postcard, pretend it's from me. Get her to go somewhere far enough away that she'd be bound to stay the night.'

'Send her a— I can't! What would I put? And where should she go? It would never work.'

'Of course it would. Somewhere like – well, like Canterbury. I've got a card . . .' He patted his pockets, pretending he did not know where to find it but putting his fingers unerringly into the right one. Tashie watched him in stunned disbelief.

'You got the card already. Wonderful planning.' Her voice was bitter, but he nodded rather proudly.

'You know me, get everything organised. There you are. You could put some little joke on it, something she'd recognise. I could jot something down, if you like.' He produced a scrap of paper and a stub of pencil. 'Let me see . . .'

'If you can write it on a bit of paper, why not write it straight on the card and send it yourself?'

he looked shocked.

'Oh, I couldn't do that! Not to Phoebe! It would be too cruel!'

Tashie stared at him.

'And it's less cruel if you tell me what to write, and I do it?'

He gave a sheepish shrug.

'Well, it doesn't feel as bad, somehow.' Tashie found herself despising him, and pushed the feeling away. With just this kind of self-deception she had seen him, she now realised, get other people to do his dirty work for him before. Delegation, he had called it, and she had believed him. If it had been anyone else, anyone other than Phoebe who was to be the victim, she would have turned from him in disgust, but her hatred was enough to soothe her with a vision of Phoebe's pain.

'Right, then,' she said dully. 'I'll let you know. When it's done.'

'That's my princess.'

'Don't call me that. Don't call me that, ever again.'

Chapter 14

Phoebe's card arrived on Tuesday. A postcard, open for all to see. At first Phoebe scarcely glanced at it. There was quite a large pile of mail, much of it advertising, with a few bills and a newsletter from her old school. A flimsy letter with exotic stamps was addressed in Millie's flyaway handwriting, and with a little lift of her spirits Phoebe filled another bowl with the sugary cereal she was currently indulging in, poured a cup of creamy coffee, and settled down to read.

Millie wrote as she spoke, full of enthusiasm and enjoyment. Everything interested her, and she derived enormous pleasure, Phoebe sometimes thought, from the odd glimpses, the unusual juxtapositions or the sudden small joys of a flower, a reflection, a wafting scent. Her letters, though rambling and sometimes disjointed, often transported Phoebe away from her present surroundings and misery. Each time, reading them, she thought that she should have gone with Millie, but after a few moments of daydreaming she returned to the reality of not being able to find the energy or the will to make the efforts involved.

Millie, from Japan, wrote of thronging cities, of crowds and noise and speed and shops where, incessantly, everyone bowed to you. She wrote of snow-blanketed mountains, of forests that looked like monochrome ink-brush sketches, of temples and meals and sleeping in luxury hotels and country guesthouses where one slept on the floor and soaked away the cold in deep wooden tubs. Phoebe read, and let the cereal grow soggy.

Finishing the letter she sighed, then picked up her spoon with one hand and riffled through the rest of the mail with the other. The postcard looked at least more interesting than the junk mail, so she pulled it out.

The picture – not a conventional photograph – was in a 'medieval' style, the people drawn in an angular and slightly distorted two-dimensional way, as if in imitation of a manuscript illustration. A legend, in Olde Englishe script, read 'On Pylgrimage to Canterburye they wende'. Phoebe looked at it without much interest, disliking the fussy artwork almost as much as the spurious spelling. Turning it over, she saw a sprawling, untidy handwriting that was totally unfamiliar.

"Lovely to be back in the dear old city!" it enthused. 'As pictureskew (!!) as ever, 'specially the Dane John gardens and the buzzem mound! Wish you were here for the weekend!!!' It was signed, more clearly than the message, 'Lulu'.

Must be for someone else, thought Phoebe vaguely. I don't know anyone called Lulu. Thank goodness, too, if she talks the way she writes. I'd better stick it back in the box. She looked at the address. Mrs Phoebe Miller, she read. How strange, someone with my name. Mrs Phoebe Miller. And the address which followed was her own, including the postcode. Phoebe frowned at it, re-read the message, then pushed it to one side and tipped another mound of cereal into her bowl, and added a sliced banana before pouring on the milk.

As she crunched her way through the cereal, she contemplated the card. Could she possibly have forgotten knowing someone called Lulu? It was true that her memory, at the moment, was suspect because nothing interested her very much, and so things didn't stay in her mind. But this card implied an old intimacy, as if they had known one another for years, had even shared a previous holiday in Canterbury. Well, that was ridiculous, for a start. The only time she'd been to Canterbury had been with Leo, when they had stopped for a few hours on their way to Dover for a weekend of wine and food buying in France.

With sudden attention, she picked up the card again, looking at the message. Pictureskew, she thought. That had been their own joke, the mispronunciation of picturesque that one of her class had once used. Unable to laugh at the time because she didn't want to hurt the girl's feelings, she had treasured the word for her private amusement, and shared it later with Leo. And the buzzem mound? She hadn't noticed the word, at first, reading it as 'buzzing' and thinking it some kind of reference to insects – bees, perhaps. But there were no insects in February, and certainly not bees.

She remembered walking along the city wall, looking down on the gardens below. It had been a perfect summer day, which was why they had been tempted to break their journey for a few hours rather than spend them all on travelling. They had reached the mound, with its snail-shell paths and surmounting stone memorial.

'What a lovely round shape,' she had mused, looking up at it. 'Like a pudding. One of those turned-out ones.'

'Nonsense, it's a breast,' Leo had responded, with a lascivious look at hers.

'Oh, hush, Leo,' she had laughed, glancing round at the nearby people.

'Rubbish, they're not interested.' It was true that the only people near them were a small group of Italian tourists, and a couple of smallish boys who were trying, industriously, to start a fire with a magnifying glass. Phoebe's teacherly soul had risen up at the sight.

'Oh, don't you think we ought to stop them—'

'Nonsense, leave them alone,' Leo had urged. 'Good clean fun, and they'll never manage it, those twigs are far too big and they're green, too, not dry. No, they're responding to the spirit of the place. A sacrifice, a burnt offering to Mother Nature.'

'Why Mother Nature?'

He gestured, his hand arcing, cupping.

'The great Earth Goddess, and this is her breast. The bosom of Mother Nature. Only I'm sure she doesn't talk like that, it should be more countrified. Owld Muther Nacher's buzzums, bain't that roight, me dearie-oh?'

'And folderol to you too, you clown. Anyway, it looks more like one of those Prussian helmets, with a spike on top. Kaiser Bill.'

'Ach,' he had grunted, taking her hand and pulling her, laughing, up the steep winding path to the memorial. 'Ach, you hef no soul, you Britishers. But ve hef vays of making you kiss us, nicht wahr?'

Oh, God, thought Phoebe. Lulu. It was written with two capital Ls. Looking at them, Phoebe felt her heart give one enormous thump. It shook her, as if someone had clouted her on the back to stop her choking. She closed her eyes for a moment, then opened them again. It was true. The two capital letters were formed just as Leo had made his.

Her hands shaking, Phoebe turned the card over and looked again at the picture. Canterbury. There could be no mistake. At last, when she had given up hope, Leo had contacted her. He would come back, and everything would be all right. She looked round the kitchen, noticing the cobwebs high up in the corners, the dirty windows, last night's washing up still standing on the draining board, not even soaking. She jumped up, gathering the dishes from the table. Feverishly she ran hot water into the sink, adding so much detergent that the foam rose up higher than the top of the bowl. She dumped the dishes in, and went to get a cobweb brush. On her way to the cupboard she passed the telephone, and for some reason this made her realise that he would not be able to come back here. Perhaps she would go with him? Common sense began to reassert itself.

Leo wasn't going to come back here. Indeed, now that the first rush of emotion had died down, did she really want him to? She told herself that she was better off without him, that he had done damage enough already. How, after all she had gone through, could she contemplate his coming back again? And yet that had been her first thought, she realised ruefully. Anyway, Leo coming to the cottage wasn't yet on the cards. Meeting him in Canterbury, however, surely was. Phoebe diverted her footsteps to the stairs.

In the bedroom she opened her wardrobe door, and looked in dismay at the row of garments hanging there. Dresses, suits, skirts, trousers – and not one of them would she be able to cram herself into. Impossible, even if she starved herself, to lose enough weight in two days to enable her to wear any of them. She thought of a hurried trip to London, of a frantic shopping session. Her heart quailed at the thought, and besides, changed as she was, would Leo even recognise her in new clothes? The thought of his missing her was intolerable. No, she would have to make do with what she had.

In the end she fixed on the stretchy trousers that she could still, just, do up. A pullover was easy enough, and there was her old coat. It was one she had bought in her teaching days, a loose flowing coat that had been expensive at the time and which she had bought for its ageless lines. She had deliberately chosen something that would go over a warm pullover – playground duty could be cold – and since she had worn it when they first met and he had remarked on its deep red colour, she thought he would be sure to recognise it.

Above all, she must be certain they didn't miss one another. She was not sure, in spite of her initial reaction, whether what she wanted was to throw herself into his arms, or to scream out all her misery and hatred of what he had done. Her mind wanted revenge, to hurt as deeply as she had been hurt. Her treacherous body, however, wanted him back. Her flesh ached for his touch, her body glowed. She despised herself for it, but half hoped and half feared that it would be her body which won.

She spent that day and the next in preparation. Impossible to do much about her figure, which appalled her when she actually looked at her reflection properly for the first time in months. She went to Tunbridge Wells and had a good haircut, a massage and a manicure, though, and bought some new make-up and expensive underwear while she was there. On Friday morning she put a small suitcase into the car, locked up the house which she had spent the previous afternoon cleaning, and set off.

The sky was iron grey, the ground frost-free but hard and the air relentlessly cold. Inside the car the air was warm, but the knowledge of how cold it was on the other side of the windows somehow made her chilly. Canterbury, she thought, would be colder still, with nothing to stop the bitter wind sweeping in from the sea.

She had shied away from going to a hotel. That seemed somehow too formal, too much like a holiday or an assignation. Instead she had telephoned the tourist board, and been given a list of bed and breakfast places. The first one she tried, chosen because it was relatively central and yet looked as though it would be quiet, had plenty of room.

'In February?' A warm, amused voice came down the line. 'No, we're not full. In fact, we're not expecting any guests at all. We don't really function at full strength at this time of year, it's usually so quiet.'

'Oh – are you not open, then? I mean, do you want . . .?'

'Of course we want.' The voice was matter-of-fact, reassuring. 'It's what we do, at least, it's what I do. My husband teaches.' That had been encouraging, and Phoebe had found herself chatting for a while before making her booking.

'Um, I'm not quite sure what I might be doing,' she said. 'I'll probably be out quite a bit, but I might be meeting an – some old friends – so it's all a bit vague . . .'

'That's fine. You can come and go as you like, I'll give you a key. And if you want to bring your friends back for tea, or a drink, that's fine too.'

It sounded so friendly. Phoebe could have wept. She drove into Canterbury, glimpsing the tower of the cathedral between the buildings, following the directions to Magnolia House. It was easy to find, the imposing façade coloured to match its name, its lines softened by windowboxes full of pansies. Two neat green balls of trimmed box in urns flanked the gate, and other evergreen plants relieved the formal appearance of the house. As she parked the car and went to ring the bell, Phoebe wished suddenly that this were no more than an innocent visit, a chance to explore the city and the cathedral. She felt, instead, like a criminal.

The door opened.

'Mrs Miller? I'm Ann Davies. Come in, it's such a cold day. Would you like a coffee, or a cup of tea?'

Phoebe found herself ushered through a narrow hall ('Guests' sitting room on your right, and this is where we serve breakfasts') to a dining room overlooking a garden that, even at this dead time of year, was beautiful in its lovingly tended neatness, with colour from variegated evergreens and a few early spring bulbs.

'Nothing to drink? Sure? Then I'll show you your room.' The inside layout of the house seemed complicated and mysterious, steps up, steps down, doors everywhere. 'There you are – I've put you in this double, as you're our only guest. I hope you'll be comfortable, and do come and find me if there's anything you need.' Tactfully, Ann Davies was leaving her alone. Phoebe put down her case, looking round the room.

It was a long time since she had stayed in a bed and breakfast. She had expected basic amenities, minimum comfort – part of her mind had called up the kind of seaside lodgings with linoleum floors and skimpy mattresses that were surely no more than a memory. What she had was comfort, even luxury. The room was, to her eyes, straight out of a glossy magazine with its pretty flowered drapes and bedcover, with walls and other soft furnishings co-ordinating or contrasting. The bathroom, though small, was cleverly arranged and held not only large fluffy towels but, she was amused to see, magnolia-scented soaps. A television on a bracket, a hair drier and shoe-cleaning equipment in the wardrobe, a kettle and a tea tray stocked with different brands of tea, coffee and chocolate, completed the equipment. There was even a clock radio.

Feeling unexpectedly cosseted, Phoebe kicked off her shoes and turned on the kettle. A hot chocolate, with sugar in, she thought. No point in trying to diet now. I need it, to warm me up. To comfort me.

Afterwards, when she had unpacked her clothes and set Leo's photograph, in its silver frame, beside her bed, she went out into the town. Friday lunchtime could scarcely be classed as the weekend, but she felt compelled to go anyway. The gardens, so green and lush when she had seen them before, were bleak, the leafless beeches silvery cold in their thin skins, the formal beds set out with frosted plants. At first she walked along the city wall, as she had done before with Leo, but the icy wind soon sent her down to the more sheltered paths below. There were no boys with a magnifying glass – indeed, Phoebe thought wryly that she might have been inclined to encourage them in their pyromanic tendencies – and the only tourists were a grimly determined-looking Japanese couple, in padded jackets so pneumatic they looked as though they might bounce off any hard surface.

Phoebe loitered in the garden until the early winter dusk began to tinge the grey daylight with dusty blue. The schoolchildren taking short-cuts had all gone home, and only a few hardy dog-walkers still strode briskly by. She was reluctant to go back past the ugly modern buildings to the High Street. Earlier, she had seen a group of older children playing on the outside staircase of the multi-storey carpark, dropping something that looked like snowballs but was more probably handfuls of wet paper towels onto passers-by. Instead she left the gardens at the other end, and on an impulse followed the sign to the Norman castle. She still had plenty of afternoon to use up before she could reasonably go and find supper, and it was good to have some end in view.

The castle, when she reached it, proved to be in ruins, a square of crumbling flint-faced walls surrounded by rough grass. The old arched entrances, which looked more like big mouseholes than something included by design, were closed off with iron railings. Inside, when she peered through, rank vegetation vied with blown or thrown rubbish. A sign said that restoration was in progress. Restoration, thought Phoebe. This place is being restored rather like I'm getting my life back together.

She walked back down Castle Street. There was a sudden transition to bustle as she reached the far end, and the pedestrianised High Street seemed relatively crowded. She found that she was searching the faces of people she passed, checking every man to see whether it might turn out to be Leo. Several times she glimpsed a man with the right shaped head, or a familiar walk, but always he would turn and reveal himself to be a stranger. The tension was exhausting, but it was impossible not to do it.

It was dark by now, and lights shone out from shops and restaurants. A loud mechanical voice came from a converted church where there was a Canterbury Tales tour, complete with almost life-size models of the characters and the pilgrims. It looked cheerful and cosy, and Phoebe was nearly tempted to go inside, but decided it was too late in the afternoon.

In the High Street she hesitated. If she turned left, she would soon be at the West Gate and almost at Magnolia House. The lure of the little tea tray in her room was great, but the High Street was still full of people, so she went straight on down the narrow little street that led to the cathedral.

Inside the cathedral, in that echoing atmosphere redolent of age, stone and the musty book smell that every old church seemed to possess, she walked aimlessly round. She stopped for a few minutes by the place of Becket's martyrdom, then moved on. Then she saw, ahead of her, a man's backview that looked so like Leo's that she hurried to catch up with him. Running up some stone steps she paused at the top to catch her breath and thought that he had vanished, then turned her head and saw him leaving the cathedral by a side door. Following, she nearly fell down a steep flight of stairs that led to the cloisters. She saved herself by grabbing at the handrail, then ran down after him.

He was already striding through the cloistered passage, his feet ringing on the stone flags.

'Leo!' She tried to call out, but she was breathless and her lips were numb with cold and shock. As he reached the low archway at the far end she caught up with him, grabbed at his arm. 'Leo, oh, wait, Leo!'

He turned, and it was not Leo at all. Close to, he didn't even look anything like him. Phoebe's hand fell away from his sleeve as if it had burned her. 'I'm sorry,' she mumbled. 'I'm very sorry . . . I thought you were someone I knew.'

A group of tall boys brushed past them. They seemed to be in fancy dress, with winged collars that shone white against their black jackets. Phoebe found herself wondering, deliriously, if they were some kind of substantial ghostly manifestation, then saw they each had an armful of books and remembered the school that shared the precincts with the cathedral chapter. The boys mumbled an apology, forging through the passage with hunched shoulders and a hint of suppressed laughter at the embarrassing little scene.

The man shrugged and moved away. Phoebe dithered, not wanting to go back into the cathedral but reluctant to appear still to be following him. She stood for a few minutes as if admiring the cloister, dimly lit and mysterious, then carried on through the arched passage that opened into a large square court, like a college quad. Several more groups of pupils, girls as well as boys, passed her by, intent on their own business and regarding the ancient walls matter-of-factly, as no more than boring adjuncts to their school buildings. Phoebe walked round the lawned square and out of a further gate into a dimly remembered narrow street, picturesque with timber-framed houses that overhung their ground floors or leaned, drunkenly, against their neighbours.

More by instinct than knowledge, she navigated herself back to Magnolia House. Tomorrow was Saturday, the weekend proper. She had the whole day during which, surely, she would see Leo. And there was still Sunday. In her room, the curtains were drawn shut and the warm air welcomed her like an embrace. She would have a cup of tea and a long, hot bath before going for a meal at the Mexican restaurant she had seen round the corner. Suddenly, for no real reason, she felt optimistic.

Tashie sat on the bus, her head turned to the window out of which she was staring blindly. Her legs ached, partly because she had scarcely slept the night before, and partly because it had been quite a long walk from the train to the bus station. Longing to get the whole thing over with she had hurried, almost running. She passed a bread factory, and the air was filled with a warm yeasty smell that should have been appetising, but which made her feel sick. She had had to wait nearly an hour for the bus, filling in the time wandering round the newly built mall.

She could still scarcely believe she was doing this. The little café/restaurant where she had spent her Saturdays serving had, not very surprisingly, replaced her with someone else. She had been round after school the previous day not expecting anything else, but at least they had paid what they owed her. The money rested, comfortingly, in her pocket. It had seemed easier not to tell her mother, so she had dressed and left that morning at the usual time. She had drawn the line at her father's suggested disguise, feeling that a girl of her age in an anorak might actually be more eye-catching than the regulation black she invariably wore.

The warm glow of the money in her right-hand pocket contrasted with the icy chill that seemed to come from the key on the opposite side. She felt compelled to keep checking that it was still there, though if she found it gone she knew it would be almost a relief. Every time her gloved fingers touched it they curled away as if burned.

Childishly, she had hoped that something would happen to prevent the whole thing. An earthquake, say, or at least a train derailment. She had woken that morning feeling so peculiar that she had felt a surge of hope that she might be ill, but her temperature was normal, her glands flat and there were no spots or rashes anywhere on her body, though she had checked carefully.

It was all so horribly easy. The train had left on time and so had the bus. Despite the fact that she felt so conscious of her own future guilt that she thought she must glow like a neon advertisement, no one had looked at her oddly or even particularly seemed to notice her. The bus was practically empty, the driver had not even looked at her as she paid her fare. She knew from the map she had studied that she was nearly there. She prayed for a puncture, without much hope.

The expected landmarks were coming up. She stood up, waited at the door, and was off the bus by instinct almost before she was aware of what she was doing. Her legs trembling, she walked down the road and found the expected footpath sign. She remembered, with anger, how good her father had always been at arranging things. His treasure hunts had run like clockwork, and when he arranged an outing, every detail was meticulously planned.

The muddy footpath had frozen into hard ridges that her booted feet slipped on. The air smelled of dung, a country smell that normally she would have found pleasantly rural but which today, when she already felt defiled, made her feel even dirtier. The temptation to fling the key into the hedgerow and run back to the road was so great that she could almost believe she had done it, so vivid was the image in her mind.

Her teeth ached, and she found that her jaws were clamped so tightly they were grating, the muscles in her face as hard as wood. Her legs hurt more than ever, and her feet were so cold that they jarred painfully with every step. Still she walked on, past endless ploughed fields where the soil looked so solid it was impossible to believe that any frail seedlings could ever work their way through the surface, through a small wood where the damp leaves had frozen together, and stuck in dismal clumps to her feet. Then more path, and suddenly ahead of her the lane. Already she could see the top of a roof and a chimney behind a high hedge.

Her eyes flickered wildly to either side. She dared not turn her head to see if anyone was watching her, in case it should look suspicious. She stopped as if to admire something in the hedgerow and managed to make a half turn. She could see no one. The opening in the hedge was an arch rather than a gap, the small wooden gate opened at her touch, and she was through. Instinctively she stepped to one side, to be shielded by the hedge, and the gate swung shut behind her. It sounded as final as a prison door.

She was startled by how pretty the cottage was. Smaller than her own home, of course, but with the kind of appearance that agents labelled 'period charm'. It looked right, as though it had always stood there, or had grown naturally from the soil and rocks beneath. Tashie, hating it, muttered 'chocolate box' to herself. She followed the stone-flagged path with its neat edging of silvery lavender, came to the door where the prickly stems of two climbing roses were trained to frame the porch – 'Roses round the door,' she muttered scornfully – and slipped the key in the lock. A spyhole set in the door stared accusingly at her, and having gone beyond fear she glared back. The key turned smoothly and sweetly, and the door swung silently open. There was no alarm, no barking dog, no calling voice. She knew at once that the house was empty.

About to step inside, she saw that her boots still had bits of soggy leaves sticking to them. Retreating to the garden, she brushed them off against some longer grass by the hedge, then stood in the porch to take them off and carried them inside with her. It made her feel vulnerable, in case she should need to get away in a hurry, but she realised she could scarcely leave footprints all over what was, she saw already, an immaculately clean and beautifully decorated house.

After the high-ceilinged rooms at home the cottage rooms seemed low and intimate. The air smelled of hyacinths – several bowls of them, the colours blending with the rooms – and, faintly, of woodsmoke and coffee. More than anything in the world, Tashie wanted to damage it. To attack the expensive curtains with scissors or, preferably, something hooked and sharp that would tear, like claws. To smash mirrors, glass and china and leave them in sharp pieces on the floor. To take handfuls of ash from the fire, or mud from the garden, and rub them into walls or grind them into carpets. Instead, she went doggedly upstairs following her father's directions, and found the case of jewellery exactly where he had said it would be.

Opening it, her eyes widened. Even on this dismal day (she had not dared to put on any lights) the diamonds sparkled like magic, like the glitter of childhood pantomimes. Tashie's lip curled. How vulgar, she thought. How crass. *My* mother would never wear anything like this. But then, my mother wouldn't have the chance. And she hasn't even got her pearls any more. Her eyes filled with tears of pity for the mother who, when she was with her, she could scarcely manage to speak to. She scooped up the jewels, wrapped them in a handkerchief, and stuffed them in her pocket. Then, her mind boiling with hatred and bitterness, she went through the house.

It was like immersing herself in acid. Without disturbing the contents, she opened and examined every drawer, every cupboard. She saw the clothes, the linen, the intimate secrets of bathroom and dressing table. She looked in freezer and fridge, checked the contents of the kitchen cupboards, read the names of books and magazines; even the wastebins (disappointingly empty) did not escape her. Everything she saw was fuel to the flames of her fury. She hated it because it was, in terms of taste, so much what her mother or she herself would have chosen (given the money), and yet it had been chosen by that woman. She loathed its perfection, its rightness, its attractiveness. At last, with hands shaking so hard she couldn't do them up, she put her boots back on, and locked the door behind her.

Chapter 15

'What do you mean, the claim will be disallowed?' Kate heard her voice rising to a shriek. The telephone call to the medical insurance company had been a formality, merely to ask for a claim form and to notify them. She took a deep breath. 'We are covered', she said slowly and calmly, 'for hospital treatment. We are not covered for out-patient treatment. This is hospital treatment. I have paid already for the consultant and the scans. So why are you telling me that the claim will be disallowed?'

'I'm sorry, madam.' The singsong telephone voice expressed as much sorrow as the speaking clock. 'I'm afraid that your policy covers you for hospitals in band B and downward. The National Hospital for Neurology and Neurosurgery is in band A.'

'But it's a National Health hospital! It's not one of those plushy ones like a five-star hotel! Why should it be band A?'

'I'm afraid I don't know, madam. You'll have to find another hospital, if you want to claim. One that's in band B.'

'This is brain surgery we're talking about here,' said Kate through clenched teeth. 'My son isn't having his wisdom teeth out, or his appendix, or even his hip replaced. They're going to cut a hole in his skull and mess about with his brain. What do you suggest I do, go down to the nearest health centre and ask if they'll have a go? Shop around for this week's special offer? How many hospitals do you think there are that are equipped for brain surgery?'

'That's right, madam.' The girl's voice was smug. 'That's probably why it's band A.'

Kate began to feel as though she had blundered into some kind of *Alice in Wonderland* place.

'All right, then,' she said carefully. 'What's the difference between band B and band A?'

'Band A is more expensive, madam.'

'I realise that. What I was going to say was, can we make a band B claim, and top it up? Pay the extra?'

'Oh, no, madam.' The singsong voice was almost triumphant. 'I'm afraid not. We would—'

'Let me guess,' Kate broke in. 'You would disallow the claim.' She imitated the characterless voice.

'Yes, madam.' There was no reaction at the other end. Was she speaking to a computer with a voice simulator? She might just as well have been. Had there not been an artificial, metallic timbre to the '*Ju*lie speaking, how may I be of *ser*vice?' with which she had answered the call.

'So what am I supposed to do?' Kate asked dully, scarcely expecting an answer beyond a bright 'The claim will be disallowed.'

'You'd better talk to your surgeon again, madam.' The voice, though still brisk, was suddenly faintly sympathetic and Kate immediately felt her throat close up.

'Thank you,' she whispered.

As one might have predicted, the surgeon, Mr Fogarty, was at a conference in Geneva for a week. His secretary could not have been kinder but said that there was nothing she could do until he returned. Kate rubbed her forehead, felt how it was corrugated and tried to pull it smooth. 'Um, suppose I paid for it myself? How much would it be?'

'Oh dear.' She had obviously been hoping not to be asked. 'It's pretty bad, I'm afraid. Very bad, actually. You see, they have to take a worst-case scenario, so they allow for problems, for him having to stay up to eight days, all that kind of thing. It's money up front – though they'd refund the extra, of course, but still . . .'

'Go on,' said Kate gloomily. 'How much?'

'Well, at least twelve. Twelve thousand.'

'Twelve thousand pounds. Twelve. Thousand. Pounds.'

'Yes. Though that's the extreme, as I said. It probably wouldn't be nearly as much. More like ten. Or even eight . . .'

'No wonder the insurance company want to wriggle out of paying,' said Kate with a laugh that cracked in the middle. 'I can't raise even a quarter of that, not in the time. Oh, bugger. Sorry.'

'It's all right. I've heard it before. Please don't worry, Mrs Miller. I'm sure we can sort something out, when Mr Fogarty gets back.'

'Yes.' Kate forced her voice to sound calm and optimistic. 'Yes, of course. But you'll keep the operation date for Sam for as long as possible, won't you?'

In a welter of renewed assurances she finished the call. Then she drifted into the kitchen and stood in the middle of the floor, gazing vaguely around her. The house was empty: the children were at school, the weekend guests had departed that morning, and Joyce was at a day-care centre that had recently opened a few streets away. Kate had been reluctant to suggest it to her mother, feeling that she might take offence, but fortunately Joyce had seen it quite differently.

'Poor old things,' she said kindly, 'sitting there all day, poor lonely souls probably, living by themselves. I'd be happy to help out.' Kate was unsure how far Joyce really believed this fiction but the result was good: three days a week Joyce went to the centre where she joined in all the group activities with gusto. It was true to say that she was healthier than many of the other members, and less confused than some except on her bad days, and in helping to serve morning coffee, lunch, or afternoon tea, or picking up a dropped stitch, she was able to keep up the fiction that this was merely her voluntary work.

Kate wandered upstairs. In the boys' room she stood as she had done in the kitchen, looking about her with unseeing eyes. Gradually the reality of it seeped into her consciousness. The room, as abandoned that morning, displayed Nick and Sam's personalities as clearly as if they had been there themselves.

Practical and pragmatic, they had adapted without much complaint to sharing a room. After trying various arrangements, they had simply split the room in half, with beds against opposite walls. The demarcation down the middle was so clear that they might as well have painted a white line.

Nick, on the far side, kept his books and his desk in immaculate order. A detailed revision timetable, in different colours for the various subjects, was stuck to the wall over the desk, and on the flat surface all the essays and notes were arranged in coloured folders. His CDs and cassettes were also carefully kept. His clothes, on the other hand, were mostly on the floor or under the bed, which had not been made for several days. The three posters on his wall were carefully chosen: one from the Tate and two of rock bands.

Sam, on the other hand, had no books other than the remnants of his childhood collection (mostly comic annuals) and his school textbooks. All were treated with sublime disrespect, battered covers and dog-eared pages displayed as they lay wherever he had abandoned them. His cassettes, too, were seldom in or even in the vicinity of their boxes. On the other hand, his collection of sporting pictures was stuck to the wall with loving care, rearranged almost every week, and while it could not be said that his clothes were folded or hung up, they were at least confined in a cupboard. Recently, as a relaxation and perhaps in response to the stress of events, he had taken out the space Lego that had a year ago been deemed too childish. A complicated construction that was half vehicle, half city, sat in the middle of his desk. The sight of it recalled the days of innocence and tranquillity. Kate turned her eyes resolutely away from it, and gathered up an armful of washing before leaving the room.

Outside Tashie's room she paused. Unlike the boys', the door was firmly shut. There was a suggestion of 'keep out' about it, whereas in the past Tashie would never have bothered to leave it shut when she wasn't in there. Still, Kate thought, I am entitled to go in. I mean, I'd always knock if she was in there, but as she's at school . . . Still feeling faintly uncomfortable, she turned the handle.

The room was painfully, almost ascetically, tidy. The bed was as smooth as if it had been in a spare room prepared for a guest. There was something wrong with it. Kate frowned as she examined the plumped, squared-off pillows, the precisely tweaked duvet, then realised that the bear was missing. Tashie's old teddy, that she had for years been unable to go to bed without, no longer occupied his place of honour. He was nowhere to be seen, nor, now she came to notice it, were any of the other soft toys that had used to sit in a friendly row on top of the bookshelves. Their place was bare, the painted wood polished clean. The desktop, too, was empty. All the clutter of books, papers, make-up, hairbrushes and jewellery had ruthlessly been swept away, and the collection of photographs and postcards was gone from the wall. Even the bin was empty.

Kate shivered. For years she had complained, resignedly or acerbically according to how she felt, about the state of Tashie's room. From time to time she had issued an ultimatum, knowing full well that there would be little beyond a surface effect. It had been a game, a kind of contest that both had moaned about and, beneath it, enjoyed. Now Kate had what she had thought she wanted, and it frightened her.

Feeling guilty of intrusion, she tiptoed to the cupboards and opened the doors. Clothes on hangers, clothes on shelves, all neat. Not very many of them, either. A major clear-out had obviously taken place. Desk drawers displayed a similar appearance, and when Kate peeped into the one sacrosanct place – the drawer of the bedside table, long a repository for secrets – it was completely empty. All the old Valentine cards, the empty cigarette packets, the photographs and letters and sweet wrappers gone as if they had never existed, and the drawer wiped clean. Kate felt a shiver somewhere deep inside her. It was as if Tashie were erasing herself, or at least erasing her previous existence; wiping the slate clean of the past, with nothing of the present or the future making any mark.

Kate shivered again, on the surface of her skin this time. The room felt cold, although the radiator was on and she knew that it was actually the same temperature as the rest of the house. The chill was more like the kind of psychic effect that was supposed to be produced by the presence of a ghost. It was true that to Kate the bedroom felt haunted – the wandering spirit of the happy little girl seemed to cower in its pristine corners, while the unknown presence of a new Tashie spread a miasma of nothingness over all.

When did all this happen, Kate wondered? She tried to remember when she had last come into Tashie's room. Now that she was busy with the bed-and-breakfast guests, all three children had agreed to clean their own rooms, and although Kate knew that the vacuum cleaner was scarcely ever touched or a duster used, she left them to live in whatever kind of squalor they created, hoping that they would eventually be driven to adopt cleaner habits. Wary of invading their privacy she seldom went in when they were there – in the boys' case they only went there to sleep or to do their homework, spending the rest of their time in the kitchen or in front of the sitting room television. Tashie, it was true, was more inclined to shut herself away, but remembering herself at that age Kate had thought it best to leave her alone. Now, however, she wondered.

Friday, she thought. I put her clean washing in here on Friday, and it was all normal then. Saturday . . . wasn't the door open on Saturday? I'm sure I remember going by, and seeing the clothes I'd left on the bed lying on the floor. Yes, I did. She had gone to work. Just as usual . . . she was a bit silent . . . I was relieved about that. Oh, God, what a bad mother I am. She came home, and spent the evening up here. Saturday evening, when she's usually at someone's house or at the cinema or something, she's never in on Saturdays, it's like wearing a sign saying I AM A SOCIAL FAILURE in luminous paint. And I was relieved, again! Glad that she was staying in for once. What's the matter with me? How could I be so blind?

She crept out of the room like a departing burglar, feeling that she ought to wipe over handles and places she had touched to obliterate possible fingerprints. It's Sam, she told herself as she went downstairs, trying to ease her conscience. I've been so concerned with Sam, it's only natural I shouldn't have so much time for the others. And Nick, what about poor Nick? With his A levels only a few months away now, and all those universities he's been offered provisional places at and I can't even remember which ones they are, except that they seemed to be so far away like Edinburgh and Durham and Dublin, for God's sake, and all I could think was how expensive the fares would be, and how we'd hardly see him.

I'll make a big effort, she thought. Starting this evening. I'll make an extra nice supper, and try and talk to them while we're eating. Show them I care, I'm interested. They know that really, don't they? They know I love them to distraction. Do I ever tell them that? We all make sick noises when they keep doing it on TV, but shouldn't I say it more? Or would they find it embarrassing?

Back in the kitchen she put the kettle on, out of an instinct to warm away the inner chill she still felt. I wish I knew what to do, how to do it, she thought. Other people do – at least, they seem to. Half the time I think I do and say too much, and then spend the other half worrying that it's not enough. It was all so easy when they were babies. Toddlers, even. Those tantrums, the battles of will, they seemed such a big deal then, but they were simple really. Straightforward. I knew how to handle them, or thought I did, which was much the same. Now I'm lost in the wilderness with no map, or compass, or guide. No helpful how-to books and magazines. Colic and tantrums you could look up. There aren't any chapters on bigamous absconding fathers, or brain surgery, or teenage girls who suddenly tidy their rooms.

She imagined ringing some kind of helpline.

'Oh, please tell me what to do! My daughter's room is so tidy, I'm worried sick!' She imagined the dismissive amusement, the 'You should be so lucky!' that she would get in return. I'm on my own, she thought, not for the first time. Down, but not out, she told herself firmly as she went to the freezer and rummaged for chicken breasts she had been saving for a special occasion.

'So, how was school?' As soon as the words were out, Kate felt that she had spoken too brightly, as if to five-year-olds.

'OK.'

'All right.'

'Eurrch.'

Nick, Tashie and Sam answered predictably, the older two in automatic grunt-speak, Sam with a wild gesture and a certain amount of flying spit that made his siblings turn on him.

'Gross! All over the table! Great hunks of gob!'

'I'm not eating here, it's defiled. It will all have to be disinfected. Autoclaved,' added Tashie, who was a fan of medical dramas.

'It was hardly anything.' Sam wiped the tabletop with a quick swipe of his arm. 'Anyway, my spit's perfectly pure. At least, it's as pure as Tommo Tomlinson's, and I didn't see you objecting to his when he was putting his tongue down your throat the other week.'

'Sam!' Tashie was scarlet. 'He was not! And it's nothing to do with you even if he was, you disgusting little pervert.'

'He was too! I saw him, slobbering and snuffling all over you down on the sea front! Sordid, I call it. Setting a bad example to me. I could be emotionally scarred by seeing that sort of thing, at my age.'

'It won't be your emotions scarred, it'll be your body! What were you doing? Spying on me?'

'Certainly not, nothing could interest me less than what you get up to when you disappear. Like you've done the last two weekends, for instance.'

Tashie's red face drained of colour so quickly it was as if someone had opened an artery in her neck.

'You little *shit*! How dare you spy on me! I could kill you!'

Her eyes were hot with fury in her white face. Kate, in the act of taking the stuffed breasts out of the oven, burned her wrist and dropped the dish back on the oven shelf with a clatter, then stood staring at the furious creature her daughter had suddenly turned into. Nick leaned back, tilting his chair, his attention for once withdrawn from the cerebral universe he was currently inhabiting.

'Steady the Buffs,' he growled. It had been one of Len's catch-phrases. Tashie looked at him wildly, then ran from the room. Nick nodded. 'Thought so,' he said. Kate, suddenly conscious of the pain in her wrist, disentangled her hands from the oven gloves and went to turn on the cold tap.

'What do you mean, you thought so?'

Nick brought his chair back to the floor.

'Something to do with Dad,' he said succinctly.

'What's Dad got to do with Tommo Tomlinson?'

'Something to do with your *father*?' Kate ignored Sam. 'You mean, she's over-reacting because she's still upset about him?'

'If you like.' Nick looked at her warily.

'That's not what you meant. So, what?'

'Tommo Tomlinson's new this term. He's never even *heard* of Dad.' Sam, doggedly in pursuit.

'Shut up, Sam. I mean, just give me a moment, darling. I don't think Tommo Tomlinson is really germane to this issue.'

'Tommo's not German. He's not even Italian, like you'd think, because his real name's not Tommo, it's Nigel, he's just called Tommo because his name's Tomlinson, and he comes from Wales actually only he's not Welsh either—'

'Sam!' Kate's shriek cut through the torrent of explanations. 'We're not talking about Tommo Tomlinson. I am not *interested* in Tommo Tomlinson, or where he comes from, or anything about him!'

'Well, I think you should be, because he was practically eating Tash alive when I saw them, and—'

Nick stood up.

'Enough,' he said, quite quietly, but looming over his brother. Sam's mouth shut with a snap, while Kate's fell open. She had never seen Nick display so much mastery over his obstreperous younger brother, and for a moment she looked at him with awed amazement. He's grown up, she thought with a mixture of pride and sadness. He doesn't need to threaten, or shout, he just believes it will work, and it does.

Nick turned his unfathomable eyes on Kate.

'I think Tashie's heard from Dad.'

Sam opened his mouth to speak, caught Nick's glare, and closed it again. Kate took her arm from under the tap and walked to a chair, feeling for it as she sat without taking her eyes off Nick. She left the tap running.

'Heard from Len? But . . . nobody's heard from him. I was beginning to think . . .' It was her turn to look wary. The corner of Nick's mouth curled slightly.

'That he was dead? It would be a solution, wouldn't it?'

'Dominic!' The use of his full name was a symptom of profound shock and disapproval.

'Well, it would. Don't tell me you haven't thought so, too. After all, as far as we're concerned, he might as well be, mightn't he? And we could claim on the insurance, too. You wouldn't have to worry about Gran, and the bed and breakfast, and everything.'

'I don't mind the B and B, and Gran's OK for the moment. But Nick . . . you surely don't wish your father dead, do you?' She could not deny that it was a solution that had been lurking in the pit of her mind, but she could not bear to think that her children should sully what she still saw as their innocence with such a thought.

'Not wish it, no. I wouldn't wish anyone dead. But that's how I've been thinking of him. It's easier, you see. Cowardly, perhaps, but easier.'

The corners of Sam's mouth were turning down.

'Dad's not dead, is he? Mum?'

Kate held out her arms to him and he came awkwardly into her embrace, huddling against her.

'Of course Dad's not dead. That's the one thing we'd be sure to have heard about. It's just Nick's way of coping.'

'I don't understand!' It was a wail. Nick went to turn off the tap, then came and sat next to his mother. He put his hand on Sam's back.

Sam flinched, but Nick kept his hand firmly on his shoulder, gripping and giving it a small shake.

'If I think of Dad going off like that, leaving Mum to manage on her own, even leaving that other woman too, it makes me so angry I want to throw up. It feels horrible, like swallowing boiling oil or something. But if I think he's died, then I can be sad about him, and miss him a bit, and even feel sorry for him. See what I mean?'

'But he's not dead?'

'No, he's not dead.'

Within Kate's arms, Sam's breathing eased.

'And he might still come back?'

'No.' Nick spoke baldly, and Kate drew in a breath to protest. His eyes met hers with an unmistakable message – leave this to me.

'Not ever?'

'Not ever. It wouldn't be fair to Mum, or to us either. You can see that, if you think about it.' He spoke as one adult to another. Kate felt Sam nod. Then he released himself from her hug and stood upright.

'I just thought he might come back. And that everything would be the way it was. You know.' It was a question, and Nick answered it.

'It wouldn't be, though, would it? Not the way it was. Dad coming back, that's just a daydream. If he really did, it would be awful. The bank. The woman. All that hassle. We don't need it. And we don't need him.'

'I s'pose.'

'S'pose is right, bro. Look at you, dealing with all that brain surgery and shit. Mr Cool, that's you. I reckon you're more grown up than he is, already, poor old Dad.'

'For real?'

'For definitely real.' They were talking like a television show, Kate realised, to defuse the emotion. And it was working. Sam was relaxed now, standing tall, his head up. Her throat tightened with pride, and she blinked rapidly. Somehow, she thought, I've got to live up to all this.

'And Tash? What about Tash?' Sam had remembered what Kate, momentarily, had forgotten.

'She thought he'd be coming back, too. She'll get there, in the end. Girls see things differently, sometimes. Well, pretty often. And you know our Tashie. She thinks she can make things happen just by wanting them enough.' The tone, now, was man-to-man. Kate, a mere woman, kept quiet.

'But you said you thought she'd seen him.'

'I thought she might have heard from him. Or she might think she had. The way she's been searching the personal columns of the paper, and checking the post and her pigeonhole at school, she'd be liable to think that any bit of junk mail was a coded message. I shouldn't worry about it.' He was speaking, Kate saw, as much to her as to Sam. 'Tashie's pretty tough, and she's no fool. At least, she might let herself be fooled by Dad, but not for long.'

Sam, who was not unnaturally more concerned with himself than with his sister, was satisfied. Kate was less so, but reluctant to disturb the upbeat mood that Nick had managed to engender.

'I'd like to go and talk to her.' It was more of a request than a statement. Goodness, thought Kate. Any minute now I'll be asking Nick's permission before I do anything. Oh, well, I suppose I could do worse.

'Good idea.'

Kate's arm stung as she moved, reminding her.

'Goodness, the supper! I hope it's not ruined. Why don't you eat yours straight away?'

'No, we'll wait for you, and perhaps you can persuade Tashie to come down and eat too. I'll put it in the warmer.'

'Thank you, darling.' Kate spoke gratefully, and it wasn't the supper she was talking about.

'Tashie? Tashie, can I come in?'

In the face of a profound silence, Kate opened the door. Tashie was curled up on the bed, with her back to the door. The room was dark, the only light a glow from the window where the curtains were open. Kate shut the door behind her, and went to sit on the edge of the bed. Tashie's breath was so slow and even that she was almost certainly only pretending to be asleep. Kate put her hand on her, as Nick had done to Sam. She felt the shiver of skin and muscle beneath her touch.

'Oh, Tashie. Darling Tashie. I'm so sorry.' The words came from deep within her, unbidden. They were not at all what she had meant to say. Beneath her hand, the quiver stilled.

'Not your fault.' Her voice was muffled, but calm.

'No, it isn't. But I feel as though it is.'

'It's Daddy's fault, but he doesn't think it is. Not at all. Not one bit. I hate him.'

So, she had heard from him. Spoken to him, or even seen him. Kate felt her own flesh contract, but she kept her hand steady and her voice level.

'No, you don't. Not really. Or if you do, it's only because you love him. Don't hate him, because the only person who'll be hurt by it is you. Be angry with him. Pity him, if you can. Hate what he's done, but don't hate him, because truly he can't help it. He just doesn't know any better. Oh dear,' she said, with a shaky laugh, 'I sound like one of those advice pages in a magazine. I wish I knew the right things to say, I wish I could help you.'

'I don't help you. I haven't even wanted to.' The honesty was habitual, the humility less so.

'You don't have to. I'm all right. In fact, if it weren't for Sam, I'd be fine, really. I'm sorry, Tashie, but I don't really miss your father all that much, you know. I only really miss him on your behalf, if you know what I mean.'

For a moment Kate hoped that Tashie would turn towards her, to hug and be hugged as Sam, the uncomplicated, the young, had done. She stayed curled like a hedgehog, however, and only her hand came out and reached for Kate's. Kate, remembering her own teenage inhibitions and horror of adult emotion, accepted the movement for what it was. She squeezed the hand, and felt a returning squeeze.

'Sam's all right, isn't he? That operation, I mean? It's not dangerous, is it?'

'Not specially. It's the thought, more than anything. He's being very brave.' Too late, she wondered if Tashie would take this as a criticism, but fortunately she didn't.

'Yes. I'm sorry about tonight.'

Kate squeezed the hand again.

'Not a problem. You know I trust you, don't you?'

'Not to make wild, passionate love under the pier with Tommo?' Tashie was recovering.

'I can certainly trust you not to do anything so uncomfortable! That, though, and . . . well, whatever.'

There was a pause while Tashie struggled with her conscience.

'There's something I ought to tell you about. But not yet, I just can't. Is that all right?'

'Of course. Tell me when you're ready. Even if it's three o'clock in the morning.'

'And will you tell me things, too?' The voice was childish, but the plea was not.

'Darling, I'll tell you anything you want to know. I just didn't want to worry you.'

'Not knowing worries me.'

'Of course it does. I keep forgetting how grown-up you all are,' said Kate with a sigh. 'Well, the thing on my mind at the moment is the beastly insurance company. They're trying to get out of paying for Sam's operation.'

She told, in full, the tale of her conversation. Halfway through Tashie turned round and sat up straight.

'But that's ridiculous! How dare they!'

'Very easily, I'm afraid.'

'But Sam's got to have this done. Can't we sell something, raise the money somehow, and fight to get it back off them afterwards?'

'It's too much, I'm afraid.' Kate told her the full amount, and Tashie, for once, was silenced. But not for long.

'Don't worry, Mum,' she said firmly. 'It'll be all right. You'll see.'

'Of course it will,' said Kate automatically. It did not occur to her until afterwards, when it was too late, that Tashie had spoken not in tones of encouragement, but as someone who means to make things happen. It did not occur to her, that is, until the following day when Tashie failed to return from school. When she discovered, in fact, that her daughter had left the school at the beginning of the morning, and that no one had seen her since she had left, her schoolbag bulging, at ten o'clock that morning.

Chapter 16

Tashie sat, once again, on the bus.

It was horribly familiar. If anyone had asked her, she would have said that she had scarcely any recollection of her previous journey to the cottage. At the time she had felt that she existed inside a bubble, an invisible skin that insulated her from her surroundings. A kind of mobile environment, such as might be worn in a science fiction book by a chlorine-breathing entity from the far reaches of the galaxy. Like that being, she had felt at once set apart from the world, and as though everyone she passed were staring at her. The cynosure of all eyes, as she had once read in a school set book. She wasn't very sure what a cynosure was, but she thought she was it.

In her efforts, then, to be invisible, she had looked around her as little as possible. The childish principle of 'I've got my eyes closed, and you can't see me' had seemed to make a certain amount of sense. If she was careful not to meet anyone's eyes then they might not notice or remember her. She had stared unseeingly out of the window, the countryside unreeling before her as artificially, to her, as if it were truly a back projection in a cheap sixties television programme.

In spite of that, her mind must have retained more than she knew. This second journey seemed to be an exact repeat of the first. The train journey, of course, was one she had done more times than she could count, since it was the beginning of the London line. She knew every house, every tree, every stretch of tunnel. The Balcombe Viaduct, usually a pleasure as it carried the train over fields and woods, was no more than an unpleasant reminder that she was nearly there. At Three Bridges the station was empty, the commuters and schoolchildren long since gone, even the cheap-day-return shoppers in London already revelling in the exhausting delights of Oxford Street. She walked out of the sloping tunnel, the sound of her feet on the concrete floor bouncing off the white plastic panels of the walls, past a sandwich bar where the smell of frying bacon should have been appetising but today turned her stomach. A little florist's kiosk, bright with bunched flowers, made her think not of celebrations and gifts but of funerals, and her aching head swam.

As she walked down the long busy roads to the bus station her arms ached. The carrier bag with her school clothes and shoes inside had not seemed heavy when she set out, but now she kept having to change hands. The plastic bag cut into her fingers even through her gloves, her fingers stiffened and cramped with cold and strain.

If only she had been able to sleep, perhaps she wouldn't feel so peculiar now. Was it the memory of the endless hours of the night, when her thoughts had chased each other so fast in circles, that made her giddy now? The aching in legs and arms was tiredness too, surely. That, and the strain of trying to act normally this morning while her body wanted to be rushing about on the plan she had evolved during the night. She had turned over and over in bed, sweating, seeking a position where her body might be able to relax into sleep.

Her mouth dry, she had drunk endless glasses of water and then needed several trips to the bathroom. Out of bed she shivered, back in bed she was soon too hot again. Pictures of her father as she had last seen him, of Sam on an operating table while faceless men in white coats drilled into his skull, of her mother's controlled face, floated before her eyes, stretching and deforming like cartoons. She felt bloated with anger, with frustrated misery, with fear and with guilt. The turmoil within her demanded action, and with feverish energy she had planned.

It had been ridiculously easy. The clothes she wanted to change into went into her schoolbag, her books hidden under the bed. Going downstairs early she rifled at the back of the kitchen drawer for some carrier bags and the spare garage key. The garage, in a separate block at the end of the street, was used for general storage as well as for the cars. She was careful to leave at the normal time and without doing or saying anything out of the ordinary. At school she made sure her presence was verified, and sat like a zombie through the first lesson before going to her tutor, Miss Lambert.

'I don't feel well. Can I go home?'

Miss Lambert looked at her. A sleepless night had left Tashie pale, with pink-rimmed eyes. An experienced woman, Miss Lambert knew how easily teenage girls who wanted a day off school could think themselves into looking really quite ill. She was wise to most of the tricks – the skilful application of make-up, the mouth rinsed with hot water to register a temperature on a thermometer, the difficult-to-disprove period pains, the tears – and she thought Tashie was probably genuine. She was aware, too, of her father's departure and Sam's health problems, and was not unsympathetic to the strains Tashie must be feeling.

'Off you go, then. Is anyone at home? Should I give your mother a ring?'

'She's at home,' said Tashie listlessly. 'You can ring her if you want, but I'd rather not worry her. She's got a lot of things on her mind at the moment. My brother's got to have an operation.' This was, she thought, rather clever. Nothing would be more likely to arouse suspicion than a downright refusal of a telephone call. She was right.

'Yes, I'd heard. I'm very sorry, Tashie. You know you can always come to me, if you need someone to talk to. Don't try to carry it all yourself.'

Tashie looked at her with a blank gaze that concealed her contempt. With the arrogance of fifteen she could not imagine how this, to her, dried-up old spinster could possibly think she might be able to help her. How, come to that, could anyone help her? Her life, once so sheltered and boringly predictable and safe, had turned into a nightmare labyrinth of dead ends, traps and pitfalls, with all the paths that had been direct now deceptive and probably leading in entirely the wrong direction. Her anger and hatred had been directed against everyone: her father, his other wife, her mother, her brothers, and most of all herself. She wanted to lash out, to hurt as she was hurting. Someone must pay for all this, and Phoebe was the obvious target. An easy target, too, since Tashie now knew where she lived, and even still had in her possession the key her father had given her and forgotten to ask for again.

The need to complete what she had planned made it easy for Tashie. She gave a little brave smile.

'Thank you, Miss Lambert. It's really kind of you. I'll bear it in mind.'

Miss Lambert, whose mind-reading skills were tolerably well developed, sighed internally. Would they come to her more readily, she sometimes wondered, if she were to highlight her hair and wear trendy clothes instead of the sensible skirt and flat shoes that were so comfortable and practical? Probably not. Children and young people had an unerring instinct for these things, and would see them for what they were, a veneer covering, but not hiding, a person who had without regrets abandoned the search for a husband and children of her own in favour of caring, endlessly, for the children of others.

Tashie, she thought, was very much in need of someone to talk to. It was in fact no accident that Miss Lambert had been picked as her tutor – she was frequently asked to take the more difficult ones and

Tashie, even before the present troubles, had never been easy. In strong contrast to her elder brother she was in general self-absorbed to the degree that one member of staff had wondered, quite seriously, whether she might be mildly autistic. Miss Lambert, more experienced, had correctly put it down to her age and her father's spoiling. She was one of the few members of staff on whom his charm had not worked, and was consequently unsurprised by his disappearance.

It might be that Tashie would one day see beyond the dowdy clothes to the generous spirit within, and talk to her tutor. That time, however, had not yet come, and Miss Lambert was too wise to press her. She therefore nodded to Tashie's assurances with an appearance of bland acceptance, and let her go. It was true that the girl looked far from well, and there had already been several cases of what looked like a nasty 'flu virus that morning.

Feeling pleasantly superior, Tashie left the school and headed towards home. On the way she stopped at a public telephone. It was carefully chosen, on a quiet corner where the only background noise would be passing traffic. Pushing in a pound coin – it would never do to run out of money before the call was over – she dialled the number, scarcely needing to check it on the little corner of paper she had copied it on. When Phoebe answered her stomach lurched, but she clenched her muscles tight and spoke. Only the high pitch of her voice betrayed her nerves, and the woman would not know it was different. She thought once again that she had been rather clever, and a warm glow replaced, for a little while, the block of ice that seemed to have formed within her.

She walked on, using a longer route that would take her down streets she never normally took on the journey to and from school. It meant she approached her road from a different direction, further from the house and nearer the garage. By the garage block she paused and checked down the street, but seeing no one she knew she let herself in and pulled the door to behind her, leaving a crack for light. It was cold and dank, and she shivered as she changed out of uniform and into her own things.

At the bus station she found what was surely the same bus, driven by the same man whose moustache, forgotten earlier, now assumed the status of an old acquaintance as it twitched over a smile. Her fellow passengers were surely identical too. There was the woman in the brown coat with a bulging basket and knitted hat. The old man who smelled of cigarettes and fried food, like a walking chip shop. The fat woman whose ankles overflowed her shoes and who had a laugh like water going down a drain, and a smile as sweet and innocent as a baby's. The young woman with the toddler in a pushchair who looked, through the encrustation of snot, as though he had more experience of the seamier side of life than the fat woman.

They couldn't really be the same people, of course, Tashie told herself. The looks of recognition she thought she had seen on their faces could be no more than her imagination playing tricks. Looking out of the bus window at the winter landscape, she told herself that no one would possibly remember one ordinary-looking girl on a bus. Nevertheless, she pushed the bag containing the distinctive uniform further out of sight beneath her seat, and slouched down, her head lowered.

As before, she left the bus early and walked. Once her memory betrayed her, and she found herself heading into a newly built housing estate, the gardens still raw earth or, worse, planted with straggly, depressed-looking twiggy shrubs. Hastily she turned and left – such a place could be full of watching eyes behind the swagged and frilled net curtains that veiled each window. Back on course she stopped, yet again, to change the carrier bag to the other hand, and to check for about the hundredth time that the key was still in her pocket. She could not acknowledge that she rather wished to find it gone. It was not. She could feel its shape through the fabric of pocket and gloves.

In the lane leading to the cottage her feeling of being overlooked increased, but she told herself it was still just imagination. Her head was aching badly by now, so that she had trouble locating the key in the lock, and her stomach was churning. She swallowed, then wished she hadn't as the movement of her throat muscles made her stomach heave. Dropping the carrier bag she ran by instinct and memory to the downstairs cloakroom, and was violently sick. Afterwards, when she had rinsed her mouth and face with cold water, she wondered why she had bothered to find a lavatory. A nice puddle of sick in the middle of the new carpet would have been a good start to trashing the house. She went back to the door for her carrier bag.

She had pushed the door roughly shut behind her, but the corner of the bag had caught and she had to open the door to free it. Outside in the porch, where she had not seen it before, stood a red plastic can, the kind her mother carried in the boot of her car in case she ran out of petrol. It seemed to glow with a lurid light of its own, and almost without knowing what she was doing Tashie put out her hand and picked it up. It sloshed heavily: when she unscrewed the cap and gave a cautious sniff, the unmistakable reek of petrol fumes made her eyes water and her stomach heave again. Hastily she replaced the cap, then edged back into the house and shut the door behind her. The petrol can was still in her hand.

Tashie shivered again. One of the pictures that had haunted her night had been of the cottage in all its perfection. Everything newly bought, carefully arranged. Curtains, carpets and soft furnishings spotless, antique wood polished to a deep reflective shine, the glitter of silver and copper and brass handles. Tashie's body had twitched as she imagined what she would like to do to it, how she would smash and tear and defile. Now, in her hand, she had the power to do more than that. A great deal more. The thought terrified her, and it was the terror that drove her to take the can upstairs with her, along with her carrier bag.

It was all just as she remembered it from last time. Tidy, pretty without being over-decorated, it could have been lifted from the pages of a magazine. Tashie, remembering her mother's lonely bed behind a screen in her grandmother's room, let the rage she felt boil over, frothing and spitting and steaming. Without even bothering to look for anything of value she wrenched open cupboards and drawers, sweeping the contents out wholesale to be trampled on the floor.

She had imagined, all the time, that it would give her pleasure. What she felt, instead, was disgust. The fabrics, good quality wools and cottons and silks, faintly perfumed or smelling of clean washing, felt unpleasant against her skin. She wanted to think that the clothes themselves were slimy and defiled, but knew that it was her own touch which was that. The more she did, the dirtier she felt. Often, as a small child, she had revelled in being dirty. Mud, paint, jam, all had been happily plastered over clothes and body, face and hands. The naughtiness, the certainty of a scolding followed by a warm bath, so that she ended feeling clean and fresh and cherished, had been a pleasure unlike any other.

She had thought it would be like that, only more so. A cleansing, a catharsis, from her hatred and her anger. Instead the emotions changed, became warped and unclean instead of hot and righteous. She felt dirty but the dirtiness came from within her, from the feelings she could scarcely control. Her stomach heaved again, but she had nothing left to vomit and she swallowed the sour saliva in her mouth, continuing grimly with her self-imposed task. The more she hated what she was doing, the more she felt compelled to continue it. The hatred and disgust fed on itself and on her actions, in a self-perpetuating spiral of despair.

Then she caught sight of her father's face. It was like a buffet of icy wind, or a cold wave crashing over her head. His photograph stood, in a pretty silver frame, on the dressing table. Open, smiling, the loving face she had thought he kept for her alone. Even in black and white it seemed to glow with life and energy.

The memory of her last glimpse of him rose in her mind as the vomit had risen in her throat, unwanted, burning, horrible. With the diamond set safely hidden in a left luggage locker and the key to it tucked into her boot, she had met him at Victoria station. She had insisted on a public place, though he had been reluctant, because she had had a week to think things over and did not mean to give him what he wanted without getting something in return. He had tried to talk her round, but had crumbled in the face of her stony resistance to every trick of cajolery or bluster he could summon. She did not fear him, and though she had loved him deeply she had never respected him as she did her mother, so the habit of obedience was lacking.

They met, not in the station, but in the shopping mall behind it. He had been waiting for her at the top of the escalator, a place so open to public view that his choice of it was a signal of his desperation. As before, they had gone for a meal and coffee.

'You have got it, haven't you?' His first words showed his anxiety.

'Yes, I've got it.'

His relief was all too apparent. He relaxed enough to eat the food she bought him, but when at the end of it she showed no sign of handing over what he wanted, he grew restless.

'Well, what about it? You did say you've got it, didn't you.'

'Yes, I've got it. I've put it somewhere safe. I must know, Dad. You must tell me what you're going to do.'

He glanced round, as if expecting the whole of the restaurant to be listening to his every word. Leaning forward, he fixed his eyes earnestly on her face.

'I'm going abroad, Tashie. This country's had it, let's face it. Economy's up the spout, government's incompetent, even the cows are bloody well mad. The old Communist bloc countries, they're the place to be.'

'They're hardly models of order and economic stability.' He looked surprised. This acerbic and incisive Tashie was not the daughter he was used to.

'No, they're not, but at least they *know* they're not. They're in a state of flux, they need people with expertise, ability – there's a lot I could achieve, there. I've got contacts, too. All I need is a bit of money, to get me started. I've a bit put by here and there round the world, but I can't get at it until I can scrape enough together to go and recover it. That's where the diamonds come in. So you see . . .'

'Yes. Yes, I see. And where does that leave us, precisely?'

'You? Surely your mother's got all that under control? You said—'

'I know I did. And she has. But what about the future? Where does she stand?'

'You mean, am I coming back? Darling, of course I am! Just give me a few months, a couple of years maybe, and then see! I'll come back, and make it all up to you! To all of you!'

His eyes shone. He really believed it. Tashie could have wept, but she wouldn't give in to that kind of weakness in front of him.

'You won't be coming back,' she said stonily. 'Whatever happens, it won't be that, and you know it. If you show up again, particularly if you show up with money, the bank will be on to you.'

'So . . . so I'll stay abroad. Find somewhere wonderful. Sunshine, beaches, palm trees. You can all come and join me.'

It was so much like her earlier imaginings that Tashie was disgusted.

'And if we don't want to?'

He blinked.

'Then you won't come. But, princess . . .'

She saw that he was putting on an appearance of minding, but that in fact he had already moved on. She did not doubt that he would miss her, miss them all, but the moments of sadness would be passing ones. They would also, she knew, be something he would make use of, to work on others' sympathies. She felt sickened.

'No, Dad. We won't be coming, and we won't want to. So, if you want your new life, if you want the diamonds' – he hushed her frantically with his hands, but she continued unregarding – 'then there has to be a *quid pro quo*. Remember the *quid pro quo*, Daddy?'

His sadness, this time, was genuine. The phrase had been a private joke. Tashie, he would say, little princess, I've got a small *quo* for you. And there would be a little job, like fetching something he had forgotten, or making him a cup of tea, and in exchange a pound coin, always new and shiny as a foil-covered chocolate sovereign, for her to put in her money box. There you are, princess, there's your *quid* . . .

'Oh, my darling . . .'

'No, Dad. I'm giving the *quid* this time, against your *quo*. And the *quo* is, that you sign this.' She produced the paper she had laboured over for half the night. He read it through. Disbelief, amusement, sadness and something else that she recognised, without much difficulty, as calculation, chased each other across his face. In simple language, as clear and unequivocal as she could make it, the paper stated that he, Leonard Miller, would not contest any attempt by his wife to divorce him, and would at no time make any claims on her or his children. 'I know it's probably not legally binding,' she said, 'but it should stand for something.'

'What are you going to do with it?' She noticed that for the first time ever he was speaking to her adult to adult, and was both saddened and elated.

'Keep it. Give it to Mum, when the time is right.'

'She wants a divorce?'

'I don't know. Probably. Perhaps not yet.'

'Is there . . . has she?'

'I don't think you have any right to ask, but no, as a matter of fact, she hasn't. I shouldn't be surprised if you've put her off men for life.' Tashie suppressed the thought of what she had until this moment scarcely noticed, the frequent telephone calls that Brian Harper made to her mother, and his visits. 'I just don't see why she should be tied to you for however many years it is before she can have a divorce. So as well as signing this, I want your promise that you will contact us once a year, minimum. At Christmas, perhaps. Or New Year. That might be appropriate.'

'Angel, of course I'll be in contact! How can you say such a thing! And more than once a year, too!'

'Really?' Tashie's sarcastic tones came through a tight throat, as she remembered the previous Christmas and New Year. 'I wonder why I don't find it altogether easy to believe that?'

'Tashie . . .' He shook his head. 'You hate me, don't you?' His voice, the rich voice which she had always loved and which he used as some used a musical instrument, to play on emotions, dropped even deeper.

'No. No, of course I don't. I just don't like you very much, at the moment. So, will you sign it?'

In the end, of course, he had. There was no choice, since he needed to get the diamonds from her. At the end, saying goodbye, she had clung to him for a moment, feeling the familiar shape beneath the unfamiliar clothes and the alien smell of him. As he walked off he had turned to wave, smiling.

'See you soon!' he had called. 'Very soon, Tashie! I'll call you, send you a ticket, something . . .' His smile expressed boundless confidence, and like a mother seeing her child off to his first day of school she had forced herself to smile back.

Now the same smile looked up at her from the photograph. With a moan she snatched it up, staring at it. She wanted to clutch it to her. She wanted, also, to tear it into little pieces. She wrenched at the frame, but her hands were shaking too much to find the trick of undoing the back. In the end she dropped it, too, on the floor, and stamped hard. Beneath the solid sole of her boot the glass shattered with a satisfying crunch, as good as wet shingle on the beach or scissors slicing through thick hair.

She turned her foot, grinding the grass into splinters so that the photograph below would be sliced, torn into confetti. No, not confetti, that was for weddings. Into chewed-up fragments fit only for burning or putting into the kitchen bin with the eggshells, the bits of chewed gristle and bone, the muddy potato peelings and the soggy teabags. The frame twisted, jagged edges of silver scratching on the leather of her boot, so that she had to kick it off like a sticky sweet wrapper, discarded and trodden on in the street.

That made her feel a bit better. Grimly she returned to her task. After this room she would go to the bathroom, tip out all the bottles on to the carpet and trample them in, smash the mirrors and the flasks of perfume. Downstairs, she would attack the kitchen, use what she found in cupboards and fridge to mess up carpets and cushions in sitting room and hall. She had glimpsed a conservatory – the windows there would be at the back, it would be possible to smash them without anyone seeing or hearing from the lane. There would be knives and scissors in the kitchen, too, perhaps even a cleaver that would ruin the delicate surfaces of antique furniture. And after all that, the petrol.

Her head was fiery hot, spinning and bursting with it all. She was so rarely ill that she failed to realise that she had a raging fever, that the demons within her were the product of her churning emotions heated to white hot in the furnace of a high temperature. She was no longer sure whether she had already done the things she envisaged, so clear were the images in her mind. She saw herself taking the top off the can, heard the gurgle as she poured and splashed the petrol, smelled the sharp reek of it, a smell she had always hated. This time, however, she would not hate it. This time it would be a clean smell, like polish or new paint. It would be the smell of a pyre, of a cleansing flame that would destroy all the dirtiness and disgust. The fire would consume all the pain, all the hatred and fury. She would be free, they would all be free. Even this woman, whom she had never met and could only imagine, would be free and it seemed to Tashie, then, that she should be grateful.

Tashie stood in the middle of the room. She saw herself surrounded by flames, heard the crackle of burning, smelled the smoke. In her mind she moved through the flickering orange tongues unconsumed, the flames following her, doing her bidding, rising and falling to her gestures.

Then the madness receded. She saw, instead, herself on fire. Hair and clothes burning, her arms flailing in a useless attempt to put out the flames. She wailed aloud, feeling her skin crisp and curl, her flesh melt from her white-hot bones. She put her hands up to her face, half expecting to feel the bones of her skull, but found instead smooth familiar skin. Her face was hot, her hands cold, and their touch was soothing. She held them to cheeks and forehead, pressed icy fingertips against her eyes, and the nightmare faded.

She remembered, at last, what she had really come for. The destruction was secondary, what mattered was her mother, and Sam. She must concentrate on that – later, perhaps, there would be time for punishment and revenge. For now she must find anything valuable, and portable. There would be silver downstairs, she had seen a few pieces in hall and dining room, she could use the plastic bag to carry them in. And up here, the jewellery. No longer the diamond set, unfortunately, but there would be other things.

Lowering her hands from her face, she went unerringly to the drawer where she had, on that earlier day, found the jewellery cases. Methodically she took them out, all but the one from which she had taken the diamond set, and opened them. She didn't bother to check the contents – she herself would never have believed that the other pieces were real stones. One by one, the boxes were emptied into her hand and then into her pockets. She was so absorbed in her task that she quite failed to hear the sound of the front door being unlocked. The faint noise of footsteps on the stairs was masked by her own rasping breathing. It was not until the door was pushed wide that she looked up to see retribution, in the shape of two female figures, confronting her.

Chapter 17

Surprisingly, the effect on Phoebe of her abortive trip to Canterbury was not as disastrous as she would have expected. She came home on Sunday evening with the beginnings of a heavy cold, caught no doubt by getting thoroughly chilled after hours spent in the Dane John gardens. Sneezing and shivering, she nevertheless found that the crushing depression she would have expected to feel had not overwhelmed her. Tentatively examining her mind, like someone with a lost filling tenderly exploring the cavity for twinges, she found that she felt, if anything, peaceful. Not happy, of course, not even optimistic. But able to accept the present, if not to look forward to the future.

As she opened the front door of her house she felt the welcoming warmth of the heating. The air, though a bit dead after two days of emptiness, smelled sweetly of the bowls of hyacinths everywhere. It was pleasant to be home, pleasant to kick off her shoes, to fill the kettle for tea and to look forward to supper on a tray by the fire. Although it was eight o'clock she did not, as she would have done the previous week, pour herself a drink. This too she noted with a kind of astonished pride, as a kind of achievement.

She was very tired. The past two days had been spent almost entirely in the Dane John gardens, where it had been too cold to think of sitting down, or even standing still for long. A brisk wind had cleared away the clouds, and a pale blue sky hung, fragile as an eggshell, over the ancient walls and the distant tower of the cathedral. The deep tolling of the cathedral clock, sounding through the hum of traffic, seemed like a natural phenomenon, as though some giant were striking the dome of the heavens. Grass and trees were crisped with frost that lingered in the shadows, slate blue.

On Saturday Phoebe had scarcely left the gardens, going for a quick cup of coffee or bowl of soup only when her feet and hands were numb, and her head aching from the cold. On Sunday morning, in a spirit of rebellion, she had gone to the cathedral. Not to ask for help or favours – it seemed unreasonable, since she was not sure that she believed in God, to expect him to bother with her – but simply to be with people in the serene beauty of the old building. There were signs outside the doors, warning tourists that they could not visit. Hesitantly, she slipped inside.

'I'm afraid the cathedral is closed for services, madam.' A man in black cassock and a blue gown eyed the bulky clothes she had put on for the gardens, and summed her up as a tourist.

'Um, I wanted to come to a service, actually. I'm afraid I'm not very suitably dressed . . .'

His face softened into a smile.

'You don't need to worry about that. Very few people dress up now, even for the cathedral. And the heating, you may have noticed, isn't always up to the weather, though we do what we can. Do you want cathedral mattins, or school eucharist?'

'I don't know.' Phoebe must have looked as helpless as she felt.

'Cathedral mattins is a spoken service, in the choir. School eucharist – that's the King's School, you know? – is a sung eucharist, in the crypt. It's a bit longer, of course, but if you like the music . . .'

'Oh, yes. But I'm not a parent or anything, and dressed like this . . .'

'It's open to visitors, and frankly, half the parents turn up in jeans, nowadays. You can go down these stairs, or round the outside.'

Phoebe went down the stairs and stood, bewildered, at the bottom. The pillared crypt was full of young people, girls as well as boys. Both looked formal in black jackets and grey striped trousers or skirts, the boys with black ties below their winged collars, the girls with enamelled brooches instead. Serious and intent, with a few recalcitrant groups of whisperers and gigglers, they were filling in the rows of chairs. Seeing her lost, a boy with a purple robe over his uniform came up to her.

'Do you need any help? Are you looking for someone, your son or daughter?'

'No, I'm not a parent. I just wanted to come to the service. I don't know where to sit . . . I don't want to be too conspicuous.'

'I shouldn't worry about that. But you'll need an order of service, and things. They're over by the door, I'll show you.'

Phoebe walked with him. His purple robe rippled as he went, and she eyed it with fascination. People melted from their path. She felt as though she were being ushered by a minor deity.

'Are you in the choir?' she hazarded.

'Good lord, no! The choir master at my prep school said I had all the musical skill of a hedge-trimmer,' he responded cheerfully. 'No, the robe means I'm a monitor. Like a prefect,' he amplified. 'Black robes are the scholars. The choir don't wear anything. Well, they wear their uniforms. Pity, really.'

'Yes, a naked choir would add a certain frisson to the proceedings.'

'They'd be doing more than frisson-ing. It's bloody cold out there. And I don't suppose the dean would like it.' He still sounded regretful. Phoebe felt her spirits rise.

'The headmaster might not care for it either.'

'No. Though you never know with the Duck. He may be strict, but he's a bit of a free spirit, underneath.'

'The Duck?' Did he waddle? Quack? Play cricket?

The boy pushed out his lips.

'You'll know when you see him. He'll be preaching, he's a canon.'

'Not a loose one, I hope.' Phoebe was beginning to feel a bit lightheaded.

'Well, you wouldn't expect him to be tight, would you? Particularly not on a Sunday morning.' Phoebe laughed. There couldn't be much wrong, she thought, with a school that could produce a young man of this calibre.

'There you are,' he said, giving her a printed booklet and a red service book. 'Why don't you sit there? Not too near the front, and if you stay at this end you can make a quick getaway. Or a break for freedom, if it all gets too much for you.'

'Do you think it might?' His perception was alarming.

'Only if you're another hedge-trimmer,' he said soothingly. 'Anyway, I hope you enjoy it. If one's supposed to enjoy this sort of thing. Be uplifted, perhaps.'

'I could do with a bit of uplift.' Phoebe felt a bit sad and pathetic, but he grinned at her.

'Then I hope it helps,' he said, smiling as he walked away.

The service was surprisingly moving, given that Phoebe almost never went to church and had to struggle with unfamiliar words. She was a bit daunted by the modernity of the language, and was amused to feel slightly affronted by finding herself addressing the Almighty as 'You' rather than the 'Thee' and 'Thou' of her childhood memories. It seemed rather a social lapse, like calling an older person *tu* in France when you'd only just met them. She told herself briskly that God, if He existed, would scarcely be worried by notions of etiquette.

The headmaster preached, not from a pulpit (there wasn't one in the low-ceilinged crypt) but from a simple wooden lectern placed in the front of the aisle. Phoebe smiled to herself when she saw him, for it was true that his lips were full enough to make the comparison with a duck's beak not altogether out of the question. He spoke, however, in a voice that was vigorous, and would have been harsh if it had not been so sonorous. Phoebe, prepared to be bored or to switch off her attention, found herself listening intently. He spoke with devastating clarity and precision, his reasoning direct and his arguments succinct. Phoebe found herself following his words intently, carried along by the force of his certainty.

When it came to the communion itself, she had intended to stay in her chair, but went instead, book in her hand to show that she was not taking the bread and wine, to receive a blessing. There was no altar rail; they stood in a semi-circle between the ancient carved pillars. The words the headmaster spoke over her were equally firm: she felt that he was not merely repeating a formula, and also that any God worth His salt must surely be paying attention.

The singing, from the (fully dressed) choir, was effortlessly beautiful, the young voices filling the pillared space, ebbing and flowing like tidal water in a grotto. At the end she left in the middle of a crowd of chattering boys and girls who carried her up the echoing ramp and out of the door into the cloisters. She went back to the Dane John gardens and felt somehow insulated from the cold, as if wrapped in a protective cloak. At lunchtime, instead of swallowing a quick bowl of soup, she went to an Italian restaurant in Castle Street that Ann Davies had recommended. After a dish of pasta *al arrabbiata* that was hot with chilli as well as the oven, and half a carafe of house red, she went glowing back to the gardens.

An hour later she saw, in the distance, a figure that looked heart-stoppingly familiar. Leo, she thought. Surely that's Leo. She started to move towards him, her pulse thrumming through her body and her skin netted with electrical tingling. It was not until she drew nearer and saw that it was not Leo at all, but someone of the same build and with a similar walk, that she realised that what she was feeling was not joy or even excitement, but dread. The realisation came after the acknowledgement that when she saw it was not Leo she was overwhelmed with a flood of relief.

After that she stayed until it was fully dark, but more out of a sense of duty than from conviction. When, at last, she walked on numb feet out of the gardens and back down the High Street, all she felt was pleasure that the ordeal was over, and anticipation of the hot cup of tea she intended to have before driving home. She rather regretted not having said that she would stay another night at Magnolia House, since she could have gone straight back to a hot shower, but her things were packed into the car and it didn't seem worth the upheaval. Her journey back, with the heater on at full blast, was easy and fast, and she entered her cottage with a sense of being welcomed home.

Unpacking, she came upon the silver-framed photograph of Leo that she had taken with her. Before he had left it had stood on the bedside table where she would see it as soon as she opened her eyes in the morning – a habit she had acquired during the time when he had supposedly been abroad during the week, and had somehow never changed. Now, taking the picture from her suitcase, she looked at it with distant sadness. She almost felt like putting it away in a drawer, out of sight, but ended up standing it on the dressing table. It was a small difference, but significant to her, and she felt pleased.

This feeling of tranquillity lasted into the beginning of the next week. Although tired – her legs ached from the hours of walking up and down – she felt invigorated. The house was cleaned from top to bottom, and she even found herself thinking of changing things, renewing the decorations to make the place properly hers alone. Until now the lottery money, although it had saved her from being homeless, had also cushioned her too much. She had been able to afford to take refuge in food, to dull her misery with drink, and to hide herself from the world. Cocooned in the silken toils of riches she had been able to snuggle self-indulgently in the fusty warmth of her own misery. Now the cold of the Dane John gardens had cut through those cobwebby clouds.

As a first step to confronting the outside world, Phoebe telephoned Jennifer Dobson. Jennifer had accepted Phoebe's frequent rejections of her well-intentioned offers of help with equanimity: straightforward herself, she never took offence at others' plain speaking. Besides, her days were already so full that she scarcely needed more responsibilities. However, she was not immune to curiosity, and accepted an invitation to lunch with alacrity.

Phoebe, to her own astonishment, found herself telling the whole story. Jennifer's face was a study in conflicting emotions: disbelief, amazement, pity, envy and, finally, inadequately suppressed hilarity, flitted over her weatherbeaten features. Phoebe looked at her, and felt her own laughter fizzing in her chest. Her lips quivered, then she gave a little laugh. Jennifer gave a snort, and within a few seconds they were both whooping with hysterical laughter. If some of the tears that ran down Phoebe's cheeks were not of laughter, they still had their cathartic effect.

'Oh, dear!' Jennifer mopped her eyes with her sleeve, and sniffed. 'Oh, dear, I'm sorry to laugh. And of course it's not funny. Not funny at a-a-all . . .' She wailed into laughter again, then sobered. 'Poor you. It must have been awful.'

'Yes, it was. And the worst thing, looking back, is that I've been such a fool. I accepted it all – being away all week, not having any family or even any friends, not wanting people to see him – without even wondering, let alone asking, whether he was up to something. And the money, too . . . it was all so easy. Too easy.'

'Gift horses, my dear. We'd all be the same.'

'What *is* it you find when you look in a horse's mouth? I've never been too sure.'

'In his case, a set of false teeth, I should think.'

'Yes! The joke sort comedians use, that clatter.' Phoebe mimed the movement with her fingers and thumb. 'What is it they say? All talk and no trousers?'

'Red hat, no knickers, my grandmother used to say. That was rather different, though. Or was it?'

'His wife – his real wife – calls him Len,' said Phoebe meditatively. 'I thought Leo was rather distinguished, but Len . . . if I'd known he was called that, I don't know that I'd ever have married him.'

'Well, you certainly wouldn't if you'd known it was his wife who called him that. What's she like? I mean, forgive me, it's awful for you but it must have been ten times worse for her. Three children, and no lovely lottery money.'

Phoebe felt a pang of guilt.

'Yes, I suppose so. I'm afraid I've not thought of her much. Too busy being sorry for myself, I suppose.' She pulled a face, despising herself.

'Not surprising. If I were her I'd resent you quite a lot. And I expect you resent her.'

'No, I just feel guilty about her, though I know it wasn't really my fault. The trouble is, you can't help disliking the people you feel guilty about. Do you suppose I ought to do something? See if she's all right for money, I mean? After all, I can afford it.'

'I should think she'd say no thank you, in spades. That wouldn't just be salt in the wound, it would be sulphuric acid, I'd say.'

'Yes. Oh dear, what a mess. Bloody, bloody man. Bloody men, come to that. Thoughtless. Selfish. Unreliable.'

'Oh, come on, not all of them. Though of course,' Jennifer mused, 'women *are* more reliable, generally. Though for reliability, give me a dog any day. Or a horse. You know where you are with a horse.'

'On your bottom in a ditch?'

Jennifer grinned. 'But that's *never* the horse's fault! Seriously, though. Do you ride? It's good exercise.' She eyed Phoebe assessingly, as though she were planning to enter her for a dressage class.

'And I could do with some exercise, I know. I did have some lessons, as a child, but it was in town, all streets and parks. All right, then. I'll have a go, if you'll teach me.'

'Splendid! Oh bother, look at the time, I've got to fetch the girls in twenty minutes, I must dash. I'll give you a ring later, we'll sort something out. Are you free tomorrow?'

'Tomorrow, and tomorrow, and tomorrow.'

'I know that,' said Jennifer proudly. 'It's Shakespeare. Or is it the Bible? Anyway, it's a quotation. Perhaps you'll be able to educate me, in return for riding. I was a complete dunce at school, spent my whole time drawing horses' heads and reading those pony books.'

'It doesn't seem to have done you any harm. Look at you, nice husband, lovely daughters, beautiful house, position in the community . . .'

'Blah blah blah. It's all just luck. The run of the cards.'

'The rub of the green.'

'The fall of the dice.'

'The great lottery of life. There you are, I've used up all my luck in one go, winning the lottery.'

'If you call that lucky. I know, it saved you from losing the cottage, but otherwise? I'd say the luckiest thing was that Leo – Len – left you when he did.'

'Luckier if I'd never met him.'

'Do you think so? It's all experience, isn't it? Would you really want to have one of those lives that just potters on day after day, with nothing new and exciting? I'm not sure I would.'

'Is anyone's life like that?'

'Some must be. I've always assumed that's how it is, for most people. The ones you don't hear about.'

'Ah, but it's the people like that who suddenly slaughter all their relatives, or run amok with a machine gun or something. The ones whose neighbours say they kept themselves to themselves, and never did much.'

'Well, you won't need to do that, will you? That's a comfort.'

'It certainly is. You'd better go, you'll be late for the girls. What are you doing, having them shod?'

'More or less, only the other end. Orthodontist, to have train tracks fitted to their teeth. Hideous expense, and they'll do nothing but get mouth ulcers and moan, and refuse to smile for photographs.'

'Chewing gum.'

'What is?'

'I mean, give them chewing gum. When it's chewed out, they can stick little bits of it over the sharp places, protect their mouths. No mouth ulcers.'

'Brilliant! Is that what they teach you at teachers' training colleges these days?'

'Nothing so useful, I'm afraid. In my day it was all "surround them with beautiful things, and they will want to learn". You must *go*!'

'Yes, I must. Ring you later. Byeee!'

There was a clomping sound as Jennifer stamped her feet back into her boots, and she was gone. Phoebe sat back in her chair, amazed. She would never have imagined that she could make a friend of Jennifer but somehow, just like that, she had done.

The telephone rang the following morning, just as Phoebe was about to go riding with Jennifer. Standing in the hall in an ancient pair of jeans that were uncomfortably tight round the waist, and a disreputable but warm anorak over a pullover, she almost didn't bother to answer it. Only the thought that it might be Millie made her hesitate, and pick it up.

'Mrs . . . Miller?' A girl's voice, slightly breathless, lacking the polished boredom of a telesales person.

'Yes?' It occurred to Phoebe, not for the first time, that she really had no right to that name, and that it was time she did something about it. She thought with a sinking heart of all the forms she would have to fill, the letters to write.

'Mrs Miller.' The girl repeated the name with emphasis. 'I have a message for you. From . . . someone.'

'Well, it would be, wouldn't it?' Irritated by the prospect of the forms and letters, Phoebe was in no mood to be patient.

'He doesn't want me to use his name, in case anyone's listening. He said you'd know who it was.'

'If anyone's listening, I'd have thought that all sounded far more suspicious than if you'd just said his name.' The sharp answer came from the top of her mind. Underneath she was thinking, feverishly. Oh no. Not again. I don't want to hear from him again.

'I'm just doing what he said.' The young voice was plaintive.

'Sorry. But I'm not sure that I really want to hear from – whoever it is. Why did he ask you to call? Why not do it himself?'

'In case anyone's listening,' the girl repeated, with a touch of impatience. 'I don't know why. I don't know anything about it. He just said to tell you to come to Brighton, now, as soon as possible, and meet him on the pier. In the hall where the machines are.'

'Machines?' Phoebe wasn't really concentrating.

'The ones you play on. They're in a big room in the middle of the pier.'

'And I have to go there now?'

'Yes. Straightaway. He said it was urgent. He said he had things he must tell you, explain.'

'Is he there? Can I speak to him?'

'No, he's gone. He gave me the message and the money, and went.'

'And who are you?'

'Me?' The voice was wary. 'I'm no one. Just someone he met. Listen, are you coming, or not?'

'Oh yes, I'll come. Of course I'll come.'

'Right, then.' The girl rang off. She had sounded oddly relieved, for someone who was just giving a message for a stranger. Phoebe put the phone down, then picked it up again and dialled four numbers. The recorded voice enunciated in her ear: o one two seven three. That was the Brighton code, sure enough. She dialled a second time.

'Jennifer? I can't make it, I'm afraid. Sorry, but something's come up. I can't really explain just yet, but I've had rather a strange phone call. No, not *that* kind of strange. Not threatening either, no. Just . . . strange. I need to think about it. No, don't. We can't both let the horses down, poor things. I'll come tomorrow instead. Right. Bye.'

After that, she went upstairs to her bedroom and stood looking around for several minutes. While unpacking on Sunday evening she had once or twice felt the whisper of a suspicion that someone had been there. Nothing was missing, nothing was wrong, but it seemed to her that there were subtle changes in the position of things, that once or twice she caught a drift of an alien scent. She had discounted it as over-active imagination, but after that strange phone call, she wondered. Presently she took off her anorak and jumper, pulled on a thermal vest and leggings left over from an old ski-ing trip, then dressed again in salopettes. In the kitchen she filled a thermos with coffee and made sandwiches, then hunted in the hall cupboard for Leo's old binoculars. Everything went into a shopping bag. She left by the front door, shutting it loudly and conspicuously behind her and locking it, before setting off in the car down the lane to the village.

In the village she went into the shop, bought two newspapers, then stood near the door pretending to examine the choice of paperbacks on a revolving stand. The road outside was empty. Leaving, she drove briskly down the road and, after a swift glance behind her, swung into a farm track and parked out of sight of the road. Locking the car she took her basket and the newspapers, and cut across two fields. She ended up behind the hedge that bordered her lane, but on the opposite side to her cottage. A tree stump provided a convenient seat and was well hidden behind a thick patch of holly. With the newspapers as cushion and insulation – how lucky it was, she thought, that newspapers now had so many sections, even on week days – it was not too uncomfortable, and she could see enough of her gateway to know if someone came to it. They could, of course, get in through the back, but the hedged boundary was thickly grown and armed with fierce thorns, presenting a daunting prospect to all but an experienced pole-vaulter.

Time passed. A solitary dog trotted down the lane, looking purposeful. The sky was overcast, but it was dry and still, and less cold than Canterbury had been. After an hour, when she began to feel chilled, Phoebe took out the thermos and poured herself a mug of coffee.

'Having a picnic?' The voice behind her made her jump, and she had to choose between spitting out the coffee, and choking. She spat.

'Daphne!'

'Sorry. Couldn't resist it. Didn't mean to make you drown in your coffee.'

Phoebe wiped her chin.

'You frightened me half to death. I didn't hear you coming.'

'You were concentrating too hard on watching the lane to think about anything behind you.' With her habitual reticence Daphne refrained from asking, as most would, what on earth Phoebe thought she was doing. Phoebe shuffled sideways on her stump, rubbing at her numb buttocks.

'Sit down and join me. Have a coffee. Oh, no, sorry, I forgot you don't drink it. Well, sit down, anyway.' Daphne perched so that they were almost back to back. Millie, had she been there, would have remembered her first meeting with Daphne, and smiled. Phoebe still kept her eyes fixed on the lane. 'I haven't seen you for ages. I did come round to your cottage a couple of times, but you were out. Did you get my notes?'

'Yes. Thanks. And Sorry.' Daphne paused and Phoebe, sensing that she wanted to say something, waited. 'Been a bit under the weather, actually,' said Daphne finally, with some difficulty.

'Daphne! I'm so sorry. Why didn't you tell me? You weren't lying there in the cottage all the time, were you? Only the cats were all outside, and there was no smoke from the chimney, so I thought . . . oh, how awful!' Visions of Daphne lying immobilised, unable to light her fire, haunted Phoebe for a moment.

'No, no, nothing like that. As a matter of fact, I've been in hospital. Didn't want to tell anyone, just got a couple of people to go and feed the cats every day – they're pretty used to fending for themselves when they have to.'

'And are you all right now?' Phoebe hesitated to ask what had been wrong. She knew Daphne's dislike of being fussed over, and guessed that she had preferred to keep her health problems a secret.

'Fine.' Phoebe felt Daphne stir and stretch, was aware of her breathing in a long breath. 'Fact is, I found a bit of a lump, just before Christmas.' Her hand moved, touching her stomach. 'Quite a big one. Frightened me a bit.'

'I should think it would! Were you in pain? I did wonder, at Christmas.'

'Yes. Sorry about that. No, no pain. But that don't necessarily mean there's nothing wrong, I believe. Truth is, it put me in a bit of a panic. I don't mind *dying*, you see, but not like that . . . slowly, in a hospital, never *alone*. Yet I couldn't face getting something done about it. Daft, really. Thought I was more sensible than that.'

'I don't blame you. I'd have been in a blue funk too. I wish I could have helped you.'

'You did. After Christmas – I'd felt so sick and so terrified, I couldn't eat a thing and couldn't even talk – I realised I couldn't go on like that, so I went off to the quack and had it checked. He whipped me into hospital pretty smartly, and the long and the short of it is, it was a cyst. A damn big one. Size of a grapefruit, he said. But benign. Funny word, isn't it? Benign – makes it sound like Father Christmas. Still, there you are.'

Phoebe felt her eyes fill with tears.

'Daphne, I'm so glad. And you're all right now?'

'Right as rain. They made me go to some convalescent place afterwards, said I couldn't be on my own in the woods. Set me right back, that did. I never did like communal life. Still, I'm home now. Got back a couple of days ago, thought I'd come and see you. And here I find you, communing with nature on a tree stump. What *are* you doing, Phoebe?'

'I had a funny phone call from a girl, telling me to go to Brighton. It was supposed to be a message from Leo.'

'And you don't think it was?' Daphne pitched her voice quietly, not turning her head.

'I'm not sure. Last weekend I had a message to go to Canterbury, but he didn't turn up and I had a feeling there might have been someone in the cottage while I was away.'

'Leo?'

'No, I don't think so. It wasn't like that. I can't explain it, it's just a gut reaction. So I thought I'd just do a stake out. As it were.'

A small tremor of laughter shook Daphne's back.

'And how long have you been here?'

'About an hour and a half. I've got some sandwiches, too. Don't laugh.'

'I'm not laughing. I'll keep you company, in case it's a gang. What's in the sandwiches?'

'Cheese and chutney. Ham and mustard. And banana. Not all together.'

'Banana! I haven't had a banana sandwich for years.'

'Have one now.'

They munched in silence. Time went by. Looking at her watch, Phoebe saw that it was after three o'clock. She had been there for more than four hours. In another hour it would start to get dark. It was a chilling thought. She was uncomfortable, too, in other ways.

'I shouldn't have had that coffee,' said Phoebe after a while.

'Need a pee? Plenty of bushes over there. Or you could creep back to the house?'

'No, that would spoil the whole point of it. Bushes it is.' Moving as quietly as she could, Phoebe crept to where a patch of uneven ground had remained unploughed. Her legs were stiff, her bottom numb, and it was good to move. The air was icy on her bare flesh when she pulled down trousers and underwear, and icy bits of grass tickled her when she crouched down. As always under such circumstances her bladder control locked and it was several moments before she could relax it enough to pee. A cloud of steam rose from the little puddle that swiftly sank into the leaf-littered ground. She had wiped herself with a tissue from her pocket and was trying to poke it into the soil with a stick when she caught a flicker of movement out of the corner of her eye. Through the bushes and trees she could see a small patch of the lane, and someone had crossed that patch.

Struggling to pull up her underwear and zip her salopettes, she stood up and lurched back to where Daphne was sitting. She had the binoculars clamped to her eyes, and was beckoning furiously with the other hand. As Phoebe came up to her she lowered the binoculars, and grabbed her arm to pull her down to the tree stump.

'Someone went in at your gate. A girl, not very large. And I don't want to alarm you, but she's let herself in to your cottage. With a key.'

Chapter 18

'Call the police, or have a go ourselves?' asked Daphne succinctly.

'Have a go,' said Phoebe grimly, still struggling to do up the zip on her salopettes. 'Blast this zip. I've caught it on my jumper.'

'Leave it. If it's stuck to the jumper, they're not going to fall down. We'll have to be quick. There's a gap in the hedge down here, I think we can get through it. Have you got that mobile phone with you? We ought to have it ready to call the police, just in case.'

'No, sorry. I shoved it in the drawer, and it's not charged up. I never thought.' Phoebe did not want to admit that she had been unable to bear the sight of the thing, let alone use it. 'Anyway, there's only one person and she didn't look very big.'

'Small doesn't mean not dangerous. And she might have a knife. Or a gun.' Daphne, nevertheless, was quickly leading the way down the side of the field, moving with the unhurried stride of an habitual country walker that effortlessly eats up distance. Phoebe stumbled behind her, catching her feet in tussocks and trails of bramble.

'Not a gun, surely. She looks so young, and she doesn't sound the type.'

'How do you know what the type is? And how can you be sure what she sounds like, come to that?'

'Not absolutely sure, but I think she's the girl who telephoned me earlier. She sounded . . . educated. You know.'

'You mean she spoke properly. Don't you read the newspapers? The jails are full of ex-public-school boys who've taken to crime.'

'She didn't sound like that,' Phoebe insisted stubbornly. They were speaking in a breathless murmur, and now came to what, if it was not a gap in the hedge, was at least a place where the growth was thinner. Some barbed wire had been woven between the trunks of the little trees. Phoebe tried to climb through it, and instantly snagged her clothes on the wire. She struggled, and embedded it deeper.

'Hold still.' Daphne pulled a pair of wire cutters from the depths of her poacher's pocket and ruthlessly snipped the wire apart, unhooking it.

'Daphne!' Phoebe, town-bred, had the new country person's reverence for the countryside code.

'Field's empty,' Daphne pointed out. 'I'll repair it, later on. Can't afford to waste time. Who knows what she might be doing? Come on.' She pushed through the narrow space, the ends of the barbed wire scraping uselessly against the armoured surface of her waxed jacket.

In the lane they paused while they were still out of sight of the house.

'I'll go round to the back door,' said Daphne. 'You go in by the front. We'll have to get to the doors quickly, in case she sees us from the windows. Now, are you sure this is how you want to do it?'

'Yes, I'm sure. The police will take hours to get here. Unless you don't want to?'

'Have-a-go Joe, that's me. Right, then. Now!'

Phoebe sprinted for the front door. It opened to her hand – it hadn't been locked from the inside. Phoebe shut it quietly behind her, and turned her own key in the lock. She could hear sounds from upstairs. The intruder was making no attempt to be quiet, obviously believing that Phoebe had rushed off to Brighton. Phoebe went to the back door and unlocked it for Daphne.

'She's upstairs.'

'We've got her trapped, then, unless she jumps out of a window.'

'They've all got locks on.'

'Right, then.'

Feeling rather silly, Phoebe picked up the rolling pin as she went through the kitchen. Daphne, she saw, was already armed with a serviceable stick from the stack of sawed branches by the back door. They went up the stairs. Phoebe, knowing the house, kept to the side next to the wall and automatically skipped the seventh step, which creaked. Daphne followed suit. In the doorway of Phoebe's bedroom they paused, looking on a scene of desolation. Every cupboard door was open, clothes and shoes flung haphazardly over the floor. Drawers had been pulled out and tipped upside down. The girl stood by the dressing table, a pile of discarded jewellery boxes as mute evidence of her activities beside her. She whirled round.

'You little bitch!' Phoebe was outraged. The picture of Leo which she still, more from habit than anything else, kept in its silver frame on the dressing table, had been thrown down and stamped on, by the look of the splinters of glass and the twisted frame. She dropped the rolling pin and stepped forward, her hands out to take the girl by the shoulders and give her a brisk shaking.

There was a glimpse of a pinched face, white and desperate. The girl said nothing, but put her head down and charged for the door like a diminutive American footballer. As Phoebe reached to grab her she brought up her knee and rammed it into Phoebe's stomach. The air left Phoebe's lungs like the cork from a shaken champagne bottle and she doubled up, retching and gagging for air. Daphne, wirier but older, hit out with the stick but the intruder ducked. Abandoning her weapon, Daphne made a spirited attempt to seize her but the other was now moving fast. She fended off Daphne with her hunched shoulder, crashing her against the door frame. Daphne, her hands clenched in the fabric of the stranger's jacket, hung on. The girl kicked out, her feet in heavy black boots hacking viciously at Daphne's shins. Daphne gave a grunt of pain but her hands still gripped tight. With a frenzied heave her attacker pulled herself free, leaving the jacket uselessly in Daphne's hold, and went in a clattering run down the stairs. Finding the front door locked she pushed herself off from it and ran for the back door.

Daphne looked at Phoebe who was still doubled up, her face pale green and sweating.

'Phone for help,' she said, and hobbled down the stairs. She unlocked the front door and went out. Phoebe, clasping her arms round her body but managing to pull air into her starving lungs, staggered to the window. From above she saw the girl, diminutive in black trousers and shirt, and with a broad leather belt round her waist, run down the drive to the lane. Daphne, limping badly, went after her but was obviously not going to be fast enough to catch her. She stopped half way down the drive.

'Stop, thief!' Daphne shouted, her deep voice with its cut-glass enunciation ringing through the double-glazing on the window. 'Stop, thief!'

In the lane the girl hesitated, then lurched off. Daphne gave an impotent wave of her arms, and gave one more cry. The ancient words sounded not inappropriate, though at any other time Phoebe thought she would have laughed to hear them.

There came an answering shout, and a clatter of hooves. Jennifer, whose large ungainly body looked normal, even graceful, when she was mounted on her mare, came down the lane at a canter. Leaning forward over the horse's neck she urged the horse after the fleeing girl, who glanced behind her and put on a desperate surge of speed. Two legs could not, however, outrun four. Inexorably Jennifer was drawing closer. When she drew level with the girl she leaned down from the saddle, hooked her hand neatly into the girl's leather belt. With a jerk she lifted her off her feet and heaved her up to hang, face down, over the shoulders of the horse.

The girl flailed her arms and legs, the horse tossed its head and skittered sideways, and Jennifer administered a sharp slap on the small bottom conveniently to hand. Her mouth moved, and Phoebe dimly heard her ringing admonition as she turned the horse back towards the cottage. It was trotting, now, the girl bumping painfully on her stomach. Phoebe, whose gasps of horrified laughter were hurting her abused diaphragm, felt little sympathy.

The horse trotted in the gateway and stood in the drive. The girl wriggled again, but Jennifer kept her capable hand firmly clamped to the belt. Phoebe hurried downstairs and joined Daphne in the drive.

'Is this what you wanted?' Jennifer's cheerful voice boomed out into the cold air. The horse tossed its head, the jets of steam from its nostrils making it look like an illustration in a children's book. It looked, as far as Phoebe could read a horse's face, rather smug. 'If you wriggle like that, the mare will probably buck,' Jennifer said happily, 'and you will come off, probably onto your head. Now, I don't much mind, and I don't suppose Mrs Miller does either, but you might.'

The girl stopped squirming but said nothing, though Phoebe had expected a torrent of abuse.

'Do you want to tie her up, before I let her go?' Jennifer was quite serious. Phoebe, remembering well publicised stories in the paper of householders taken to court for defending their own property, was appalled.

'No, no, we can hold her,' she said hastily.

'As you like.' Jennifer tugged the belt, and the girl slithered backwards to the ground. She staggered as her feet thudded down. Phoebe and Daphne took hold of her as much to steady as to restrain her. She stood between the two of them, staring sullenly at the ground.

'Do you want me to stay? Only it's too cold to leave the mare standing out here. When you said you were busy, I put off my ride till this afternoon. Thought I'd come and check whether you were free yet. Good thing, really! I could come back when I've stabled her, it wouldn't take long.'

'We'll be fine,' said Phoebe gratefully. 'You were wonderful. I've never seen anything like it!'

'If I'd stopped to think, I'd never have dared do it. It's not really much different from the games they play at the Pony Club, but of course it's rather more dangerous with a live person.'

'You could have killed me,' muttered the girl. Jennifer glowered at her.

'Worse than that. It might have injured the mare.' Without waiting for an answer she wheeled the horse round, and trotted out of the gate.

'In you come,' said Daphne grimly. The girl trailing between them, they went back into the house. Daphne closed and locked the front door, removing the key and putting it in her pocket. They went into the kitchen, and Daphne locked the back door too. The girl sat at the table, her hands tightly clasped in her lap, her head bowed. With Daphne perched on the table nearby, Phoebe went upstairs to the bedroom. When she came down again she was carrying the girl's jacket, and also a plastic carrier. It was heavy. She hefted it on to the table and set it down, pulling away the bag to reveal a plastic container that sloshed gently as it sat. Its shape and colour were unmistakable, and Phoebe remembered that she had left the can under the bench in the porch the day before, and forgotten to put it back in the car.

In silence, Phoebe put the can down. She took up the jacket again, and turned out the pockets. A little heap of jewellery piled up on the wooden tabletop, along with a day return ticket from Brighton, a bunch of keys, and a handkerchief. The girl reached out her hand to snatch at the crumpled square, but Phoebe was faster. Smoothing it out, she looked at the nametape so carefully sewn on to the corner. She looked at the girl, who kept her head down. Phoebe took hold of the girl's chin and, after a silent struggle, lifted her face. At first the girl screwed up her eyes as if, childishly, she thought she would be invisible if she could not see anything. Then she opened them again, staring defiantly up at Phoebe's face with hazel eyes. The irises, strikingly, were rimmed with a darker brown, making them look larger and more liquid by contrast. Beautiful, familiar eyes. Leo's eyes.

'Natasha.'

Tashie jerked her head sideways out of Phoebe's slackened hold, but did not lower her face again. She glared defiantly, with hatred, with despair. Her lips wobbled and she compressed them, the smooth skin of her chin corrugating with effort.

'You know her?' Daphne, without moving, withdrew herself from the confrontation.

'Natasha Miller. Leo's daughter.'

'Ah.' There was a rich texture of meaning in the monosyllable. Tashie transferred her glare, briefly, to Daphne.

'What do you mean, ah?'

'I mean, ah, so that's how you got the key. And ah, like father, like daughter. No respect for other people's property. Or for their persons, come to that.' Daphne pulled up the leg of her disreputable trousers. A crust of blood was drying on her shin, and the flesh round the cut was bruised.

'Sorry,' muttered Tashie. 'I'm sorry.'

'That trick with your knee is dangerous,' Daphne pursued relentlessly. 'Mrs – Mrs Miller could have been seriously injured.'

'She's *not* Mrs Miller!' The high voice was suddenly childish. 'My *mother* is Mrs Miller. Not her!'

'And that makes it all right for you to steal from her? And what about the petrol? You weren't carrying that around in case you met someone whose car had run dry, were you? Or to fill up your cigarette lighter? You, my girl, are in serious trouble. Burglary, attempted arson, assault . . . You won't get away with that with just a slapped wrist. If you're not old enough for prison, it'll be a detention centre. On the whole, I don't know that they're not as bad. Worse, even. Though perhaps not quite as shaming for your family.'

Tashie burst into tears.

'Oh, Daphne! She's only a child!'

'People who are only children go round committing murder these days, haven't you heard? I don't believe in being soft on them. She should pay the price, learn what crime really means.'

Tashie sobbed.

'Look,' said Phoebe. 'Don't think I'm not grateful, but this isn't exactly the average crime, is it? Oh, it's a crime all right, don't get me wrong. Several crimes. But the circumstances . . . I'm practically Natasha's stepmother.'

'And that makes it better?'

'No, of course not. But it means that, even if wrongly, I feel a bit responsible for her. After all, there's really not much harm done – except for your leg, and I'm very sorry about that – and I really think Natasha and I should have a talk about things. I want to hear about it from her, not secondhand from some police report. And I don't see why I shouldn't have my say, too.'

Daphne snorted.

'Like I said. Too soft. Still, it's your lookout. I know I'm old-fashioned, and I'm not used to dealing with young people like you are. My father would have taken a horsewhip to her.'

Phoebe, remembering Daphne's description of her father, said nothing but looked at her steadily.

'All right. All right, my father's way was wrong, too. I'll go, leave you to have your talk. Rather you than me.'

Daphne stood up. Phoebe reached up and kissed the weather-roughened cheek. Daphne shied, rather like the horse, but seemed not displeased.

'Thank you, Daphne. You're one in a million. I'll never forget your help today.'

'Hmf.' Daphne gave a gruff snort, but she gave Phoebe a friendly buffet on the shoulder before leaving. Phoebe, just to be on the safe side, locked the door behind her. When she came back to the kitchen Tashie was crying in great gasps, her body heaving with the effort. Her tear-reddened eyes were dry, but frightened. Her hands reached out aimlessly, clutching at nothing. Phoebe, accustomed to dealing with over-emotional teenagers, resisted the impulse to slap her, sighed resignedly and fetched a paper bag. As Kate had done weeks before she held it up to Tashie's face, speaking calmly, slowing the breathing until it was back to normal. Then, prosaically, she handed Tashie the handkerchief with her name on it, and went to put the kettle on.

Phoebe put two mugs of tea down on the table. As an afterthought she fetched the biscuit tin. As she set it down, the little heap of jewellery shifted. An earring rolled in a lazy circle, and a loop of gold chain snaked out, like a tendril from some unlikely plant. Looking at the jumble of necklaces, rings, bracelets, brooches and earrings, some real but mostly fake or fun, she realised that something was missing. The rather vulgar set of paste diamonds that Leo had insisted on giving her, and that she had scarcely ever worn, was not there. Since the heap included even the most obviously plastic beads, it seemed strange.

Phoebe glanced at the girl, who was slumped in her chair and snivelling quietly to herself. Doors and windows were all locked, the keys removed. She went upstairs, cursing her bruised stomach muscles and Natasha who had bruised them, shuffling through the clothes on the bedroom floor to reach her dressing table. Sure enough, though every other box had been opened and cleared, the leather case for the missing set had been put aside, still closed. It was not a great surprise to find, on opening it, that it was empty.

Back in the kitchen, Natasha had not moved. Phoebe sat down opposite her and sipped at her tea. She pushed the other mug nearer the girl, who ignored it and continued to sniff. Irritated, Phoebe went and pulled a handful of kitchen roll from the wall dispenser, and pushed it into the girl's hand.

'For heaven's sake, blow your nose,' she snapped.

For a moment she thought she would get a flat refusal, but fortunately common sense asserted itself. Natasha blew and mopped.

'Now drink your tea.'

There was a defiant glare, but Natasha picked up the mug and sipped obediently. Phoebe sat quietly, not looking directly at her. At that moment, she felt she couldn't bear the sight of Natasha, which filled her with so complex a mixture of anger, bitterness and guilt. After a few moments the girl reached out absently, and took a biscuit. When the mug was empty, Phoebe refilled it. Then she pulled the jumbled heap of jewellery towards her, and began to sort it. It was tangled, one fine chain in particular having knotted itself round everything else. Phoebe picked at it, keeping eyes and hands busy.

'They're not worth much, you know,' she said in carefully conversational tones. Natasha said nothing. 'Even less than they cost, when you come to try and sell them. And that would be tricky, too. They ask questions, when people go into shops with handfuls of stuff to sell, particularly people of your age.' A silence. Phoebe glanced swiftly across the table, caught the remnants of a curious expression. 'Or was it not you who would do the selling? Who, then? Your brother? Your mother?' The girl gave a sudden jerk, instantly stilled. 'Not your mother, then. I apologise. I didn't think she sounded the type to be inciting her daughter to burglary. So, who? Oh, of course. It was your father, wasn't it?'

She had already worked it out. Who else could have sent the original postcard, or have given Natasha the key? Phoebe wanted to make the girl confront what she had done, and intended to do, by coupling it with the rest of her family. Natasha said nothing, but picked up her second mug of tea and drank, hiding her face, concentrating her gaze on the drink.

'You came last weekend, didn't you? Came with the key, while I was away in Canterbury, and took the diamond set. They were only fakes, you know.'

'No, they weren't. They were real. He gave you real diamonds, and you were too stupid to realise.' There was triumph in her voice. The words 'so there!' floated, unspoken.

'How do you know? Fakes can sparkle just as brightly. Or are you an expert?'

The sarcasm stung.

'Well, you're certainly not. You didn't even notice.'

'I believed what I was told. After all, if someone gives you something and says they're real, you might wonder whether they were really good imitations. But if the person tells you they're fake, you're hardly going to suspect they're the genuine article. It doesn't work like that. So, they were a little nest egg, were they? A little hedge against inflation? I'm surprised he didn't take them with him in the first place.'

'He forgot.' Natasha sounded apologetic. 'It was a rush. And a shock. He didn't know—'

'That the bank was on to him? Yes, I can imagine that would come as rather a shaker. So, how did he find out?' Phoebe looked at Natasha. 'It was you, wasn't it? You who telephoned him?'

'I didn't believe it.' Her eyes filled with tears again, her voice tight and husky. 'I thought it was all a mistake, that he could sort it out.'

'So he sent you to fetch them. When?'

'I don't want to talk about it.'

'I don't suppose you do. But I don't think you have all that much choice, do you?'

Natasha looked at her.

'You're not going to call the police, are you?' she asked shrewdly.

'Probably not. But that's not really the point any more, is it? We have reason to dislike one another. We both have reason to feel guilty. My – being with – your father has damaged your family, but you must realise that I didn't know about you. You, however, have broken into my home – well, got in uninvited, anyway – stolen from me, and brought indoors the means to burn it down. Were you really going to do it?'

Natasha had the grace to look ashamed.

'I don't know. I wanted to.' She looked round the room, and through the open doors to the dining room, the conservatory beyond, and the hall. Her eyes came back to the table, to the jewellery that now lay in separate piles. 'My mother had to sell her pearls,' she said. 'She was going to leave them to me.'

'Oh, Natasha.' For the first time, guilt overcame anger. Phoebe's voice ached.

'It's not that I wanted them,' Tashie was at pains to explain. 'I don't care about that, they're not my sort of thing, I wouldn't be seen dead in pearls. But *she* minded. I think she thought I'd wear them on my w-wedding day, or something.' The tears were gentler, this time. Not a toddler's tantrum or teenage hysteria, but an adult weeping for another's pain. 'She needed the money,' she finished, in desolation.

'Oh Natasha, I'm sorry.' It was true, Phoebe found. This troubled girl with Leo's eyes was a victim, even more than Phoebe had been. All the anger she had earlier felt at the desecration of her home seemed irrelevant now. 'The man from the bank said it was all sorted out, he said she was all right. I should have realised . . .'

Tashie blew her nose again, made an effort.

'She is all right, really. We've got the house, and she does bed and breakfast. The pearls were to pay for doing it up a bit. Her old room, and the bathroom. She sleeps in with Granny, and the boys are in together, and I have the little room. There are students in the old upstairs rooms. It's fine.' She spoke with a pride that would have astonished Kate, accustomed as she was to Tashie moaning about the smallness of her new bedroom and the inconvenience of having guests and lodgers.

'So, why . . .?' Phoebe indicated the jewellery. Tashie's face creased.

'It's Sam. My brother. He's got to have an operation for his fits, and the insurance won't pay up, and it costs thousands and thousands, Mum's really worried. I wanted to help, and . . . I was so angry, you see. About Sam, really, and the insurance behaving like pigs, and somehow it all got muddled up with everything else, and I just wanted to . . . to hurt someone. You.'

The bald admission made, she sat back in her chair, as if awaiting the warders who would drag her away. She was very pale, her reddened eyelids puffy and half closed. As Phoebe looked at her she shivered, though the kitchen was warm. Her hand had been very hot, Phoebe remembered. She stood up, and went round the table. As she put her hand on Tashie's forehead, Tashie shivered again, her teeth chattering.

'I'm cold,' she said.

'You, my girl, have got a temperature. Quite high, I'd say.'

'I must go home.' Tashie shuddered again. 'I feel awful.'

Phoebe looked at her. Tashie, already washed out from lack of sleep and too much emotion, looked quite ill. It was out of the question to send her home on the train. Phoebe contemplated driving her back to Brighton, but it looked as though even that would be too much for her. She made up her mind.

'Come on.'

'Where? What are you doing? I don't want to!'

'You're going up to bed,' said Phoebe firmly. 'The spare room is made up, thank goodness. I'm going to fill two hot water bottles and put them in it while you telephone your mother.'

'No! No, I can't!'

'Can't go to bed, or can't phone your mother?'

'Both! I can't stay here! I won't!' Her voice was rising. She stood up, and swayed. Phoebe caught her and lowered her back into the chair.

'You're certainly not fit to be going anywhere else. But you must phone your mother. Where does she think you are – at school?'

'I can't. I can't tell her!' Tashie was crying again, childishly this time, in a panic.

'You must at least tell her you're safe. Come on, Natasha.'

'Tashie. They call me Tashie. Natasha's for when . . .'

'For when you're in trouble? Yes. Well, come on, Tashie. You know you can't not do it, and the sooner you do it, the sooner it'll be over. Or tell me the number, and I'll ring for you.'

'No! No, I'll do it. Oh dear!' Tashie wailed. 'I feel sick!'

Phoebe grabbed the washing-up bowl, which by good fortune was empty. She was just in time. She held Tashie's hot head, smoothing back the damp hair from her sweating face, then gave her a mug of water to rinse her mouth, and a wet towel to wipe her face. Wiped clean, she looked about twelve. So this, thought Phoebe with grim amusement, is what motherhood's all about. The Wicked Stepmother strikes again.

Chapter 19

Kate leaped to answer the phone, picking it up before it had finished its first ring.

'Hello? Tashie? Is that you?'

'I'm sorry, Mummy.' The high voice, the use of the childhood name, froze Kate's blood. It prickled in her veins, as though the liquid content had indeed turned to shards of ice.

'Are you all right? Where are you?'

'I'm all right. I'm really all right. Only I've got a temperature, I feel awful, and I've been sick.'

'But where *are* you? I'll come and get you.'

'No . . . I can't . . . I can't tell you. Oh, Mummy . . .' Her voice was fainter.

'Don't ring off. Listen, Tashie, whatever it is, it's all right. Can you hear me? It's all right, it will be all right. Now, are you with your father?' Kate damped down her own panic, spoke in matter-of-fact tones.

'With *Daddy*?' Tashie's voice was stronger, a shriek of astonishment. Kate had to pull the telephone suddenly away from her ear, which buzzed. Hastily she put it back.

'Well, I just wondered – Nick thought you might – anyway, that doesn't matter now. Just tell me where you are.'

'I'm all right. I'm with someone. A . . . a friend.'

'A boy? A man?' Would that be worse than Tashie being with Len, or better? Tashie's voice came back, strangely, amused.

'A man? No! Really, Mummy, what have you been imagining?'

Kate was annoyed. Even the use of 'Mummy' did not mollify her: for the last year or two, Tashie had only used it when she wanted something. Kate had thought, from time to time, that it was no coincidence that 'Mummy' sounded so very like 'money'.

'If you don't know,' she said crossly, 'you must be more of a fool than I thought. Really, Tashie, you went off without a word, I don't know how the school didn't miss you but I suppose some of your beastly friends covered up for you or something, and I've spent the last hour worrying myself sick, and wondering whether to contact the police—'

'No! Don't do that!'

'Well of course I won't now I've heard from you, they'd just say I was wasting police time and I'd probably end up going to prison or something. But I must know, *where are you*?'

'I'm – Oh God, I'm going to be sick again—' There was a clatter as she dropped the telephone. Kate dithered. In the distance, she heard the sound of retching and another voice. Then the telephone was taken up again.

'Mrs Miller?' The voice was vaguely familiar.

'Yes. Who is this?'

'I'm Phoebe. Your . . . um, I don't know how to describe myself. Leo's – Len's – other wife. As it were.'

'As it were.' Kate, uncharitably, would have called her his mistress, if not worse. 'And where are you? Why is Tashie with you? Is Len – Leo – there?'

'I'm at home, and no, he's not. Nor is he likely to be. Natasha – Tashie – came here of her own accord. I really think I'd better leave her to explain that to you, when she's able to. It's a bit of a sorry tale, but I must tell you, she did it out of love for you.'

Kate bit her lip. She felt she was being patronised by someone who scarcely knew her or her daughter. Nevertheless, by nature and upbringing she found it difficult not to be polite.

'Thank you. I'll bear it in mind. What's the matter with Tashie?'

'She's just got a high temperature, and vomiting. It's probably just a touch of 'flu, exacerbated by emotion. She's in quite a state.'

'I'll come and fetch her.'

'Come, by all means. In fact, I think you must. But I honestly don't know about taking her home, she's really quite poorly and then there's the vomiting. Meanwhile, I'm putting her to bed. She's treating me as though I'm a white slaver, which is sort of understandable, but I really don't think she's fit for anything else.'

'It's very kind of you,' said Kate stiffly.

'I don't feel I have all that much choice,' replied Phoebe honestly. 'She's here, and she's ill. I can hardly push her out into the night, like a pregnant housemaid in a Victorian melodrama.'

Kate thought that there were people who would have done just that, out of spite or lack of caring. Grudgingly, she admitted to herself that Phoebe had behaved generously, since she was pretty sure that Tashie had gone there with no good intentions. The admission made her feel resentful, as someone who is having good done to them by a person they dislike.

'I'll come straight away.'

'I'd better give some directions. And the address, unless you know it?'

'No, I don't.' Kate, unfairly, felt she was under attack. 'I don't have your phone number either, I don't think.'

Phoebe gave her both.

'It's a bit tricky, in the dark. The lane's quite small, you can easily miss it. Give me a ring if you get lost.'

'Thank you,' said Kate, through gritted teeth. She put down the telephone and turned to see Nick and Sam hovering, halfway down the stairs. Feeling that they could do nothing to help find Tashie – it was too soon to panic and go hunting the streets for her – she had sent them upstairs to study. Now their eyes pinned her in their stare, like headlamps.

'She's all right. She's at someone's house.'

'Whose house?' Sam's direct mind had no use for, or even acquaintance with, the concept of discretion.

Kate spoke with repressive austerity. 'Nobody you know. Tashie might have to stay there for a while, she's not very well. A temperature, and vomiting. I'm going to go and see her.'

'Nick's been sick too,' Sam volunteered cheerfully. 'Twice. I haven't.'

'Oh, Nick.' Guiltily Kate took the stairs two at a time. Nick's eyes, she now noticed, were too bright in his flushed face. When she touched him he gave off heat, like a furnace. 'Darling, why didn't you say?'

'I was all right, earlier. Well, just a bit shivery, thought it was the weather. Or something. Didn't see any point in worrying you.'

'Poor old love. You must go straight to bed, I'll bring you something to get your temperature down, and a drink. Go with him, Sam.'

'I'll fetch him the bucket. In case he's sick again.' Sam, in robust health, didn't mince his words. As the two boys went back upstairs and Kate turned back to the kitchen, her mother's door opened.

'You're very noisy out here,' she complained. 'I don't know why you have to talk to those people on the stairs, Catherine. And who are those boys? Did you invite them?'

With an unvoiced groan, Kate soothed her mother.

'Sorry about the noise, darling. Don't worry about the boys, they're going now. Come and sit down, I'll make you a quick cup of tea.'

'I don't want any tea.' Joyce's voice was querulous. 'I want your father. Why hasn't he come back yet? He won't want those boys in the house, shouting on the stairs. He's late. It's dark. Something might have happened to him.'

'Nothing's happened to him, Ma. Please come back to your room.'

'I don't want to. That's not my room. I want to go and look for Harold.'

Kate's mind scurried like a mouse dashing round the skirtings of a room. Impossible to leave her mother here, with Nick ill and only Sam (unrecognised, at present, by his grandmother) to take care of them both.

'All right, then,' she said, with forced cheerfulness. 'We'll go in the car. I'll need to get ready, though, and so will you. It's cold outside. You get your coat and hat, and some gloves. And a scarf. I won't be long.'

Mollified, Joyce pottered back into her room. Kate, cursing under her breath, locked the front door to prevent her mother from wandering, then went to the kitchen. A jug of water, and another of weak squash, went on a tray while the kettle boiled. A pot of weak tea and a jug of milk, along with appropriate mugs and beakers, and some dry biscuits, filled it almost to overflowing. As quickly as its weight would allow she carried it up to the boys' room where Nick was already in bed.

Kate waited until she had seen him take two pills washed down by some tea. He looked pale, but the tea stayed down and she stroked the hair back from his face.

'Poor old darling. Let's hope it's one of those twenty-four-hour things. I'll go and see Tashie now. I'll take Gran with me – she's having a bad spell and I don't want her making a fuss, or trying to wander off.'

'We'll be all right. Tell Tashie . . . oh, I don't know.'

'Nor do I. But she's not with your father. I won't say any more now, if you don't mind. It's not that dreadful, and it's not that I don't trust you, but I'm not sure what I think about things myself yet. I'll tell you all about it when I come back. OK?'

He managed a wan smile.

'Sorry, Mum.'

She bent and kissed him, feeling the heat of his skin with her lips.

'Don't be silly. Try to sleep. It'll all be fine.'

She must have sounded more confident than she felt, because he closed his eyes and seemed to relax. Kate went to her bedroom. Whatever else happened, she was not going to face Len's Other Woman without make-up. And something rather smarter than the old jeans she had put on when she had expected to spend the evening doing the ironing.

★ ★ ★

In the car, Kate made no attempt to pretend that she was searching for her father. Joyce was subdued by the darkness, like a parrot with a cover thrown over its cage, and seemed content to sit beside her, securely strapped in. As they drove out of Brighton on the main road Kate flicked a glance sideways. In the transient lights of oncoming traffic her mother's face was tranquil as a baby's, gazing with apparent fascination at the dimly seen countryside.

The village was easy to find, the lane less so, but Kate managed after turning the car twice in farm turnings or drives. As she pulled in to the gravelled drive of the cottage several outside floodlights flashed on, spotlighting her car. Kate, town-dweller, thought at first that Phoebe had done it on purpose to disconcert her, then realised that of course they were automatic. She parked with self-conscious neatness, feeling under critical surveillance. With every fibre of her being she longed to be able to leave her mother in the car, but short of finding some way of locking her seatbelt in place she could see that it couldn't be done. The thought of Joyce wandering vaguely through the dark village lanes made her turn cold.

'Come on,' she said, with resignation. The only thing to be said about her mother's disoriented state was that she asked no questions, accepting what was happening and struggling out of the car without demur. Kate helped her. On the step she looked in vain for the doorbell, then banged the knocker. Her first attempt was too soft, she was sure no one would have heard it. She was lifting the iron knocker again when it was pulled from her grasp as the door opened.

Phoebe and Kate looked at one another. Each saw, in the other, the reflection of what she was thinking. So *that's* what you look like. Not at all what I imagined. Each thought, in despair, she looks nice.

Joyce, sensing social unease, stepped into the breach.

'How do you do?' she said, holding out her hand. 'I'm Joyce Carpenter. And this is my daughter Kate. Kate Miller.' She paused, politely, to allow Phoebe to give her name.

Phoebe, bemused, shook the offered hand.

'How do you do?' she responded automatically. 'Phoebe. Phoebe, um, Humphreys. Won't you come in?'

'That's so kind of you.' Joyce was gracious. 'We're really looking for my husband, Harold. Harold Carpenter, of course. Is he still here?'

Phoebe's eyes met Kate's, her question meeting Kate's mingled embarrassment with anxiety. Something passed between them that could have been sympathy, or complicity, or merely understanding. Phoebe turned back to Joyce.

'He's not here, I'm afraid,' she answered smoothly. 'In fact, I'm not sure where he is, but he may well be back at home by now. What a pity you've had this long journey for nothing, but you must come in for a few minutes, and get comfortable. No, I insist. A drink, or a cup of tea or coffee.' She took Joyce's arm, obliging her to step over the threshold. Kate closed the door and trailed behind them as they went into the sitting room. She felt as she had done as a child, when her mother had taken over a meeting with one of her own friends, and started to run the whole show.

'Won't you let me take your coat, Mrs Carpenter? And do sit here, near the fire. Will you have a sherry, or would you rather have something hot?'

'A cup of tea would be most welcome,' Joyce said, basking in the attention as much as the warmth. 'But not if it's any trouble.'

'No, not at all. I'll just go and put the kettle on. And perhaps . . . Kate . . . would like to give me a hand.'

Together, like conspirators, they left the room.

'Sorry,' Kate muttered. 'Sorry about all this. I couldn't leave her behind, she's having one of her confused days, and Nick's gone down with whatever Tashie's got. I couldn't leave Sam to cope with both of them, she wanders off sometimes, looking for Dad.'

'It's all right,' said Phoebe. 'Look, why don't you go straight upstairs to Tashie? It's the room on the right at the top of the stairs. I'll keep your mother company.'

Kate sniffed.

'I can smell petrol,' she said, suddenly suspicious. Phoebe glanced round, and she followed the direction of her look. 'Isn't that a petrol can? What's it doing here?'

Phoebe felt, and looked, guilty. There was nothing she could say. Kate went white.

'Tashie did it, didn't she. Brought it into the house. Oh God, she didn't . . .?' Phoebe put her hand on her arm and gave it a little shake.

'Nothing happened,' she said. 'Hush, your mother will hear you. Listen, nothing happened, and I don't believe she would have done anything even if she'd had the chance. Not with the petrol, anyway. It was just a gesture. A bit of melodrama, with herself as audience. Go and see her, she'll tell you herself.' She gave Kate a push towards the door.

Kate went up the stairs wearily, feeling older than her mother. She, at least, was safe and happy enough in her misty world of the past. With corners of her mind she registered how pretty the cottage was, with colours and styles that were just right for a house like this.

In the doorway of the spare room she hesitated. The soft primrose yellow of the walls glowed in the light of two lamps, and the shades of green and blue in curtains and bedding were restful to the eye. On the bedside table was a tray that was almost the mirror image of the one she had left for Nick, only less homely: the jug of water with its matching glass (hers were plastic), and a cup and saucer where Nick's tea had been in a mug. The packet of painkillers to reduce the temperature was the same make. Even the bucket on the floor (green instead of red) was there. But what else would anyone do? She thought sensibly.

Tashie lay curled on primrose sheets and pillows under a moss-green patterned duvet. Her eyes were closed, but although Kate had made no sound she seemed to feel her mother's gaze and opened them.

'Mummy! Oh, Mummy, I feel awful!'

'I'm not surprised,' said Kate. 'In fact, I rather think you deserve to, don't you?'

'Mummy!' Kate shut the door against Tashie's wail and the ensuing sobs.

'I saw the petrol can.' Kate's voice was controlled, but it cut through Tashie's crying like a hot knife through butter. Abruptly, Tashie stopped sobbing although the tears still ran in an unnoticed stream down her face.

'I didn't do anything,' she said in a small voice.

'Because you were caught.'

Tashie swallowed.

'Yes,' she said. Her honesty touched Kate where the crying had not. She went and sat on the edge of the bed. Tashie sat up, but did not try to throw herself into Kate's arms. Kate had expected this and braced herself against the emotional appeal, but when it did not come she was obscurely hurt yet, at the same time, impressed.

'I think you'd better tell me all about it, don't you?'

Tashie nodded, and winced at the movement.

'Why don't you lie down again? You can talk just as well lying down.'

'No,' said Tashie. 'It's easier, sitting up.'

'Facing the firing squad without a blindfold?'

Tashie's smile was crooked, but a good effort.

'Something like that.'

Downstairs, Phoebe heard all about Harold. The conversation progressed to Kate, and a résumé of her birth, childhood, schooldays, marriage, and subsequent children ensued. Phoebe, her ears straining for sounds from upstairs, nodded and smiled as necessary, and was thankful that her elderly guest was so easy to entertain. After the tea tray had been cleared away, with Joyce insisting on helping to wash up, she waited a short time and then offered sherry. It was accepted, and after three glasses (Phoebe had only one, and pretended to sip it) Joyce began to look rather fuddled. The room was warm, and her eyes grew heavy.

'I really should be going,' she said.

'Oh, not yet,' said Phoebe. 'I don't think Kate's ready yet. Look, I don't know about you, but I often find I feel rather sleepy at this time of day. I usually put my feet up for five minutes and have forty winks.' The phrase, one of Millie's favourites, struck a chord with Joyce.

'Forty winks.' She nodded wisely.

'My mother always says it's the best thing. No point in fighting it, if you're sleepy. This sofa's very comfortable, and if we just slip your shoes off . . .' Not for nothing had Phoebe been a teacher. Almost before she knew it, Joyce found herself comfortably installed on the sofa, with a rug over her feet and two soft cushions for her head.

'Most kind,' she said. 'If you're sure you don't mind?'

Phoebe waited until a gentle snore signified that Joyce was asleep, then slipped quietly out of the room. Upstairs she listened for a second at the door and, hearing no sound of voices, knocked gently. After a few moments Kate came and opened it.

'Your mother's asleep,' Phoebe said quietly.

'So's my daughter,' said Kate, with the ghost of a laugh. They looked at one another.

'How about a glass of wine?' suggested Phoebe.

'I'd love one,' admitted Kate. She felt exhausted and aching, as though she had been swimming in a cold rough sea and fighting a rip tide.

They sat in the conservatory. Phoebe, who felt they needed something more sustaining than white wine, poured from a bottle of the good claret Leo had bought. Kate sipped it, and nodded.

'I know who chose this,' she said without thinking. 'At least—'

'Yes, you're right. Your husband.'

'Your husband too.'

'Not really. More yours than mine, anyway.'

'Neither of ours now.'

'No.' In strange companionship, they drank.

'I'm sorry about your jewellery,' said Kate eventually. Phoebe shook her head.

'The only things I've lost are the ones I didn't much like, even if I had known they were real. He needs the money, and I don't. It's a small price to pay . . .'

'To get rid of him?'

'Oh dear. Yes. Only if anyone were going to have the money, it should probably have been you.'

'I couldn't have taken it. Not that money, not from him. Like you, I feel it's a small price to pay.'

'We're better off without him, aren't we? At least, I am.'

'So am I. And so is Tashie, if only she'd realise it.'

'I think she does, now. She frightened herself quite badly today, realising what she came close to doing. It was partly being ill, of course, but I think . . . today might have been a good thing for her, in the long run. If you don't mind me saying that.'

'Who am I to mind? My daughter tried to rob you, and burn your house down.'

Phoebe heard the bitterness, and felt its match in herself.

'My very existence is an affront to you,' she said.

Kate nodded, not agreeing but seeing the justice of the words.

'Quits, then?'

Phoebe was startled into a grin.

'Quits,' she agreed. She refilled their glasses, and they sipped in what turned into a surprisingly companionable silence.

'If we were Muslims,' said Kate meditatively, 'it would have been quite different. We could have been . . . co-wives. If that's what you call it.'

'Yes. He'd have liked that. It's probably a good thing he never thought of it. I wouldn't have put it past him to convert, if he had.'

'It might have been better. He might not have taken the money.'

'He might have taken even more, and picked out a number-three wife as well.'

'I shouldn't have liked that.'

'Me neither.' Phoebe thought about it. 'Two wouldn't be so bad, if you liked each other. And if there was room.'

'Someone to share the cooking.'

'I like cooking.'

'So do I, the special meal sort. But the everyday "what's-for-supper-Mum-I'm-starving" sort gets you down a bit, sometimes.'

'I suppose so.' Phoebe thought sadly that she might never have that problem, now.

'It's a lot to have to share. Not just a house, and the work. His time. His attention.'

'His dick.'

Phoebe giggled.

'Well, yes. Alternate nights, do you think?'

'My dear, after all those years of marriage, I think I could easily settle for two nights a week. Or even one. Birthdays and anniversaries as optional extras, of course.'

'Of course. Does it really get boring, after a while? Oh dear, I shouldn't really ask you that.'

'Why ever not?' Kate was genuinely surprised. 'No, not boring. A bit routine, sometimes, perhaps. I'm afraid it just seems less important, now. Less – urgent, exciting. I think you'd find that what most people in my position would say they missed is the companionship, the sharing of things like problems with the children, and jokes, and memories. Well, I've got the memories, and I shall miss the jokes a bit, but to be honest he was sort of a dead loss as far as companionship was concerned. Particularly with the children.'

'Even Tashie?'

'Particularly, Tashie, in a way. It's true he spent quite a lot of time with her – when he was there – but it was the wrong sort of time. You know that phrase they go on about, quality time? Well, this was extra-high-super-charged quality time, if you like. He spoiled her ridiculously, which was bad for her when she was little, but even worse now she's grown up. It wasn't good for the boys, either, though in fact I don't think it's done them much harm. As far as I can tell, which may not be very far. Like, about an inch and a half.'

'Tell me about the boys.'

Kate's face softened.

'I must say, I know I may be just a fraction biased, but they're pretty great. Did Tashie tell you about Sam?'

'Yes. She's very concerned, though more for you than for him, I think. She knows Sam can't help being ill, but she resents the fact that you have to worry about it. Especially the money side. She told you . . .?'

'That she was going to pay for his operation by selling your jewellery? Yes. Dear silly girl, she'd have been caught out at once. Bother.' Kate sniffed, and wiped her eyes. 'If it weren't for that bloody insurance company, none of this would have happened.'

'It'll sort itself out, I'm sure it will. And if not . . . I could help.'

'No.'

'Why not? Aren't co-wives supposed to think of all the children in the family as belonging to them? Besides, I can afford it. You knew I won the lottery?'

'No, I didn't. Congratulations.'

'Thank you. It happened just before Leo left, and at the time I thought it was the luckiest thing that had ever happened to me, except for meeting Leo. Now, I'm not so sure. It meant I was able to keep the cottage, of course, and I didn't have to worry about what the bank would do to me. But it was – too easy.' She gestured to her body. 'I wasn't always this shape, you know. This has all come on since Leo left. Comfort eating, to the power of ten, and with enough money to go in for serious self-indulgence. The remnants of my Protestant work ethic make me feel it was too easy. It might have been better for me if I hadn't won.'

'Or if you hadn't met Len.'

'Perhaps. I'm still not sure about that one.'

'You don't have to have it.'

'The fat, or the money?'

'Both. Exercise, diet, good works.'

'That's what I mean. Why can't Sam be my good works?'

'Because . . . because. Well, because.'

'All right. But don't dismiss it out of hand. Keep it as a last resort. Blackpool. Benidorm.'

'Land's End. All right. And thank you.' Kate raised her glass, and drained the last mouthful of wine. When Phoebe would have refilled it she shook her head. 'I mustn't. I can't afford to lose my licence, and I must be going. Get my mother home, and check on Nick.' She was reluctant to stand up, reluctant to leave this pretty, peaceful room and the woman who, against all odds, she found herself liking.

Or was it so surprising? Len had always been consistent in his tastes. He had decided at an early age what kinds of food and drink he liked, and though with the passing years he had added to them he had never changed in those preferences. His taste in women was equally consistent. Kate remembered, during her first year of marriage, meeting an ex-girlfriend of Len's and liking her at once. With Phoebe, too, she felt the same unexpected sympathy.

It was true that much of what they seemed to have in common was superficial – a similarity in tastes. She had no way, as yet, of knowing whether it could go deeper than that. Certainly Len himself never looked much below the surface: Kate had often suspected he might be unaware that there *was* anything below the surface. That she and Phoebe had both been attracted to a man like Len was a strong bond between them, though not as strong as the fact that they had both been betrayed by him. She realised sadly that he would have been unable to grasp the reality of either of their characters, that he would have been profoundly shocked to see them making friends, and that his assumption that each would cope without him was based, not on faith in their strength and resourcefulness, but on a vague belief that it would be so because that was how he wanted it.

Kate and Phoebe were certainly on the same wavelength, finding in each other an instinctive understanding of what was said, and, more importantly, unsaid. Different though they were, in many ways Phoebe reminded Kate of herself when younger. They could, she thought, have been sisters.

'I really must go,' she said reluctantly, and stood up. They went upstairs together. Tashie was fast asleep, her face fallen from teenage sophistication into the softer lines of childhood. Even the fever-flush in her cheeks emphasised her resemblance to that younger, less complicated person. Her teddy bear was clasped in her arms. Kate had found him when she had been rapidly collecting a few things to bring her, and with some instinct to remind her of home and safety had pushed him into the bag, where Tashie must have found him. When Kate bent and kissed her she smiled, and mumbled, but did not wake.

Joyce woke refreshed from her nap, and seemed less confused.

'It's been lovely,' she said with genuine enthusiasm. 'Such a pretty house, and so kind of you to invite us.' She reached out in the most natural way to kiss Phoebe goodbye, patting her gently on the shoulder. 'You must come and see us soon,' she pressed. 'We could have lunch, or perhaps dinner. You could meet the children.' She did not mention Harold, which Phoebe took to be a good sign.

'That's very kind,' she answered without committing herself. 'I should love to see you again. Both of you.'

She sounded wistful. It came to Kate that it had been a relief for her, also, to talk to someone who knew Len as well as she did, and with whom she could be utterly open. On an impulse, she too leaned to kiss Phoebe.

'I'll be back tomorrow,' she murmured, 'to see Tashie again. And thank you, Phoebe.'

Phoebe blinked.

'I'll take good care of her,' she promised. 'Thanks, Kate.'

Chapter 20

During the night Tashie's temperature went up again. Phoebe, waking to hear a voice in a house she had become used to having to herself, was momentarily confused. Then, when the low babbling rose to a cry, she slipped out of bed and hurried through.

She had left the landing light on, in case Tashie should wake and wonder where she was. By its glow from the doorway she made her way to Tashie's bedside. Her eyes were half open, she was frowning and querulous, her face red and her hair damp.

'No,' she said crossly. 'No, I'm not going to.'

'Tashie,' said Phoebe. The watering eyes turned towards her, but did not focus.

'It's not *fair*,' Tashie complained.

Phoebe did not need to touch Tashie to realise how high her temperature was – she could feel the heat radiating from several inches away. Tashie was not altogether delirious, but not completely conscious either, and Phoebe doubted that she would be able to persuade her to swallow capsules or tablets. Hunting through the bathroom cupboard she found some soluble painkillers, and swirled them into a plastic beaker of fruit juice.

'Here you are Tashie, here's a drink. A drink, Tashie. Come on.' Tashie parted dry lips, and struggled to sit up. Phoebe put an arm under her to support her, and held the beaker to her mouth. The girl swallowed the first few mouthfuls, then turned her head away as the bitterness of the medicine reached the back of her tongue.

'Nasty,' she said.

'Drink it, Tashie,' said Phoebe firmly in the kind of voice all good teachers can produce at will. Tashie whined speechlessly, but responded to the sound of authority and obediently finished the drink. Phoebe fetched a bowl of tepid water and towels, and began to sponge her hot face and arms.

'I want Mum,' said Tashie suddenly. Phoebe kept on, dipping and wringing the cloth when it grew too warm.

'I know. But it's the middle of the night, she can't come now. She'll be here in the morning.'

'Not Daddy?'

'Not Daddy,' Phoebe agreed calmly.

'Daddy's gone.' There was both complaint and relief in the husky voice.

'Yes, he's gone.'

'I don't like it.'

'None of us likes it, Tashie. It's just how it is.'

'It's your fault.'

Phoebe knew that Tashie scarcely knew what she was saying, but it was still difficult to answer.

'No, it's not my fault.' Did she believe it herself, she wondered?

'Yes, it is. You're too fat.'

Phoebe, startled out of introspection and self-pity, laughed.

'I am too fat,' she agreed, 'but that isn't why he went. I wasn't fat then.'

Tashie's focused eyes expressed their disbelief.

'Daddy doesn't like fat women.'

'I know he doesn't. Sexist pig.'

Tashie frowned. Phoebe's breath caught in her throat. Tashie, who generally resembled her mother more than anyone, suddenly in that instant had absolutely the look of Leo about her.

'What's the matter?' Tashie, though still inclined to be grumpy, was less confused than earlier, and the brick red of her face had faded patchily.

'Nothing. You looked like your father, just for a moment.'

Tashie's lower lip firmed and jutted.

'No, I don't. I don't look like anyone. I look like me.'

'Of course you do.'

Tashie yawned suddenly, like a cat or a tiny baby. Her eyes closed. Phoebe waited until she was sure she was asleep, then took away the bowl and went wearily back to her own bed.

In the morning Tashie was lucid, but her temperature was still over a hundred and two. She complained of a headache, back ache, leg ache, all-over ache, and turned down the offer of breakfast with every sign of disgust. She drank several glasses of home-made lemon and honey, however, and Phoebe was not particularly concerned about her. She complained of being sweaty, and Phoebe agreed to her having a bath as long as she kept the bathroom door ajar. During that time Phoebe aired the room and remade the bed with clean sheets, so that when Tashie came back (smelling of Phoebe's talcum powder) it was cool and smooth, with the pillows piled up ready for her to sink back against.

'Thank you,' said Tashie, rather shyly. 'You're very kind.'

'Although I'm too fat?'

Tashie looked appalled.

'Did I say that? I'm sorry.'

'Don't be, it's true. And I intend to do something about it. Do you want the radio, or something to read? Or I've got a little portable TV I can bring up, though the reception isn't great without a proper aerial.'

'No, thank you. Perhaps the radio. I don't feel up to reading, or watching anything. In fact, I think I might go to sleep again.'

'It's amazing how tiring it can be, just having a bath,' Phoebe agreed. 'I won't be far away. Give a call if you want anything, or bang on the floor.'

Half an hour later the telephone rang, and Phoebe wasn't very surprised to hear Kate's voice.

'How is she?'

'Not too bad. Her temperature was quite high in the night, but it's down a bit this morning, just over a hundred and two. She's had a bath, and I think she's gone back to sleep. How about Nick?'

'Much the same. Doesn't want anything to eat, says he aches all over, especially his head. Worrying about his A levels, in case it's glandular fever and he's going to be ill for months. I told him it's most unlikely – Tashie doesn't work nearly hard enough to get glandular fever.'

'It probably isn't, though I'm not sure it's only the hard-working ones that get it. Do you want me to call the doctor?'

'No, not unless you're worried about her. The thing is, I can't come over today. I'm so sorry, but I just can't leave the house. I'm afraid my mother's gone down with it too.'

'Oh no! Poor Mrs Carpenter! Is she very bad?'

Phoebe could hear the tension in Kate's voice.

'Quite bad. Not so much the illness, as, well, everything else. You know. She's very confused, keeps wanting to get up and go out looking for my father, that kind of thing. I can't take my eyes off her for a second, it's like having a big toddler. Except that I can't be cross with her, or confine her in a cot or a playpen.'

And except, thought Phoebe, that she's not going to grow out of it.

'Poor you. Don't worry about Tashie, she'll be fine.'

'I feel awful, leaving her with you . . .'

'Don't. I'm rather enjoying it.'

'As long as you don't catch it too. It seems to be quite contagious.

Nick sat with my mother for an hour, the day before yesterday. He said he felt a bit tired, then, so he was obviously just going down with it. It's going through the school like wildfire, the classrooms are half empty.'

'There you are, then. Definitely not glandular fever. Just a 'flu virus. I'm not very likely to get it. I was a teacher for years, I've built up a tremendous immunity after all those years of being bombarded with bugs. What about you, though? If you go down with it?'

'I'll worry about that when it happens. I don't usually catch things off the kids, for some reason. Mainly because I just haven't got time to be ill.'

Phoebe went upstairs to check on Tashie. She opened her eyes as Phoebe went into the room.

'Was that Mum?'

'Yes. I'm afraid she can't come and see you today, after all. Your grandmother's not well.'

'She hasn't wandered off again, has she?' Tashie looked alarmed.

'No, not at all. She's just gone down with your 'flu, or whatever it is.'

'Oh no! It's all my fault!' Tashie shed tears of weakness. Phoebe went to sit on the edge of the bed.

'Of course it isn't. Your brother Nick sat with her for an hour, the day before yesterday, and he's got it too. You both picked it up from school.'

Tashie's tears fell faster.

'I never sit with Gran. Nick's always doing it. He's so bloody *nice*. *And* he works hard at school.'

'How annoying of him,' Phoebe responded calmly. 'He's really letting you down, isn't he?' Tashie looked at her suspiciously. 'I mean, the oldest one is supposed to be the trail-breaker, isn't he? The first to rebel, to break the rules, to get your parents used to how things are. Still, you're doing it for Sam, aren't you?'

'Sam can do no wrong anyway, at the moment. If you're down for brain surgery, they practically canonise you on the spot.'

'Never mind. Look on the bright side. This may turn into meningitis, then you'll have a halo too. Of course, you'll feel too bloody to appreciate it at the time, but if you survive you'll go round in an odour of sanctity for a while, you'll see.'

Tashie looked ashamed.

'You think I'm horrible, don't you?'

'No. I think you're a fifteen-year-old girl, which isn't always everything it's cracked up to be. I was one once, believe it or not, and so was your mother.'

Tashie picked up a corner of the duvet cover, and pleated it carefully between her fingers.

'It's different . . .'

'Of course it is. I'm not trying to tell you I know just how you must be feeling, there's nothing more patronising. It's different for everyone, and there aren't many fifteen-year-old girls whose fathers have done what yours did.'

'No.' The pleats grew tighter. Carefully she let them go and smoothed the fabric, then started again with yet smaller pinches of material. 'I don't know how I feel. I don't know what to *think*,' she said. 'Other things, you know, you tell your friends at school, and we all talk about it, and it gets your mind straight. Only this . . . I can't tell them. Don't want to. And Mum . . .'

'I know. So many people think that girls tell their mothers everything. Perhaps some do. Perhaps it's just a myth put about by mothers, or something. But in my experience, it's more difficult to talk about those sorts of problems with parents than anyone else, because they're too involved. You hate to see them upset, and they feel guilty if you're upset, and it all spirals into some awful out-of-control emotional whirlpool.'

'But she doesn't seem to *mind*!' Tashie abandoned the duvet cover to clutch her hands together.

'Oh, Tashie. Of course she minds. She feels betrayed, and angry, and hurt. Worse, she feels a fool. And worst of all, she feels responsible for you and your brothers, that she's failed in her care of you.'

'How do you know?' Tashie sounded truculent. 'You can't know all that. You hardly know her.'

'I know, because that's how I feel, too. All except the bit about you and the boys, of course; I'm guessing at that. But I can imagine it, and though I don't know your mother very well I think in many ways we're very similar.'

Tashie looked up at her, her eyes expressing disbelief. Phoebe grinned.

'Not to look at! I may be younger than your mother, but I don't need you or anyone else to tell me she looks about a hundred times better than I do at the moment! I mean in our temperament, our character, the way we think. It may sound ridiculous to you, but I felt I knew her. There was a *rapport*, if that isn't too precious a word.'

'Don't you hate her?' Tashie was folding, this time, smaller and smaller.

'No, of course not. I feel guilty about her, of course, but I don't hate her. I shouldn't altogether blame her if she hated me, but she doesn't seem to. Your mother is a very special person, Tashie.'

'I know she is!' Tashie flung down her folded piece of duvet cover. 'That's what makes it so difficult! She makes me feel guilty all the time.'

'Well, why shouldn't you?' Tashie gaped at her. 'Why shouldn't you feel guilty? Don't you think you have one or two things to feel guilty about?' Tashie was appalled. She had begun to think that Phoebe was on her side, and did not know how to deal with this unexpected attack.

'You're not being very nice to me.'

'Why should I be? You tried to burgle me, and burn my house down.'

Tashie burst into tears.

'It's not fair! I didn't do it.'

'Only because you were stopped.' Phoebe knew she was being harsh. She hoped that it was more for Tashie's sake than to express her own anger.

'You just hate me, because of Daddy.'

Phoebe paused, and looked that idea in the eye.

'I don't hate you, Tashie. I loved your father, and the few months I had with him were the happiest of my whole life. I still love him – at least, I love the person I thought he was. Just like you do. And because of that, because we have that in common, and because you are his daughter, some of that love has to spill over on to you. Can you understand that?'

Tashie's angry sobs eased into something gentler.

'I suppose so. But it was me that warned him. He wouldn't have gone if I hadn't.'

'And then they'd have caught up with him here, and he'd probably have gone to prison for all I know. That would scarcely have been an improvement. No, I'm glad you did. It wasn't your fault he went off as he did, without a word of explanation or farewell. The blame for that lies in his own character. The kind of person he was.'

There was a long pause. Downstairs, the telephone rang. Phoebe stood up quickly, but after one ring it stopped. To her amazement, Phoebe heard a voice in the hall. For a moment she was filled with panic, then she recognised the gruff tones of Daphne. She went to the top of the stairs. Daphne was just replacing the receiver.

'Let myself in,' she said unnecessarily. 'Hope you don't mind. I knocked at the back door, but you didn't hear. I thought I'd just make sure, well, you know. In case.'

'Daphne!' Phoebe was filled with guilt. 'I should have let you know what happened! I'm so sorry, but there hasn't been a chance . . . and with you not being on the phone—'

'I know. Silly. I was thinking, I ought to get myself one of those mobile affairs. Like the one I found in the hedge. Ghastly, really, but practical. If I had a fall, I mean, or something like that.'

'Yes, good idea. Um, who was it, on the phone?'

Daphne flushed.

'Sorry. Got sidetracked. Shouldn't have answered it anyway, in someone else's house, but I was standing right next to it, and it made me jump. Sort of instinct, to pick it up. It was Millie.'

'Millie? My mother? Why didn't you call me?' Phoebe felt quite cross. She hadn't heard from her mother for over a week, and although it wasn't unusual for them not to see one another for several months at a time, Phoebe was finding that it was a very different matter knowing her mother was practically on the other side of the world.

'No need. She'll be here in half an hour.'

'Half an hour? Where on earth was she calling from? I thought she was in Japan.'

'She was. Now she's at Gatwick Airport. She flew into Heathrow in the early hours, and took the coach down. Didn't want to wake you then, and didn't want you to have to turn out to fetch her, so she's getting a taxi.'

'Oh, Daphne! How lovely!'

'Yes, that's what I thought.'

'I'll come and make us a drink – I've got some limeflower tea I bought specially with you in mind. Come up and meet my guest first, though.'

Daphne looked down at her muddy trousers, but came obediently up the stairs, her feet silent in the thick woolly socks she wore inside her boots. In the doorway she paused.

'It is you, then. Thought so. Leo's daughter?'

'Yes.' Tashie looked at her apprehensively. 'I've got 'flu,' she offered, more as protection than in warning.

'Not to worry. I don't believe in germs and all that rubbish.'

'Then let's hope they don't believe in you either,' said Phoebe, as Daphne strode forward.

'What's your name?'

'Natasha.'

'Fancy. Russian?'

'No. They call me Tashie.'

'Why not Nat? Gnat,' said Daphne thoughtfully. 'God knows, you've been irritating enough.'

'I know. I'm sorry.' Tashie sounded unusually meek.
'Doesn't bother me. Matter of fact, it was all rather fun.'
Phoebe gave a snort of laughter at Tashie's expression. 'This is Miss Cunningham,' she told her. 'She has a strange sense of humour.'
'Not Miss Cunningham,' said Daphne decidedly. 'Sounds like an old aunt. Ghastly woman, such a snob she could scarcely bring herself to speak to anyone without a title. Call me Daphne.'
'Daphne.' Tashie sounded uncertain.
'They called me Daffy at school. Can't think why.'
'Of course you can't. Count yourself lucky,' said Phoebe. 'They called me Feeble. Come on, Daphne, Tashie ought to be resting, she's been having an ear-bashing from me. Do you want anything to drink, Tashie? Cup of tea? Or some of Daphne's limeflower?'
'Limeflower, please. Um, did you say someone's coming?'
'Yes, my mother. Don't worry, you'll like her. Everybody does, even me. She's daft as a brush, in some ways, and about the sanest person I know.'
Tashie looked reassured, but only slightly.
'Am I in her room?'
'Not really. Well, she did use this one before, but she's not at all territorial. She'll be perfectly happy in the little room.'
'I could change . . .'
'Then I'd have to change all the sheets, and get this room ready for her, all in about twenty minutes. No, you stay put.' Tashie, obediently, lay back on the pillows but her mouth was trying to frame another question. 'What else? Come on, Tashie, spit it out. You must know by now I don't bite, and nor does Daphne.'
'Only in self-defence. Like you kick,' growled Daphne. 'I'll put the kettle on.' With her rough tact she left the room.
Tashie wriggled, and asked awkwardly, 'What shall I call you?'
'Oh dear, yes,' said Phoebe. 'I see what you mean. Phoebe, I think, don't you? Mrs Miller is out of the question, of course – and I don't intend to go on calling myself that, anyway. I'm not sure I know what to call myself, though. I don't mind Humphreys, of course, but I don't feel altogether like *Miss* Humphreys any more. Miss Humphreys taught English, and had a nice tidy life in a flat. Only I can't very well be Mrs Humphreys, because that's my mother.'
'Ms?' suggested Tashie.
'I beg your pardon? Oh, I see what you mean. Ms. I suppose I'll have to, but I don't feel like a Ms either.'
'What does a Ms feel like?' Tashie yawned.
'I don't know. Very independent. Individual. Not linked to anyone

else. Efficient. Brisk. Thin.' Tashie giggled weakly. 'See what I mean? Just call me Phoebe.'

They were still sipping their drinks when the taxi drew up.

'Darling!' Millie, her hair silvery blonde from the sun, her skin a smooth golden brown, looked like an exotic butterfly in her brilliantly coloured silk trouser suit. As she stood on the doorstep with her arms held wide, the cold grey February air seemed not to touch her, as if she were surrounded by a layer of Far Eastern zephyrs. Phoebe, hugging her, almost thought she could smell the heady aroma of flowers and spices and lush tropical vegetation.

'Millie! Why didn't you warn me? Is everything all right? You surely haven't fallen out with the Abercrombies, have you?'

'Fallen out with them? Of course not, when did I ever? No, they had a crisis back home, one of their children was in a car crash. Not badly hurt, but stuck in hospital for quite a while and they felt they wanted to be there, for the grandchildren. So here I am! Darling, how are you? You were far too thin when I left . . .' Millie leaned back, and surveyed Phoebe. Her eyes were bright as a bird's. You would never believe, thought Phoebe, that she had just endured a flight of more than twelve hours.

'And now I'm too fat. I know, but I'm fine, and I'm going to do something about it. For goodness' sake, let's get you out of the cold. Come and say hello to Daphne, and then you must meet my guest.'

'A guest? How lovely, darling. Shall I tactfully disappear?'

'When you've only just got back? Not likely. Besides, it's not that sort of guest. I think I'll let her tell you who she is. Only you mustn't go too near, she's got some kind of 'flu.'

'Oh, you know I never catch things like that,' said Millie blithely. Phoebe knew this was true – Millie not infrequently volunteered to nurse sick friends, and never caught anything from them. Another example, she thought, of how extraordinarily tough the older generation could be.

Sure enough, when Millie finally went up to the spare room she breezed happily right up to the bed, and took Tashie's hand as if she hadn't noticed how reluctantly it was offered.

'Hello, my dear. I'm Millie, Phoebe's mother.'

'I'm Tashie.' Millie smiled encouragingly. 'Tashie Miller. My father is . . . was . . .'

'Is, surely?' Millie, who was no fool, had seen the resemblance straight away.

'Not as far as I'm concerned. I disown him.'

'Ah, well. Nobody chooses their parents, unfortunately. Ask

Daphne. Or me, come to that. Anyway, the only reason to worry about who your parents are, or were, is genetic. Dodgy genes apart, the rest is up to you. Unless you were planning to exhibit yourself at Crufts?'

Tashie giggled.

'I don't think I'm obedient enough. Did Phoebe tell you why I'm here?'

'No. She said you'd do that.'

'I came here to steal all her jewellery. And her silver. And to burn the house down,' said Tashie with some relish.

'How dramatic,' said Millie calmly.

'Aren't you shocked?'

'Nothing shocks me. There are things I don't like. Spitting, for example. Cruelty to children, or animals. Fanatics of any persuasion. Slugs. But they don't shock me.'

'What about people who have two wives, and steal money and run away?'

'Well, I don't like that, either. But shocked? Not really.'

'Why? I thought old – older – people were easily shocked.'

'Some are. So are some young people. It just struck me, fairly early on, that it was rather a waste of time and energy. My parents found everything shocking. Perhaps that's why; I had aversion therapy to being shocked and turned right against it.'

'Shock tactics?' Tashie was grinning.

'In effect, only of course they didn't mean it to happen. And you can guess how they reacted, can't you?'

'How shocking?'

'Precisely. Terrible example of lack of moral fibre in youth of today. And I thought, there must be a difference between moral fibre and being trussed up in a straitjacket, so I escaped.'

'Like Houdini.'

'Rather like. It's all in the mind. So, do tell me, have you overcome your incendiary tendencies, or should we keep a bucket of water handy?'

'I think I've escaped from that, too.'

Phoebe, well satisfied, left them to it.

Chapter 21

When Kate telephoned that evening, to speak to Tashie, she sounded exhausted.

'No, I'm all right,' she said wearily, in response to Phoebe's question. 'Just tired. Nick's been quite bad, poor old chap, and though he's very undemanding he's needed quite a lot of attention. Thank goodness for Sam. I've kept him home from school, which is a bit awful of me but I don't think I could have coped without him to fetch and carry for me. I just can't leave my mother for a moment.'

'Oh, dear. Is she very ill?'

'Not really. At least, she's not as bad as Nick in terms of temperature and so on, though of course these things are more dangerous in the elderly. No, she's just so confused. More than confused, really. Half the time she doesn't seem to know where she is, or recognise anyone. It's awful to say it, but it would actually be easier if she were more ill, because at least then she'd stay in bed. As it is, I've twice caught her on her way out of the front door – Sam keeps forgetting to take the key out of the inside of the lock – and the second time we actually had a dreadful sort of struggle on the front doorstep, and someone called the police.'

'Oh, Kate!' Phoebe was appalled. 'Do you want me to come and help? I mean, I'm probably the last person you want in your house, but I could sit with your mother. I've got my own mother here, and she could easily take care of Tashie.'

'It's sweet of you, but no. Not that I'd mind you being here in that way. It's funny, but since he went,' (no need to specify which 'he', between the two of them) 'I've slightly lost touch with most of my old friends. Not all of them, of course, but except for one or two of the oldest, people I was at school with, I find I don't know what to say to the others. I just don't feel comfortable with them. One's in such a funny position, and I don't feel able to talk to them about it. It's easier with you.'

'Quite. I found the same. Even my mother – she was wonderful, but

I was almost relieved when she went away. So, are you sure you don't want me to come?'

'No. Nick's a bit better today. By tomorrow he may be able to sit downstairs and keep her company for a few hours. That'll make all the difference. I'll ring in the morning.'

In the morning, however, the telephone did not ring. Phoebe waited until about ten o'clock, imagining that Kate was busy overseeing the washing and breakfasting of her invalids. Between ten and eleven she was listening out for the phone, and at eleven o'clock she took the cordless phone to Tashie, and suggested that she ring home.

It was answered after half a ring, and although Phoebe was halfway across the room from Tashie's bed, she could clearly hear the high, anxious voice.

'Hello? Who is it?'

'Sam?' Tashie pulled herself upright in bed, as if the anxiety in her brother's voice acted like a string attached to the top of her head. 'Sam, what's the matter?'

'Oh Tashie! Gran's gone missing, and I don't know what to do! Mum's got flu, and she keeps wanting to go and look for her, but I don't think she should, she looks awful. I went and checked the usual places, but there's no sign of her and nobody's seen her.'

'Oh, poor Mum! Can I talk to her?'

'Yes, she's here. She won't go to bed.'

'Mum? Oh, poor Mum, don't worry, I'll come back and look for her.' Phoebe heard Kate's protest. 'What do you mean, not well enough? What about you? Yes, I know, but . . . oh, all right. Yes, she is. Yes. Yes, I will.' Tashie held the phone out to Phoebe. 'She wants to talk to you.'

'Kate.'

'Phoebe, I'm sorry, but I'm at my wits' end. I don't know how she managed it – she must have taken the keys from my handbag to open the door. I had a bad night, and dozed off at about six, I just didn't hear her go. I've been on to the police, but there's no sign of her, and she's been gone for hours. I can't bear it. Of all the times . . . I know it's not her fault, but it couldn't be a worse time. I feel awful . . . I meant to phone, but the piece of paper with your number on it has vanished, and I just couldn't remember it at all. I knew you'd phone in the end. Oh dear . . .'

'I'll come,' said Phoebe firmly. 'At least she's met me, and I know what she looks like. Try not to worry.'

Phoebe hastily threw together an overnight bag, in case she needed to stay.

'Will you be all right? I'm sorry to leave you with Tashie, when you've only just got back.'

Millie was tired, her internal clock not yet having adjusted, but her eyes and voice were as bright as ever.

'Get along with you, don't be daft! Tashie and I will be just fine, and if there are any problems we can always call Jennifer. And I know Daphne will be round, too.'

Phoebe drove to the village, where she stopped at the shop and stocked up with basics like eggs, cheese, lemons and other fruit. Loading the bags in her car she realised that more than an hour had passed since her telephone call, and she drove off quickly. In a hurry, she decided to take Blackwater Lane, the narrow lane that led to the main road and cut several miles off the journey. Since Daphne had found the mobile telephone there Phoebe had felt an irrational dislike of it, though even before she had seldom used it since there was virtually no passing space and too many people tended to drive down it too fast, but she thought that at this time of day it should be all right. Still, she hooted at every blind corner and was ready to stop abruptly, which was just as well, as she came out of a bend to find a figure in the road, flagging her down.

Braking fiercely, Phoebe did not at first recognise Daphne. With no coat or hat and her hair flying in all directions, looking more like a distinguished scarecrow than usual, Daphne dropped her outheld arms and strode round to the driving door of the car.

'Phoebe! Thank goodness, I thought it might be you, but I'm hopeless at recognising cars. Look, I've got a problem. Found this old dear wandering, can't get much sense out of her, and I'm afraid she's pretty ill.'

'I'll go and call an ambulance.' Phoebe had already put the car in reverse. 'See me round this corner, there's a farm gate where I can turn.'

'No time for that. You know how long it takes ambulances to get here, we're miles from the hospital and they invariably get lost. She's dreadfully cold, and practically unconscious by now. I couldn't lift her, but between us we could get her into the car, and back to the village.'

Phoebe saw that she could not, in all conscience, refuse to help. Her mind on Kate, she pulled the car as far into the verge as the overgrown hedges would permit, and climbed reluctantly out.

'All right, then. Where is she?'

'Just back here. She was sitting on the wet bank when I found her, and I managed to get her to a fairly dry tree stump. I put my jacket round her, and gave her my hat, but she's chilled to the bone. I didn't dare leave her to fetch help, there isn't a house for at least two miles and I was afraid she might wander away from the lane, and I'd never find her again.'

The word 'wander' struck a chord in Phoebe's memory.

'What does she look like? Do you know her name, or anything?'

'Not a thing. She doesn't seem to have a handbag, and there's nothing in her pockets. I can't get any sense out of her, she just keeps talking about someone called Harold.'

A large, cold hand clutched at Phoebe's stomach.

'Harold! Oh no, it's not – it *can't* be – what on *earth* is she doing here . . . Can't remember her name, dammit – Carpenter, that's it. Where is she?'

'Steady,' said Daphne. 'Just here. I propped her up. Only place I could find to sit her down. There's a bit of shelter from the wind.'

The little figure looked pathetically small, slumped on a tree stump against the fallen trunk of another tree, wrenched from the earth during the great storm of eighty-seven and left to rot. In Daphne's coat and hat she was almost invisible, the faded olive cloth blending with the undergrowth. Her head had fallen forward so that only the crown of the hat showed. Phoebe hurried to her and crouched down, trying to look up into her face. Shadowed by the hat, it was indistinguishable, and she stood up, putting out a gentle hand to lift the head.

It was heavier than she would have expected, so that she had to use some force, and the flesh felt cold and soft. As she had feared, as she had expected, she was looking into the face of Kate's mother, Joyce Carpenter. Still supporting the weight of the head with one hand, Phoebe pulled off Daphne's hat and put trembling fingers inside the collar of the thin coat, pressing them against a neck that felt thin and sinewy as a bird's. For a moment she felt nothing, then she moved her fingers and there it was – faint and slow, but a pulse.

'Mrs Carpenter! Wake up, Mrs Carpenter. Joyce! Joyce!'

At some time that morning she had put on make-up, the foundation and powder blotchy on skin now an unhealthy greyish colour, the pink lipstick crooked so that it overshot the creased borders of her lips. The wrinkles in her eyelids still held traces of blue eyeshadow, like random biro lines. When her eyelids quivered they looked as though they were wriggling. Joyce looked blearily up at Phoebe. Her lips trembled like a child's.

'Cold,' she whispered. 'Harold . . .?'

'You're very cold, Mrs Carpenter. We must get you back to the warm. Come on.'

Phoebe tried to lift the old woman to her feet, but with surprising strength she resisted, flinging out her arms. One fist connected with Phoebe's cheekbone, the sharp thud ringing through her head bones so that she felt deafened.

'No! No! Harold!' The little voice cracked as she wailed the name. Daphne came to the other side of her, taking hold of her arms.

'Harold's not here,' she growled firmly. 'We're going to find him.' Whether it was her deep-toned voice or the firmly spoken lie that did the trick, Joyce quietened down. This time, when they pulled her to her feet, she tried to stand, but her legs could not support her and she sagged between them like a sack.

'Can't drag her along like this,' said Daphne. 'We might damage her shoulders, or her spine. Have to carry her. Link hands.'

It was easier said than done. Phoebe remembered doing this for fun, at school, and how she had clasped her own wrist with one hand, and someone else's with the other, to make a square seat. That, however, required the third person to be conscious, and co-operative. The best they could now do was to keep one arm each supporting the top half of the limp body, while clasping hands beneath her as best they might. It was not the weight that was the problem, for Joyce weighed very little, but her semi-conscious state. Unable to help them by holding on, she was yet aware enough to know that something uncomfortable was happening, and make awkward little movements that threatened to unbalance their precarious hold. Step by tiny step, they edged themselves sideways towards the car.

'I'll prop her up,' puffed Daphne. 'You open the door.'

Phoebe was just in time to help catch her as Joyce tried to fight herself free of Daphne's hold. Unceremoniously they heaved her on to the back seat.

'Thank goodness it's not a two-door,' puffed Phoebe. 'You get in the other side, and hang on to her. What do we do with her?'

'Back to your house, I'd say, if you know her. Take too long to get her to the hospital. Got to get her warm. Pity she's not a lamb.'

'A what?' Phoebe, hastily starting the car and driving forward to find a turning place, thought she must have misheard.

'A lamb. Put her in the oven. What you do, if they're orphaned and get chilled. Who is she, anyway?'

'A lost sheep,' said Phoebe with the ghost of a laugh. 'Otherwise, Tashie's grandmother. Leo's wife's mother.'

'Sounds like one of those puzzles. My father's son's daughter, that kind of thing. A bit addled, is she?'

'Just a bit. And she's got Tashie's 'flu too, which doesn't help. She went missing this morning early, Kate's frantic – that's Tashie's mother – but she's gone down with the bug as well. Heaven only knows what she's doing here, though, or how she got here.'

'Looking for Harold.' The croaking voice startled them both. Phoebe glanced in the reversing mirror. The sound of familiar names had roused Joyce for a moment, but her eyes were closed again.

'Harold?' Daphne mouthed it rather than spoke. Phoebe met her eyes in the mirror.

'Her husband.'

'*En retard*?' Daphne spoke the words with a forthright English accent. Phoebe interpreted, translated, and gave a nod. Late. Her late husband.

'Yes. Why didn't I bring the mobile phone? I must be mad, we could have called for help.'

'Nearly there. Call the doctor.'

'Not nine nine nine?'

'Doctor's quicker. He calls to see Mrs Ford on Wednesdays, about half past twelve. Should catch him, if we're lucky.' This, thought Phoebe, was village life at its best.

'Why, is she very ill?'

'Not very. Not unless you call having large breasts and a small brain ill. On Wednesdays her husband goes to market, doesn't come home for lunch.' Phoebe gave a snort of laughter. 'But she's not his patient, so it's quite legal.'

'I'm surprised they haven't been caught out, if everyone knows about it.'

'Not everyone. And her husband chases every woman he meets between the ages of sixteen and sixty. Knocks her about a bit, too.'

'What about the doctor's wife?' Phoebe, in spite of worrying about Joyce, was fascinated by this insight into village life.

'Dead. Cancer, two years ago. Tragic, really, she was only in her thirties. No children, fortunately. Or not, perhaps, I don't know.'

They pulled into the drive, and she parked as near the front door as she could.

Between them, they manoeuvred Joyce indoors and onto the sofa. Phoebe lit the fire, which fortunately she had already laid that morning, and Millie filled hot water bottles and fetched pillows and blankets while Daphne telephoned. The doctor promised to be with them in five minutes, and Phoebe tried hard not to let her imagination dwell on the fact that he was probably putting his clothes back on. She went up to reassure Tashie, and to persuade her that it wouldn't help anyone if she came downstairs.

Phoebe went to the telephone in her bedroom to ring Kate.

'She's here. Don't worry.' Why did I say that, she wondered? Of course she's going to worry.

'Where are you?' Kate, of course, thought that Phoebe was on her way to Brighton.

'I'm at home. A friend of mine found your mother in a lane not far from here. I was on my way to you, and she waved me down. We've brought her back here, and the doctor's on his way.'

'How bad is she?'

'Pretty confused, and very cold. She's only semi-conscious, I'm afraid.'

'How did she *get* there?' Kate, feverish, sounded startlingly like Tashie. 'It's miles!'

'In a taxi, I think. Didn't you say the piece of paper with my address and phone number was missing? Perhaps she found it, when she went looking for the keys. You know she was convinced that your father was here. She must have found a taxi, and given him the name of the village. For some reason he didn't bring her right here, or we'd have been all right. She must have been wandering for quite a while, and somewhere along the line she seems to have lost her handbag, poor old love. Anyway, she's safe here, and I'll keep you posted. The doctor may want to move her to hospital, so there's no point in you rushing up here.'

Like Tashie, Kate had to accept the unpalatable truth that she could do nothing to help except keep out of the way and not do anything to make her own illness worse.

'I'm sorry. I'm afraid my family are messing up your life in a big way at the moment.'

'Not really. He did that for me. The rest of them – well, I think they're probably doing me quite a lot of good. Stopped me thinking about how miserable I am all the time, that sort of thing. There's a car, that'll be the doctor. I'll ring as soon as he's seen her.'

The doctor was small and dapper. Phoebe thought inconsequentially that he didn't look at all like a man who has just come from an illicit bed. Phoebe gave the medical history as far as she was able: the onset of Alzheimer's, the attack of 'flu, the amount of time she must have been wandering the countryside.

'Hmmm.' That's what doctors always say, Phoebe thought, when they need a bit of time. 'Hmmm. It's the cold I'm worried about, of course. She's basically well nourished and quite healthy, but getting as cold as this, on top of the onset of 'flu, is unfortunate. Could well lead to complications. The daughter's ill too, you say?'

'Yes. Could you speak to her? She's dreadfully worried.'

'Yes.' He scrubbed at his face with both hands. 'She'd be better in her own home, but there's the journey to consider, and her daughter's state . . . I'd better try to get her into hospital, to be on the safe side.'

He was on the telephone for half an hour. At the end of it he put the telephone down decisively.

'Can't find a bed nearer than London, I'm afraid.' He looked thoughtfully at Phoebe. 'On the whole, it would probably be better for her to stay here. If you don't mind? I can get one of the practice nurses to come over, bring you some things you might need. And of course, if you're worried, you can ring me any time.'

Phoebe, looking at his concerned face, thought what a nice man he was. She also found herself thinking that it was a pity she found him so completely unattractive, in a romantic or a sexual sense. A good, caring man like this, she told herself, was just what she needed. The thought made her want to giggle, which on the whole was probably a good sign, though of what she could not have said.

Joyce was a good patient, to Phoebe's relief. She slept much of the time, and obediently swallowed drinks, soup and tablets as they were offered to her, and used without complaint the disposable bedpans the nurse brought to the cottage. Though unsure who Phoebe was, she seemed to respond positively to her and Millie, and all in all showed remarkable equanimity for someone who found herself in a strange room, being cared for by someone she hardly knew. When Tashie, looking terrified but trying hard to hide it, came in to see her, she smiled, clearly knowing who she was. Phoebe was deeply relieved, and since Tashie was now well enough to sit, well wrapped up, in an armchair, she left the two of them together for much of the day.

On Thursday Joyce sat up, ate a little breakfast, and seemed so much brighter that Phoebe brought her the mobile phone and suggested she speak to Kate. Leaving the room, she stayed on the landing in case of problems. Joyce, however, seemed completely her old self.

'Darling, I'm so sorry about this. It must have been the 'flu, I was quite batty to come over here. No, I don't remember much about it, but I suppose I must have taken a taxi, and then lost my bag with the address. Phoebe's had half the village out looking for it, but no luck yet. Still, I'm fine, and what about you? And Nick? And Sam? Good. No, you mustn't dream of coming out. I'll get a taxi to bring me back, when I'm allowed, and Tashie too. Or maybe that nice Phoebe . . . Yes, of course. Yes, I'll tell her.' She gave a little chesty cough. 'Nothing. Just a tickle.' She coughed again. 'I'll speak to you soon.'

By the evening she was coughing more, and when the nurse called that evening Joyce was once again very confused, though quiet.

Phoebe checked her several times in the night, and she was restless, but sleeping. By the following morning Phoebe was worried about her, and when the nurse arrived she too shook her head.

'I don't like the sound of her chest, and she seems very lethargic. I'll get doctor round as soon as he can come.'

The doctor came, and shook his head a little.

'I was afraid this would happen. I think we must get her into hospital at once. I'll call an ambulance. Her daughter lives in Brighton, doesn't she? I'll see if I can find her a bed there.'

Phoebe, after consultation with Kate, went in the ambulance with Joyce.

'I don't want her to travel all on her own. With just the ambulance men, I mean. Or do you think Tashie . . .?'

'Certainly not,' said Phoebe firmly. 'Tashie's still convalescing, and apart from that, she's still tearing herself apart with guilt over her grandmother's illness. She's decided it's all her fault, and you know what they are at that age – she's all ready to punish herself by some daft and heroic action. Besides, Joyce really doesn't look too good. I don't think it would be good for Tashie in other ways . . .'

'Oh dear. All right. I seem to spend my whole time thanking you for taking care of my family. I'll be at the hospital, then, when you arrive.' Kate had insisted on that, and although she was obviously far from well it was impossible to say no to her. Phoebe was only thankful that a bed had been found at a Brighton hospital.

In the ambulance they fitted Joyce with an oxygen mask. Phoebe was afraid that this would worry her, but in fact she lay quietly, her eyes almost closed, and Phoebe found this acquiescence pathetic and alarming. She was more glad than ever that Tashie was safely at the cottage, being cared for by Millie and Daphne. Tashie, to everyone's surprise and particularly her own, found Daphne easy to talk to and, in her gruff, forthright way, comforting. Daphne said exactly what she thought, without regard to Tashie's sensibilities, and her abrasive personality was invigorating. Tashie felt that Phoebe and Millie, however kind, stood in a parental relationship with her, whereas Daphne treated her as an equal. Kate would have been astonished to see how she accepted even the severest criticism from Daphne.

At the hospital, Phoebe and Kate faced one another across Joyce's bed. The curtains had been closed round them, but any faint illusion of privacy was rendered stillborn by the intrusion of noises from the rest of the ward: footsteps, coughs and sighs, conversations and creaks, the rustle of newspapers and magazines. Between them, Joyce was propped against piled-up pillows, her little legs scarcely seeming to lift the thin cotton blankets above the level of the mattress. An oxygen mask obscured her face, a drip was taped to her arm and some kind of monitor was clipped to her fingertip. She seemed remote, an alien being existing in an inimical universe. Phoebe felt awkward, but when she had tried to leave Kate had looked so panicky that she had stayed. She sat next to the machines and drips. Kate, on the other side, held her mother's free hand, her thumb stroking and stroking the thin, freckled skin.

'I didn't think it would be like this,' whispered Kate. Phoebe looked puzzled. 'For her, I mean. My mother. I thought – I always hoped – that it would be at home. In her sleep, perhaps.'

'They don't think she'll . . . There isn't much hope, then?'

'What do you hope for? What does the future hold, for her? The consultant says that her memory won't improve. Well, one knows that, with this kind of thing, but before she was ill, she remembered more than she forgot. Now he says that what he calls her lucid periods are likely to be fewer and shorter. I'd keep her at home for as long as possible, of course, but how long would that be? How can I keep her safe? I've not done very well so far.'

'It's not your fault,' said Phoebe. She seemed to spend all her time saying that. Not Tashie's fault. Not Kate's fault. Not even her own fault. Leo's fault? Perhaps. But how futile, now, to hold him accountable. If one could free oneself of guilt, she now thought, one could be rid of the sticky tendrils of blame that linked one to others, as if they were flies caught in the same web. It would be freedom, of a kind.

Chapter 22

Joyce died two days later.

By then, all her family had been able to visit her, and though she had not appeared to recognise them she had smiled, aware that they were dear to her even if names and relationships escaped her. Tashie had amazed everyone. Not only did she not cry at the bedside, as Kate had feared she would do and upset her grandmother, but she had behaved with a kind of calm strength that helped all of them, particularly Kate. At home she comforted Sam, still miraculously free from 'flu and also fits, since the medication was finally controlling them. The pills made him sleepy, however, and also ravenously hungry, a side-effect that Kate had not taken into consideration. Tashie produced endless snacks for him without complaint, and refrained from teasing him as she would once have done.

'Is this really Tashie you've sent back to me?' Kate asked Phoebe over the telephone. 'Or is it a changeling? No, changelings were always naughty, weren't they? I've often thought they were an early way of explaining autism. A robot, then? Like the one on *Star Trek*, Data. Looks almost like the real thing, but impossibly perfect.'

'Don't worry. It probably won't last. Just enjoy it while it does. She's risen to the occasion, that's all. It does happen.'

'I know I'm over-reacting. Before she ran away, I panicked because her bedroom was so unnaturally tidy. Now I'm worried because she's so *nice*. Do you suppose there's something wrong with me?'

Phoebe laughed.

'Just an overload of events. You're probably blown out a few circuits, and you're making dud connections.'

'*Star Trek* again. I suppose so. I know I never used to be so pessimistic. I expect things go wrong all the time, then worry if they don't because I think something worse will happen. Perhaps I need a shrink.'

'Isn't it axiomatic that anyone who says they need a shrink probably doesn't? It's the people who think they're normal that need to have their heads read.'

'Maybe. I don't think I'm up to that kind of subtlety at the moment.'

'Sorry. How are you getting on with the funeral arrangements?'

'It's all fixed for Tuesday of next week. Two-thirty, at the church, and the crematorium afterwards. It was that or this Friday, which is such a rush and I wanted to make sure we were all over the 'flu. Um . . . can you be there? If you want to be, of course. I mean, don't feel you've got to . . .'

'I'd like to be there,' said Phoebe. 'If you're sure.'

'I think it would be right. You looked after her. Besides, you're family. Sort of.'

Phoebe felt a warm rush of pleasure.

'Sort of is right. How will you explain me away?'

'No one to explain it to. I haven't a large family – my mother was an only child too, like me.'

'Same here. The odd cousin. And when I say odd . . .'

'Heavens, you don't have to tell me. What's the collective noun for fruitcakes?'

'I don't know. An indigestion?'

'Probably. Anyway, they don't need to know who you are, you're just a family friend. And even if they find out, what does it matter?'

'It's embarrassing. I feel a fool.'

'Not any more you don't.'

'I'm sorry?'

'The fool's gone. Sorry. A bit coarse.'

'Not really. And you're right. I haven't done anything to be ashamed of.'

'Neither of us has. Solidarity, that's the thing. Maybe we should form an action group.'

'Why not? Everyone else does. What shall we call ourselves?'

'Wives Of Leonard Miller. WOLM. Not a very good acronym.'

'Ex-wives. EWOLM.'

'Co-wives. Ex-co-wives.'

'Mm. Ex-co. Sounds like an oil company.'

'Kate and Co,' said Kate dreamily. 'Sounds a bit twee. Miller and Co. That's a solid, respectable kind of name.'

'For an action group? I thought we needed aspirations?'

'No, that's trades unions. Action groups have ideals. No problem. Any old ideal will do. World domination. Bring back *Blake's Seven*.'

'Free the Renault Five. Where were we?'

'Joining our relatives, I think.'

This time it was Kate's turn. 'What?'

'In the cake shop. With all the other fruitcakes.'

'Oh, yes. Oh!' Kate felt her stomach fizzing with laughter. It erupted into something between a sob and a hiccup. At the other end of the telephone she could hear, between her own helpless gasps, a kind of wheezing noise which she knew was Phoebe struggling for breath between paroxysms of giggles.

'What a ridiculous conversation,' said Kate at last. 'What is the matter with me? I haven't laughed like that since I was at school.'

'Nor have I. I expect it's reaction. My stomach aches.'

'So does mine, and my mascara's run halfway down my cheeks. You know what?'

'No, what?'

'I reckon he did us a favour, after all.'

'Going off?'

'Well, yes. But I was thinking more, I'm glad I've met you.'

'Me too.' Phoebe felt rather shy. 'You know those stories you read in the paper, about adopted children seeking out their natural mothers? I feel a bit like that.'

'As if I were your natural mother?'

'No, of course not. But as if . . . well, I always wanted a sister, when I was a child. I used to be jealous of other girls. When they said they hated their sisters, and did nothing but fight with them, I used to think it wasn't fair, they didn't deserve to have sisters at all if they didn't appreciate how lucky they were.'

'All siblings fight,' said Kate with feeling. 'We would have done too. If we'd been sisters.'

'But not now.'

'No, not now.' Kate drew in a long breath, expanding her lungs until she felt she would float upwards like a balloon. She breathed out slowly, feeling the oxygen revive her slow-moving blood. 'I feel better.'

'Good. It's pretty awful, this patch between the death and the funeral, isn't it?'

'Yes. I can't wait for the funeral to be over. Is that awful of me? It's not that I want to be rid of her . . .'

'Of course it isn't. I don't think you can start mourning properly until you get to the funeral. I suppose that's what it's for. Do you want me to do anything, on the practical side? Are you having people back afterwards?'

'I suppose I should. Some of them will be coming from further away. What should it be? Funeral baked meats, whatever they are? It always sounds so dried up. Sherry? Something stronger?'

'If the funeral is for two-thirty, it'll be teatime. Sandwiches, cakes, that kind of thing. Tea, of course. Something stronger available, but most people will be driving so you won't get many wanting to drink. Look, will you let me do the food? I've got nothing to do, now Tashie's gone, and it would be nice to feel useful.'

Kate accepted gratefully. She was not, herself, particularly busy. She had cancelled the few bed and breakfast bookings she had had, telephoning round to make alternative arrangements and receiving much gratitude from the new hosts. Soon she would have to sort through her mother's remaining things, but most of what she owned had been winnowed out when she first came to live with them, and what remained was mostly family furniture and books, which she would keep. In a week or two, she supposed, she would rearrange the downstairs room.

Her mother's capital, which she had earlier expected to be needed for the expense of a nursing home, would come to her. She could probably manage, now, without the bed and breakfast guests or the students. Wearily, she contemplated moving everyone around again: the boys back upstairs, Tashie and herself to their old rooms, perhaps a quiet guest in the downstairs room. It all seemed such an effort, and meanwhile she continued to sleep downstairs. Her old room no longer felt like home.

The funeral passed in a kind of dream. To Kate it simply did not seem possible that her mother could be contained in that wooden box, which looked so pathetically small and yet so horribly solid. She noticed with detached pleasure that the service went well. The hymns that she had carefully chosen from Joyce's favourites were not too gloomy, and the small choir the church was able to provide ensured that the singing lacked the embarrassing thin, dragging sound that frequently attends such occasions. Nick, bony and intense in a dark suit, gave a short address that filled her with so much pride that it brought her nearer to weeping than anything else. On her other side, Tashie and Sam concentrated silently, and got through the service with decorum.

Kate was only dimly aware of anyone other than her immediate family. She knew that later she would be pleased to remember how full the church was, how many friends made the effort to be there. At the time she was vaguely conscious of Phoebe, with her mother and Daphne, sitting near the back. The only other person who registered with her was Brian Harper. He had telephoned her every day, with undemanding kindness and occasional offers of help that were carefully non-invasive. He made no attempt to visit, but Kate still had a warm subliminal feeling of being cared for.

The crematorium was harder to deal with, particularly since none of her three children had ever been to one before. Kate had warned them how it might be, but was relieved to find that there was no opening of doors and trundling of the coffin through, only a curtain coming down and hiding it. They had kept the service there to a minimum, and it was a relief when it was over and they could, after a polite inspection of the flowers, go back to the house.

Phoebe, as promised, had brought plates of little sandwiches, cakes and home-made biscuits. There were also savoury tartlets, and tiny pizzas. Tashie, who had helped bring them indoors and unwrap the clingfilm, found herself with a willing helper in Sam. If he ate more than he offered round no one complained, and with the guests warmed by cups of tea or glasses of ginger wine, the noise level soon rose to the convivial heights frequent at such occasions.

Kate, moving on auto-pilot round the room, greeting and thanking, responding suitably to expressions of sympathy that she would, at that moment, rather have done without, picked up tag ends and snippets of other conversations and used them as a barrier to thinking.

'. . . such a good daughter. Pity about the husband . . .'

'. . . happened to him? Bit of a mystery there. Of course, I always thought he was a bit . . .'

'. . . some problem with the boy? Diabetes, I think. Something like that, poor kid. Still, they can do wonderful things, nowadays. Kidney transplants . . .'

'. . . don't believe we've met? Friend of Kate's?'

'Yes, that's right.' Phoebe's voice, full of uninformative friendliness.

'Poor Kate, this is a sad time for her, particularly in view of Len . . .'

'Yes. Very sad. But she's coping magnificently, don't you think?'

'Oh yes, Kate always copes. Have you known her long?'

'Not long. You know how it is. There are some people you get on with straight away, and some people you don't.'

'Oh, yes.' Phoebe's questioner sounded uncertain, as though she suspected that she might be one of the latter. Kate, keeping her face straight with difficulty, thought that she was right.

Brian, who had offered to help, was in charge of the alcohol. The ginger wine had been his suggestion.

'It warms you up, which is what you need after a funeral. And there's something rather comforting about it, more so than sherry.'

He had been right, she saw. Several of the older people, who had been brought in someone else's car, were happily accepting a top-up. He caught her eye, and smiled. It occurred to her that he had a nice smile. His eyes crinkled at the edges, and he had good teeth that were just uneven enough still to be his own. Presently, when he had been round the room, he joined her.

'Going well,' he said in a voice pitched below the conversation level, so that although he spoke quietly she could easily hear him. 'The service was just right. Nick did well, didn't he?'

She nodded with a tight throat.

'Excellent tea, too,' he continued, giving her time. 'It's amazing how much people eat at this kind of thing. Comfort, of course, and relief that it's over. There's something very soothing,' he said judiciously, 'about a really well made sandwich.'

Kate achieved a shaky laugh.

'They are well made, aren't they? Phoebe did the tea.'

'Yes, Tashie told me.'

'Tashie did?' Kate didn't quite keep the surprise out of her voice. He smiled.

'Yes, we had quite a chat. She was telling me about Sam.' It was his turn to keep his voice neutral.

'Yes, I'm sorry. I know I should have told you about it. I would have done. It's just . . . I didn't want you to feel obliged to offer to help. With money, I mean.'

'When it comes to health, money is an irrelevance. You know you can always come to me.'

'I know I can. And I would have done, if it had been crucial. But I don't see why the insurance company should wriggle out of paying, and I wanted – oh, I don't know . . . to do it myself, you know.'

'Of course I know. And you can win this battle on your own. Of course you can. What's the state of play now?'

'Impasse again. We've found another hospital, but they're still stalling. It makes me so *cross*. What's the point of paying for insurance if it isn't to use it at times like this?'

'Don't let them get you down. You've just got to keep on fighting.'

'Yes, but *how*? When I telephone, I just get those girls with the voices, you know what I mean, and they don't know anything except what the rules say. They can't make decisions, and they won't put me through to anyone who can.'

'May I suggest something?'

'Oh yes, I wish you would. Independence is all very well, but I'm getting desperate!'

'Write to the chief executive. Send the letter – or better still, fax it – and make it clear that you're prepared to make a fuss. Not threats,' he added, seeing her doubtful face. 'Just firmness. Obstinacy, if you like. Show them you'll fight. Mention the Ombudsman, that usually gets them hopping about like performing fleas.'

'Goodness. I'd never have thought of that.'

'I've always found there's nothing like going straight to the top.'

'Oh, Brian, I could hug you!'

'Do,' he invited. 'Any time.'

Looking at him, Kate knew that he meant it. She wondered, for a moment, what it would be like, and decided that it would be pleasant. Not, perhaps, the fireworks and volcanoes of her first encounters with Len, but something more comfortable. Safety, and kindness and companionship. Her mind, conditioned by the funeral into prayer-book lines, came up with the words from the old marriage service – 'the mutual society, help and comfort'. Good words, and something worth having. She looked at Brian, and saw behind the neat, plump face and the controlled manner, a friend. A man who, though he would never set the world on fire, could be depended upon in good times and bad. She saw that he would be reticent, that he would never do or say anything that would make her feel embarrassed, or uncomfortable.

'I'd like to ask you to stay to supper tonight, but I think I should spend this evening with the children. But what I'd really like . . .'

The smile that was already in his eyes travelled down to his lips.

'Yes? What would you really like?'

'I'd like to go out to dinner somewhere really nice, next weekend. On Saturday. Just the two of us. I'd like to be me. Not Len's wife, or Joyce's daughter, or the kids' mother. Just me, Kate, having a proper meal that I haven't had to shop for, or cook, or think about. With a friend. With you. Can we do that?'

His face did not change, but she saw the tremor, quickly stilled, in the hand that still held the bottle of ginger wine. Kate, who felt herself to be beyond feeling or inspiring passion, was moved.

'I'd like that very much. I'll make a booking, and pick you up. Seven-thirty?'

Kate knew, as she agreed, that he would go to a lot of trouble to find somewhere special. She knew also that he would make no assumptions. The fact that she had asked him to take her out would not lead him to expect that she would be accessible in other ways. There would be no fending off, no awkwardness when he brought her home, or when they said goodbye. He would kiss her cheek, as he had done on meeting and parting for some years, and it would be up to her to decide what, if anything, should happen next. She wondered what her children would think, or say, then decided that for once she didn't care.

As if at some invisible signal, everyone began to leave. Kate was suddenly aware that her legs and back ached as if she had just run a marathon, that her cheeks ached from smiling and her head from just enduring. Phoebe, she saw, had with Millie's help quietly cleared up the tea things.

'There's a chicken casserole in the fridge, with dumplings,' she said. 'I thought you probably wouldn't feel like cooking tonight.'

For the first time that day, Kate felt her eyes fill with tears.

'Bless you,' she said. 'I wish I could do something for you, in return.'

'Lend me Tashie, from time to time? And the others, if they'll allow it. You're so lucky, Kate.'

'I know I am.' Kate gave her a hug. 'I really am. And you will be, too. There are other men in the world, you know.'

'I know. Pebbles on the beach. Fish in the sea. But how do you find the right fish, the right pebble? It took me so many years to find one, and then I picked wrong, after all. How do I go about it? I haven't got much time, you know.'

'Poor Phoebe. I'm sorry. It's ticking away, is it?'

'The old biological clock?' Phoebe grimaced a smile, tried to joke. 'It certainly is. Any day now it'll strike twelve, and I'll be turned into a pumpkin.' She sniffed, fishing for a handkerchief. 'Sorry. I'm being silly. It's my period, I always get a bit weepy, and it's worse now, because for the last few months I kept hoping . . . even after he'd gone, you know, I thought I might just be . . . of course not now, it's far too long, but it sort of *reminds* me . . .'

Kate edged them both out of the room. The hall, mercifully, was empty, and she whisked them into Joyce's room and shut the door.

'Sit down,' she said, rummaging in a cupboard. 'Have a drink. We'll both have a drink. My mother was partial to the odd glass of Scotch, there should be some . . . Ah, here it is.'

'I shouldn't. I'm driving.' Phoebe was making an effort, but her voice still wobbled.

'One little one will be all right, on top of all those sandwiches. I'm going to have one with you.'

Kate waited until the glass was almost empty.

'So you were hoping to start a family? You and Len? Leo,' she corrected hastily.

'Yes. I'm sorry. It's just I did so want—'

'The bastard! The absolute, total, first-class arsehole of a bastard!'

Phoebe gaped at her. 'I know it's awful of him, when he already had three children to support and everything. Though of course I didn't know that, but still . . .'

'Oh, not that.' Kate dismissed her words with a gesture. 'I don't mean that. I mean, he didn't tell you?'

'Tell me what? He really seemed to want us to have a family. He used to be disappointed, too . . .' She broke off, seeing Kate's face. 'What is it? What didn't he tell me?'

'He may have been disappointed each month, but he couldn't have been surprised when you didn't start a baby.'

'Why not? You don't mean . . .? Oh, no!'

'Oh yes. He had a vasectomy, years ago. Just after Sam was born. I'm sorry, Phoebe. Phoebe?'

Phoebe's face was buried in her hands, her shoulders heaving. Kate moved to comfort her, but Phoebe lifted her head and Kate saw that she was laughing. Laughing perhaps rather hysterically, but still far from the desperate weeping she had feared.

'That was the one thing left,' said Phoebe when she was calmed. 'The one thing I still minded about. I didn't want him back any more, not as a person. All I wanted was the chance of a baby. And it was never there, anyway. Ironic, isn't it?'

'That's one way of looking at it.' Kate looked at her searchingly. 'Would you still want it, knowing what you now know? Knowing what kind of person he is? Not such a good bet, genetically, I wouldn't think.'

'Is being a bigamist genetically inheritable? Besides, how can you say that? Look at your three. They're all his children, and they're wonderful.'

'Possibly. So, shall I tell you something even more ironic?'

'What?'

'You can still do it.'

'Still do what?'

'Have a baby. His baby. If that's what you want.'

Phoebe stared at her speechlessly.

'No, I haven't gone off my rocket. When he said he wanted a vasectomy, I was upset. I was still quite young, I wasn't sure I didn't want to have any more children. It wasn't so much that I wanted another baby, as that I didn't want to think that I couldn't. You know?' Phoebe nodded. 'So I made such a fuss that he agreed to have some semen stored. As a kind of just-in-case. Of course, in the end I didn't want another child, but it's still there, as far as I know. In fact, I'm sure it is, because we had a letter only a year ago asking if we wanted to continue the storage, and for some reason I wrote back and said yes. Daft, really, because I knew I wouldn't want to use it, but I still didn't feel happy about it being destroyed. So there it is. If you want it.'

'If I . . . But what about . . . Will they let me?'

'I've no idea. I know he signed some form to give me ownership, or custody, or whatever it is you have. We don't need his permission. Of course, it means he doesn't acknowledge paternity or anything, but I don't suppose, under the circumstances, you'd really want him to.'

'Not really, no. But, Kate, are you sure? Do you really mean it?'

'I wouldn't have said it, if I didn't. It's there, it's no use to me.'

'What about Tashie, and the boys?'

'It's not really their business, is it? Well, perhaps it is, but I don't see that we need to tell them. One day, perhaps. By then, I hope, they'd think of you as a kind of relative anyway.'

'I don't know what to say.'

'You don't have to say anything. In fact, it's not a decision you should take in a hurry. It's not all roses, being a mother – you may have noticed – and particularly a single mother. Even if you've got money, and family support, which of course you'll have. You need to think hard about what you'd be committing yourself to.'

'I know. Kate, even if I don't go ahead with this, I will be in your debt for the rest of my life. I can't find the words . . .'

'Don't even look for them. He's damaged us both. Don't you think that this is the perfect way to balance the books?'

'I hadn't thought of it like that. I suppose there is a certain poetic justice . . .' Phoebe was laughing again, and Kate with her. When they had their breath back, Kate picked up the bottle and poured a little more whisky into each of their glasses.

Chapter 23

'Sam! Wake up, Sam! Open your eyes, please.'

Kate pushed her chair back out of the nurse's way, and watched the now familiar routine.

'Squeeze my hands. Move your feet. What year is it? What's your middle name?'

Sam frowned. The dressing over one side of his head looked unnaturally white against his skin which even now retained some of last summer's tan.

'I'm not telling you that!' he protested. 'It's private!'

The nurse laughed.

'Not much wrong with you! You can go back to sleep now.'

'No point,' he mumbled. 'You'll only wake me up again.' Nevertheless his breathing grew stertorous and he soon dozed off.

'Would you like a cup of tea, or coffee, Mrs Miller?' The nurse had finished recording Sam's responses and was smiling at Kate.

'Oh . . . thank you. Tea, please.' Kate still had not altogether adjusted to the amazing luxury of the private hospital where Sam's operation had, that morning, been performed. Her letter to the chief executive had indeed, as Brian predicted, got the insurance company hopping around. The hospital, bizarrely to Kate's eyes, was rated band B as long as Sam shared a room. In the event, there was no one in the second bed and Kate had actually spent the previous evening reclining on it, watching television with Sam.

In the morning she had been with him when he had been taken down to the surgical suite. He had been subdued but not sleepy – the anaesthetist had explained to both of them that a pre-med was not given because it was important that Sam should be woken up as quickly as possible after, or even during, the operation.

'Only way to check everything's all right,' he had said breezily. 'They'll be asking you a few questions, and getting you to move a bit, every quarter of an hour for the first few hours. Bit of a bore, but not too dreadful. All right?'

Sam had been round-eyed but calm. Kate had said a cheerful 'Good night, sleep tight' as he went under the anaesthetic, then rushed back to hide in his room and have a good cry. She already knew, from when Nick had had his tonsils out, how upsetting it was to see one's child pass into unconsciousness.

She had heard the surgeon's voice out in the corridor, talking to the nurses.

'Yes, very good,' he said. 'Most enjoyable.'

Enjoyable! Thought Kate. He's been making holes in my baby's head, and he found it enjoyable! He breezed into the room, and she stood up.

'All done, Mrs Miller! Went very well, too, all exactly as we'd expected. You can go down and sit with him now, if you like.'

Kate had taken the time to telephone home, where Nick and Tashie were waiting to hear from her. They had wanted to be at the hospital, but Kate had thought it better that they should wait. For one thing, she wanted to keep things as low key as possible for Sam. The other reason, kept to herself, was that she felt it was likely to be as much as she could do to bear her own anxiety, without having to worry about theirs.

She repeated the surgeon's words to them, and said they could come and visit Sam that afternoon.

'Phoebe rang,' said Tashie. 'Shall I ring her?'

'Yes, do,' Kate agreed. She thought how ironic it was that the person wanting news of Sam should be, not his father, but his father's other wife. She had wondered whether she should try to get some kind of message to Len, but the only thing she could think of was to put something in the personal column of the newspaper, which if he had gone abroad was unlikely to reach him. In the end, since Sam never mentioned his father, she had done nothing. Len knew that Sam had been ill, she reasoned, and hadn't bothered to get in touch then. If the worst happened – her mind shuddered away from the possibility – then she would do her best to inform Len. Otherwise, she wouldn't bother either.

The nurse came back again. Another quarter of an hour gone by already.

'What's your favourite TV programme, Sam? What date is your birthday?'

In a cubicle down the ward a child cried inconsolably. Kate was unworried, knowing that it was not the patient crying but his little sister, who was bitterly resenting the fact that her parents were too preoccupied to play with her. Kate might have offered to help, but they spoke no English and the mother was heavily veiled. Her brown eyes had regarded Kate's bare head and arms revealed by a short-sleeved shirt (the hospital was very warm) with blank disapproval. The hours crept by, slowly but with somnolent calmness. Sam continued to be woken three or four times every hour.

There was the sound of footsteps, rubber soles squeaking on the polished floor. Kate, since she was listening for them, recognised the rhythms and was already on her feet when Tashie and Nick came round the corner of the cubicle. They eyed Sam with some alarm, taking in the hi-tech equipment to which he was connected, and the dressing on his head.

'Hi, Mum. Are you sure he's all right?'

Kate smiled reassuringly.

'A bit of a headache, not very surprisingly. And a little bit dopey from the anaesthetic, though they didn't give him much. Otherwise, fine.'

Sam opened bleary eyes.

'Hi, Nick. Hi, Tashie.'

'How you doing, bro?' Nick stood awkwardly by the bed.

'All right. I'm thirsty.'

'I'll get you a drink,' said Tashie eagerly. She rushed off to find a nurse, and returned with a glass of water and a straw.

'There you are.' She stood watching while Sam drank, obviously reassured by this normal behaviour.

'Do you want to sit with him for a bit while I go and stretch my legs?' asked Kate. She thought they would be more relaxed without her.

'Sure. Oh, Phoebe's out there somewhere.'

'Phoebe is? Why didn't you say?'

'Forgot.' Nick was already investigating the monitors to which Sam was wired. 'She brought us up. Tashie rang to tell her, and said we were coming, so she met us at Three Bridges and drove us. She said she'd hang around for a bit, when she'd parked the car.'

Kate went to the reception area, where she found Phoebe reading a glossy magazine with half her attention. She jumped up when she saw Kate.

'Kate! How is he?'

'Amazing. I can't believe it.' It seemed natural that they should embrace. 'Thanks for bringing the kids up.'

'No problem. I was glad to have an excuse to come. Not that I want to be a nuisance, of course. I thought I'd have a day's shopping.'

'New clothes?' Kate stood back and eyed her. 'You've lost weight.'

'Yes, thank goodness. Sensible eating and a lot of riding. You wouldn't believe how much energy you use, just sitting on a horse. Or maybe it's the falling off. A kind of extreme form of massage. Anyway, I thought I'd reward myself. Want to come?'

'I'd have loved to, but I don't really want to leave Sam just yet. It's been very successful, and he's fine, but . . .'

'I know, I'd feel just the same. Another time.'

'I wouldn't mind a little while off – Tashie and Nick are down with him. Do you want to come and have a coffee or something in his room? It's wonderfully plushy, hot and cold running nurses and bottles of champagne in the fridge.'

'Love to.' They went upstairs. Phoebe admired the private bathroom and peeked in the fridge. 'Really champagne – I thought you were joking!'

'I know. All the nurses keep telling me not to touch it, they charge like wounded bulls for extras. Tea and coffee are all right, though. I think it's warm enough to sit on the balcony, don't you?'

'Definitely. As a matter of fact,' Phoebe fished in her capacious bag, 'I brought a bottle of champagne with me. I thought you should celebrate a bit. It won't be as cold as the one in the fridge, but I put one of those insulated jackets on it, so it shouldn't be too warm.'

'Oh, Phoebe, what a lovely idea! I'll find some glasses.'

It was one of those early spring days when the temperature was high enough to deceive one that winter was a thing of the past. They sat on the balcony overlooking Lord's cricket ground and sipped their champagne. The sun was warm on their faces, and Kate felt the tension slipping away from her.

'I really think the worst is over,' she said. 'Touch wood,' she added, looking vaguely round her.

'With Sam? I'm sure it is.'

'With Sam, and everything else. Len. Leo.'

'Yes.' Phoebe finished her glass, and sat with it held loosely in her hand, waiting for Kate to be ready for some more. 'I've been thinking.'

'About Len?'

'In a way. About what you suggested, the day of your mother's funeral. You remember?'

It had from time to time crossed Phoebe's mind that Kate's offer had been the result of a combination of alcohol and stress, and that she might have forgotten or at least regretted it later.

'Of course I remember. You having Len's baby. Do you want to go ahead with it? I meant it, you know. You can, if it's what you want.'

'That's just it. It's so kind of you, Kate, such a generous offer. It seems almost churlish to say no.'

'But?'

'But. I can't do it. I've thought about it so much. Of course I want a baby. It had been on my mind before I even met Leo, in an "if only" kind of way. In fact, it's one of the reasons I was so eager to take him at face value, I see that now. I was dreadfully disappointed when nothing happened, and especially in those first two or three weeks after he'd gone, when I went on hoping . . . but I'm not *desperate* about it. Not desperate enough that if you hadn't made your offer, I might have considered going for AID. I just wouldn't have been prepared to go that far.'

'Aids?' Kate was confused. The warmth and the alcohol were making her drift into a kind of half-trance. Phoebe smiled.

'Not Aids! AID – artificial insemination by donor. Like what we discussed, but from an anonymous man.'

'Oh, that. Goodness.'

'Yes. Anyway, when I realised that, I also realised it would be completely wrong to accept your offer. Wrong for me, wrong for the baby. For you and your family too, come to that. Leo is the past, for all of us. The last thing we need is to resurrect him like that. I do want a baby – very much – but I want him or her to be part of a relationship that has some hope of a future.'

'None of us can guarantee that,' said Kate mildly.

'Of course not. And I don't doubt I could do a pretty good job of bringing up a child on my own – after all, my mother did it. It's just that I don't want to saddle a child with a father who didn't even hang around long enough to be there for the conception, let alone the birth. Does that make sense?'

'Of course it does. You of all people know what it's like to have a father who's a bit of a mystery.'

'Yes. I suppose I do, though to be honest until you said it I hadn't really made that connection. I can honestly say that I never particularly felt the lack of a father – some of my friends at school had such horrible ones I was just thankful I didn't have one at all. Even when Millie told me about him, it didn't seem especially relevant to me or my life, except how it affected her. I suppose that's my subconscious mind suppressing things, or something.'

'I'm all for a bit of suppression, myself. About some things, anyway.'

'Me too. Anyway, imagine watching some poor little creature growing up, and seeing little bits of Leo coming out. It doesn't bear thinking of.'

'What will you do? Go back to teaching?'

'No. I'm going back, but not to school. To university. I'm going to take a course in educational psychology.'

Kate sat up, her glass tilting perilously. Hastily she righted it, and took a gulp.

'Phoebe, what a wonderful idea! Where?'

Phoebe looked abashed.

'Well, Brighton, if I can. Sussex University. I really want to keep the cottage, I find. I've got to know so many more people in the village now, and of course there's Daphne, I couldn't bear to lose touch with her, or Jennifer either, come to that. Brighton is near enough that I can drive up and down.'

'What a pity. You could have come and lived in our bedsit, experienced student life properly.'

'It's tempting. Beans on toast, and trips to the launderette . . .'

'*My* lodgers are allowed to use the washing machine. By prior arrangement.'

'Naturally. But I'm afraid even that inducement isn't enough to make me abandon the cottage. I'll call in from time to time, if I may.'

'I certainly hope you will. It's a fabulous plan. I'm quite jealous.'

'Nothing to stop you doing it too. Why not? We could go together, it would be fun.'

Kate shook her head decisively.

'No, it's not for me. I haven't the time, for one thing, and I'm more of a do-er than a studier, I think. I'm going to look for a part-time job, now I haven't got to be at home all the time. I think I'll give up the bed and breakfast – it was fun, but dreadfully time-consuming and an awful tie. If I get desperate, I can let my mother's old room as well as the bedsits.'

They were both silent for a moment, contemplating the future. Kate was surprised by how disappointed she felt that Phoebe had turned down the offer of having Len's baby. Not that she particularly wanted to see another little Miller, it was just that the idea of a baby had been so appealing.

Her mind wandered to Brian. He had been so supportive over Sam. They had been out to dinner several times, decorously enough it was true, but she knew without any shadow of a doubt that she had only to make the tiniest hint for that to change. Neither of them was young or impetuous, Kate at least was reluctant to rush headlong into anything so soon after Len, but even so . . . Deep within her she felt a certainty that there would come a time, not too distant, when she and Brian would be together. It was a wonderfully comforting thought, like seeing the name of your destination on a road sign when you had been driving for hours. Not home yet, but soon . . . soon . . .

She felt her moment of mourning for Phoebe's not-to-be baby slip away. After all, she was not so old yet. Not too old, perhaps . . . and Brian, she thought, would make a wonderful father. Why not? She smiled, half laughing at herself, but half in love with the idea already.

'Poor old Leo,' she mused. 'I wonder where he is.'

'So do I, sometimes. I rather feel he's probably all right. What do you suppose the diamonds were worth?'

'No idea. A lot, though. And since they're legally his – at least, in the sense that he must have a bill of sale to prove they aren't stolen – presumably he can sell them for what they're actually worth.'

'And Tashie said he'd told her he had some money here and there abroad. I expect he's found some other poor mug, and sweet-talked her into taking care of him.'

'Almost certainly.' The thought caused little pain now. 'Perhaps we should start a club.'

'Mm. I don't think so. Two's company.'

'Yes.'

They smiled at one another. Phoebe refilled their glasses.

'To Sam,' she said, raising her own. 'A complete cure, and lots of rugby.' They drank. 'Your turn.'

'Absent friends? I don't think so,' said Kate without heat. 'I think we should just drink to us. Phoebe and Kate.'

'Miller and Co,' said Phoebe, reaching across to clink her glass against Kate's.

'Yes, why not. To Miller and Co.'

'I'll drink to that,' said Phoebe.